Amazon R___
Double D___

C000151994

"A great read, witty and funny. Once you pick it up, you won't want to put it down. Ordinary people looking and sounding like famous people lead similar exotic lives! ... This book has all the makings of a good thriller. It would make a fabulous film, with an audience gripped to their seats laughing, crying ... never knowing what's coming next, with some wild love scenes!"

"It was one of those unusual books that you don't want to put down! ... some of the twists were so well spun... I sincerely hope there will be more from this talented author."

"Brilliant book full of twists and turns, with a touch of 'ooo la la' thrown in for good measure..."

"Great book... author knows how to keep you captivated throughout. Must read!"

"I really enjoyed this story ... entertaining, and there was lots going on. The style is very tongue-in-cheek, which is fun..."

"Being in this industry myself, it really sheds a light on the lives of real top lookalikes! I love the humour in this book along with the lust and thriller side...!"

About the Author

L ondon born with an Irish father and Italian mother, Barbara Angela Kealy was the fourth of seven children. Enjoying her younger years in a loving, noisy household, she remains close to her siblings and many nieces and nephews. Never a shrinking violet, Barbara, together with her sister Sandra, attended the local dance school at an early age, loving the opportunity to perform on stage whenever the teachers arranged shows for the public.

A bright student at school when she wanted to be, Barbara's first employment was as the office junior with a highly regarded travel agency in London's West End.

When still a teenager, Barbara left her home, family and friends, to follow the American dream, becoming an au pair with a wealthy American family in New York. After a few months, she left her position, and temporarily lived with her mother's relatives in Brooklyn. Soon after, she successfully found employment with a bank on Wall Street and thoroughly enjoyed working in this affluent part of the Big Apple. It was during this time that she eventually moved into an apartment on East 82nd Street with three young ladies from Scotland. Thus, the fun began!

Some time later, Barbara decided to move back to London, returning to the same company she had worked for prior to moving to New York. Always a performer at heart, Barbara joined the Lissenden Players, an Old Time Music Hall group in North London, as a performing artiste and eventually also becoming secretary. Barbara continues to be part of the very popular Lissenden Players.

Shortly after forwarding her portfolio to a prestigious agency in London, Barbara became a lookalike for the iconic actress Dame Joan Collins, and began travelling around the United Kingdom and Europe in her exciting new show business career. This has fuelled her life experiences, and certainly her two books!

Barbara is a passionate storyteller and throughout her life, people have often told her she should write a book to capture all her entertaining stories and fascinating experiences. At long last, she has now accomplished this. *Duplicity* is Barbara's second book and is the sequel to *Double Deception*. Barbara is married and lives in London.

Keep in touch with Barbara!
www.barbaraangelakealy.com
Twitter: @kealybarbara

*The dark, fast-paced sequel to Double Deception
will thrill you more as it races to its climax...*

DUPLICITY

by Barbara Angela Kealy

First published in Great Britain in 2023
by Book Brilliance Publishing
265A Fir Tree Road, Epsom, Surrey, KT17 3LF
+44 (0)20 8641 5090
www.bookbrilliancepublishing.com
admin@bookbrilliancepublishing.com

A CIP catalogue record for this book is available
at the British Library.

ISBN 978-1-913770-53-2.

Typeset in Adobe Caslon Pro.
Printed by 4edge Ltd.

This is a work of fiction.
Names, characters, businesses, places, events, locales, and
incidents are either the products of the author's imagination or
used in a fictitious manner. Any resemblance to actual persons,
living or dead, or actual events is purely coincidental.

Dedication

To my dear brother,
Anthony Stephen Frank Kealy (recently deceased)
FOREVER MISSED.

Acknowledgements

Thank you to Brenda Dempsey, my publisher, for your guidance and support.

Thank you to the Book Brilliance Publishing team: Olivia Eisinger, my editor, for her encouragement and dedicated hard work for guiding me; and to Zara Thatcher, for her creative skills in typesetting and proofreading of this book.

Douglas Donaghey, my husband, who has always supported me.

To special friends throughout my life, for believing I could do it...

Contents

Character List

All characters in this novel are fictitious.

Name	**Pseudonym**
Frank Lanzo	Gene Capalti

Name	**Lookalike Character**
Belinda Flynn	(1st) Dame Joan Collins
Chloe Radlett	(2nd) Dame Joan Collins
Camp Freddie Lawlor	Liberace
Tanya Christianssen	Pamela Anderson
Lady Denise Ava	Madonna
Molly Rose	Taylor Swift
Marina Greenslade	(1st) HM Queen Elizabeth II
Louise Rickman	(2nd) HM Queen Elizabeth II
Spencer Carlisle	Prince of Wales (Duke of Cornwall)
Max Rushton	(1st) Prince Harry
Jeff Williams	(2nd) Prince Harry
Ada Demir	(1st) Meghan Markle
Louise Clarke	(2nd) Meghan Markle

Bernard Shaftoe	President Donald J Trump
Kay Carney	Ex-Foremost Marilyn Monroe
Crystal	(1st) Marilyn Monroe
Melita	(2nd) Marilyn Monroe
Luke Cohen	Charlie Chaplin
Vicky Sutton	Ex-Foremost Elizabeth Taylor
Stephanie Jones	(1st) Elizabeth Taylor
Grace Simmons	Audrey Hepburn
Kevin	Boy George
Ruby Clement	Diana Dors
Elaine Catini	Sophie Loren
Charlie Fox	Tom Cruise
Huey Lewis	Sean Connery 007
Meyrick Sheen	Jack Nicholson
Rob	Elvis Presley
Neil Patterson	George Clooney

Chapter 1
Jailhouse Blues

B eing held by the Italian Police in Venice not only caused immense concern and pain for Frank Lanzo, but gave him a sense of desperation which, try as he may, he could not shake off. His mind lingered constantly on his lover, Belinda in London and his son, Mikey, in New York.

The policy of the high security prison where he was being detained by the Italian Polizia di Stato allowed just one telephone call. Frank had used this to speak with the Society's hierarchy in New York, who assured him they were doing everything in their power for his imminent release on bail and that instead, Count Luigi Boggia would carry out the crucial meetings for which Frank had been sent to Venice. Knowing that Count Luigi Boggia, his dearest friend, was working alongside the Society for his release, made the American less troubled. He had asked the Count to call Belinda at the Top Drawer Lookalike Agency in London and explain to her that he had been detained in Venice due to a mix-up but that he would call her at the first opportunity once he was released. Confident the Count would not let him down, Frank relaxed a little. They were, after all, like brothers and Frank trusted Count Luigi Boggia completely.

Daily, Frank would check his fingertips, dreading what he might find there; to his relief, his fingerprints had not, as yet, shown any sign of reappearing. With a slight shudder, Frank recalled being extra harsh with them just before he left New York for Venice, rubbing them out of existence and now he prayed they would take much longer to reappear, or not at all.

This morning, yet again, he had rubbed his fingertips on the stone floor of his tiny cell until they were bruised and swollen, knowing only too well that once they did reappear, his true identity would be out in the open and his days of freedom would be over.

Summer was fast approaching, and Frank's cell was becoming unbearably hot. He found it hard to tolerate such heat. Although he was a man who always took great pride in his appearance, since his incarceration, he had become uninterested in how he looked, allowing his wiry grey hair to grow and his beard to become unruly. With no appetite to speak of these days, Frank was beginning to lose weight and his dancing brown eyes, that Belinda adored so much, were now vacant and inexpressive. Frank, unquestionably handsome, thick-set and extremely attractive, was becoming unrecognisable.

On a particularly hot morning early in May, shortly after a bland breakfast in the noisy dining hall, Frank Lanzo waited together with several other prisoners for the guards to accompany them back to their tiny cells. Nonchalantly nodding to one or two familiar faces, Frank then dropped his gaze to the floor, lost in thought.

As he reached his cell, one of the guards, Alfonso, a skinny young man with a quirky manner and shiny black hair, which he wore parted down the middle, informed Frank that the Governor wanted to see him immediately.

A grinning Alfonso then marched the puzzled American quickly towards the Governor's office on the floor above.

The Prison Governor, Cesare Rizzi, a short thickset man in his mid-sixties with a face to rival a British bulldog, held, with immense pride, the record for the longest reigning Governor of the prison ever. As Frank was ushered into the office by the skinny Alfonso, Cesare Rizzi rose slowly from his chair behind the mahogany desk.

"Ah, Signor Lanzo," he said in broken English, smiling faintly at Frank. "You are a lucky man! You have been granted a special visit!" he added quickly, turning towards a figure standing by the window.

Frank's heart fluttered as his expressionless eyes recognised the other person. It was Marty Di Carlo, the Society's highly-regarded Supremo Lawyer.

Educated at the elite Columbia University in New York, suave, tall and charismatic Marty Di Carlo smiled as he walked over to Frank and stretched out his hand in greeting to the Society's Capitano Numero Uno. Turning his beaming smile towards the Governor, Marty Di Carlo spoke fluently in Italian, greatly impressing Governor Rizzi, who nodded in agreement to what the younger man was saying. Reluctantly moving towards the door, his dark eyes glancing fleetingly towards Frank, Governor Rizzi hesitantly left his office, allowing the American lawyer and the American detainee privacy for their brief but crucial meeting.

"Frank! The Society have sent me to put your mind at rest and to assure you they are doing everything in their power to bring you home," announced the lawyer, speaking quickly under his breath as he watched Frank closely.

Meeting the younger man's gaze, Frank, his voice faltering, thanked Marty as he tried to control his beating heart.

"Okay!" said the lawyer, walking over towards the window again, the sun revealing the slightest tinge of auburn in his hair. Turning to face Frank, he continued. "For a very high price, Governor Rizzi has allowed us thirty minutes alone, so let's take a seat and I will explain precisely what the Society has decided to do in order to get you out of this dump."

Gingerly sitting on the edge of a deep-red cushioned chair, Frank kept his eyes on Marty Di Carlo as the lawyer opened his tan leather briefcase, retrieving several documents. Handing them to Frank, Marty then leant back in his chair and watched Frank's expression with interest, as his eyes scanned the pages, absorbing every word. After some time, glancing up into Marty's face, Frank nodded his head in agreement to whatever was proposed. Of course, Frank Lanzo, being the Society's most revered Capitano, was fully aware that his bosses had Associates in the prison system, not only in Italy, the USA and Europe, but all over the world.

Just before the meeting came to an end, Marty reconfirmed that it was unfortunate but necessary that the Capitano Numero Uno would have his non-dominant arm broken by another inmate, who, of course, was an Associate of the Society. Marty went on to explain there would be a mock quarrel then fighting amongst the prisoners, resulting in Frank needing urgent medical attention. The other prisoner had already been briefed without causing suspicion.

"Sorry to do this to you, Frank, but there is no other way for us to get you out of here quickly," offered Marty, apologetically. "We have been informed that the Italian Authorities are 'digging their heels in' where your bail is concerned," Marty divulged, shaking his head as he picked up the document before placing it back neatly into his briefcase.

"We have to urgently get you out in case the Italians become unaccommodating," he added, as an afterthought.

Before Frank could reply, the door opened and Governor Rizzi entered the air-conditioned office, a wide smile spreading across his bulldog-like face.

"I presume you have had enough time for your discussion, Signor Di Carlo?" he asked in broken English, walking up to the young lawyer and shaking his hand.

"Yes, indeed we have," replied Marty, nodding his head before continuing. "The Society will not forget your comprehension and co-operation in this matter, Governor Rizzi."

With a sly grin, the Governor turned, nodded to Frank then called the guard to take the detainee back to his cell. As Alfonso arrived, his crafty eyes taking everything in, Marty half-whispered "Okay?" to which Frank replied by nodding to the lawyer. He then followed Alfonso out of the coolness of the Governor's office to dwell chillingly on what was to take place within a few days.

Chapter 2
A Rendezvous with the Count

Belinda had taken a black London taxi to Villa Di Geggiano in the fashionable Chiswick area of West London where she was to meet Count Luigi Boggia for dinner. Her mood had become melancholy, even mournful since she had received his telephone call yesterday. What could the Count possibly have to say about Frank that was so secretive he couldn't relay it to her over the telephone? Her imagination played havoc with her nerves and she knew deep in her soul that Frank was in some kind of terrible trouble, otherwise he would have contacted her weeks ago.

Count Luigi Boggia was as charming and attentive as ever. Just seeing his classically handsome face again seemed to lift Belinda's spirits, albeit briefly.

"My dearest Belinda, it is so wonderful to see you again. Thank you for agreeing to meet me, my dear," said the Count, taking her hand and pressing it to his smiling lips.

Blushing slightly, Belinda answered quietly,

"It is lovely to see you again, Count Luigi, although I am confused and very concerned about what has happened to Frank."

Nodding his elegant head understandingly, he took Belinda's elbow and ushered her towards the entrance of the elaborate, fifteenth-century Villa Di Geggiano. Once seated, Count Luigi explained everything to Belinda about Frank's arrest in Venice, until her ears refused to hear what he was relaying to her. Noticing the colour had drained from her stricken face, he asked gently, "Belinda, my dear, did you understand what I have just told you?"

Turning her soulful eyes towards her dining companion, Belinda nodded slowly but her senses refused to accept the devastating news. She felt as if the whole world could hear the screaming inside her head. At last, finding her voice and close to tears, she asked, "But, Count Luigi, why would the police detain Frank in prison? What are they accusing him of? Why are the Italian authorities taking so long to sort this mess out?"

The Count reached across the cream tablecloth and wrapping his hands around hers, focused his eyes on her as she searched his face for answers.

"Because, my dear Belinda, they are morons and have taken Frank to be an elite diamond thief, whom they have been searching for, for the last thirty years!" replied the Count, lowering his voice to a near whisper before glancing around quickly.

"But that's ridiculous!" retorted Belinda. "How can they think this diamond thief is Frank?" she added indignantly, surprised and a little angry at the absurdity of it all.

"I have no idea why this mix-up has occurred, Belinda," lied the Count, shrugging his manly shoulders slightly. "Please try not to fret so. Frank's bosses and, of course, myself, will sort this insane business out and have Frank released as soon as possible," he added encouragingly, pouring red wine into their tall crystal glasses.

Count Luigi's assurances managed to lift Belinda's low spirits somewhat and as she allowed the delicate wine to work its magic, she found herself giggling at everything her charming companion was saying during their sumptuous dinner together in the splendid restaurant.

As the evening drew to a close, Count Luigi called a taxi to take Belinda home to Clapham Old Town, some six miles away. Before he closed the door of the shiny black taxi, the Count leaned into the open window and gently kissed Belinda in true Italian style, on both cheeks, causing her to feel like a treasured child.

As expected of the traditional London taxi driver, the elderly gentleman chatted non-stop throughout the journey south, but Belinda's mind was elsewhere and she blushed in the darkness of the back seats as she recalled with shock how her heart had jumped just a little, as Count Luigi's lips touched her cheeks, warmed by the splendid wine.

The following day at Top Drawer Agency, Camp Freddie and Dawn Jarvis looked somewhat anxiously at each other as Belinda walked slowly into the office, her sad eyes downcast. Queenie ran up to her and wagged his furry tail, turning over on his back for her to rub his little tummy. Belinda began to smile at the little dog's insistence that she pay him full attention.

"Darling Belinda," stammered Dawn, her voice faltering in her throat as she rose swiftly from her chair, walking towards her dear friend and junior partner. "What on earth was it the Count had to say about Frank?" she asked, a look of concern shadowing her face as she wrapped her arms around Belinda supportively.

Slowly shaking her aching head, Belinda smiled weakly at Dawn then turned towards Freddie and drew him into the group hug, little Queenie yapping to be included. For some time, the three close friends held each other in a comforting way, each knowing that they could completely rely on the other two for love and compassion, no matter what.

When Freddie had made them all a welcomed cup of coffee, Belinda explained exactly what Count Luigi had told her regarding Frank's unbelievable circumstances and why he was being held by the Polizia di Stato in Venice.

"Belinda, darling, I am sure with the support of his employers and the Count, Frank will soon be back home again in New York," encouraged Dawn. "You wait and see!" she added, glancing fleetingly at Freddie and raising her newly microbladed eyebrows.

"Count Luigi said the exact same thing to me yesterday!" revealed Belinda, trying her hardest to hold back the hot tears. "But I am devastated and sick with worry about Frank."

Dawn gently put her arms around Belinda reassuringly before advising, "Now, now, darling, you have to put on a brave face, if not for yourself, then for Frank!"

"At the risk of me sounding like an old agony aunt," she continued, "you really must not give up hope, Belinda! You'll see, everything will work out fine. I am sure of it!" However, deep down, Dawn was dubious about her own words of encouragement.

The one thing Dawn had started to believe was that the Count had a secret passion for Belinda. Quickly dismissing this thought from her mind, she gently patted the younger woman comfortingly, then returned to her office.

It was mid-afternoon and Dawn's usually good mood was now returning. One of Top Drawer Agency's clients in the Netherlands were requesting to see photos and videos of their foremost Meghan Markle lookalikes. The Royal wedding could not have come at a better time for the agency and Dawn knew only too well that lookalikes who portrayed members of the British Royal Family were some of the most sought-after artistes on her books. Dawn's motive for deciding to hand over responsibility for this prestigious job to Belinda was to keep her partner fully occupied, so that there would be little time for her to ponder on the disturbing circumstances in which Frank Lanzo now found himself.

Chapter 3
Irrational Reality

L ying awake in his cell in the dead of night, Frank could not sleep. Apart from the loud snoring of his cellmate, Dario Mazzarini, Frank's mind was full of turmoil. He worried deeply about the mock fight that was to happen in a couple of days and the unpalatable thought that he would have his left arm broken. To help quell his anxiety, Frank would conjure up thoughts of Belinda, of their time spent together sharing passionate and sensual love. Somehow, these thoughts had the power to make him feel peaceful and he lay in the darkness during the hot Italian night, longing again to be in her arms.

All too soon, dawn had descended in the Italian skies, witnessing an exhausted Frank as he mustered all his courage to drag himself from his bunk, joining the other prisoners in the morning 'slop out'. He knew this was the day before the mock fight was to take place and a perturbed Frank blessed himself at the very thought of it.

Sometimes throughout life, circumstances happen that seem to be marked by the intense irrational reality of a dream that cannot be explained, as if a higher being had intervened. As Frank joined the long queue of prisoners to enter the canteen for breakfast, one of the guards walked up to him and whispered in his ear, "Vieni con me, Signor, subito!" *(Come with me, mister, right away!)* Slightly confused,

Frank followed the guard, who marched him directly to the Governor's air-conditioned office. Entering the room with a look of concern on his ruggedly handsome but sullen face, Frank was shocked to see Marty Di Carlo sitting opposite Governor Rizzi at the large desk. It was eerily quiet as, rising directly from his chair, the Supremo Lawyer walked over to Frank and shook his hand.

"Frank! Great news, my friend!" beamed Marty, dark eyes shining with excitement as he resumed. "In the last twenty-four hours, the Italian authorities have decided to drop all charges against you. You are a free man again!"

Trying to comprehend exactly what Marty was saying to him, Frank looked over to the Governor, who, grinning, nodded his head, confirming the Supremo Lawyer's words were indeed true.

Motioning Frank to move closer, Governor Rizzi pointed to some papers laying on his desk.

"Sign here, here and here, Signor Lanzo," he ordered, pointing with a stubby finger to boxes marked with an 'X', waiting for Frank's signature. Next, opening a small metal case, the Governor emptied the contents onto his highly polished mahogany desk.

"Please confirm these are your personal possessions and sign for them," he instructed, pushing the papers towards Frank. Frank quickly identified his vintage Rolex wristwatch, his mobile phone, his wallet still containing euros and his lucky silver dollar, given to him by his beloved maternal grandfather many years before. Hand shaking, he signed in the appropriate boxes before sliding the papers back to the Governor.

Watching in silence and with trepidation, Marty rose quickly from his chair, walked across to a confused Frank and slapped him heartedly on the back.

"Governor Rizzi, I believe you are also in possession of Signor Lanzo's suitcase containing his clothes which was confiscated from him at Marco Polo Airport?" enquired the Supremo Lawyer, turning away from Frank and addressing the Governor.

"The suitcase? Ah! Yes, of course, Signor Di Carlo. I have it right here," replied Governor Rizzi, bending down under his desk and retrieving Frank's dark brown leather suitcase.

Accepting the case from the Governor, Marty handed it to Frank who, quite dumbfounded at what exactly was happening, accepted his belongings silently.

"Governor Rizzi, the Society is highly satisfied with the way you and the Italian authorities have handled this unsavoury case against their Capitano Numero Uno. As you have been briefed, you will be hearing from them personally," declared Marty, walking over to the Governor and shaking his hand enthusiastically, his perfect straight white teeth causing the Governor to subconsciously compare them to a keyboard.

Picking up the telephone, Governor Rizzi arranged for two of his top prison guards to escort the American lawyer and now ex-detainee, Signor Frank Lanzo, off the prison premises and on the road to freedom again.

His head thumping painfully with the surreal situation unfolding around him, Frank was conscious that he managed to keep in step with the Supremo Lawyer, who ushered him along very quickly.

On reaching the gates, the two burly prison guards handed a foolscap sheet of paper to one of the four guards on duty, who after briefly reading it, glanced at Marty Di Carlo and nodded. Turning to the other guards, he instructed them to unlock the gates to allow the Americans to pass through. In the blink of an eye, Marty Di Carlo had opened the back door of a waiting deluxe limousine, climbing in behind Frank before they were driven off at speed.

It took some time before Frank could apprehend what had happened and accept that he was now free from the nightmarish ordeal he had been living; for him, it felt like a fairy-tale ending.

"How the hell did you pull this off, Marty?" queried Frank, breathing deeply and swallowing to clear his dry mouth.

"Frank! Frank! The Society's hierarchy have reserved the right to relay everything to you once we are back home again," replied Marty, turning to the elder man. "Come, let's enjoy the flight back to New York, where everybody awaits your return."

Leaning closer to Frank, the Supremo Lawyer half whispered in his ear, "Remember, you are the Capitano Numero Uno. The Society would pay a king's ransom for your release in order to bring you back to the Family."

Frank began to thank the young Supremo Lawyer but a lump in his throat refused to allow the words to flow. Understanding completely, Marty smiled and nodded, glancing out of the window to admire his ancestors' beautiful Italian scenery as the limousine sped towards Marco Polo Airport.

Frank gratefully began to close his eyes, and allowed his good fortune to flow through his senses, raising his hopes and spirits into a state of euphoria. He begun to thank God for his blessings before the lovely face of Belinda came tenderly into his mind.

Just two days after Frank Lanzo had been released from the Italian prison, a dull but warm late spring morning found Belinda busy at her desk at Top Drawer Agency. She was closely studying dozens of photographs sent in by young women hoping to become professional lookalikes, many who had been told, at least once, that they had a resemblance to Meghan Markle. Sorting them in two separate piles, 'Good' and 'Not Good', Belinda stretched out her arms then got up from her chair and walked into the kitchenette to make herself another cup of coffee. She was drinking far too much coffee these days and silently promised herself that she would cut down.

It was Friday and Dawn had taken the morning off, but Camp Freddie and his little poodle Queenie were due to arrive at any minute. As Belinda poured the coffee, her mobile phone, still in her dark blue leather handbag, rang out loudly, completely invading her private thoughts. Rushing back to her desk, she reached into her handbag to retrieve the insistently ringing mobile.

"Good morning, Belinda Flynn here," she said quietly, sitting down at her desk.

"Amore mio, mi sei mancato tanto!" *(My Love, I have missed you so much!)* came the deep throated tones of Frank. On hearing his voice after all those lonely nights she had spent crying herself to sleep, Belinda could hardly believe she was talking to her beloved Frank!

"Frank!" she screamed into the mobile, "Where are you? Count Luigi told me you were being detained in a Venetian prison. I have been sick with worry!"

He could hear the panic in her voice. To calm her down, he gently explained what occurred regarding his mistaken identity.

"Belinda, my darling. I am back home in New York. It is a long story and I can't discuss it now, but I promise I will tell you every single detail when I see you in person."

Camp Freddie and little Queenie arrived. Seeing Belinda in deep conversation on her mobile and the look in her eyes, Freddie blew her a kiss then slipped off his green bomber jacket and hung it on the mahogany coat stand. Queenie, tail wagging ferociously, ran to Belinda and directly rolled over on his back. Smiling widely, Belinda bent down to oblige the little dog, then half-whispering into the mobile, her voice full of emotion, she exclaimed, "I am so, so happy! I thought I had lost you forever, my darling. I can't wait to be with you again!"

On hearing the news that Frank had been freed without charge by the Italian authorities, Dawn and Camp Freddie were almost as happy as Belinda herself. For some weeks now, they had seen how their dear friend and colleague had become desperately saddened by her lover's detainment and the fact that he was not allowed telephone calls made it unbearable for her. Belinda, eyes still shining with unexpected happiness, explained to them that hopefully in a few weeks, she would be visiting Frank in New York.

"All credit to Frank's employers for securing his freedom with the Italians!" declared Dawn, looking pensive. "If I didn't know better, the word Mafia would rear its head!" she added, glancing at both Belinda and Freddie before returning to her office, the pensive look still clouding her face.

The Society had decided that their Capitano Numero Uno needed much rest and care after his terrible ordeal, and had strongly recommended he take time to recuperate and gain the weight and the confidence he had lost during his incarceration. It was further decided that Frank should spend some weeks at one of their retreats in Southern California where he would be nourished and pampered, bringing him back to his former 'good health' as soon as possible. Although he was their revered Capitano, the hierarchy were conscious of the fact that Frank, like many of them, was a man of advancing years.

With only himself and Marty Di Carlo present at a meeting with the hierarchy of the Society, Frank was informed that an exorbitant amount of money had been paid to the Italian authorities in order to secure his release with all charges dropped, thus allowing him to continue to travel back and forth to Venice on official business when necessary. Frank was also informed by his superiors that no matter what, the fact that he was the elite of the elite Capitano, a king's ransom would most definitely have been paid for his release. And it was!

Frank learned that when he had first been detained by the Polizia di Stato in Venice, the Society had commissioned Sergie Belladoni in London to fly to Venice immediately and, together with Count Luigi Boggia, carry out the extremely sensitive meeting for them in Frank's absence. The event was a success in favour of the Society but, as was pointed out, it had taken two, rather than just one, elite Capitano to 'pull off the coup'. Frank Lanzo was undeniably their 'king pin.'

During the following week, the Society organised a wonderful evening for Frank's homecoming, although Frank craved only for rest and to be with Belinda again. How he missed her!

Count Luigi Boggia, accompanied by his trusted driver and bodyguard, Alessandro Longo, had flown to New York to attend the lavish party. Deep in his heart, the Count was genuinely happy and thankful for his closest friend's freedom but also, deep in his heart, he was mindful of his own growing passion and longings for Belinda.

Knowing it would be some weeks before she was able to fly to New York to see Frank, Belinda kept herself busy with the agency and the forthcoming shows with Lissenden Players Olde Tyme Music Hall.

Recuperating under the biggest and brightest of skies, Frank had telephoned Belinda several times from Southern California. Sometimes Frank would call her in the middle of the night apologising for the time difference and for wakening her, but Belinda always reassured him that she lived to hear his voice, no matter what time of day or night it was.

Occasionally, the charismatic image of Belinda's deceased husband, Matt Flynn, would linger in her mind, causing desperate feelings of sadness to sweep over her. Both their families continued to mourn Matt's untimely death in James Swift's BMW on that cold, dark night many months before. The rain had been merciless then and ever since, Belinda found she hated the sound of its heavy patter, always bringing to mind that tragic night. Although she had fallen out of love with Matt, they had been married for many years and were very fond of each other. There would always be a special corner in her heart for Matt Flynn.

Sidney Stone, Matt's retired senior partner in the betting shops and the man who had given her deceased husband his chance in the 'bookmaker world,' often telephoned Belinda enquiring how she was but primarily to reminisce about his prodigy Matt, whom, he divulged to Belinda, he greatly missed. To Sidney Stone, Matt Flynn had been the son he and his wife had sadly never been blessed with.

Chapter 4
The Sparkle of Markle

Although many photographs and videos had already been received by Top Drawer Agency in relation to Meghan Markle lookalikes, Dawn had announced an 'open day' for all wannabes. Judging by the amount of telephone calls to the agency during the past two weeks, Belinda and Freddie were expecting a very busy and exciting day interviewing and auditioning potential lookalikes for the Duchess of Sussex. As Dawn had reiterated to them time and again, the more Meghan Markles taken on by the agency, the better. Being the astute lady that she was, Dawn knew how popular and in demand the Royals were throughout the world and as far as she was concerned, Top Drawer Agency would never disappoint their clients. She would make sure that even if 15 different lookalike jobs came in for Meghan Markle on the same day, then Top Drawer Agency could, and would, accommodate them all.

At ten o'clock sharp, Freddie jumped up from his desk to answer a knock at the agency's door. Little Queenie leapt up alongside his master and trotted after him. Freddie caught his breath as, upon opening the oak door, his deep blue eyes took in the apparition before him. Standing outside and giggling amongst themselves, stood six wannabe Meghan Markles.

"Ah! Good morning, ladies, or should I say, your Royal Highnesses!?" quipped Camp Freddie, bowing in his usual flamboyant way. This encouraged the girls to giggle even more loudly. Pulling open the door, Freddie waved the potential lookalikes inside and asked them to take a seat as they stood, looking around the office. Two of the ladies petted and patted little Queenie as he performed his party trick by turning over on his back and demanding his tummy be tickled.

As the girls made themselves comfortable on the gold-coloured chairs situated along the side of the mirrored wall, Freddie handed them each a four-page document.

"Please complete the whole form, answering every question. If you have any issues, do let me know," he announced, handing out the biros.

"The agents will be interviewing together today so each of you will be called in separately," he added, scooping up little Queenie and walking over to the water fountain.

"And please help yourselves to coffee or tea, ladies," he gestured, pointing to the little kitchenette. "Sorry I haven't got anything stronger!" he joked, tutting in mock disgust, setting the potential lookalikes giggling again.

Another knock at the door caused Freddie to jump before rushing over to open it. Glancing at the visitor before lowering his voice, he said smiling to the young woman, "Sorry, sweetie, we are only interviewing Meghan Markle lookalikes today!"

On hearing this, the newcomer rushed quickly past Freddie and into the agency office.

"Yes, I am quite aware of that!" she snapped. "You are definitely overdue a visit to the opticians. I am the double of Meghan Markle!" she scoffed, her North London accent very evident. Camp Freddie was conscious of the fact that the other girls, sitting quietly in the room, had, unfortunately, witnessed this unsavoury little scene and were nudging each other in disbelief at the terseness of the latecomer.

Ever the professional and never consciously wanting to offend anybody, poor Freddie replied apologetically to the furious young woman.

"Oh, yes, of course, silly me!" he stuttered, handing her a form. "Please take a seat," he gushed, showing her to a chair. She did not look happy and glared at an embarrassed Freddie.

By the end of the day, thirty-one Meghan Markle wannabes had arrived at Top Drawer Agency, all interviewed in turn by Dawn and Belinda. After much discussion and several cups of coffee later, the two agents had taken on twenty-two new impressive lookalikes of the Duchess of Sussex.

The terse young woman, Freddie was surprised to hear, was one of the successful candidates. When he queried this decision with Belinda, she had explained to him that the girl, Ada Demir, although not having a strong resemblance to Meghan as some of the others had, was more than capable of imitating an authentic American accent and impersonating the Duchess of Sussex perfectly.

"In actual fact," remarked Belinda as an afterthought, "Ada Demir is even prettier than the real Meghan Markle and most people will know who she is portraying!"

"Actually, I thought she was a real little diva!" declared Freddie, pursing his full lips as he collected the used coffee cups then carrying them into the kitchenette.

Belinda glanced at him and let out an amused laugh. "Yes, she is a little opinionated, I agree. Apparently, her parents are Turkish, although she was born here in London. We will definitely find work for Ada Demir."

Swanning around the office then taking his green jacket from the coat stand, Freddie replied, "Well, she may be prettier than Meghan Markle but, personally, I didn't take to her! If you ask me, Ada Demir is trouble!"

"Oh, come now, Freddie, darling! I am sure she is a charming young woman who will become a real asset to the agency in her forthcoming career," coaxed a smiling Belinda.

"Well, I hope you are right, sweet pea," came Freddie's response, as he pulled on his jacket.

Blowing her a kiss, Freddie and little Queenie disappeared through the door.

Chapter 5
Hail, the American Bosses

Sergie Belladoni and Joey Franzini were a dynamic partnership as they stepped into the shoes of Matt Flynn and James Swift – both now deceased – running and overseeing the three London betting shops, now under full control of the Society.

Joey found he was still mourning his deceased lover, James Swift. Although he now moved in James' circle of friends and had recently met some lovely women, Joey began to accept that he was indeed bisexual. Ever since James opened his eyes to gay sex, Joey found himself looking at beautiful men as well as beautiful women. Unfortunately, for Joey, nobody, as far as he was concerned, male nor female, could 'lace James' boots'. He knew in his aching heart that it would take a very long time before he would be free of James' haunting memory, if at all! In the meantime, he would laugh, love and be merry, if only to keep his sanity.

The Society's decision to place Sergie in the vacant position in London, arisen by Matt Flynn's untimely demise, was a stroke of genius as far as Joey was concerned. He knew that without the gregarious Sergie working closely with him and living nearby, he may have never survived his broken heart.

The employees of all three London betting shops had settled down quickly with their new American bosses, first and foremost because every one of them had been given a generous pay rise. Sergie was a real favourite on the shop floor and the employees enjoyed his bombastic, happy-go-lucky character. A Yank he may be, but as far as they were concerned, Sergie was another 'diamond geezer'. This greatly satisfied the hierarchy of the Society, since they were very aware that Matt Flynn would be a very hard act to follow. The employees often mentioned their late boss and how shocked and saddened they all were by his unexpected tragic death.

Joey continued travelling to and from New York, carrying thousands of forged twenty-pound notes of the Society's money into the UK. Being a 'Man of Honour', he was always confident, and this confidence showed as he passed undetected through customs.

When Joey wasn't partying with James' circle of friends, he liked to spend some leisure time with Sergie. Being a single man, Sergie loved to visit the best restaurants London had to offer, and it had plenty to offer in the way of some of the finest culinary to be found anywhere in the world. Joey enjoyed eating and sampling the best wines with Sergie, often ending up at one of Sergie's favourite casinos, The Ritz Club at St James'. This was a remarkable place to spend an evening, mused Joey, the first time Sergie ushered him through the opulent swing doors into the sumptuous surroundings. The restaurant and bar were decorated in red and gold, and Joey agreed with Sergie that there was a great range of high-quality food and the very best of the world's wines on the menu.

Apart from excellent food and wine, Sergie's passion was gambling – poker, roulette and blackjack. He would stay for hours, winning, losing, then hopefully winning back his money from the bemused croupiers. Joey liked to dabble just a little but, although he took a serious gamble each time he carried the Society's dirty money into the UK, fully aware he would lose his liberty if apprehended, gambling his own money away was not one of his favourite pastimes.

Easter had come and gone, unexpectedly bringing the most beautiful warm and sunny days, which everyone thoroughly enjoyed after the long, dark, miserable cold months of winter. Sergie and Joey had settled down well into their new adopted city and soon found themselves yearning less and less for New York. Occasionally, Sergie would fly back home for a quick visit or to attend one of the Society's meetings. He, too, had newfound buddies in London, many from the casinos he frequented, as well as from the betting shops' employees. For Sergie, there did not appear to be one special lady. He loved them all and would often be seen with a different attractive woman hanging on his muscular arm, in and around London's fashionable casinos.

On many occasions, Sergie would mention Frank to Joey, admitting how much he missed having Frank come across 'the pond' to work with them in London. Like all other members of the Society, Sergie held Frank in great esteem; he knew he owed much of his own success to Frank and for that reason, he would always be in the revered Capitano's corner.

Early on a dull afternoon in late April, following the hectic past few weeks of dealing with the Cheltenham Cup and the formidable Grand National, Sergie sat in the back room of the Soho betting shop, sipping hot coffee from a takeaway cup, brought in for him by one of the employees. As he browsed the day's racing form in the newspapers, his mobile phone rudely interrupted his thoughts as it impatiently rang out.

"Sergie Belladoni," he whispered into the mobile.

"Good morning, Sergie Belladoni!" came the deep tones of Frank Lanzo's voice in reply.

"Frank! How the hell are you, buddy?" responded Sergie, dropping the newspaper as a wide smile spread across his rugged face.

"Yeah, good, thanks, Sergie. It took some time but I'm really, really good now," came Frank's answer. "Called to let you know that I shall be coming to London the week after next. The Society will be letting you know but I've only just heard myself and thought I would break the good news to you first," he continued, his voice catching a little with emotion.

"WOW! That's awesome, Frank!" enthused Sergie. "So pleased you are back, buddy! We've missed you, Joey and me. When will you be arriving? I'll collect you myself," he added.

"May 7th. A Monday, I think. I will call with the finer details in a few days. How is Joey?" enquired Frank, his voice becoming morose.

"Hey, Frank, Joey is ace! Been doing great over here, as the Society would have informed you. Yep, Joey is a good kid!" replied Sergie, nodding his head at the mobile.

"Great!" replied Frank. "I know that boy will go far. Just wanted to get it straight from the horse's mouth! By the way, I am still Gene Capalti while in London. Don't want to confuse our work colleagues over there, do we?"

"Of course, Frank… I mean, Gene!" responded Sergie playfully then added, on a more serious note, "I will make sure Joey is informed, Frank."

"Okay! Good work, Sergie! I know I can always rely on you. Thanks again, buddy, stay safe! Ciao!" he uttered, before ending the call.

Drinking down the remains of his now cold coffee, Sergie switched his attention back to the day's racing form, delighted at the prospect of having Frank Lanzo back again in the hub of London.

Chapter 6
A Lady Visits

Belinda was over the moon. Frank had just called her at Top Drawer Agency and explained that the Society were sending him to London very soon. Obviously, this meant she would not be flying to New York now; not for the time being, anyway. Although a little disappointed at not to be visiting the Big Apple, it made little difference to Belinda where in the world it would be when they next met. The images now flooding her mind caused her to blush like a schoolgirl.

"That's fabulous news, Belinda! I am so happy for you both!" declared Dawn when she and Freddie heard about Frank flying to London again.

"I really think, once and for all, you should make an honest man of him," she joked, smiling and winking at her friend and partner.

"Yes, you should do!" agreed Freddie, looking up from the pile of post he was sorting through.

"I wish Claudio would make an honest woman of me, darling!" he added, waving his long slim arms around in the air sending Dawn and Belinda into uncontrollable laugher.

For the rest of the day, things ran smoothly. Top Drawer Agency was enjoying a busy summer. As many as twelve Meghan Markle lookalikes were contracted out on different jobs. Dawn was extremely confident with the new recruits and marvelled at how popular the Duchess of Sussex had become since marrying into the Royal Family. Belinda was pleased to see that Ada Demir, the young woman whom Freddie did not care for, was proving to be one of the top Meghan Markle lookalikes on the agency's books.

Both Dawn and Belinda agreed that the more one looked at Ada, the more she seemed to resemble the Duchess, albeit Ada was altogether prettier.

"Another job has just come in for Meghan Markle," announced Dawn, getting up from her desk and handing Belinda the email.

"It seems the Duchess of Sussex is rivalling HM Queen Elizabeth II these days!" remarked Belinda, her eyes skimming quickly over the email received from one of their clients in the Netherlands. "Oh! I see they are asking for DVDs of all our Meghan Markles," she added, glancing up at Dawn quizzically.

"Yes, you know how the clients like a choice. So let's give them what they want!" replied Dawn, returning to her office. "Belinda, send only DVDs of the very best fifteen girls, would you? I am sure our Dutch clients will be extremely satisfied and probably spoilt for choice!" she retorted, letting out a throaty laugh, feeling a real sense of pride with Top Drawer Lookalike Agency, now arguably the best in the world.

Just before the end of the working day, there was a light tap on the door which caused little Queenie to run to it and bark consistently, until Belinda rushed over to open it.

"Well, hello… Lovely to see you! Please come in," Belinda said, smiling at the unexpected visitor.

"Thank you, darling, don't mind if I do!" giggled Lady Denise Ava, the top Madonna lookalike, pecking her agent fondly on the cheek. Belinda noticed she was wearing the most wonderful ruby-red trouser suit, teamed with a purple chiffon blouse.

"I was passing, so thought I would see if my contract was ready to sign for the Beirut job," gushed the Lady, sweeping swiftly into the agency, glancing around and finding Freddie busily attaching a blue leather lead to little Queenie's studded collar.

"Lady Ava!" exclaimed Freddie excitedly. "You look amazing, as always. Unfortunately, I have to catch the post office before it closes. Hope to see you when I get back?" he added, flamboyantly bowing before kissing Lady Denise Ava's left hand.

"Oh, Freddie! You are hilarious!" giggled the Lady, flirting like mad with her most ardent admirer. "Sadly, I can't stay as I have a friend waiting for me outside in her car. We are having dinner with some influential colleagues of hers in less than an hour. She's a barrister, you know!" offered the Lady smugly, bending down and stroking little Queenie under his chin, as his tiny tail wagged and wagged with excitement.

"Never mind, Freddie," chirped Belinda on seeing disappointment sweep across his face. "We must invite the Lady for dinner ourselves very soon."

"Yes, we must definitely do that!" enthused the Lady as Freddie kissed her hand again murmuring,

"Toddle pip, my Fair Lady! Until soon!" before he swept out of the heavy oak door with little Queenie at his heels.

Suddenly, Dawn came out of her office and seeing the visitor, smiled broadly as she kissed Lady Denise on both cheeks. Dawn was an expert judge of character and she liked the Lady immensely, although the agent was fully aware how much of a gossip her Madonna tribute act was. In many ways, this was helpful to Top Drawer Agency in that Lady Denise kept her ears and eyes wide open and had a knack of finding out who was doing what with whom in the lookalike/tribute act world, be it good or bad! Both Dawn and Belinda were fully aware that being the gossip she was, the Lady revealed every modicum of news to them. She was indeed better informed than the media!

"How lovely to see you, Lady Denise. Your contract is right here and ready for you to check and sign," said Dawn pleasantly, handing her a three-page contract. "Be sure to come and visit us as soon as you are back from Beirut. I am very interested to know your opinion on our new clients over there."

"Yes, of course. I shall come in directly when I return and relay everything to you!" answered the Lady, grinning broadly, showing off the famous Madonna gap in her front teeth, which was uncannily authentic. She took her elegant leave.

"I know the Lady is very capable of looking after herself, but Beirut is a far cry from London," exclaimed Dawn, looking a little thoughtful.

"Oh, she will be fine. Her singing has improved immensely and they will love her over there!" encouraged Belinda, trying to calm her partner's growing concern. "Besides, Adam told us he was treated like the real Johnny Depp when he was recently there."

"Yes, darling, I know, but Adam is not the image of Madonna and just as sexy!" replied Dawn, furrowing her brow. "My concern is they might love her too much!" she added, biting her bottom lip.

Chapter 7
The Intensity of Love

L ooking up at the Sherlock Holmes Hotel, close to Regent's Park and one of Frank's favourites in London, Belinda felt the butterflies dancing excitedly in her tummy. The hotel stood gleaming in the bright early May sunshine and she took a deep breath before ascending the front entrance steps and into the familiar foyer. After speaking with the hotel receptionist, Belinda walked nervously into the lift, up to the third floor, and her lover.

She noticed her legs could hardly keep from shaking; the adrenalin had reached every fibre of her body and she felt weak. Slowly walking towards his room, she took deep breaths and tried her hardest to appear natural. Too late... a door opened a few yards away and he stood there in the entrance. Catching her breath, Belinda then ran the short distance between them and literally collapsed into Frank's open arms.

Pulling her quickly into the room, out of sight of inquisitive eyes, they held each other for a long time. Frank, she noticed, was slightly shaking, their emotions and love for each other overwhelming their senses. At last, when he spoke, it was in Italian and his deep voice cracked, "Pensavo di averti perso per sempre, amore mio." *(I thought I had lost you forever, my love.)* Belinda heard her own voice whisper his name; she felt as if she were in a dream, witnessing this tender scene from afar. She could feel his body pressing on her and the overwhelming love she felt for this man became her only need in life.

Within seconds, after carrying her to the sumptuous bed, he had removed every piece of her clothing. His tanned hands found her heaving bosom and gently, he caressed them. Bringing his strong head down, Frank sucked and softly bit her nipples as they stood up hard and waiting. Unaware that she was moaning in ecstasy, Belinda's hands sensually touched her lover.

Laying together now, Frank masterfully pushed open his lover's creamy legs, lips kissing the inside of Belinda's thighs, then using his talented tongue, he found her honeypot until she could feel her juices flowing to him in response, as she was brought to a sensational climax. With their bodies glistening and on fire, Frank urgently entered his lover, uttering something in Italian, which she could not understand. His manhood as hard and erect now as she had remembered before he had been detained in Venice. For Frank, he could not get enough of this lovely woman and like a piston, he thrust into his lover as she arched her back, answering and responding to his great need for her. Reaching paradise together, moans of love escaping from their throats, until fully spent, they lay in each other's arms, happy, contented and still as passionately in love as ever. Intimately, he pulled her close to him.

Belinda could see that Frank had lost some weight, which she thought a good thing. They chatted endlessly and she listened with tears in her eyes, as he relayed to her what had happened to him and how, his heart broken, he had felt he would never see her again and that he would probably die in the Venetian prison.

"Frank, why don't you sue the Italian authorities? Surely you would have a good chance of winning the case?" asked Belinda, a little timidly, as she remembered how Frank did not like discussing his private business in too much detail.

"No! No, my darling!" came his quick reply. "The Society are dealing with the Italian authorities. I shall be informed of any outcome when the time comes. Don't you worry, my sweet," he added, leaning over and pressing his lips to her ear. "Questo e ora nel passato!" *(That is now in the past!)*

Frank mentioned to Belinda that he would be flying back to New York the following morning when, in fact, he was scheduled to remain in London for a further day and night. There were a lot of files and invoices to deal with in the betting shops and together with Sergie, he was expected to sort these out. How he hated deceiving Belinda, but there was no other way at the moment. Even though both Matt and James were deceased, Frank did not want Belinda to ever learn that he had been a good friend and colleague of her husband Matt before his fatal accident. He knew she would never forgive his deviousness, hence Frank still insisted on being known by his pseudonym, Gene Capalti, while in London, apart from when he was with Belinda.

For the remainder of the day, the lovers brought sensual pleasure to each other, making love again and again, the temptation ever compelling.

"Making up for lost time, my darling?" asked Frank, winking, prompting her body to quiver for his touch. Calling the reception desk, he ordered a wonderful dinner with the finest wine to be brought to his room so there was no need for them to dress and leave their love nest at all.

All too soon, today had turned into tomorrow, and the sadness Belinda always felt at their partings returned to darken the very fibres of her soul.

"Frank, you know we can't go on like this forever," she half-whispered to her lover before leaving the hotel room.

Turning and holding her as close to him as he could, Frank whispered back to her. "I promise you... one day, we will always be together, be it in New York or London, but, please, give me time to get back to my life after the nightmare in Venice."

Seeing the sincerity in her lover's eyes, Belinda assured him that she understood perfectly and would be patient. "When you are next in London, Frank, you must stay at my place," she suggested, trying her best to hold back the tears that were threatening to spill over. "We have no need for hotels now," she declared.

"Yes, of course, my love, if that makes you happy," came his reply, bending down and kissing her sensually on her lips.

"Yes, it will make me very happy" she smiled weakly, as she turned to leave.

"I will call you tomorrow, Belinda," he called out, watching her closely. "Ricorda, io ti amero e ti voglio sempre!" *(Remember, I will always love and always want you!)*

The morning for Frank passed all too quickly in the Soho betting shop. There was much to go through but he found it difficult, almost impossible, to keep his mind on the job at hand. Images of his beloved Belinda lingered persistently in his mind. Sure, it was good being back in London with all the employees who treated him with great respect, even though Sergie and Joey were running the show there now.

Frank always felt a strange nostalgia when in the Soho betting shop. His unlikely bond with Matt Flynn had been very close. The two men in Belinda's life had become firm buddies, despite the deception that surrounded that friendship. Frank missed the charm and charisma that made Matt so unforgettable.

"Joey's doing good these days, don't you think, Frank?" asked Sergie, when Joey had gone to lunch with a couple of his colleagues. Stretching in his chair and placing a handful of papers down on the mahogany table, cluttered with dozens of slips and accounts brought over from the Maida Vale and Victoria betting offices, Sergie glanced at Frank for his response.

"Yeah, he was telling me earlier that he loves being in London. I'm real glad he bounced back again after the James Swift episode. We have you to thank for that," replied Frank, also stretching and getting up from his chair and walking over to the water cooler, filling a paper cup then allowing the refreshing liquid to slid down his dry throat.

"Not really, Frank," came Sergie's modest reply. "Joey was in a dark place for a while there. I know he is still cut up about James, even now, but Joey is a survivor, like you. He crawled his way back from that dark place all alone, although I was here for him whenever he needed me."

"Listen, buddy, you are far too modest," came Frank's quick response. "The Society have placed Joey here in London alongside you because you are the best mentor for young Mr Franzini! Now, let's finish this pile quickly then take off for lunch," he suggested, tapping Sergie on the shoulder as he sat down again at the table.

Later that evening, after closing the Soho betting shop and at Sergie's suggestion, the three Americans decided to visit The Ritz Club at St James' for amazing food, drink and, in Sergie's case, gambling. Frank followed them both through the elaborate entrance into the elegant restaurant. Frank had been to the club before, although not for some time, but nevertheless, he let out a low whistle as his eyes took in the classic décor of the room in which they were to eat. He recalled the last time he had been there. It had been with Matt Flynn and despondency for his friend swept over him.

The following morning, silver wings flying through the heavy clouded sky carried Belinda's lover back to New York even before she had opened her eyes to the new day. Frank, heavy of heart, was already missing Belinda and knew, in the not too distant future, he would ask her to be with him forever.

Life settled quickly back to normal for Belinda. The agency was beginning to pick up business and she desperately tried to bury herself into every aspect of her job as junior partner, although always hoping for more lookalike work for her own character, Dame Joan Collins. She needed something to keep her mind off her sadness of being separated from her American lover.

Frank had contacted her a couple of days before from London Heathrow Airport, just as he was about to go through duty-free, when in fact he was still working at the Soho betting shop when he made the call. Although he hated lying to Belinda, Frank had decided he had no other choice. As difficult as it may seem, he swore his lover would never learn the truth of how her deceased husband had been deeply involved with the Society and, of course, Frank himself.

Chapter 8
The Precariousness of Life

At Top Drawer Agency, Belinda was very concerned. Vicky Sutton, the agency's ex-Elizabeth Taylor lookalike, had sent her a very short, almost illegible letter from West Africa. It was little more than six months since Vicky had given up her career as a successful lookalike, her charming one-bedroom flat in North London, and her family, friends and life, flying to Nigeria to work alongside fellow born-again Christians, to spread the gospel of Jesus Christ to the poor people and to teach underprivileged orphaned children the English language, hopefully preparing them for a better life in their adulthood, but first and foremost, to teach the gospel of Jesus.

It was barely fifteen years ago that The Sunrise Church had sprung to life in the small basic lounge of Anthony Devine, a one-time police officer from Wood Green in North London. Anthony Devine was now the number one evangelist not only of North London, but the whole of London and beyond. The Sunrise Church had a congregation so large now that it was beginning to be a concern to the Roman Catholic Church. Anthony Devine no longer held his Born Again meetings in his modest lounge at home, but in schools and theatres throughout the UK and Europe.

Vicky was a member of The Sunrise Church and she had never been happier. Finding Jesus Christ, her Saviour, changed her life completely, and although others thought her peculiar, giving up her exciting lookalike career in order to spread the gospel of the Lord, she prayed for them and their ignorance. As far as she was concerned, she had been saved through finding Jesus and she knew deep within her heart, she would be an evangelist for HIM until her last breath.

Excited about moving to and working in Nigeria, Vicky couldn't wait to be there. Desperately needing to prove her unconditional love for Jesus, her life seemed blessed and complete as she landed in West Africa. There were twelve members of The Sunrise Church assigned to this project, most of them carefully chosen by Anthony Devine himself. Vicky, along with her fellow evangelists, were hand-picked for their passion for Christ and their dedication to spreading His word.

Belinda read Vicky's handwritten note slowly to Dawn and Camp Freddie, both frowning as they listened quietly.

"Well! She doesn't say much, does she?" exclaimed Freddie, tutting disappointedly. "I thought we were going to hear that she had actually met Jesus!" he quipped, pursing his full lips and shaking his head in mock disbelief.

"Oh! Stop, Freddie!" giggled Belinda. "I can just about make out her writing!" she added, moving into a brighter light and reading Vicky's letter through again, her eyes squinting.

"Perhaps she was busy and wrote this very quickly?" suggested Dawn, taking a sip of hot honey tea, her eyes following Belinda.

"Yes, I think you are probably right," agreed Belinda, looking thoughtful again.

"She says she is well and loving what she is doing, but I also know parts of Nigeria are surrounded by al-Qaeda extremist groups and we know how much they despise anything to do with Christianity," she added, a worrying frown appearing on her forehead.

"Oh, come now, Belinda!" exclaimed Dawn. "You know a lot of what we hear from the media is either hearsay or just plain exaggeration. Besides, surely Vicky would have been made aware of any such dangers before she agreed to go. Do stop worrying!" she urged, finishing her tea and checking her lipstick in a small hand mirror. "Reply to her letter and ask her what exactly is going on over there. I'm sure she will tell you everything is okay."

"Yes, of course, I will write to her this evening but I have heard all about these al-Qaeda splinter groups aiming to create an Islamic State across Iraq, Syria and now Africa. I just wish Vicky would come home and preach the gospel of Jesus to the unbelievers in the UK instead!" replied Belinda, genuine concern for her friend suddenly flooding her mind.

"Please give her my love when you do write," said Freddie, taking his brown leather bomber jacket off the coat stand then clipping Queenie's lead onto the little dog's diamanté studded collar.

"I shall send her lots of love from all of us, letting her know she is greatly missed," said Belinda, looking up from her computer with a smile.

"Off to the post office, ladies. See you in a bit!" Freddie called over his shoulder as he and Queenie disappeared out of the door.

Although Top Drawer Agency's number one Marilyn Monroe, Kay Carney, had more or less taken charge of her own career these days, she occasionally accepted the more affluent jobs that the agency had to offer. Dawn had left a voice message on Kay's mobile, explaining that a marvellous lookalike job had just come in and that both Belinda and she felt they should ask Kay's availability first because, even though she self-managed these days, they felt she just may be interested in this job in Monaco.

It was almost three o'clock before Kay telephoned Top Drawer Agency in response to Dawn's message regarding the very prestigious job. After the initial niceties, Dawn explained to Kay exactly what the client was expecting from the chosen Marilyn Monroe lookalike, who would attend the 70th Red Cross Ball Gala in Monaco in the presence of Prince Albert and Princess Charlene.

"The clients are requesting three songs from you directly after dinner and speeches. One of those songs must be *Diamonds Are a Girl's Best Friend* but you can decide yourself which other two you will perform. Are you happy with this arrangement, Kay?" asked Dawn, raising her eyes to the ceiling when Belinda glanced in her direction.

Belinda knew Kay's answer was favourable when Dawn punched the air, mouthing 'YES'.

Finishing the call, Dawn set about writing up Kay Carney's contract to portray and perform as the most iconic icon woman at the most iconic ball.

Out of curiosity, Belinda Googled the Monaco Red Cross Ball and was highly impressed to learn that the first Monaco Red Cross Ball was organised in 1948 by Prince Louis II of Monaco.

"How lucky Kay is to be attending such an event!" remarked Belinda, envy showing in her eyes.

"Yes, she certainly is, but you never know, they may request La Collins next year!" replied Dawn, glancing up at her friend. "Your eyes have turned emerald green, my darling! Isn't that a sign of jealousy?" she teased, and they both laughed knowingly.

Chapter 9
If Music be the Food of Love

Just lately, Freddie was beginning to feel uneasy in his relationship with Claudio, his Italian opera singer lover. Each time Claudio flew back to Italy for a show, he would stay longer and longer. At the beginning of their relationship, Claudio would fly straight back to London after his performances whenever possible, but these days he made excuses to Freddie about feeling tired and needing to stay over for an extra day or two. Deep in his heart, Freddie knew it had been common knowledge that Claudio was indeed a 'player'. How many times did Belinda and Dawn warn him off of continuing his relationship with the opera singer, but Freddie was deeply in love, and when Freddie was deeply in love, there was no use trying to make him see sense.

Only last week, Freddie recalled his conversation with Claudio regarding a friend of theirs known as Bertie Big Balls, for obvious reasons... Poor Bertie Big Balls had the hots for Camp Freddie, and Claudio apparently had got wind of this.

"You must have encouraged Big Balls in the first place, cara mia," accused Claudio, pacing the wooden floor in their two-bedroomed apartment, dark Italian eyes flashing at Freddie.

"Encouraged him!" shrieked Freddie in his own defence, causing little Queenie to whimper. "I would throw up if Big Balls touched me! And you know it, Claudio! Do not try to create an argument over this. I have never looked at another man since we have been together. Accusing me of flirting with Bertie Big Balls. How dare you!" he screeched, now pacing the room himself, his dark blue eyes, directed at Claudio, blazing with fury.

"Okay, okay, calm down, cara mia. We shall forget about Big Balls now," came Claudio's reply, not relishing an all-out argument with Freddie. "I am tired and have to leave early in the morning for my flight to Milano, so let us now be calm, have a nightcap and retire," he added, walking over to Freddie and playfully pinching his bottom. Little Queenie began to wag his furry tail, sensing that all was well again with his master.

Camp Freddie recalled the two men had kissed and made up which had led to an amazing night of passion but yet again, Claudio had called him from Italy after his performance the following evening, informing Freddie that, due to exhaustion, he would stay a couple of extra days in Milano in order to rest after his sell-out performance.

"Cara mia, remember I told you this particular opera was a one-off performance here in Milano?" Excitedly, he continued. "The management have now invited me back next month for a whole week!"

Before Camp Freddie could congratulate his lover, Claudio added quickly, "Ciao, cara mia, I shall see you in a few days, molto amore, fina a presto!" *(much love, until soon!)* As the line went dead, a feeling of unexpected fear clawed at Freddie's heart.

Unfortunately for poor Freddie, the deception of Claudio was still prevalent. He was indeed enjoying a new romantic fling in Milan with a young man who was part of the chorus line in the show. As soon as Claudio's wandering Italian eyes lay on the latest cast member, Fabrizio, his heart fluttered.

After introducing himself to the young countertenor – who was able to sing even higher than a tenor, although this voice actually falls within a female's voice range – Claudio mustered up all his charm and charisma to win the young man over. Fabrizio was completely fascinated with Claudio and virtually on the brink of falling in love for the first time in his young life.

Three days after Claudio had telephoned Freddie from Milan, he arrived back at London Gatwick Airport, situated in the beautiful West Sussex countryside, just outside London.

With a satisfied smile playing on his lips, he sauntered through customs, enjoying the curious looks from everyone, which caused him to play to the crowd. Claudio was a natural flamboyant, shown not only in his taste of clothes and colours, but in his exaggerated walk and distinctive feminine mannerisms.

Many of the airport employees had seen Claudio several times before on his way to and from Milan and one or two waved to him as he sauntered through. Claudio gracefully nodding his head in reply, as he would often do to his adoring audiences. During the short, slightly bumpy flight, his mind had been full of his new young lover, and he was not at all surprised when he felt butterflies in his tummy. After all, the young countertenor was not only beautiful, with his almond shaped eyes the colour of the sea, but he had also fallen deeply in love with Claudio. A pang of guilt struck him as Freddie entered his thoughts. Claudio was saddened that he would have to hurt his English lover of whom he was very fond indeed. Then again, maybe he would keep quiet about Fabrizio for now and, like the sailor boys, have a lover in every port!

Freddie was so happy to cook a wonderful dinner for Claudio, who arrived at their flat an hour before Freddie and little Queenie had returned from shopping. Today, his lover's homecoming, Freddie had taken time off from the agency because he wanted to prepare a wonderful meal for the opera singer. He was, after all, up against strong competition as everyone knew that Italian cooking was held in the highest regard throughout the world.

As Freddie let himself into the flat with little Queenie running in ahead of him, he was aware of the sound of snoring coming from the master bedroom. Instantly, excitement shot through him and he pushed the bedroom door gently ajar, revealing the sleeping body of his lover. Moving quietly to the bed, Camp Freddie looked down with love on Claudio as the latter continued snoring loudly. Pulling the door gently closed, Freddie set about his labour of love as his nimble fingers created a delicious English roast beef dinner.

"That was magnifico!" exclaimed Claudio, swallowing the last morsel of his tasty roast beef before pushing his plate towards the middle of the round table. "You are quite the master chef now, Freddie," he retorted as Freddie smiled and glowed from his lover's praise.

Drinking down the remainder of his Italian red wine, Freddie asked many questions about Claudio's performance and how he had spent the extra days in Milan. Of course, Claudio lied, telling Freddie that he literally just ate and slept.

"It's been a long time since I was last in Milan. I must accompany you when you perform there again next month," suggested Freddie, clearing the used crockery from the table.

Surprised and taken aback by Freddie's words, Claudio poured himself another glass of wine before replying.

"Cara mia, you know very well that you hate opera and besides, my next booking is for a whole week. What will you do while I am performing each night and rehearsing each day? You don't understand the language. You will be bored to death, I guarantee it!"

Returning to the lounge, Freddie felt disappointment at Claudio's response.

"No, THAT is not true, Claudio. I do not hate opera, I don't particularly like it, but hate? No, no, no, not at all!"

A furrowed frown appeared on the otherwise wrinkle-free forehead of Claudio as he answered, irritation creeping into his voice.

"Cara mia, let's not get into a squabble this evening. I am still very tired and really cannot deal with this right now. We shall discuss this another time."

Getting up from his chair then wiping his mouth with a serviette, Claudio turned briefly to Freddie who was beginning to look crestfallen, kissed him lightly on both cheeks and slowly walked into the bedroom to sleep.

Chapter 10
Sisterly Love!

"Darkness cannot drive out darkness; only light can do that.
Hate cannot drive out hate; only love can do that."
Martin Luther King

Although having worked in many of the most affluent cities of the world, Kay Carney was nonetheless amazed at the glamorous and prestigious ambience of the Monaco Red Cross Gala. This year, a legendary English singer had taken centre stage at the gala and Kay felt highly privileged to have her dressing room next door to his. She had made it her business to meet with him and found him to be a very friendly albeit terse personality. He was several years her senior, yet she was amazed at how young he looked and behaved. The legend had told her he often saw her on Twitter and thought her a remarkable lookalike for the iconic Marilyn Monroe, to which Kay fluttered her fake eyelashes at him and blushed like a schoolgirl under his admiring gaze.

The evening was an overwhelming success. Kay was asked by the clients to help with the traditional tombola before the sumptuous meal, after which His Serene Highness Prince Albert II of Monaco opened the ball. The first notes of the concert to raise funds for the Monaco Red

Cross where then heard on the stage of the legendary Salle des Etoiles.

Straight after the speeches, Kay was determined to win this affluent audience over during her performance. Of course, even before she came to the end of *Diamonds are a Girl's Best Friend*, the whole place were shouting for "More!" Win them over, she did!

Later during the traditional fireworks display that lit up the Monaco sky, delighting the guests and marking the close of a wonderful ball, the famous English legend remarked to her, "Kay, you deserve the accolade of the world's most famous icon. You were mesmerising up on that stage this evening; simply smashing, my dear!"

Giggling, she looked up from under her eyelashes and replied coquettishly, dropping her voice an octave. "Thank you so very much, Zac. A compliment like this coming from one of the world's biggest legends means the world to me. Thank you!"

Kay Carney wanted to go places.

As the world was aware, the legendary singer was gay and Kay knew only too well he would never be interested in her as other men were but, to be one of his many acquaintances and even better, friends, would open up a whole new world for her.

For the following hour, Kay and her newfound friend drank, danced and laughed together. He was, of course, surrounded by many of his admirers, some of whom complimented Kay on her tribute act as the iconic Marilyn Monroe. For Kay, the highlight of the evening, apart from meeting Zac Lewis, was being introduced to HRH Prince Albert and his beautiful wife, Princess Charlene.

Zac was mesmerised by Kay and invited her to one of his famous parties in the South of France in November.

Kay's own life seemed to be evermore imitating the famous icon she was portraying.

Kay Carney was definitely going places.

൙

Back at Top Drawer Agency, Dawn was looking at several photographs that had just been delivered from all over the UK and Europe of potential lookalikes and tribute acts. One photograph in particular caught her meticulous eyes. It was of a young blonde woman promoting herself as the next top Marilyn Monroe on the planet. Dawn was impressed and let out a low half-whistle as she scrutinised the professionally taken photograph.

"Belinda, take a look at this, will you, darling?" she asked, eyes still studying the photograph.

Belinda exclaimed, "Wow! She is fabulous!" then added, glancing at Dawn, "A definite possibility to fill Kay Carney's iconic shoes, I would say. Who is she?"

Walking across to the large window, glancing up at the rolling clouds, as she handed Belinda the photograph, Dawn replied, "Crystal. Just one name, Crystal. Read her attached letter, Belinda. I think you are in for a surprise!"

Picking up the single sheet of notepaper clipped to the photograph, Belinda's eyes scanned the full page of text quickly, finding some words difficult to decipher. Turning back from the window in order to watch her friend's reaction, Dawn raised her recently microbladed eyebrows questioningly at her partner.

"Sisters? So this Crystal is Melita Morgan's younger sister? Melita has never mentioned the fact that she had a sister, especially one that looked more like Marilyn Monroe than Marilyn Monroe!" exclaimed Belinda, bewildered.

"Seems that way, doesn't it?" agreed Dawn.

"Melita is excellent as Monroe," offered Belinda, "but I hate to admit it, this girl has probably the closest resemblance to Marilyn I have ever seen, and that includes Kay Carney!"

"Let's bring her in as soon as possible," suggested Dawn returning to her office and picking up the telephone receiver.

"Please call Melita and mention this. We don't want to make her feel that the agency has been underhanded in any way."

"Yes, of course. I will do that straightaway. Poor Melita, such a lovely girl. I was hoping that now Kay is managing her own career, the Marilyn Monroe crown would go to her, but I suspect she will now miss out to her own sister!" replied Belinda, searching for Melita's contact number on the agency's online Artistes List.

"C'est la vie, I'm afraid. You must remember the greatest icon of all is Marilyn Monroe and there will always be contenders for her crown. May the best imposter win!" exclaimed Dawn, shrugging her shoulders.

Dawn had made arrangements for Crystal to come into Top Drawer Agency the following Friday for an interview. Crystal seemed very keen to become a professional tribute artiste and had informed Dawn that she had been singing and dancing from an early age.

After unsuccessfully trying to contact Melita, Belinda decided to leave a message on her voicemail. Less than an hour later, Melita returned Belinda's call, anticipating that a potential job had come in for her.

Of course, disappointment set in when Melita learned that the call was not about a job but that Crystal's photographs had been received and that she had expressed hope of becoming a Marilyn Monroe lookalike herself.

"Oh! Crystal? Yes, she is my half-sister. Different mothers. I don't have anything to do with her or my father," explained Melita. "She must be twenty-five years old now, I suppose. I haven't seen either of them for years. Obviously, she probably does look a little like Marilyn Monroe as I do."

"Yes, Melita, but she is extremely like Marilyn, not just a little," replied Belinda. "Dawn and I are concerned about how you'd feel about having your sister working for the agency and, in a way, being one of your rivals," stressed Belinda, feeling quite sorry about how life often throws unlucky blows at some of the nicest people.

Slightly stuttering in order to make herself sound unconcerned about this troubling situation, Melita assured Belinda that as long as she and her sister did not have to work together, she was quite relaxed about them taking Crystal on their books as another Marilyn Monroe lookalike.

However, when the call had ended, Melita's heart shattered into a thousand tiny pieces.

Knowing how ambitious Dawn was regarding Top Drawer Agency, Melita was sagacious enough to realise that even if she had expressed her dislike of Crystal being on their books, the agency would have taken her sister on nonetheless. Anyone Dawn and Belinda decided to take on their books would indeed have to be 'top drawer' and this fact caused Melita serious concern. It had only been a few weeks since Kay Carney began managing her own career, enabling the Marilyn Monroe lookalike crown to sit precariously upon Melita's own blonde head.

Friday had arrived and Camp Freddie sauntered towards the big oak door when a gentle tap was heard. "Coming!" he sang out quickly, as little Queenie followed in his beloved master's footsteps.

On opening the door of the agency, Freddie's blue eyes took in the beautiful apparition of the visitor outside. Crystal stood there with such an astonishing resemblance to Marilyn Monroe that Freddie had to catch his breath and blink several times.

"Hello," said Freddie, again noticing how very beautiful the girl was. "You must be Crystal?"

Smiling, Crystal swayed slowly past Freddie, and replied sweetly in a voice that was a perfect replica of the famous icon's, "Why, yes. I am Crystal, how clever of you!"

"Clever? No! No! Your resemblance to Marilyn Monroe is extraordinary!" gushed Freddie, offering Crystal a seat in his usual flamboyant manner as little Queenie ran up and started sniffing her black suede stilettos. Crystal did not bend down to stroke the little dog or even acknowledge him.

Both Dawn and Belinda were also mesmerised upon meeting Crystal. Not only did she look exactly like Marilyn Monroe but her resemblance was even closer than Kay's and far, far closer than Melita's. Dawn was ecstatic.

After all forms were completed and photographs and videos taken, Crystal finally said goodbye and left her new agents, leaving them under the impression that she was a very sweet, young lady. As she walked down the steps of the agency into the pale sunlight, Crystal felt elated. Knowing how fabulous she looked as Marilyn Monroe and how wonderfully she could perform the icon's songs, her lifetime obsession to destroy Melita's life had just begun.

Unbeknown to the outside world, beautiful Crystal suffered from an antisocial personality disorder.

Chapter 11
Las Vegas Daydreams

Frank Lanzo frowned as he hung up the phone. The Society was sending him to California for some time. Las Vegas would be his home from home while he set up and dealt with underhanded dealings within the Society's gambling structure. He was fully aware that something had been brewing on the West Coast for some time now and it had affected one of the Society's major concerns there. Of course, he had no choice but to agree to go.

It was being debated whether Aldo Lamarina was to accompany Frank to Las Vegas rather than pulling Sergie back from London and sending Aldo to London in Sergie's place.

The Society was extremely satisfied with how the London concerns were being run by Sergie and Joey, so decided not to upset the apple cart in the UK. It was finally arranged that Aldo would support Frank in Las Vegas and the two men would remain there until the Society's massive West Coast concerns were back on song.

Frank felt saddened. His move to California would put another three thousand miles between himself and Belinda. For the next few months, he would not be flying into London and this thought begun to depress him.

Pouring a large Jack Daniels and drinking slowly, he decided to call Belinda later that evening and explain everything. Of course, she would be able to fly out to visit him and he consoled himself with the fact that she would have beautiful blue skies and sunshine, no matter what time of year she visited.

Knowing the work could take months in Las Vegas, Frank was sure it would be close to Christmas by the time he and Aldo had completed all the necessary business for their bosses. The biggest challenge, of course, was to make sure they caught the culprits red-handed, so there could be no doubt whatsoever. Frank felt a surge of confidence that he, with support from Aldo, would hopefully successfully wrap up the Society's business by Thanksgiving at the end of November.

Although Frank was a little disappointed that Sergie would not be accompanying him to Las Vegas, he was also happy because it meant he could now ask Belinda to join him for a week or two. Belinda had never met Aldo but she had met Sergie at Matt's funeral and knew that Sergie had been friends with Matt. Under no circumstances, Frank repeated to himself, must Belinda ever learn that he and Matt had been very good friends and colleagues.

"But, Frank, you and I will never be together at this rate!" exclaimed Belinda down the telephone, her voice sounding sulky.

"Listen, mia amore, it doesn't matter whether I am on the East Coast or the West Coast, we are still apart!" replied Frank, his voice taking on a cajoling tone before adding quickly, "You can fly out to Vegas and enjoy the beautiful sunshine. Will you do that for me, mia amore?"

"Of course I will, Frank. It's just that I sense we will never really be together. The Society will always come between us."

"Nonsense, darling!" replied Frank. "How many times do I have to tell you that soon we will be together for always!"

❧

The following morning at the agency, Freddie frowned as he studied a photograph from a pile of wannabe Boris Johnson lookalikes.

Belinda interrupted his thoughts. "Do you think I should go to Vegas to see Frank?"

"Go for it!" Then rising, he pranced around the agency office, checking out his face in the mirrored wall before winking at her. "Go for it!" he echoed.

"You know, Freddie, it's six thousand miles to California from London, twice as far as New York!"

"And?" replied Freddie, turning back from admiring his reflection in the mirror to look Belinda in the eye, hands outstretched in an exaggerated gesture.

"I am not the best flyer in the world and six thousand miles is a long time to be airborne, my friend," she remarked, picking up a tourist guide and flicking through its pages, a frown furrowing her brow.

"Oh, come now, sweet pea," encouraged Freddie, looking aghast. "If you become nervous, just close your eyes and think of England, or even better, have a stiff drink! Now that will definitely send you off to sleep for the remainder of the flight!"

"Freddie, darling, what would I do without you to make me see sense?" replied Belinda, giggling.

"Exactly, darling. Now book that flight and when lover boy is busy during the working week, you can have a wonderful time sunbathing and shopping with his credit card! How exciting! Las Vegas! You lucky girl! I am so, so jealous – look! My beautiful blue eyes have turned green with envy!"

"Oh, Freddie, you are so funny!" giggled Belinda again, walking over to the water cooler to pour herself a drink.

"Yes, as long as I am funny 'ha ha' and not funny 'peculiar'," quipped Freddie, attempting a pirouette in front of the mirrored wall, causing little Queenie to whine as he watched his beloved master's antics.

"Morning!" came the dulcet tones of Dawn's voice as she rushed in, slipping off her blue cashmere jacket and hanging it on the mahogany coat hanger.

"Morning, Dawn!" replied Freddie, finishing his amusing frolics and sauntering into the kitchenette to fill the kettle for coffee.

"Good morning, Dawn!" said Belinda, looking up from her desk, still giggling at Freddie's horseplay.

"What have I been missing so early in the morning?" asked Dawn, smiling as she went into her office.

"Oh, Freddie has been keeping me entertained!" replied Belinda.

"Really?" queried Dawn, flippantly.

"Yes, really!" replied Belinda. "I'll tell you all the latest while you unwind."

Chapter 12
The 'S' in Sin City

July and into early August had been unusually warm in London and Belinda stopped to remove her orange tweed jacket, laying the garment on top of her Bellagio four-wheel spinner suitcase. Hurrying towards the Virgin Atlantic desk at Heathrow Airport, she was aware of butterflies building up inside her tummy. It had been some time since she had been with her lover, and her mind and body ached for him. The queue was quite long and Belinda's heart sunk, hating the fact that she would be flying the furthest she had ever flown, and alone. However, the thought of being with Frank again managed to calm her nervousness.

As the Virgin flight touched down smoothly at McCarran International Airport, Belinda put her Bleu de Cartier wristwatch back eight hours to Californian time. Momentarily, sadness overwhelmed her as she remembered her last birthday when Matt had presented her with the beautiful gift, which she knew she would always treasure, as she would always cherish his memory. How unpredictable life had been over the past two years, she reminisced, as the sign to secure seat belts was flashed off. Passengers got up from their seats quickly, grateful that the long flight from London was over and they could at last stretch their weary legs, Belinda amongst them.

Following the other passengers down the steps, Belinda became very excited as she felt the hot afternoon sun caress her skin. Glancing upwards, Belinda realised that she had never seen such a huge sky before! Cutting through her thoughts, one of the air stewards asked her to hurry along into the waiting airport bus that would carry passengers into the main terminal. Standing amongst the throng of people, looking out of the bus windows, Belinda continued to marvel at the azure sky which seemed to promise her a warm stay in Las Vegas.

As she hurriedly followed the other passengers, passing quickly through customs and immigration control, and then the baggage retrieval, with her duty-free purchases clutched tightly in her left hand, Belinda became very excited as she passed smoothly through Anything to Declare and into Las Vegas Airport itself.

Frank stood there looking tanned, handsome and a little leaner than usual, grey hair and Roman-style beard accentuating his brown eyes. He smiled and waved when she appeared. Upon seeing him, Belinda could not keep the tears inside any longer.

Like a child, she stood in front of him, deliriously happy. His eyes mocked her a little as he took her in his arms and held her close to his body. A quiver began deep within her, and for a few brief seconds, she was in a private place with Frank, the only two people in the whole world.

Strongly, he held her at arm's length from himself and whispered, "Ringrazio Dio che sei qui con me!" *(I thank God you are here with me!)*

Frank drove Belinda to his luxury suite on the top floor of one of the more exclusive hotels, the Majestic, owned by the Society. Belinda caught her breath as her eyes took in the opulent surroundings. Frank ushered her across the large lounge and out onto the equally large balcony where she gazed at the stunning sights of Las Vegas, as far as the eye could see.

"You wait until dark, my darling; the view is spectacular!" declared Frank, placing her case down.

"It is all so beautiful, Frank, I love it!" Belinda enthused, removing her suit jacket then popping to the bathroom to freshen up.

When she reappeared, Frank had poured them both a large glass of red wine which he handed to her. His amused eyes locked with her own and they sipped their wine slowly, melting in the fact that they would be imminently sharing passionate love.

An excited sound escaped her throat as his lips found hers which she parted enabling his tongue to flicker in and out. Every fibre of Belinda's body screamed out for him. This lover of hers held the key to everything she craved; like no other man before, he knew how to fulfil her every need. Deftly sweeping Belinda off her feet, Frank carried her quickly into the master bedroom and gently lay her on the Emperor sized bed, which was dressed in ruby and gold brocade.

Before Frank could climb above her, Belinda opened her legs as wide as possible, causing him to catch his breath, his manhood standing up proud as he lowered himself onto her, feverishly entering his lover's quivering body. Feeling him inside her again after so long, Belinda moaned in ecstasy as she felt the whole length of his manhood bringing her to a glorious climax.

Las Vegas is known as the Gambling and Entertainment Capital of the World. The city's nightclubs are open all night for eating, drinking and dancing. Known as Sin City, you can find all kinds of adult entertainment there.

Both Frank and Aldo had worked in Vegas several times during their careers with the Society but Frank, unlike Aldo, was becoming weary of the lifestyle that it had to offer. He knew his outlook on life had changed dramatically over the last year, even to the extent that he hardly recognised himself. He also knew this change was largely due to his falling deeply in love with Belinda.

Frank and Aldo had the privilege to eat and drink in whichever restaurant that took their fancy within the hotel complex. There were three five-star restaurants, each serving world-class food from Italy, France and Japan. Frank and Aldo favoured the Italian one but Frank decided he would take Belinda for dinner wherever she wanted to go, wanting her to love every minute of her stay.

That evening, Frank introduced Belinda to Aldo and all three had dinner together in Uccellino (*little bird*), the Italian restaurant within the hotel. Belinda liked Aldo; she found him quite charming with a dry, deadpan humour. Aldo could deliver a hysterically funny line without cracking a smile or raising an eyebrow, causing Belinda to continuously giggle and laugh.

Leaning towards her, Frank placed his suntanned, manicured hand over her own and smiling, focused his gaze on Aldo, remarking, "Darling, you'll get used to Aldo in time. He is a frustrated stand-up comic. Isn't that correct, Aldo?"

"Me, frustrated, Frank? No way, buddy, I'm in Las Vegas, how can I be frustrated?" replied Aldo, winking knowingly at both Belinda and Frank, causing them to laugh heartily.

"Aldo, your humour is very British!" remarked Belinda, taking a sip of her red wine and allowing it to slide slowly down her throat, appreciating the fruity aroma.

"British comedies often produce great examples of your type of humour," she added, placing her empty wine glass on the crisp white tablecloth.

Pouring more wine into all three crystal glasses, Frank mouthed to Belinda, "Ti amo."

❧

The following two weeks passed so quickly, Belinda could not believe her time with Frank was almost at an end.

Although she could see and sense that her lover was beginning to feel a little weary of his jet set lifestyle, she knew deep in her heart that he would not be burning his passport any day soon; he lived and breathed his position with the Society. Belinda knew only too well, no matter how Frank tried to placate her, that it would be a long time before they could always be together.

"I have another name for Las Vegas," she told Frank as he joined her in his suite at a little after four o'clock that afternoon.

"Do you?" asked Frank, raising one of his eyebrows.

"Yes, I do. Copycat City!" announced Belinda with a giggle. "And I should know all about copycats!" she added with a wink, as Frank pulled her close to him.

"Copycat City, eh?" replied Frank, frowning before adding, "Yes, I guess I'll go with that, seeing as the hotels are copies of cities around the world."

"Exactly!" she agreed. "They are lookalikes!"

Belinda smiled up at him as he brought his mouth down to hers.

Chapter 13
Farewell to Las Vegas

With a heavy heart, Belinda landed in London on a sunny but windy late August afternoon. For the duration of the flight until the Virgin Atlantic plane touched smoothly down at Heathrow, Belinda's thoughts were full of her time with Frank, deliriously happy together in the sunshine of the exciting Copycat City. She reflected on their flight from the helicopter terminal off the Strip, with aerial views of the Hoover Dam and the iconic Colorado River, before the aircraft descended to land deep in the Grand Canyon for a Champagne picnic lunch, hosted by their private pilot. Belinda would never forget the gorgeous red mountains of the Mojave Desert and the cool, calm waters of Lake Mead.

Being accustomed to their long-distance love affair did not make it any easier each time she had to be parted from her lover. When she had spoken with Dawn just before her flight back to London, Belinda was pleased to hear the agency was flourishing. Dawn had suggested Belinda take the following day off due to possible jet lag but she decided to go into the agency the following afternoon to have a quick catch-up on business, to spend time with Dawn and Camp Freddie, to help take her tortured mind off Frank.

"Wow, look at you!" squealed Freddie, as Belinda arrived at the agency, suntanned and relaxed. "You look amazing, darling! Queenie and I have missed you so much!" he said, walking over to Belinda as she unbuttoned her light cream jacket.

Pecking her on both cheeks, Freddie let out another squeal before wrapping his long arms around her and hugging her. Smiling, she handed Freddie a duty-free bag.

"Pressies for Freddie! Oh! Thank you so much, sweet pea. What is it?" he asked excitedly.

"Open it and see!" coaxed Belinda, stroking little Queenie who was becoming excited.

Quickly taking the gift out of the bag, Camp Freddie let out a long whistle.

"Creed Aventus Eau de Toilette!" he exclaimed. "You naughty girl! This is mega expensive. You really shouldn't have!" he added, hugging his dear friend again.

"Dawn is at the bank right now, so come sit down and tell me all about it," he encouraged, becoming increasingly flamboyant, causing little Queenie to bark while he lay on his back and insisted Belinda rub his furry tummy.

"Oh, Freddie! I won't bore you with how miserable I feel right now. This is precisely why I came in today. I can't bear being alone at home with the pain and sadness of being away from Frank," revealed Belinda, eyes downcast.

"Now listen to me, sweet pea! I could never be bored with you, my darling. You and I are two of a kind! Far too sensitive for our own good! Now come along, tell Freddie everything of how amazing Vegas was!" he cajoled, squeezing Belinda's hand.

As Belinda relayed to Freddie everything about the wonderful places she had visited with Frank in Las Vegas, every so often, an excited squeal would escape from his throat, especially when she mentioned about the beautiful gay community that sauntered up and down the Strip nightly, alongside some of the most glamorous men and women in the world.

"I must tell Claudio as soon as possible about Las Vegas!" enthused Freddie; blue eyes sparkling. "Hopefully, he may agree to go with me once his singing commitments have quietened down."

"Oh, yes, you must tell him! I would think Las Vegas is right up Claudio's street!" remarked Belinda. "By the way, when will he have a break from all his theatre bookings?"

"Oh! Don't ask me, sweet pea, he is forever on the go! Back and forth to Milan. Non-stop these past few months," replied Freddie, sighing deeply.

"Welcome home, Belinda!" came Dawn's throaty voice, snapping Freddie out of his troubling thoughts.

Turning towards the door, Belinda smiled, and walked over to her business partner and close friend. The two ladies hugged each other in genuine friendship before Dawn stepped back and whistled in a most unladylike manner, reducing Belinda to a fit of giggles.

"You look fabulous, my darling. What a superb tan you managed to acquire! I can see you didn't spend the whole time in bed with lover boy then!" joked Dawn, winking.

"Of course not!" replied an embarrassed Belinda indignantly. "Lover boy had heavy work commitments, that is how I managed to sunbathe," she added before continuing, "Mind you, Dawn, the time we did have together was magical. I miss him dreadfully."

"You must tell me everything, darling girl, I want to know everything! Come with me!" instructed Dawn, winking at her again.

Carrying another duty-free bag, Belinda followed her partner into the office, hoping she would be strong enough to hold back the tears that were welling up inside her.

❧

Two days later, back at the agency as Belinda read through her emails, she suddenly exclaimed, "You won't believe this!"

"Really? Try me," replied a subdued Freddie, playing with his ballpoint pen.

"Our most influential Dutch clients have chosen Ada Demir as Meghan Markle for their new TV commercial!"

Freddie's blue eyes opened widely.

"I don't believe it! You mean to say the client chose Ada over Charlotte?" he queried, looking baffled.

"Yes, they did," she replied. "Didn't I tell you Ada Demir has something special or even mysterious about her and will go far in this business?" she remarked, looking at Freddie for a response.

"Well, I still think Charlotte, or even Amanda for that matter, have a closer resemblance to the Duchess of Sussex than Ms Demir!" retorted Freddie, fidgeting on his chair and tutting to himself.

"C'est la vie, Freddie! I guess we all see things differently but I am over the moon that we have won this extremely important contract and, of course, Dawn will be ecstatic!" said Belinda, looking under the letter D in the long list of names for Ada Demir's contact details.

Suddenly, the telephone rang in Dawn's office. Freddie jumped up and trotted in quickly to answer the persistent ringing. Making excuses for Dawn's absence, Freddie informed the Dutch client that he would transfer the call to the junior partner.

After a short discussion with the caller from the Netherlands, having replaced the receiver, Belinda let out a squeal, wakening Queenie from his afternoon nap, which caused him to stare at her bewilderingly.

"What is it?" asked Freddie, looking even more bewildered than his little dog.

"The client has also requested Max Rushton as Prince Harry for the TV commercial. This is going to boost Top Drawer Agency more than ever in Europe," declared Belinda, then muttering almost to herself, she added, "I must call Ada and Max immediately for their availability then I will leave a voice message for Dawn on her mobile."

Chapter 14
Antics in Amsterdam

On a clement day in early September, Max Rushton, the Prince Harry lookalike, bent down in a gentlemanly-like manner, brushing Ada Demir's left cheek in greeting when they met at the British Airways desk at Gatwick Airport for their early morning flight into Amsterdam. Max noticed that Ada stiffened slightly when he pecked her cheek. They had worked together just once before, in London some two months earlier, but had not spoken much to each other, as there were three other young women on the same photo shoot, all portraying Meghan Markle.

At first glance, although he thought her quite stunning, Max was not impressed with Ada's resemblance to the Duchess and thought Charlotte and the two other girls had the edge. Amazingly, after the make-up artistes and hair stylists had performed their magic on all the lookalikes, Max was astonished to see how Ada had been transformed into Meghan Markle's double.

Now as he was chatting with her, Max was no longer surprised that she had been chosen for the prestigious TV commercial promoting one of the Netherlands' favourite alcoholic beverages Jenever. After checking in, Max asked Ada if she would like to have some breakfast in one of the many restaurants in the airport. Accepting his offer as she cast her eyes downward, he noticed a slight suggestive flutter of a grin at the corner of her mouth.

Max had worked in Amsterdam several times but this was Ada's first visit to the land of tulips, windmills and canals. She found the Dutch people and the country charming. For the two days they were there, she vowed to herself that she would return some day to spend more time exploring this fascinating country.

"I love the Netherlands already!" exclaimed Ada, gazing out of the shiny black limousine's window as they were driven from the airport by Jan, the client's personal chauffeur, to their hotel in the heart of the effervescent Nine Streets neighbourhood. They were both wide-eyed as the chauffeur pulled up and stopped outside the Pulitzer Amsterdam which overlooked the picturesque waters of the historic central canal belt that has been the centre of social life in the city for centuries.

Promptly alighting from the driver's seat, Jan opened the back door for his regal passengers, giving Ada his hand to help her out. Opening the limousine's roomy boot, Jan quickly lifted out his passengers' luggage and led the way into the charming entrance of the hotel.

"How beautiful!" exclaimed Ada as her hazel eyes noticed the large shiny pots situated outside the entrance, each cradling the most amazing array of flowers of every colour imaginable.

Hurrying now to keep up with Jan and Max, Ada was again enthralled with her beautiful room on the fourth floor. Jan explained to them that every room was different, and each was unique and part of the exceptional heritage of

Pulitzer's canal houses. Max's room was also on the fourth floor, overlooking the serenely twinkling canals.

There was a silver bucket with ice and Champagne for each of the lookalikes in their rooms, together with a small box of handcrafted Dutch chocolates. Next to the bucket was an envelope containing a gold edged white card which stated that two of the client's representatives would arrive at the hotel by seven o'clock in order to take Ada and Max for dinner. Ada immediately called Max in his room across the hall and seemed quite excited about everything.

At seven o'clock sharp, Mila and Bram arrived in a chauffeur-driven car and waited in the elaborate hotel foyer for the lookalikes to appear. When the lift doors opened and Ada and Max walked out together giggling, Mila rushed up to them, smiling broadly with approval.

"Wow, you both look sensational!" she enthused in broken English. Mila – slim, tall and blonde – held out her hand in welcome, first to Ada, then to Max.

"Thank you," replied Ada, now beaming like a Cheshire cat. An elegant dark-haired young man walked up to the threesome and let out a low whistle as he too held out his hand in welcome.

"You approve, I take it?" laughed Max, as he shook Bram's tanned hand.

"I most certainly do, Your Royal Highness!" he responded, bowing in mockery to Max.

"I hope you are both hungry because we have a real treat for you this evening, compliments of the client," he added, in almost perfect English with hardly a trace of a Dutch accent.

"Let's get going. Your chauffeur awaits!" he declared, stepping in line with Max while Mila ushered Ada outside to the waiting limousine.

A very enjoyable evening was spent by all in the De Wallen medieval city centre, which Bram informed his guests was crossed by canals and narrow alleys. Max and Ada noticed the alleys were lined with old-school bars. Mila explained to them that the area was surrounded by the neon-lit red light district to which both Max and Ada raised their eyebrows.

A five-star Dutch restaurant had been booked for their evening meal which consisted of local appetizers, followed by a delicious soup of the day. The main course was pork tenderloin with rhubarb and mashed potatoes with vegetables on the side. Bram ordered a French wine which proved a perfect pairing for the main course.

As the four young people chatted happily, Ada's mobile phone rang out loudly, interrupting their flowing conversation. Retrieving it quickly from her purple leather handbag, she checked the number and cut the call off.

"Are you not going to answer it?" enquired Mila in her attractive broken English.

Shaking her head, Ada smiled sweetly at her three dining companions, curiosity showing in their faces.

"I really love the Netherlands!" announced Ada, dabbing her mouth with a pure white napkin, hazel eyes shining from the effects of the large glass of red wine she had consumed.

"Me too!" responded Mila and they all laughed at her wit.

Suddenly, Ada's mobile phone interrupted their conversation again. Jumping up from her chair and excusing herself, an angry look fleetingly touching her lovely face, she moved away from the dining table and into the restaurant's corridor.

Barely two minutes later, she returned to her waiting companions, acting as if she had never left the table.

"Everything okay, Ada?" asked Max, watching his Duchess closely.

"Oh, yes, fine, thank you, Max," she replied, smiling at him.

All too soon, Ada and Max were driven back to their hotel together with their hosts.

"Sweet dreams! See you bright and early!" called out a grinning Bram, leaning out of the limousine window as the lookalikes walked into the beautiful hotel foyer, different aromas from the flowers filling the chilly night air.

"We will be bright-eyed and bushy-tailed! Thank you both for such a lovely evening!" Max called out, turning back and waving.

"Yes, thank you very much for a lovely evening," echoed Ada, slightly swaying as she linked Max's arm, steadying herself.

"You know, Max, I am a lightweight. Barely two glasses of wine and I'm tipsy!" she whispered, leaning on her escort for support.

"You can say that again!" agreed Max, teasing her, which started Ada giggling.

As they exited the lift on the fourth floor, Max enquired whether his Duchess was okay.

Looking up at him, with her big childlike hazel eyes, she squeezed his arm and whispered, "Oh, yes, I'm wonderful, thank you."

What happened next completely surprised the Duke of Sussex lookalike. Reaching up, placing her slim arms around his neck, Ada pulled Max's head down to her level and kissed him sensually for what seemed a very long time, before releasing him and giggling again.

"Oh! Sorry to be so pushy! Don't know what came over me. Mind you, I've been itching to do that all evening!" she confessed demurely, eyes downcast. "I hope I didn't shock you, Max?" she asked, looking up at him seductively.

Flustered, Max, his face turning a shade of pink, replied, "No, of course not. No problem at all, Ada. I quite enjoy that kind of shock actually!"

The Duke and Duchess of Sussex lookalikes enjoyed one more drink together in Max's room, becoming a little more familiar with each other. Stopping his amorous advances before they both got carried away, Max insisted they had some coffee before escorting a giggling Ada to her room, making sure she was safe.

As he pulled her door closed behind him, he was conscious that he desperately wanted to stay all night with Ada but a voice at the back of his mind warned him that this would not be advisable. He knew nothing about her. She could be engaged or even married for all he knew! Making a point to find out more about her at breakfast the following morning, he went back to his own room, tumbled onto the king-sized bed and instantly fell fast asleep.

At seven o'clock sharp, the hotel's Reception desk called both Max and Ada's rooms, alerting them that it was time to rise and shine.

Within the hour, both were walking towards the lift to go down to the breakfast room.

"Good morning, Ms Demir. I trust you had your beauty sleep!" enquired Max, surprised to see Ada looking stunningly gorgeous first thing in the morning.

"Good morning to you, Mr Rushton. Yes, thank you, I had a wonderful sleep. A couple of glasses of wine always does the trick, don't you agree?" she answered, smiling sheepishly.

As the pair got into the empty lift, both felt a shimmer of excitement shoot through their young bodies.

At breakfast, Max asked several questions about Ada's life, the normal questions asked by new friends and acquaintances. He was surprised that she appeared ready to talk about herself and he listened soberly.

Ada revealed to Max that although she was born and bred in London, her Turkish Muslim family were very old school and she would be expected to marry a Muslim boy, preferably from another good Turkish family.

Max asked whether the mobile calls during dinner last evening were from her family, but Ada told him that both were from her betrothed, Mehmet, and that Mehmet was a very jealous person.

Upon hearing this, Max's heart sunk.

He had never been lucky in love and the few girls he had fallen for in the past were unavailable, as was Ada, it seemed.

Seeing the disappointment in his eyes, Ada explained to Max that she did not love Mehmet but that he had been accepted by her family because he was an educated, ambitious young man who came from an extremely good Turkish family and was deeply in love with her.

Continuing, she told Max that she liked Mehmet, he was very kind to her, but that she could never love him.

When Max asked her why she would contemplate marrying a man she was not in love with, Ada stressed that she was brought up to understand that even if she did not feel love for her betrothed at the beginning, she would eventually fall in love with him and be happy.

Ada also explained to Max that it was not good for her to go against the wishes of her family, especially her father and his three brothers.

"So there is no hope of us ever getting to know each other better?" asked Max, suppressing his inner voice, alerting him again to be careful.

"Max! Believe me, I already have strong feelings for you but I must be very, very cautious. You have no idea about my religion and how impossible it is for me to go against both mine and Mehmet's families."

Drinking down the last drops of her orange juice, she continued. "I am angry deep down in my heart that I cannot fall in love with whoever I choose."

The two Royal lookalikes finished breakfast just as Bram walked into the elaborately decorated breakfast room.

"So, indeed you are bright-eyed and bushy-tailed this morning!" came Bram's perfect English accent, echoing around the room.

Max and Ada followed Bram out of the hotel and into the waiting chauffeur-driven limousine.

After a thirty minute drive, the limousine pulled into a large compound with Czar Studios emblazoned in gold on the front of a red-brick building.

Within two hours, Ada and Max were out of make-up and standing in character in front of several TV cameras, together with producers, executive producers, directors, production managers and others milling around the set.

The lookalikes were briefed about what was expected of them. The promotional commercial was for Jenever, a clear, botanically rich malted spirit, made only in the Netherlands and Belgium. The lookalikes had to stand close to each other, smiling into the camera, each holding a tulip-shaped glass of ice-cold Jenever, while a male voice-over stated in Dutch, *"A Regal Spirit for Royalty."*

The British Airways flight carrying Max and Ada landed smoothly in the evening at Gatwick Airport at nine-fifteen precisely. Both lookalikes had a good feeling of satisfaction, knowing that the Dutch clients had been extremely impressed with them and had already decided to use them both again.

As they entered the arrivals lounge, Max sensed Ada stiffen by his side. Looking down at her, he asked, "Are you all right, Ada?"

"Yes, yes, of course, but I have to go now. Mehmet is waving to me. I will call you!" and with those words ringing in his ears, she was gone, rushing over to a stocky man of medium height with black hair and an olive complexion, whom, Max noticed with envy, held out his arms to Ada as she went to him.

Jealousy is one of the hardest emotions to endure and as he walked past Ada and her fiancé, still embracing, he kept his eyes straight ahead, hurrying out to the waiting taxis.

Chapter 15
A Match Made in Heaven

The following day, Dawn Jarvis was thrilled when the Dutch client personally telephoned her complimenting the agency on their Duke and Duchess of Sussex lookalikes, jokingly stressing that the Royal couple were indeed 'top drawer'! The client went on to say that he would be contacting the agency again very soon regarding a forthcoming photo shoot for the British Royals but that he was unable to say at the moment which of the Royals they would hire. The agency was to be informed as soon as everything was confirmed his end.

"Stars!" exclaimed Dawn, as she replaced the receiver before walking out of her office to Belinda's highly polished desk, strewn with documents.

"Good news, obviously?" remarked Belinda, smiling up at her partner.

"Yes, indeed! Very good news! Our Dutch clients are even more impressed with Top Drawer since working with Max and Ada!" replied Dawn smugly, taking a sip of cold water from the cooler.

"I knew Max and Ada would have chemistry," declared Belinda, raising her arms above her head and stretching. "I wonder how they really got on though," she added as an afterthought.

Throwing her empty paper cup into the recycling bin, Dawn replied, "Oh, I'm sure they got on like a house on fire. Max usually calls after his jobs to keep us in the loop. He probably will do tomorrow."

"Can't wait to hear!" said Belinda, picking up her mobile phone and checking incoming messages.

Disappointedly, there was nothing from Frank today so far.

When Dawn had left for the evening, Belinda telephoned her close friend Tanya, the Pamela Anderson lookalike, asking if she would like to join her for dinner that evening. Tanya readily agreed as the two friends had not seen each other for a while and both had a need to catch-up. Much to her delight, Tanya's lookalike career had started to pick up again after a long quiet spell. She had also briefly mentioned to Belinda over the telephone, that she had met an attractive man a couple of weeks earlier. The two friends arranged to meet at Aquavit London, a contemporary Nordic restaurant which had excellent reviews.

Belinda arrived at Carlton Street off of Piccadilly a little after six-thirty and was surprised to see the notoriously 'late' Tanya already waiting for her. The two friends embraced and hurriedly entered the restaurant.

Tanya had visited the Aquavit London several times but Belinda had never dined there before and was very impressed with the dining room's decor. Apparently, she learned from the receptionist, the designer had fashioned it after the Gothenburg City Hall in Sweden but kept the original bricks and mortar of the Grade II listed building, adding layers of blue, green and white, timber, polished brass, trimmed chairs and lamps. Tanya pointed out the abstract wall hangings which caused Belinda to unexpectedly whistle under her breath, setting the two friends laughing like a couple of schoolgirls.

As a faint blush swept over her beautiful face, Tanya proclaimed that she had met her new man, Aarne, in this very restaurant when she was celebrating a birthday with a group of friends. Aarne was also Finnish and came from a small town barely six miles from where Tanya was born and grew up.

"What a small world!" declared an emotional Belinda. "I'm so happy for you, Tanya, darling!" she enthused, genuinely feeling happy for her dear friend.

"Hey, take it easy, Belinda!" replied a laughing Tanya. "We're just good friends, nothing more at the moment. Mind you, I do like him but you know me, I take things slowly," she said, taking a sip of her wine, "especially where men are concerned!"

The evening past far too quickly and it was close to eleven when the two friends kissed goodbye, promising to meet up again as soon as possible.

"Say hello to Frank for me when you next speak to him!" requested Tanya, calling out before walking towards her bus stop then blowing Belinda a kiss.

"So glad it's Friday again!" whispered Freddie, arriving late at the agency the following morning. "Sorry that Queenie and I are a little behind, sweet pea, but I simply overslept!"

"No problem! As long as you are happy, then so am I!" replied Belinda, smiling up at him.

"Oh, we're okay, thank you, darling; just blooming tired!" replied Freddie removing his black leather jacket and hanging it carefully on the coat stand before disappearing into the little kitchenette to make coffee.

"Been racing around, as you can imagine, trying to make everything lovely for Claudio. He arrives very early tomorrow morning!" squealed Freddie, clasping his hands, a wide grin spreading across his face. "I'm so pleased to have next week off, darling! Let's have lunch today and I'll tell you all about it, sweet pea," he added turning on his computer. "Must crack on now, I'm well behind!"

Suddenly, Dawn rushed into the office, her face flushed.

"So sorry. Late this morning. I'll make it up some time," she announced. "Traffic is always bad, but this morning, it was ridiculous!" she groaned, slipping out of her stylish tartan coat and hanging it up.

Before anyone could respond, Dawn's telephone rang in her office and she walked quickly to answer, making herself comfortable in her office chair as she listened intently to the caller.

A short while later, she walked out of her office and over to Belinda's desk. "That was Max Rushton, keeping us updated about his job with Ada Demir in the Netherlands," she announced. Smiling as she accepted the hot cup of coffee handed to her by Freddie, she added, "Says he'll pop in sometime this week."

"Was he happy working with Ada?" asked Belinda, glancing up at Dawn who shrugged her shoulders thoughtfully before replying.

"Not really sure, Belinda. Says he has something important to discuss when he comes in."

Walking back into her office, Dawn, the cup of coffee still in her hand, said reflectively, "I'm curious to know what he has to tell us."

"I do hope the two of them got along because I think they will be seeing a lot of each other! In a professional way, of course!" Belinda quipped. "It does seem that suddenly Ada is becoming a favourite with the clients," she added as an afterthought.

"Yes! I believe you are right," agreed Dawn, glancing through her many emails.

"Well! I still think Charlotte has the edge portraying the Duchess of Sussex," muttered Freddie, pursing his lips indignantly.

"Proof is in the pudding, Freddie," responded Belinda smiling at him, "proof is in the pudding!"

"I bet Max did not get on with Ada any more than I would have done!" exclaimed Freddie, satisfied that he had had the last word on the subject, but both Belinda and Dawn decided to ignore his last comment.

During lunch in the little Greek restaurant two streets away from the agency, Freddie and Belinda sat outside in the chilly late September sunshine, enjoying doner kebabs and glasses of red wine, while Queenie sat at his master's feet under the round table. Freddie mentioned that Claudio was spending more and more time in Milan these days and never asking Freddie to join him like he used to.

Trying to reason with Freddie, Belinda stressed that Claudio was probably very busy with his nightly performances at the Opera House and his coaching lessons which were ongoing in order to keep his voice as pure as possible.

"Yes, I understand this, sweet pea, but when I bring up the subject of visiting him in Milan, Claudio becomes offish and defensive. I am beginning to think the worse," admitted Freddie, looking forlorn.

"Well, maybe you should pop over there some time and surprise him!" suggested Belinda, a feeling of angst welling up inside her as her mind flashed back momentarily to when she and Tanya had flown to New York to surprise Frank.

"It will put your mind at rest if nothing else!" she cajoled, placing her hand on her friend's arm.

"You know, Belinda, I have thought about doing that myself for some time now. You are right, I should take the bull by the horns and do just that!" exclaimed Freddie, looking happier again.

"Why not go for Claudio's birthday at the end of November?" suggested Belinda, arched eyebrows raised enquiringly.

"Why not indeed?" echoed Freddie. "Why not?"

Chapter 16
Unrequited Love

"... unrequited love does not die; it is only beaten down to a secret place where it hides, curled and wounded."
Elle Newmark,
The Book of Unholy Mischief

At Top Drawer Agency the following Tuesday afternoon, as Belinda and Dawn were busy dealing with telephone calls and emails, the office was eerily quiet. How they missed Camp Freddie who had taken the week off.

Suddenly, a tap was heard at the door. Dawn was first to get up to answer it.

Looking through the spyhole, she quickly opened the door and in greeting exclaimed, "Hello, Max! Lovely as always to see you. Please come in!"

Max Rushton, smiling broadly, followed his agent into the office and bending down, gentlemanly kissed her cheek. Walking over to Belinda, who had now risen from her chair, he kissed her also.

"Great to see you, ladies, and may I say, how well you both look!" he remarked, straight white teeth showing as he smiled broadly at them both.

"Yes! You may say how well we look all day long, Max!" quipped Dawn, prompting a giggle from Belinda.

When all three were sitting comfortably and enjoying their coffee, Max began to explain to his agents how, in his opinion, the Dutch TV job went with himself and Ada. Dawn and Belinda sat in silence taking in everything he was divulging to them regarding his time spent in the Netherlands and how he began to develop certain feelings for Ada.

Neither of them had any inclination that Max would fall for one of the Meghan Markle lookalikes, although he worked closely with them. As far as they were concerned, everyone was under the impression that Max was sweet on Kay Carney, even though the two hardly worked together. Max looking a little embarrassed, admitted that he had been besotted with Kay for a very brief time, but that was all. It was no more than a crush.

More than an hour and several cups of coffee later, Max handed Top Drawer Agency a big problem. Since he had fallen in love with Ada who was engaged to somebody else, Max had asked Dawn if she would offer the clients either Charlotte or Amanda for future Meghan Markle jobs that he might be involved with rather than Ada.

When Dawn strongly objected to his request, stressing that it would not be possible, he hunched his shoulders in defeat, his troubled eyes downcast.

"Max! You are asking us to be underhanded towards a fellow artiste and, more importantly, our good clients!" Dawn stressed, shaking her neatly coiffed hair. "Taking Ada off our availability list is not the answer. She is becoming the number one choice and I will not sabotage her career on a mere whim! I'm quite sure you are just infatuated, Max. Please do not expect this agency to stoop so low!" she added, her voice rising, as a flush of anger swept across her pretty face.

"Listen, Max," placated Belinda, placing her hand on Dawn's arm and patting it. "Dawn and I are well aware how difficult it must be to think you are in love with someone yet can't be with them but, as Dawn has unequivocally stated, this agency will not succumb to this kind of request. It is unfair to the other lookalikes and it is definitely unfair to the clients. Please try to understand it from our point of view," she implored, continuing to pat a fuming Dawn's arm soothingly.

"Of course, I understand, ladies, but as the foremost Prince Harry lookalike in the UK and Europe, surely you could bend things a little for my sake?" came Max's reply, his eyes pleading.

Having composed herself again sufficiently, Dawn swiftly responded. "Okay, Max. Now why don't you think about this for a few days and then come back to us. Yes, you are the foremost Prince Harry on our books at the moment, but please don't use this to your advantage in order to control another's career opportunities. I am frankly quite shocked that you have taken this selfish line of action."

"I am truly sorry, Dawn, but I seriously know I could not cope with being in Ada's company feeling the way I do about her. That is my problem, I know," replied a miserable-looking Max, before taking his leave.

Dawn and Belinda looked at each other in disbelief after saying their goodbyes to Max, who promised to give his problem a lot more thought over the next few days and come back to them.

Suddenly, the telephone in Dawn's office shrilled on her cluttered desk and she rushed to answer it.

After replacing the receiver, she walked over to Belinda and informed her that Ada Demir, as the Duchess of Sussex, had just been chosen by one of their clients in Germany to attend the Essen Motor Show. This was for a two-day duration at the end of November. Marina Greenslade, as HM Queen Elizabeth II, and Max Rushton, as Duke of Sussex, had also been chosen.

"Well, I never! Talk of the devil!" exclaimed Dawn, lowering her voice somewhat before continuing. "Belinda, darling, please contact Ada to check her availability for those dates. I will call Marina myself."

Walking back into her office and without turning her head, Dawn announced, "Personally, I think we should check Jeff Williams' availability before contacting Max. He looks much better now that his nose has been reshaped."

Freddie was over the moon having Claudio back with him for a full week, or at least that is what poor Freddie thought. No sooner had Claudio pecked his waiting lover on both cheeks after walking out of customs into the arrivals lounge, than he mentioned to Freddie he would only be staying in London until the following Tuesday. Rehearsals for his forthcoming show were going into full swing the following week and he could not miss even one of them.

"After all, cara mia, I am the primo uno, the principal male singer. I know you will understand my predicament."

Looking upset by his lover's unexpected announcement, Claudio put a tanned arm around Freddie trying to console him.

"I'm in London now, cara mia, so please let us enjoy the time we have together!" he coaxed, in his charming broken English. "Come now, cara mia, let us stop for some real Italian coffee."

Camp Freddie decided to snap out of his despondency and enjoy a wonderful few days with the opera singer.

Any amount of time, no matter how short, spent with his beloved Claudio was better than none at all, and Freddie really didn't want to make the Italian angry.

The following few days were almost perfect for Freddie. Claudio seemed to be more charming than ever, even complimenting Freddie on his cooking after their late dinner on Sunday evening.

"Assolutamente delizioso!" cried Claudio after finishing his meal, pushing his dinner plate into the centre of the small round table, covered by a beautiful cloth hand embroidered in Capri.

"Glad you enjoyed it, my love," said a glowing Freddie, hooking a blue leather leash onto Queenie's studded collar, ready to take the little dog for a quick walk. "Put your feet up, darling, and relax. I won't be long then you and I can go to bed early!" suggested Freddie, grinning back at his lover as he followed Queenie out of the door.

It was less than twenty minutes later, as Freddie and Queenie arrived back at his flat, that he was surprised and hurt to see that Claudio had already gone to bed but not in the master bedroom. The Italian had fallen asleep in the small second bedroom on top of the black silk duvet after removing his shoes, socks and jeans. Throwing a blanket over his sleeping lover, Freddie began to fret about how distant Claudio had become. Not once had he made an attempt to make love to Freddie during the last two days and now, listening to the opera singer's heavy snoring, he knew things were not about to change. Only yesterday, when Freddie confronted Claudio about the Italian's lack of passion towards him, he waved his arms frantically in the air, accusing poor Freddie of being selfish and only interested in one thing.

"Have you no consideration!" yelled Claudio at him, causing little Queenie to whimper and hide under the table. "Can't you see? I am totally exhausted!" he screamed, bringing tears to the sad blue eyes of his English lover.

Poor Freddie tried to pacify the angry Italian until Claudio begrudgingly apologised to Freddie for his outburst, pinching his lover's cheek playfully.

They had chatted then for more than an hour, revealing their day-to-day lives while apart from each other. Freddie's astuteness began to cause him to question most of what Claudio was saying, yet at the same time he understood that the opera singer was exhausted. After all, was he not the primo uno?

Chapter 17
Murmur of Deceit

Wrestling constantly with his conscience since speaking to Dawn and Belinda about his unexpected feelings for Ada, Max tossed and turned during the night, unable to sleep. Up he would get to drink a glass of water, followed by a glass of wine before switching on his Samsung QLED TV, staring unseeingly at the screen.

Max knew he had acted completely out of character requesting his agents drop Ada from future jobs involving himself. Working and being in her presence, Max sensed, would cause him unbearable pain. He was a sensitive man, realising with shock that he had fallen deeply in love with another man's fiancé. With desperation, he longed to take Ada in his arms and make passionate love to her, asking only in return that her love for him was greater than she had ever felt towards another.

"How can I have her so close and not be able to make her my own?" he asked himself as he glanced wearily at his tired, sad reflection in the bathroom mirror, dark circles shadowing his young eyes.

Suddenly, like a knife cutting through his secret thoughts, his mobile shrilled noisily in the bedroom. Startled, he jumped out of his daze as he rushed out of the bathroom to answer the call.

The astonished expression on Max's face did not portray how he was really feeling deep in his heart after listening mesmerised for some time. Mumbling his goodbyes, voice faltering, Max sat for a few minutes to make sure that he had completely understood the surprising turn of events before jumping up and yelling, "Yes! Yes! Yes!"

Ada had confessed to Max that she had been wrestling with the thought of breaking off her engagement to Mehmet without causing too much upset in the family. Ada explained to Max that hers was an arranged union, although with her agreement at the time. While she respected Mehmet, she was not in love with him. Like many Muslim women before her, Ada would have to 'make do' with her chosen husband and hopefully, in time, learn to love him.

Resignedly accepting her fate, until she had fallen deeply in love with somebody else, Ada confessed to Max that it was he whom she was in love with. Becoming emotional, she further relayed sadly that there was little hope of them ever being together, because the two Turkish Muslim families would go to great lengths to ensure her betrothal to Mehmet was indeed honoured.

A feeling of jubilation swept over Max and swearing his dying love for her, he assured her that he would find a way for them to be together.

Before saying their loving goodbyes, Ada, lowering her voice as an added precaution, declared, "The only light for us at the moment, Max, is that we will be working together often and that way we can make sure our feelings for each other are genuine. Wait for me to call you some time tomorrow. It is safer that way," then she was gone.

"Oh no!" yelled Max distraughtly, recalling his conversation with Dawn and Belinda at the agency the day before. "I must call them right away," he muttered to himself, pressing Top Drawer Agency's number on his mobile.

No answer.

Max Rushton checked his watch laying on his grey Portland bedside cabinet, it showed 11:33.

Calling the number again, he let out a sigh of relief as Belinda answered. Keeping the fact that he had spoken with Ada from her, Max explained that he had had a chance to think things over, as Dawn had suggested he do, and was now happy to work with Ada Demir.

As Belinda listened quietly, he reiterated that she and Dawn were completely right in surmising that his feelings for Ada were simply a little crush and nothing more.

"I'm so glad you realise that now, Max," came Belinda's response, sounding genuinely pleased at his change of heart. "After all, sweetheart, there was a time you thought you were madly in love with Kay Carney!" she reminded him playfully.

"By the way, Max, another job came in just after you left the agency yesterday," she informed him, "for Essen in Germany at the end of November. Only this morning, Ada and Marina have been booked on it. The client also requested a Duke of Sussex but obviously, Dawn could not offer you because of your stipulation of not working with Ada. I must tell you, Max, that Dawn called Jeff Williams this morning but unfortunately, he is not available for those dates."

She could sense that Max was anxious.

"Dawn was about to offer the clients the ever-popular Prince Charles lookalike instead but now that you have changed your mind, I will let you know of her decision once she returns from the bank."

A hot flush swept over Max's face. It was imperative that he see Ada as soon as possible. He knew it was difficult for her to find time away from both her fiancé and family but as the end of November drew ever close, and assuming that he was booked on the Essen job, then he could wait patiently.

"Belinda, please explain to Dawn that I am terribly sorry for my stupidity yesterday. I assure you, there will be no more silly infatuations for me!" rendered Max, hoping that Belinda would put in a good word for him with Dawn.

"Of course I will, Max! Now don't worry about a thing," assured Belinda understandingly. "I am sure Dawn will appreciate you alerting us so quickly that you are now in favour of working with Ada."

Unfortunately for Max, and in turn, Ada, Dawn had in fact booked Spencer Carlisle as Duke of Cornwall on the Essen job. Due to Prince Charles' popularity throughout the world, and the fact that he would eventually be King, the German clients were happy to book him in place of the Duke of Sussex.

"I am truly sorry, Max, but Spencer has changed a prior engagement in order to be available for the Essen job and as you will appreciate, I cannot do anything for you now," declared an adamant Dawn to a very morose Max Rushton.

"You must remember, Max," she continued tersely, "Top Drawer Agency will always put the clients first. We have to strike while the iron is hot in order to keep this agency the foremost in Europe and the UK. If a particular lookalike is not available, then we make sure the client has excellent alternative choices!"

Max slipped back into a dark place. He was desperately longing to be with Ada but conscious that due to his own stupidity, the pair would have to wait until further job opportunities arose for the Duke and Duchess of Sussex. Max had decided to text Ada and explain about the Essen job and why he had failed to be included. He must have the courage of his convictions and ask her to deceive Mehmet, pretending that another lookalike job had been booked for her in Brighton. Hopefully, then they could meet and spend the afternoon together without causing suspicion to anyone.

Ada knew she was playing with fire when she agreed to meet with Max as soon as possible. Mehmet was extremely proud of his beautiful betrothed and very interested in her successful lookalike career. He often enjoyed boosting about her to his friends and work colleagues, who were curious and fascinated about the surreal world of lookalikes and tribute artistes.

Cunningly, Ada chose the date for her falsified Duchess of Sussex job as the same organised by Mehmet's employer for an important training day for the company. Being aware that this was crucial to his career, Ada assured him that she would be working in Brighton for the afternoon and into the evening, possibly arriving back in London close to ten o'clock. There was no need for him to meet her at the station; she would take an Uber straight home. Although reluctantly agreeing, Mehmet admitted he would possibly have a raging headache from the intensive studying that day. He did offer that his cousin Attila collect her at the station but Ada managed to decline his kind offer without causing any suspicion.

With that settled, Ada called Max who was over the moon with the realisation that he would soon be with his love again – alone with the beautiful Ada. They sensibly arranged to travel separately from London to Brighton, he in his Mini Review car and Ada taking a train. Every tiny detail had to appear usual and above suspicion.

Chapter 18
The Haunting of Africa

Vicky Sutton, the ex-Elizabeth Taylor lookalike, found it incredulous that already six long months had passed since leaving her comfortable life, full of fun and frivolity in London, to work in Africa teaching underprivileged children and adults about the Saviour. Although she was also employed to teach them the English language, Vicky's passion was to Spread the Word. How happy she had become since her spiritual rebirth!

During her time in West Africa, learning quickly to become both a teacher and a disciple, Vicky often found herself reminiscing about her past life which now she abhorred. Asking for His forgiveness, Vicky would constantly pray silently to Jesus, desperate for him to take her tormented guilt away caused by her previous soiled existence.

Of course, being a born-again Christian, she felt and looked at life differently now, and her aspirations had completely changed, seeing only through the eyes of Jesus Christ. The usual sins of nature, wealth, pleasure, power and honour that most are guilty of desiring, were blown out of proportion in Vicky's mind. As far as she was concerned, they now represented the Devil.

Some weeks before, she had received a letter from her close friend, Belinda. Vicky smiled remembering the fun she and Belinda had had together on their lookalike jobs, travelling all over the UK and Europe. Whilst Vicky had replied to her friend shortly thereafter, she had been informed by the Senior Post Collector in the camp that often the letters did not get out successfully. Vicky had decided to write again to her family and one or two of her closest friends, Belinda being one of them.

Early in November, during the dry season on a late Friday afternoon, Vicky noticed, with surprise, a young African boy standing alone by the side of the little red school building. Walking quickly towards him, she recognised him as one of the pupils in her class. She recalled he was a quiet boy, a loner who did not mix well with the other children.

"Jafari, what are you doing here at this time?" Vicky asked, wiping her perspiring face with a white cotton handkerchief. How she hated this dry heat! "You've missed the school bus. Do you think your father will come to collect you now?" she enquired, a worried expression descending on her sunburnt forehead.

"Sorry, Miss," replied Jafari, eyes growing wider as he began to whimper.

Hugging the eight-year-old boy to comfort and sooth him, she asked curiously, "Where were you when the other children were getting into the bus? How did you miss it, Jafari?"

"Sorry, Miss," he repeated again and again, now whimpering louder.

"Now, Jafari, please stop whimpering," cajoled Vicky, hugging the boy again. "I will ask the Pastor if he will allow me to drive you back to your village. Your poor mother will be sick with worry!"

At these words, the little boy immediately stopped whimpering then glancing up, gave his teacher a weak smile.

"Now, come with me," she urged, taking him by the hand and running into the school building.

"I can't understand why the bus driver didn't realise you were not on the bus!" she remarked, confused. "They know they are supposed to call out every child's name before leaving the school," she added, more to herself than to Jafari.

This was beginning to prove an unfortunate and trying situation for Vicky who could not find the Pastor, or the janitor, or anybody else for that matter.

Conscious that the janitor would have to lock the school before leaving for the evening, Vicky scribbled a note to him, explaining that she had taken one of the old cars on site in order to drive a young pupil back to his village before nightfall.

She remembered that her colleagues had been anxious to leave for the weekend, desiring to return to their commune living quarters less than half a mile away and in the opposite direction to the villages. Each teacher had been issued with a small bedsit where they could relax and unwind after the hectic days and weeks in the dry African heat. Vicky was no exception and was looking forward to having a long cool bath while reading the Bible when she finally arrived at the commune.

With Jafari holding tightly to her hand, she hurried quickly outside. His village was one of several surrounding the complex of the school. With dismay, Vicky realised she would be breaking the missionary rules about vigilance and never leaving the site unaccompanied, but Jafari's village was one of the closest to the school and Vicky knew she could drive there and back within half an hour.

Vicky had always been a spontaneous character and had now decided the boy arriving home safely to his mother for the weekend took precedence over her being reprimanded by the Pastor. After all, he should know that Jesus Christ would keep her safe.

Driving out of the school complex as fast as she would allow herself, Vicky turned the car onto the dusty dry tracks leading into Jafari's little village. Encouraging the boy to cheer up now that he was on his way home, Vicky noticed he appeared fretful and disquieted.

As they drove along, the skies now beginning to take on its twilight mantle, Jafari kept looking around anxiously.

"It is not in the stars to hold our destiny but in ourselves." These words echoed in her mind. It seems as if this Shakespearean phrase was written especially for Vicky, driving through the African outback as night descended quickly, enveloping the earth in darkness.

Suddenly, Jafari started whimpering again, so Vicky took her eyes briefly off the road ahead.

Before she could ask him what the matter was, Jafari started shouting, "Sorry, Miss," over and over. "Sorry, Miss!"

Startled, Vicky stopped the old car abruptly. Looking down at the troubled boy to discover exactly what was upsetting him, she did not see the open-top Jeep parked across the dirt track, no more just thirty metres ahead, directly in her path.

"What is it, Jafari? What is it that upsets so much?" implored his teacher, becoming very concerned for the boy.

By this time, Jafari was sobbing uncontrollably.

Vicky, now completely confused, became a little irritable. "Jafari, you will be home in less than five minutes. Please stop crying, there's a good boy," she coaxed.

Suddenly, there was a loud bang on the roof of the little car which startled her. Glancing up and squinting her eyes to make them focus more clearly in the darkness, she noticed they were surrounded by at least eight men in uniforms. She recalled fleetingly having seen these outfits somewhere recently, possibly in a book or newspaper.

Before she could enquire about what was going on, the driver's door was forcibly pulled open and Vicky Sutton was dragged out by her thick, dark hair. Screaming in pain as she was thrown to the ground, her first thought was for Jafari who had also been taken out of the car but in her fearfulness, she did not see that Jafari had been taken by two men into a second open-top Jeep.

She had no way of knowing that he was driven the short distance to his village where he was rewarded with money for his part in the capture of one of the evil Christians who taught African children about their Devil.

When after nightfall on Friday Vicky had failed to return to the commune, the Pastor called the ruling police force who shook their heads in dismay, alerting the missionaries that this was not an unusual incident in the area.

"You have always been made fully aware that you must consistently be extra vigilant out here!" reminded the Chief of Police, a massive African with eyes that bulged at the Pastor in exasperation.

"Over the last few years, several people have been kidnapped and only a few months ago, two Americans went missing and have never been seen or heard of since!"

The Pastor, trying to calm the situation, apologised profusely to the Chief of Police and begged him to have a search party ready for Vicky as soon as dawn broke.

It was hardly daylight when the search party came across the pitiful, lifeless body of Vicky Sutton. Covering the wretched corpse with dust sheets, the search was immediately abandoned.

The following Monday, Jafari did not attend school as usual. It was widely felt, once the janitor had showed the Pastor Vicky's scribbled note informing him that she was going to drive Jafari back to his village, that the militant soldiers had terrorised the boy beforehand into submitting to their demands in assisting them with the capture of a missionary. The first enlightenment of the born-again Christian is forgiveness and so the missionaries forgave Jafari. After all, he was but a child and would not be held responsible for the loss of their dear sister Vicky.

Occasionally in life, situations occur that are mysterious. In the series of events culminating in Vicky's tragic, untimely and senseless death, this was one such surreal happening. It seems as if an invisible hand was picking characters and placing them like pieces on a chessboard into situations that cannot be easily explained.

On that fateful night, grisly events fell into place finding Vicky vulnerable. What happened to the ex-lookalike was abhorrent and heinous. Being brutally raped over and over by several Islamic militant soldiers, she was then subjected to abominable torture as she prayed silently to Jesus to take her quickly.

Vicky Sutton, bleeding, in terrible pain and close to death, finally stopped breathing as her slim throat was slit from ear to ear, ending her life in the darkness of night on a dusty dirt track somewhere in West Africa. Her last thought was of sadness that she had not more time to serve her Saviour longer on this earth. Vicky's crime, as far as the militant soldiers were concerned, was that she was an evil Christian ruled by a Devil and had to be destroyed.

One week later, a heavy sadness descended upon Top Drawer Agency, overpowering and weighing heavily on anyone entering its doors. Belinda was inconsolable and Dawn kept mumbling, almost unintelligibly, to herself that she could not comprehend what had happened, and why, to the lovely Vicky. She suggested Belinda go home and rest after the terrible shock they had both had after receiving a sombre and distressing call from Vicky's sister, Melanie, barely half an hour earlier.

It was Friday, and Belinda had arranged to meet Bryanne, Simon and Eileen for dinner in Soho but she was aware her deep sorrow for Vicky would spoil the evening for everyone. Furthermore, there was always a feeling of loneliness when she arrived in Soho as if she could feel Matt's spirit. Reminiscing on his tragic and untimely death as well as Vicky's, Belinda knew she would not be good company.

There was a new restaurant/bar recently opened to rave reviews that Bryanne and Simon wanted to try, and had invited Belinda and Eileen, her friend from the Lissenden Players Music Hall. A good catch-up was long overdue, Bryanne had enthused, so everything had been arranged. After persistent persuasion by Dawn and Camp Freddie, Belinda decided she would go after all.

The new restaurant turned out to be a not-so-new restaurant in Soho, but one that had closed for a time enabling a new refurbishment. Nonetheless, Café Bohéme was full of liveliness and spending time there would hopefully help Belinda to forget briefly her sadness.

Being the last to arrive at the rendezvous, she tried to smile as she kissed her three friends affectionately. Bryanne immediately grabbed her and went straight into a tango dance, leaning her backwards towards the floor, his white Elvis quiff bouncing about, causing everybody to burst into laughter. How she loved Bryanne's sense of outrageous humour, his air of debonair, his intellect on life, his warmth and kindness! Simon, his bridegroom of barely a year, also amazing, handsome, stylish, amusing and generous, gave her a huge hug. Belinda thanked God for her wonderful friends.

After the four had exchanged sentiments, Belinda noticed Eileen watching her closely with a look of curiosity on her face. If there was one person she could not mislead, it was Eileen Hobbs.

"Belinda, your eyes have lost their glow. They portray sadness. Is everything okay with Frank?" she asked, looking at her questioningly.

Trying with difficulty to hold back her threatening hot tears, Belinda assured Eileen she was fine but that once settled at their table, she had something to tell them all but that it had nothing to do with Frank.

Café Bohéme was wonderfully French: French wine, French food, French music, French waiters. Staying true to its roots, the interior retained that belle époque vibe, with classic Bentwood chairs and tiled flooring. Almost every square inch of blank wall space had been uniquely covered in photos, paintings and mirrors.

"I love it here!" squealed Bryanne. "It reminds me of a Parisian bordello!" he laughed, waving over a weary looking waiter.

"How do you know what a Parisian bordello looks like?" queried Simon, grinning at his charismatic husband, setting Eileen and Belinda giggling.

"Yes, how do you know?" repeated Eileen, winking at the other two.

"Oh! I know everything, darling girl!" came his sweeping statement, pursing his generous lips in a pout. "I know exactly what a bordello looks like, be it Parisian or otherwise!" he added, his white Elvis quiff bouncing about on his head. "Positively everything, darlings!"

"Well, it's positively Bohemian here and I for one adore it," responded Simon, smiling as he began to read from the red and gold embossed wine list to the others.

After the dessert of baba au rhum had been served, when Belinda, her voice sounding emotional, announced, "I have very sad news but did not want to ruin the evening, so will tell you now."

Three pairs of empathetic eyes, shining with curiosity, focused on her. Deciding not to elaborate on the distressing details of her dear friend's last hours, she gave them a meagre, rather sketchy outline of Vicky Sutton's tragic death, wishing not to upset her friends and ruin their evening altogether.

When she had finished speaking, as if on cue, all three jumped up from their chairs and group-hugged her, showing they were truly, truly sorry for what happened to Vicky, each shaking their heads in disbelief at such a terrible tragedy.

In spite of all the sadness, the evening turned out to be mostly enjoyable and as is often the case, the fine wine helped sooth Belinda's melancholy, albeit temporarily.

As the four close friends kissed and hugged each other before departing their separate ways, Bryanne, swaying slightly, placed his hands on Belinda's shoulders.

Looking at her solemnly, his wine-infused breath causing Belinda to catch her own, he declared, "From the most glamorous female in London to the second most glamorous – I love you!"

Turning then precariously, he and Simon, together with Eileen, trotted off unsteadily towards the nearest tube station. Smiling as she watched them fading into the distance, Belinda hailed a black taxi to take her safely home to Clapham Common.

Later that same evening as Belinda made ready for bed, Frank called her from Las Vegas. Upon hearing his voice, the tears began to flow uncontrollably as she tried with difficulty to explain to him what had happened to Vicky.

Of course, Frank was shocked and appalled, trying for a long time to calm his lover, soothing her with words of wisdom and love. In an attempt to cheer Belinda a little, he reminded her that they would soon be together.

Eventually, they reluctantly murmured their loving goodbyes.

Frank's face wore the mask of uneasiness. It was the second week of October and the crisis regarding the Society's Las Vegas gambling concerns were still outstanding. Although he and Aldo were closing in on the culprits, Frank knew they had to be unreservedly sure that their suspects were indeed the guilty perpetrators.

If Frank was anything, he was a fair man, conscious of the fate that awaited the guilty. The Capitano Numero Uno was determined to make sure, without a shadow of a doubt, that he and Aldo were unconditionally accurate in their accusations.

Chapter 19
Disturbance in Saint-Tropez

The music legend, Zac Lewis, held a birthday party in the South of France in October, which saw Kay Carney at her most spectacular. As requested by the icon earlier in the year at the Red Cross Ball, the Marilyn Monroe Tribute Artiste arrived at his opulent home in Saint-Tropez. Not only was Kay part of the cabaret for the birthday celebrations, but she was also a special guest and friend. During the past few months since meeting Zac, Kay had chatted with him many times over the telephone and occasionally, time permitting, she would Skype him. Now becoming one of his closest confidantes, Kay found she understood much about the legend and the fact that he was married to a man.

Having been to Saint-Tropez several times before in her glamorous career as a lookalike and tribute artiste, Kay felt relaxed as the plane touched down in the French Riviera. The beautiful coastal town of Saint-Tropez, long popular with artists, attracting the international 'jet set' in the 1960s, remains known for its beaches and nightlife. Kay was excited about spending a few days tucked away in this elaborate corner of the world and in such distinguished company.

The chauffeur-driven car stopped smoothly outside high custom-made wrought iron gates, forbidding entrance without an invitation. Driving through, the Bentley weaved its way along grounds lined with tall elegant trees, standing proudly to attention as they protected the amazing yellow and white house, causing Kay to catch her breath at its beauty.

It was more than a house. It was a château, a palace, built in the 1920s with all the opulence and glamour borne of that jazz age era. Kay noticed the large elaborate swimming pool dominating the front entrance, artistically surrounded by the most exotic blooms and flowers known to man. Whistling unladylike under her breath, Kay realised she was actually in the playground of international socialites, something, she mused, she could very easily get used to.

The tall dark-haired chauffeur alighted from his seat, briskly walking around to open her door in the back of the deep burgundy Bentley.

Following the luggage-laden chauffeur into the château, her eyes gleamed with pleasure as they focused on the beauty surrounding her. Imitating Marilyn Monroe's famous movements, Kay purposely shimmed across the cream marble floor then slowly up the marble staircase, carpeted in the finest to be found anywhere in the world.

Cutting suddenly into her secret fantasy world, Kay glanced up towards the landing, hearing a distinctive London accent in greeting.

"Darling, Marilyn! Welcome to my 'humble abode!'"
He stood there grinning, arms outstretched. He wore a light pink jump suit, his fine, unkempt hair bringing instantly to mind a young street urchin.

"Zac, darling!" she squealed, hurrying up the remaining stairs and kissing him several times while the smiling chauffeur stood by, still holding her luggage.

"Thank you so much for inviting me!" she gushed.

Returning her affectionate kisses, Zac then asked the chauffeur to show Miss Monroe to her suite so that she could unpack and relax for a while before dinner. Kay was mesmerised; although she had stayed in many beautiful hotels all over the world in her glamorous career, she had never seen such spectacular beauty. How she wished she had the talent of Zac Lewis, then she too could own a home like this!

Kay was completely overwhelmed, as her suite was also breathtakingly beautiful. With a four-poster bed with white chiffon curtains hanging from the posts, gold cherubs adorning not only the bed itself but mirrors and furniture, she felt like a princess.

At dinner, Zac's partner, Daniel, joined them and all three chatted happily about the forthcoming extravaganza scheduled for the following evening. The music legend explained to her that he had organised a 39-piece band for his birthday celebration and a sound check was arranged for the following afternoon, allowing all the performers a chance to make any last-minute changes to their acts.

"By tomorrow afternoon, the château will be filled with performers and their personal stagehands," he explained "You will have a chance to meet them all at the sound check, darling, so please don't worry!" he encouraged, winking at her.

"Oh! Zac! I am completely in love with your château. I feel like Cleopatra!" giggled Kay, accepting another glass of wine from Daniel.

"Cleopatra, eh?" laughed Zac "Well, darling girl, I can assure you there will be many snakes sliding about around here tomorrow, so you had better keep your guard up, sweetheart!" he warned, winking again, prompting Daniel and Kay to burst out laughing. She adored Zac and his sharp London sense of humour.

Kay thought Daniel quite beautiful and could completely understand how Zac fell madly in love with him. She noticed the young man had the most amazing bone structure and lips that would put Angelina Jolie to shame. His hair was streaked blonde, enhancing those amazing piercing green eyes. She liked Daniel and thought he would make Zac very happy, at least for now!

Time as always rushed by and after a wonderful dinner, served by the crème de la crème of French waiters and waitresses, Kay Carney, more starry eyed than ever, affectionately kissed her host and his husband goodnight, fully aware that she needed a good night's sleep for the rehearsal, the show and, of course, the fabulous party that would follow.

Waking the following morning, a little later than she anticipated after forgetting to set her alarm clock, Kay climbed slowly out of the four-poster bed and walked towards the heavy draped curtained windows, again catching her breath at the spectacular scene in front of her.

Rushing down for a late breakfast, she jokingly declared, "You know, Zac, darling, if it wasn't for the fact that you are already spoken for, I would make a beeline for you just so that I could see the view from my suite every morning!"

Affectionately kissing Zac as he sat reading *The Times* newspaper at the otherwise empty breakfast table, she gushed, "It is unbelievably gorgeous!"

"Now, now, darling girl! You know quite well you are not my type! And you are well aware which team I bat for!" came his brazen reply, eyes shining mischievously.

Laughing and chatting together while they enjoyed breakfast, Zac suggested he show Kay his wonderful gardens and grounds before "all hell breaks loose" in the form of performers, musicians and stagehands.

Strolling leisurely, her arm familiarly in his, Kay was enthralled with everything she was shown. The upkeep of his magnificent château, gardens, trees, tennis courts, swimming pools and staff, were exorbitant but worth every penny earned purely by Zac's amazing talent.

The sound checks and rehearsals for the evening's show was carried out to the finest detail, making sure the spectacular evening would indeed be spectacular. There were two well-known female singers on the programme together with a very famous Scottish rocker and two boy bands, one extremely famous and the other an up-and-coming group of five young men from North London, whom Zac had spotted on a TV chat show some weeks earlier. Kay was the only tribute artiste on the programme but she was Marilyn Monroe incarnate and as far as Kay was concerned, she was just as famous as the others, if not more so.

Making friends came easily to Kay, especially among the male populace. Kay was feeling good. Zac had arranged for all the performers to dine together, encouraging everybody to get to know each other a little before the evening's extravaganza.

The two female singers were very friendly towards Kay, invigorating her to feel extra special during the sound check when they had jumped up simultaneously, applauding loudly after she had performed the famous Monroe songs.

Noticing that one of the stagehands assigned to the famous boy band kept staring at her during dinner, Kay thought he was hot and started to flirt outrageously with him. From a very early age, Kay was a natural femme fatale. How she adored encouraging the opposite sex until they were putty in her lily-white hands.

The landmark birthday celebrations for one of the globe's richest musical icons was carried out to perfection. Held in Zac's elaborate ballroom, it involved many carefully arranged parts and details by several of the world's top party planners.

Not one pair of eyes, who had the luck to witness such exquisite beauty, could believe what they were being shown. Several highly polished round tables, each placed for ten diners, were strategically situated around the enormous dance floor, spectacularly covered in gold lame cloths edged with pink rose buds with each chair matching the dressed tables. Sparkling chandeliers in abundance hung from the sky-high ceiling, featuring a replica of Botticelli's *Birth of Venus*. Amazing flowers of every hue adorned the ballroom, their exotic perfumes filling the air, causing the guests to catch their breath in wonderment. Handsome men in black tuxedos, together with gorgeous ladies adorned in black net stockings coupled with tiny gold bikinis, lined the ballroom ready to ensure the music legend's guests would want for nothing and remember this evening forever.

The 39-piece band, made up from the finest musicians both London and Paris had to offer, jumped at the chance to play for Zac Lewis long before they knew that their fees were to be exceptionally generous. Each band member felt elated as they took their seats carefully, climbing steadily onto the large stage, anxious to give their greatest performances. Their ruby-red tuxedos coupled with frilly ivory shirts, complemented the beautifully dressed tables and chairs.

The whole room full of guests shimmered as they jumped up one by one, applauding and stamping their feet, showing their appreciation for the performers. As far as the guests were concerned, declaring their preferences, not bothering to lower their voices, Kay's tribute act to Marilyn Monroe was joint favourite alongside the Scottish rocker. Zac quickly made his way onto the stage, trying to calm his guests down.

"What a truly marvellous show!" he gushed, provoking the audience to whistle and shout ever louder in agreement.

Turning to the performers he continued. "Thank you so, so much, you beautiful, talented people. You have indeed made me a very happy man!" He then graciously bowed to the thunderous uproar.

Kay was feeling good; she knew how wonderful she had been during her tribute act. Sexily, she sauntered backstage, joining the performers, the band and the stagehands where they were to have drinks and nibbles before joining the revellers at Zac's party.

She sat down at one of the large tables where Jess and Lola, the two female singers, were sitting. Kay giggled girlishly as the stagehand called Rex, whom she had been flirting with earlier during the day, came rushing over and sat down beside her. Turning towards Kay, he gently took her right hand in his and kissed it as he looked longingly into her bemused eyes.

Playing along, Kay fluttered her eyelashes at him whilst purring under her breath. Teasing and heckling, suggestively encouraging them, Jess and Lola started to giggle as they watched the unfolding scene at the table. Rex became rapturous and wrapped his arms around Kay before kissing her passionately on her ruby-red lips. Others had now arrived and joined in, whistling as they witnessed Rex the stagehand drooling over the Marilyn Monroe impersonator.

Coming up for air but not wanting to stop kissing this amazing woman, Rex opened his deep-set brown eyes and bowed to the heckling crowd now gathered around the dining table. Pulling her dress in place and accepting a tiny gold mirror handed to her by an amused Lola, and wiping her bright red lipstick off her mouth and teeth, Kay caught her breath in shock as ice-cold water was thrown down the front of her low-cut gold evening gown, completely saturating her. Kay found herself looking into the angry face of a pretty young woman of Indian heritage.

"What the hell do you think you are doing, you stupid bitch?" The words spat out of Kay's perfectly shaped mouth.

"Cooling you down, Ms Monroe!" yelled the young woman in a refined English accent. "Keep your claws off Rex. He is with me!" she screamed in anger, her voice rising as she banged the empty water jug back on the table.

"Ajlal, are you nuts?" came Rex's furious voice, as he rushed up to her, confronting her angrily.

Ajlal did not answer him; she was staring at Kay.

Many pairs of startled eyes witnessed in astonishment what then followed, all adding to this most surreal evening.

Suddenly and without warning, Kay became a tigress, making a jump at the young woman, who, expecting some kind of retaliation, moved quickly backwards causing Kay to trip and fall against the large dining table. Immediately Rex moved in to break up the fight but was held back by two members of the famous boy band who seemed to be enjoying this female affray – this catfight!

Now once again steady on her stilettos, Kay made another wild grab for Ajlal who met her halfway, both women tearing at each other's clothes and hair.

Rolling over and over the thick carpeted floor, the rivals kicked, bit and clawed at each other until two of Rex's stagehand friends jumped in and bravely parted the two warring females. Dresses were split, stained and ripped, clumps of fake hair pulled out, arms and legs bruised. Make-up was running down the reddened face of the world's most revered icon impersonator. Poor Kay; vulnerable, looking worse for wear, dishevelled, her beautiful evening gown hanging half off her curvy toned body, prompting not only every male in the room to fall deeply in love with her, but also many of the females, especially the two lady singers, Lola and Jess.

Flashing mobile cameras had recorded the whole brawl which would imminently be all over social media. Unhappily, Rex was assisting Ajlal with her torn dress showing bruises covering her arms. Turning to look at Kay, he was not at all surprised to see she was being mobbed by almost everybody else in the room.

Quickly, the two female singers ushered Kay towards the door, determined to get her to her private suite so that she could change and retouch her hair and make-up when suddenly Zac rushed in, closely followed by Daniel.

"My God!" he cried "What the hell happened here?" he demanded, looking from Lola to Jess then to Kay. Once he was given the full story of how poor Kay had been the innocent party, not realising that Rex had a girlfriend, Zac wasted no time as he marched straight into the ballroom and dismissed Rex, demanding him to leave immediately and take his "bitch of a woman" with him. Zac could be very direct to the point of rudeness but he was a loyal friend and Kay was now one of his closest people. Zac had, however, noticed her exquisite body underneath the torn evening gown.

Much to everyone's delight, the wonderful Marilyn Monroe lookalike did join the party celebrations a little later. Dressed in another astonishing gown, hair back to its immaculate style, full make-up expertly retouched with a smile belying the horrible confrontation she had endured earlier, Kay shimmed slowly into the ballroom comfortable on the intimate arm of a beaming Zac, to a thundering applause from his many animated guests.

Of course, the photographs and videos of the cat fight were all over the media and even became the top talking point on the more popular television and radio stations. This boosted Kay's career further up the ladder, as well as triggering the sales of Zac's latest album to soar ever higher. Kay Carney was becoming almost as famous as the greatest icon she portrayed.

Chapter 20
A Sorrowful Farewell

The cremation of Vicky Sutton, daughter, sister, aunt and friend, was one of the saddest events Belinda had ever attended. Travelling by car with Dawn and Freddie to Manchester in the north-west of England, early on a cold, windy Friday morning, Belinda was grateful her business partner had offered to drive. Mindful that the tears were close every time Vicky fluttered through her mind, Belinda felt it was safer that she did not drive.

Arriving in a drizzly Manchester, the Londoners reached the pretty church, chosen as the resting place for their dear friend. Immediately, Dawn found a parking place for her cream Mercedes-Benz coupé.

Freddie alighted from the car and gentlemanly opened the doors for both Belinda and Dawn. As the three figures, attired in black, were about to walk into the heavy wooded church entrance, a woman came rushing towards them waving. All three caught their breath, for the woman had a strong resemblance to Vicky.

"Hello, I am Vicky's sister, Melanie. Are you from Top Drawer Agency?" she asked, breaking into a smile which belied the sadness in her eyes.

Moving quickly towards her, Belinda held out her hand to the young woman. Before she could answer, the tears became insistent and she found she was sobbing uncontrollably as Vicky's sister hugged her.

Noticing how grieved Belinda was, Dawn and Freddie rushed over to the two woman and a group hug ensued.

Vicky Sutton had never married. Some years before, she had had just one love interest in her life but it turned out that he himself was in fact a married man with two young children. She had become friendly with Belinda while working together in their glamorous lookalike careers; confiding in her, being undeniably certain that Belinda could be trusted. Over the years, it became apparent that the heartbreak caused by Vicky's married lover had never really subsided, prompting Belinda to believe that this loss had brought about Vicky's dependency on alcohol until, of course, she had finally found Jesus.

Often when the two friends were working together, some people would get them confused. Remembering with nostalgia when Vicky had arrived a little late for a job, Belinda recalled how the Elizabeth Taylor lookalike laughed when she remarked to her friend that the taxi driver had mistaken her for Joan Collins.

"That's because he had already mistaken me for Elizabeth Taylor!" Belinda grinned at her.

Remembering her friend with sadness, Belinda knew she would always miss Vicky and would treasure the many wonderful memories of her forever.

Although Vicky had turned her back on her Church of England upbringing to follow her destiny of becoming a born-again Christian, she would nevertheless have been overwhelmed with the beauty and poignancy of her farewell given by Vicar Dudley, her bereaved family and devastated friends. Dawn, Freddie and Belinda were welcomed with open arms by Vicky's closely-linked family and the

Londoners were happy to have paid their last respects to such a warm, kind-hearted and generous lady as dear Vicky.

Having stopped twice on the return journey for refreshments, giving Dawn the opportunity to stretch her legs and rest her eyes from the tedious motorway, the cream Mercedes at last came to a stop outside Swiss Cottage Underground Station in north-west London. It was almost eight o'clock and the dark murky evening sky caused Belinda to shudder.

"Okay, darlings. Here we are! Home safely now! See you both on Monday," called out Dawn, turning to smile at Belinda sitting in the front passenger seat. "Don't forget to collect little Queenie from your neighbour, Freddie. He will be missing you terribly by now!" she added, peering into the driver's mirror and focusing on a yawning Camp Freddie.

"Of course not, Dawn! Can't wait to pick my Queenie up!" replied a weary-looking Freddie alighting from the Mercedes and walking up to her open window. Pulling his bright red scarf up around his neck to ward off the evening chill, he leaned in, kissing his lady boss on both cheeks, before flamboyantly thanking her again.

Hugging Dawn and also thanking her for driving them all the way to Manchester and back, Belinda hurried out of the car. Taking Freddie's arm, Belinda waved at Dawn who waved back at them as she slowly drove away. Turning slowly, they entered the station together.

For Belinda, the weekend proved one of loneliness and deep sadness. Her restless mind conjured up images she had witnessed when Vicar Dudley had invited members of the congregation to come up and say their final farewells to Vicky. With the haunting hymn *Jesus, Remember Me* descending eerily around the chapel, her family and friends rose sadly from the pews they had been occupying during the beautiful service and moved slowly and silently in two single lines towards the coffin.

Belinda could see their tear-stained faces as they waited to kiss or touch the highly polished wood, encasing the corpse of their loved one. Vicky's sister Melanie and brother Jeff had to physically help their heartbroken eighty-eight-year-old mother Stella walk towards the traditional casket so she could lay a red rose on her beloved daughter's coffin. It was then lifted up by pallbearers and taken solemnly and in a dignified way to the crematorium chapel adjacent to the church.

Belinda's aching head becoming more intense, knowing she would never forget the sound of the anguished scream that erupted from Stella's wrinkled throat as her shaking hand tried unsuccessfully to place the rose for her dead daughter. It was as if her piercing scream had signified everyone present to simultaneously break down into floods of tears, as a mass of white handkerchiefs, desperately pulled from pockets and handbags, frantically dabbed at eyes.

The one highlight of Belinda's weekend – apart from Tanya inviting her to have Sunday lunch with herself and Aarne, to which Belinda graciously declined – was Frank's late-night call on Saturday.

It came a little after midnight as she was dozing in front of the large television, mounted on her main lounge wall. A long time was spent whispering words of endearment and of how they missed and loved each other, with Belinda becoming teary.

Pacifying her before they said their goodbyes, Frank mentioned he was hoping to be out of Las Vegas soon, although exactly when, he really couldn't say.

To Frank, Las Vegas had become despicable. Suddenly, after a lifetime, he was beginning to loath the iconic desert city. He felt everyone and everything were pretentious to such a degree that he was slowly losing faith in the human race. At last, after all these months, he and Aldo were unwavering in their beliefs as to exactly who the perpetrators were. Frank was a sensitive man and the culprits who had been skimming money off the Society's gambling interests were two Associates. These were young men, still wet behind the ears, and Frank's heart went out to them, mostly for their stupidity of actually believing they could deceive their bosses and escape unscathed. He contemplated talking to Aldo, asking him for his agreement not to inform the Society of their discovery, thus keeping the two young men's names off the infamous hit list.

Frank Lanzo and Aldo Lamarina went back a long, long way. They were close, and over the years Frank had helped Aldo climb the precarious ladder of the secretive Society to become a well-respected Capitano in his own right. Unlike Frank who was of a similar age, Aldo was still a very ambitious man and desperately wanted to reach the rank of Capitano Numero Uno one day.

Of course, Frank currently held this most esteemed position, but of late, Aldo sensed his good friend was growing weary of all the responsibilities the most revered position brought with it. He was conscious both he and Frank were not getting any younger, but then, who was for Pete's sake! Aldo was also conscious that under different circumstances, Frank would have moved across the pond to London, to be with his beloved Belinda.

To say Aldo was shocked at Frank's proposal would be putting it mildly.

Adamantly refusing to have any part in misleading the Society and going against the Code, he yelled, "What? Has the Vegas sun completely scrambled your brain cells, Frank?" his face turning an unhealthy shade of crimson. "You know darn well I can't go along with this crazy idea of yours. We'd both end up on the Society's hit list along with these other two jerks. No way, buddy! Use your head! I am speechless, Frank, that you have even considered such a thing!" he added, drawing deeply on his cigarette and shaking his head in disbelief.

The two men were sitting at a table in the opulent grounds of their Las Vegas hotel, taking advantage of a long break. Rising from his chair, eyes full of distress, Frank finally responded.

"Okay! Okay, Aldo! Forget I even mentioned it!" appeased Frank before continuing. "I am afraid for these two jerks. They are such young men and have no idea what is in store for them once the Society learns of their deception."

These words prompted an astounded Aldo to raise his voice in reply.

"Serves them right, Frank! Hey, buddy, you of all people know the Code of the Society. These guys have been initiated as Associates and are fully aware of the consequences of ripping their bosses off! We are here to bring the culprits to justice for the Society and that's exactly what we have to do. You know that," coaxed Aldo, stubbing out his cigarette in a glass ashtray, randomly placed on the table.

"You getting soft in your old age, Frank?" he asked impudently, lighting another Marlboro and walking over to the Capitano Numero Uno. "You worry me, paesano.

You and me still got years left in us. You know we gotta do this, so let's do it, my friend!" he cajoled, slapping Frank affectionately on the back.

Being fully aware how astute Aldo was, Frank rose resignedly from his plush garden chair and, feigning a smile at the other man, nodded in agreement.

"There you go, buddy!" exclaimed a beaming Aldo. "Thought for a minute you were serious!" he declared, blowing the cigarette smoke into the crisp winter air.

Chapter 21
The Devil makes the Pot

"What would the lookalike business be without the icon Marilyn Monroe!" exclaimed Dawn walking from the kitchenette into the office, a cup of hot coffee in each hand. Offering one to Belinda, she continued. "I hate having to explain to Melita that her sister has become the number one choice of the clients now that Kay is self-managing. I feel bad for Melita, I really do."

"Yes, I completely agree, Dawn," responded Belinda, taking a soothing sip of the hot warm liquid.

"It seems to be the Kay Carney versus Jane Baxter scenario all over again!" she added, her mind going back and reflecting on the terrible tragedy of Jane's suicide, a little more than a year ago now.

A look of sadness shadowing her face at the mention of Jane's name, Dawn slowly shook her head, the neatly bobbed blonde hair bouncing gently.

"But it's even worse now, Belinda!" she groaned. "Melita and Crystal being warring siblings! At times I dread it when the clients request Crystal! Crystal! Crystal!" Now looking sheepish, Dawn admitted, "You know, I often toy with the idea of informing the clients that Crystal is already booked and offer them Melita in her place!"

Raising one of her eyebrows at her junior partner, Dawn stressed, "But, of course, I couldn't do that. It would go against company policy. This lookalike business is what it is!"

"It certainly is," agreed Belinda. "That is why we love it so!"

"That is why we love what so, ladies?" queried Freddie, winking at Belinda as he burst through the agency's heavy oak door, little Queenie in his arms.

"The lookalike business, of course, Freddie!" replied Belinda grinning at him.

"But, of course, we do, ladies! How else would I afford my Botox!" he exclaimed, lowering Queenie onto the thick carpeted floor. Pouting as he scrutinised his reflection in the mirror which covered the entire back wall, he quipped, "Oh dear! Botox time again, me thinks!" causing Dawn and Belinda to giggle before jokingly agreeing with him.

The festive season was on the horizon and the day had been hectic.

"How I love Christmas!" announced Dawn. "We become so wonderfully busy!" she added, taking three more faxes off the machine and placing them on Freddie's cluttered desk.

"Call these people for their availability, Freddie dear, and do leave a voice message if there isn't a reply," she suggested, smiling at him. "Have a good evening, darlings. See you bright and early tomorrow," she called as she disappeared through the open door.

Glancing at the faxes, hoping to see the name of Liberace appear, Freddie was again disappointed. It had been quite a while now since he had been booked as the famous American pianist. How he envied the more popular lookalike characters. Being employed part-time by Dawn in the agency, he had first-hand knowledge of who was working and who was not. He always wished he had had the luck to resemble Elvis or George Michael – then he would have been a very popular lookalike.

"Who's on the list?" enquired Belinda, glancing up from her computer.

"Not Liberace, that's for sure," he answered sulkily.

"Oh, don't worry, Freddie, something will come in for you soon, I'm sure," she encouraged, smiling at her dear friend. She was always full of sisterly concern for him. "I'll bet La Collins isn't there either, is she?"

"Afraid not, but Marilyn Monroe is, of course!" he answered sarcastically. "Also, Taylor Swift and Boy George! Kevin will be pleased – the Boy has been rather quiet of late," he remarked, as an afterthought.

Closing her computer and getting up from her chair, Belinda asked Freddie when he would be flying to Milan to surprise Claudio for the opera singer's birthday at the end of November. Looking a little forlorn, Freddie took Belinda into his confidence and told her that he would not be going for the birthday now but instead had decided to surprise his lover during Christmas.

"But I thought Claudio was coming back to London for Christmas?" queried Belinda, looking confused.

Turning his sad blue eyes on her, Freddie raised his shoulders and explained to her that Claudio had telephoned only yesterday informing him that he was heavily committed to several charity shows in and around Milan over the Christmas festivities and it was impossible for him to leave there until the middle of January.

"Oh! I am so sorry, darling," came Belinda's sincere response. "Why not revert back to your original plan and go for his birthday?" she suggested, looking at him questioningly.

It was by now home time and, taking his dark navy jacket off the coat stand, Freddie replied, "Christmas is around the corner and the agency is already very busy. I would rather surprise him over the festive season, even though he will be on stage for much of the time. Besides, I could stay a little longer in Milan during the Christmas break."

"Listen, Freddie, you must do what you think is right; please don't worry about the agency; Dawn and I will cope for a while without you," urged Belinda, kneeling down and stroking little Queenie who immediately turned over on his furry back.

"Yes, I appreciate that, and thank you so much, my darling, but my mind is made up! I will fly on Christmas Eve," he divulged, clipping the blue leash onto Queenie's diamanté collar.

"Oh! By the way," he remarked as an afterthought, "I have asked my neighbour Big Gerty if she would take care of Queenie while I'm in Milan. Gerty and Fanny are at home all over Christmas and they adore Queenie."

"You know I would always take Queenie for you but I am not sure where I will be this Christmas. Still waiting to hear from Frank!" said Belinda, pecking Freddie on both cheeks.

"Yes, I know you would," he admitted, glancing in the wall mirror as he passed by. Suddenly turning back to his friend, he asked, "What are we like, you and I? Always waiting for our lovers to throw us a crumb!" and with that he and Queenie disappeared out of the agency door, leaving Belinda to ponder over the implications of his last remark.

Waiting for Ada to find a safe date to meet in Brighton seemed like a lifetime to Max. Mehmet's scheduled training day at his employment had been postponed for almost two weeks, and as Ada had reiterated several times to Max, this was the only real safe day they could meet. Usually where day jobs were concerned, where the lookalikes were not required to stay overnight, Mehmet would accompany his Ada to the venue, wait patiently for her, then they would travel back home together. As a Turkish male, such was his privilege and control of her.

The smitten potential lovers spoke to each other daily while they waited impatiently in anticipation of being alone together.

The chilly days of a bright October were rapidly coming to an end, signalling the beginning of the unpredictable eleventh month. It was Tuesday and excitedly Max checked the time on his dashboard as he raced his 2018 Mini Review down the motorway towards Brighton. He had booked bed and breakfast for two in the West Pier Residence, a highly recommended hotel set in the centre of Brighton. Because Max and Ada could not stay overnight, he had decided that when they left that evening, he would inform the receptionist they had to cut short their stay due to an unforeseen family crisis.

Grinning to himself for his clever deception, Max felt shivers up and down his spine as his eyes took in the grey foggy sea, crashing rhythmically against the famous Palace Pier. Stopping his car outside Brighton Station, he noticed the big clock displaying almost eleven o'clock.

There she stood, small and alone, her dark eyes surveying her unfamiliar surroundings. A worried expression on her lovely face enhancing her beauty, so he thought.

"Ada! Jump in, darling. I will get a bloody ticket otherwise!" he joked, laughing loudly.

Looking up and seeing him, Ada hurried towards the Mini and climbed in besides him. She told him the train journey down had been very quick, barely an hour, but that Mehmet had called her just before she boarded the train at Victoria Station, informing her that he had decided after all to meet her from the train later that evening.

"I am so glad that you decided to drive down because I told Mehmet I was working only with the Duchess of Cambridge lookalike," she admitted, checking her mobile and putting it on silent.

"I told him we two Duchesses were booked for a photo shoot with a Norwegian magazine!" she divulged, slipping her mobile back into her leopard-print handbag.

"That's cool! No problem!" replied Max, turning briefly to look at this beautiful young woman in the passenger seat beside him. "He sounds very controlling," remarked Max "He doesn't check your bank account, does he?"

"No! Of course not!" retorted Ada, suddenly giggling to herself.

Ada was very fond of Mehmet. He was a good man and she knew he adored her. Had she not met Max, Ada would have sailed happily enough through life with her fiancé, probably bearing his children but never really experiencing true love. Meeting Max had set off an array of strange feelings within her and she was certain that come what may, she had to spend private time with her Duke in order to determine exactly how she felt for him.

Within half an hour, Max and Ada stood together in their booked room on the second floor of the West Pier Residence. It was spotlessly clean and beautifully decorated with an en suite. The bed, situated in the middle of the very large room, was dressed in autumnal colours and Max tried desperately to restrain himself from grabbing the playful Ada and masterfully throwing her onto it.

Kicking off her walking shoes, Ada glanced up at him, her eyes wide and sincere before the couple hungrily kissed for a very long time.

"Hey! Hey! Hold on, tiger!" she laughed as she playfully circled out of his arms. "Let's get comfortable first, darling," she coaxed, sauntering into the bathroom, Max's eyes never leaving her.

Returning to the bedroom, Ada giggled when she realised Max had stripped naked and neatly laying his clothes on an armchair, had positioned himself in the middle of the king-sized bed, his manhood erect underneath the sheets. Opening the covers for her, Max tapped the mattress seductively as Ada, wearing only a red thong, slowly went to him, the nipples of her small round breasts protruding with desire.

Outside, the dismal October day passed far too quickly for the new lovers who had spent the whole day in bed, bringing joy and erotic pleasure to each other. The hours in the day were far too few for them to express their deep feelings as they sensually gave up their bodies and souls to each other.

Max had lunch sent to their room and hastily went to answer the sheepish tap on the door signalling that their refreshments had arrived. Taking the large tray from the bellboy, Max thanked him then placed a generous tip in his hand, prompting the older gentleman to whistle and wink at Max, nodding his balding head in approval as he disappeared down the staircase.

For Ada, this rendezvous was a necessity of the highest importance. She was fully aware how perilous it could be if she broke her engagement off with Mehmet and because of this, she had to be undeniably certain in her heart that what she felt for Max was indeed true love. Completely sure now that her Duke was, in truth, her soulmate, Ada was willing to fight anyone or anything who stood in the way of her true happiness. She knew beyond a shadow of a doubt that for such a man, she would go to the ends of the earth and for her, this man was Max Rushton.

At precisely eight-thirty that evening, Max ventured down to the reception desk and explained to the night shift staff that he and his partner would have to leave the hotel immediately due to an unforeseen crisis that had arisen in his partner's family. Although appearing sympathetic, the male receptionist apologetically informed Max that they could not reimburse him for the overnight stay. Max assured the man that he understood perfectly, as he paid the bill with his credit card. Making his way back to his room, he found Ada dressed and ready to leave. As he approached her, she smiled up at him. Ada could feel her heart beating faster.

At Brighton Station, standing close together on Platform 5 for London, the young lovers were reluctant to part company, but part they must.

Max gently remonstrated, "You must catch the nine o'clock train, Ada, otherwise you will not arrive at Victoria until almost midnight!" Pulling her close to him, he could feel his lover's beating heart beneath her cashmere coat.

Hesitant to leave him, Ada nodded her head solemnly as she watched the London bound train pull into the station, noisily coming to a complete stop as if it were complaining of the tiresome journey ahead.

Swiftly, kissing her ardently on the lips, Max helped his Duchess ascend the waiting train.

It was a little after nine-thirty when Max hurriedly left the station and headed towards his parked car. His heart full of loneliness, already missing the beautiful Ada, he was unaware that a group of people had also joined the London bound train on Platform 5 and that two of them had recognised Ada from photographs as the fiancé of their boastful colleague, Mehmet Tekin.

Chapter 22
Deception, Lies and Malice

When Freddie telephoned Kevin – aka Boy George lookalike and tribute artiste – the Boy was ecstatic to have been picked as part of the evening's entertainment at the upmarket Selfridges on Oxford Street. The store's retail profit margins were outstanding and the reigning Chairperson generously decided to treat the hundreds of hard-working staff to an extravagant Christmas party as a special thank you to them. A lavish sit-down dinner was to be followed by the overwhelming talents of Taylor Swift, Marilyn Monroe and Boy George – all lookalikes, of course! Kevin was readily available, quipping that it was about time the agency had found him another job!

"Yes, it's been a quiet couple of months, I know," agreed Freddie, apologetically. "Mind you, at least you have this one now, and Boy George's name also came up a couple of days ago in an enquiry regarding a mix and mingle in Leeds. We're still waiting to hear about that one," offered Freddie, hoping Kevin would feel happier now.

"That's more like it, Freddie!" giggled Kevin. "Hey, why don't you come with me on the Selfridges gig? I could pass you off as my dresser again," he suggested, sounding even more like Boy George than Boy George.

"Oh! I'd love to! Thanks for the invite. I'll speak to Dawn later and will let you know," replied an excited Freddie. He always found the Boy George lookalike quite outrageous and loved being in his company. Freddie also liked Wayne, Kevin's bodyguard and lover.

"Cool!" replied Kevin. "Wayne will be happy to see you again as well. We've missed you, darling!" he added, giggling again. "By the way, who is this amazing new Marilyn Monroe I've been hearing so much about?"

"Oh! Don't ask me! You'll find out soon enough!" came Freddie's response, a tinge of warning in his voice. "She's also been booked on the Selfridges job. Her name is Crystal, just one name mind! I'll tell you all in good time," he assured Kevin and with those parting words, the call ended.

Later that same day, Freddie sheepishly asked Dawn whether she was agreeable to him accompanying the Boy George lookalike on the Selfridges job as his dresser.

Sitting in her office, busily dealing with several contracts for the imminently confirmed jobs, Dawn peered at Freddie over the frames of her expensive Cartier glasses and studied him for a few seconds.

"Now, Freddie! I know you are a little bored of late with Claudio in Milan and Liberace not flavour of the month, but do you really think it is a good idea to accompany Kevin?"

Taking her glasses off and focusing on him, before he could reply, she quickly continued. "You know he has a talent of opening his mouth at the wrong time and landing not only himself but everyone else in hot water! Personally, I rather you did not go."

"Dawn, I really would like to see the guys again. As you know, I've been accepted as the Boy's dresser on other jobs. I could really do with some cheering up and Kevin's the one to do it!" pleaded Freddie, appealing to her more empathetic side.

"Look, Freddie, I'll have a word with Belinda when she gets back from the bank and we'll let you know then, okay?" cajoled Dawn, replacing her glasses and concentrating once again on the contracts.

Realising how forlorn Freddie was feeling, Belinda finally persuaded Dawn to agree his attending the Selfridges job.

"We all know how Kevin could pick a fight with his own shadow, Dawn, but remember, Wayne holds a black belt in karate, so Freddie will be in good hands!"

Invariably having the last word, Dawn replied curtly, "Yes, Belinda, I know all about Wayne's black belt! Let us hope it will not be put to the test when Freddie's with them!"

Freddie's melancholy mood seemed to disappear when Belinda told him that it had been agreed for him to attend the Selfridges job as Boy George's dresser, scheduled for Saturday 14th December at the Sheraton Grand Hotel, Park Lane.

Ada Demir's fiancé, Mehmet Tekin, was feeling despondent. A couple of the guys from his office had been asking questions about his girlfriend, mockingly pressing him to show them more photographs of the Meghan Markle lookalike. Danny Jones and Archie Barnes were quite certain that by pure chance they had witnessed some naughty shenanigans between Mehmet's finance and another man, who most certainly was a Prince Harry impersonator.

Attending a conference in Brighton for their company, the young men had dashed to the station to catch the penultimate train back to London that evening. Both single men, but not for the want of trying, Danny and Archie were shocked to see Mehmet's girlfriend, or at least it certainly looked like her from the photographs they had been shown at the office, standing on Platform 5, snuggled in the arms of a tall, sandy-haired chap. The two friends kept their distance but just far enough so that they could watch, with interest, every lingering kiss shared by the besotted couple.

"That's definitely her," whispered Danny Jones to his friend, pulling his thick navy overcoat up around his neck against the unpleasant dank evening.

"Yes, I think you are right! Now have a good look at her playmate!" urged Archie Barnes, keeping his voice very low as his inquisitive eyes took in the affectionate body language of the unsuspecting lookalike lovers.

"Poor old Mehmet!" smirked Danny sarcastically. "That will teach him not to be such a boastful git!" he added, his effectual Welsh lilt complementing his sultry good looks.

"Right on, Dan!" agreed Archie, glancing up at his friend.

"I can't see 'Lights, Camera, Action' anywhere so these two lovebirds are not play-acting, mate, that's for sure!" he declared, dropping his south London accent to a near-whisper, his close-shaved auburn hair glinting in the lights of the platform.

Archie and Danny watched with excitement as the chivalrous Max helped Ada onto the train, kiss her passionately once again through the open window before turning and quickly walking out of the station.

Now, joining the other passengers from Platform 5, the two work colleagues hurried onto the waiting train, thankful to be in the warmth. Walking slowly behind Ada, the two young men took up seats across the aisle from her and were privileged to the calls she made from her mobile. Nudging each other frequently as they pretended to read their newspapers, they were witness to Ada's first call to her Prince Charming, reminding him how much she loved him and how she was looking forward to being with him again very soon.

Archie nudged Danny excitedly when Ada's second call was conducted in Turkish. It was obvious to them that she was speaking to Mehmet, who apparently was already on his way to meet her at Victoria Station.

"Yes, darling, I love you too!" came Ada's half-whispered response into her mobile, this time in English, to her deceived betrothed. "Must go now. Entering a tunnel!" she remarked, her voice raising a little before ending the call.

Archie and Danny turned and mouthed to each other questioningly, "Tunnel?" Appreciating Ada's slyness and fully aware they had not entered a tunnel, the two friends begun to feel this situation was becoming quite surreal.

"She's good!" remarked Archie quietly to Danny.

"Yep! She's very good indeed!"

Disembarking the train as slowly as possible so as not to be seen by their work colleague at the barrier, Danny and Archie discussed seriously what they should do with the knowledge they now had regarding the deception of the Meghan Markle lookalike towards her intended and their unpopular work colleague.

"You've seen photos of my fiancé, guys. What's this all about?" enquired Mehmet, irritated by the cross-examination he had been receiving from two of his work colleagues over the last few days.

"Okay, Mehmet!" appeased the silver-tongued Archie. "Dan and I are having a little dispute about a woman we saw on Tuesday evening on Platform 5 at Brighton Station. I said it was your fiancé and Dan says it was not. That's why we want to have another look at your photos, mate," he added, watching Mehmet closely.

Placated now and always happy to show off his beautiful future wife, Mehmet wiped his perspiring brow with a white handkerchief then retrieved two colour photographs of Ada from his leather wallet and passed them to Archie.

Peering at the images, Archie nodded and handed them to Danny for inspection.

Letting out a low whistle, then grinning at Archie, Danny admitted, "You were right all along, Archie! I apologise! Thank you, Mehmet, for solving our little dispute."

Slapping his friend on the back, Archie jokingly replied, "Am I not always right, Danny boy?"

Getting up from his chair after carefully returning the photographs to his wallet, Mehmet admitted, "Yes, it probably was Ada you saw because she was working in Brighton on Tuesday. Besides, who else looks as stunning as my Ada?" he asked, grinning smugly at his colleagues.

"Unless it was the real Duke and Duchess of Sussex, of course!" Archie replied sarcastically, causing Danny to nudge his opinionated friend.

At this, Mehmet felt a kick in his stomach.

"What do you mean, the Duke and Duchess?" he demanded, his dark brown eyes flashing at Archie. "There was only Ada and the Duchess of Cambridge lookalike on this job," he barked, sitting back in his chair, angry eyes staring at his colleagues.

"Really?" queried Archie. "It didn't look much like the Duchess of Cambridge to us, did it, Dan?" he said, turning to the Welshman for support.

At these words, Mehmet jumped up from his chair, causing it to flip over and crash to the floor. He was thankful it was lunchtime and the office was empty.

"What the hell are you getting at, Barnes?" asked the Turk, eyes now flashing with anger.

"Hey, hey, cool it, mate! The Duchess of Cambridge didn't look that good. That's all!" lied Archie realising he had bitten off more than he could chew.

Retrieving his chair and leaving the office for some fresh air, Mehmet had decided he would not mention this incident to Ada for now. He would have to think about it first.

"Honestly, Archie! You are a liability! I thought we were going to wait before mentioning anything?" remarked a concerned looking Danny. "If Mehmet makes a complaint to HR, you are in big trouble, my friend, and me along with you!" he hissed, his Welsh lilt resounding in Archie's ears.

Pretending he had no regrets for his actions, Archie replied with hostility, "He's such a smug bastard. I really wanted to tell him everything we saw between his bird and the Prince. Sorry about that, but you must admit, I covered myself brilliantly, didn't I?"

"Yes, you did. Very conniving, I must say, but we will have to give this whole state of affairs a lot more thought before we go shouting our mouths off. Okay?" stipulated Danny, angrily.

Agreeing to hold fire for the time being, Archie assured Danny that he would not mention Ada to Mehmet again until they had both decided what to do.

Chapter 23
The Inimitable Boy
George Lookalike

Early December, although wet and dismal in London, found Belinda in high spirits. She had just received a telephone call from Frank who had told her he would be flying back to New York at the end of the week and that he wanted her to join him for the festive season. Immediately, she had booked her return flight to JFK Airport, intending to be back in the UK ready to reopen the agency on 7th January.

Although the thought of being with Belinda again lifted Frank's mood considerably, his heart was heavy with regret and guilt after he and Aldo had informed the Society's hierarchy that the culprits in Las Vegas had now been identified beyond a shadow of doubt.

The atmosphere at Top Drawer Agency was electric, not only because of Belinda's euphoric state of mind, but because Camp Freddie was also very cheerful. Apart from the Selfridges job as Kevin;s dresser, he had now been booked as Liberace for a mix and mingle at the Hilton Hotel Park Lane for an American-themed Christmas party organised by the London-based branch of a Texan oil company. There would be a continuous running buffet together with four bars, a casino and dancing to the sounds of a big band well into the early hours. Scheduled for 22nd December, Freddie breathed a sigh of relief that he would still be in London on that date and definitely available to accept the booking.

Both Belinda and Dawn were very pleased that dear Freddie was at last having some good luck.

ॐ

Kevin appeared to Freddie to be more volatile than ever when he and Wayne pulled up in their white Peugeot 308 outside Green Park Underground Station. Climbing briskly into the back of the car, Freddie felt deliriously happy to be in his friends' company again.

"I trust you will not outshine me tonight!" giggled Kevin, surveying Freddie in the driver's mirror as Wayne headed for Park Lane and the Sheraton Grand Hotel.

"Oh, very funny! A million stars couldn't outshine you, Boy!" came Freddie's quicksilver reply. "You look amazing, my friend, and your make-up is a work of art, as always!" he complimented, causing Kevin to giggle and preen.

"I couldn't agree more!" quipped Kevin before turning to Wayne, demanding he put his foot down and drive faster.

"For God's sake, Wayne, I want to get there this evening, not Christmas!" came Kevin's impertinent remark.

Freddie noticed Wayne was unusually quiet. He was very aware that life with Kevin must certainly have its downside and it appeared to Freddie's sensitive nature that the lovers must have fallen out over something. This caused him sadness. Making small talk and bringing Wayne into the conversation helped lighten the tension that seemed to be building inside the car.

"Here we are, ladies!" announced Kevin looking out of the window at the resplendent hotel, red and gold awnings flapping gently in the windy December evening as if desperately wanting to attract attention to itself.

Jumping out of the Peugeot, Kevin moved to the back of the car and retrieved his costume for the evening from the roomy boot. Handing it to Freddie, he asked, giggling, "Carry these, would you! There's a good chap!"

Before Freddie could reply, Kevin had walked over to the driver's window and peering in, declared, "Okay, Wayne, Freddie and I will be in the changing area. See you there once you've parked," and with that, he turned on his killer-heel green stilettos and sauntered into the hotel's entrance, Camp Freddie hastily following behind, trying desperately not to drop the Boy's elaborate stage costume.

Everyone turned to watch Boy George and his handsome companion stride quickly through the reception and into the changing area. Freddie had been meticulous with his attire for the event. His black sequinned three-piece suit paid tribute to his long slim legs and his frilly yellow silk blouse complimented his blue eyes. Freddie's dark brunette hair with its gentle quiff had been carefully lacquered and looked very elegant. To complete his look, he had experimented with a few strokes of black mascara, accentuating his amazing eyes. Camp Freddie was indeed a handsome fellow.

"Boy George and Beau Brummell?" exclaimed the client's representative as the two entered the changing area.

"Beau Brummell?" queried Kevin glancing around then noticed the young man was looking directly at Freddie. As sharp as a knife, answering his own question, Kevin retorted, "Yes, of course we are! Who else could look this amazing?" causing the representative to blush uncomfortably.

"There you go, Freddie. You can now become a Beau Brummell lookalike as well as Liberace! The more strings to your bow, the better, darling! Have a word with Dawn and Belinda, see if they will agree," he encouraged, as Freddie beamed at this suggestion.

"You know, Kevin, I might just do that!" replied Freddie, still beaming. "After all, Beau Brummell was an iconic figure in Regency England and for many years, the arbiter of men's fashion."

"Good for you, Freddie, and I think Beau Brummell and Liberace will rub along famously together!" quipped Kevin, giggling as he hung up his flamboyant costume on the clothing rail provided.

It was a wonderful evening. Selfridges had spared no effort for their staff, laying on a lavish sit-down meal followed by the tribute acts show, specially chosen from Top Drawer Agency. A famous DJ had also been booked to keep the employees happy and on their toes for the remainder of the evening and into the twilight hours.

Freddie managed to accompany Wayne into the ballroom to enjoy the tribute show. Screams and shouts went up from the alcohol-infused audience as Molly Rose (Taylor Swift) opened her set with *Shake It Off*, thrilling everybody until her closing number *You Belong With Me*. Freddie had never seen Molly perform live and he readily made a mental note to let Dawn and Belinda know just how marvellous she was.

If the audience's screams and shouts were loud and appreciative for the Taylor Swift tribute artiste, then the thunderous sound that followed as Boy George took to the stage was no less than ear-splitting. Strutting perilously on his green stilettos to *Karma Chameleon*, his purple velvet coat flaying around his pink silk pantaloons, the Boy had the audience in the palm of his highly manicured hands. The long red silk scarf attached to his emerald green top hat twisted and twirled in rhythm to his staccato movements. Freddie, along with the rest of the packed ballroom, was mesmerised by this phenomenon commanding the stage and his audience's full attention.

Turning to Wayne, Freddie, his blue eyes shining, exclaimed, "He is sensational!"

Wayne nodded his head in agreement as his eyes focused on the apparition lighting up the stage, not wanting to take his eyes off him.

By the end of Boy George's set, the uproar was deafening and when he yelled to the ecstatic crowd, "Have I still got it or what?", the inebriated audience screamed and whistled while some stamped their feet in appreciation of the sensational Boy George, screaming at him, "More! More!"

Still in the dressing room waiting to be announced as the last tribute act of the evening, Crystal had the briefest feeling of apprehension as she heard the standing ovation and extended applause for Boy George. Although she had only just been introduced to Kevin by the Taylor Swift lookalike, Crystal could instantly sense that there was something extraordinarily special about him. His quick sharp wit was magical and she found herself hanging on to his every word along with other people in the dressing room area.

Checking her face in the large mirror and making sure there was no lipstick on her newly whitened teeth, Crystal knew she had a very hard act to follow but she also knew that once she was halfway through *Diamonds are a Girl's Best Friend*, Boy George would be forgotten.

Crystal's confidence was sky-high. All afternoon people had been remarking on her uncanny resemblance to the world's greatest icon. Crystal was a natural, requiring no form of surgery to enhance her to look more like Marilyn Monroe. Unlike Kay, Melita and others before her, Crystal's full lips and delicate features were God-given and her hair, naturally wavy and blonde, had no need for bleach.

Aside from all these attributes, Crystal possessed something no other wannabe Marilyn Monroe ever possessed – Marilyn's beautiful haunting eyes; as if the icon's childlike vulnerability crept up from her heartbroken soul and lingered there irresistibly for the whole world to fall in love with her, and of course, it did.

The lights dimmed considerably, persuading the noisy audience to quieten. Suddenly, the spotlight fluttered around the now hushed darkened room, people twittering, excited to see who would entertain them next.

Coming to a sudden stop at the back of the large stage, the spotlight brightened as the first bars of *Diamonds are a Girl's Best Friend* struck up. There she stood, the replica of Marilyn Monroe, deep satin pink dress with matching long gloves and stiletto shoes glowing in the spotlight, while the many diamonds adorning her hair, ears, wrists and throat sparkled as brightly as her dark blue-green eyes. Deliberately walking towards the front of the stage, tight dress hugging her femininity, the whole ballroom now deathly quiet, Crystal stretched out her arms and began to sing, her voice a replica of the famous icon's.

"A kiss on the hand may be quite continental, but diamonds are a girl's best friend."

Before she had reached the second line of the celebrated song, the audience went crazy but, unlike the reception given to Boy George and Taylor Swift earlier, suddenly, a ghostly quietness descended on the audience as they became mesmerised with this beautiful apparition on stage.

Finishing her set with *I Wanna Be Loved By You*, Crystal felt completely fulfilled as the frenzied audience kept calling for Marilyn.

This time, they were not giving up. Rushing quickly on stage, the male compère for the evening tried to quieten the audience; if they stopped yelling, Crystal would perform one last song for them. Upon hearing this, the audience began whistling and stamping their feet in jubilation.

Turning to a smiling Crystal, the compère held out his hand to her as she shimmed up to the mike in the centre of the stage then, in her breathy Marilyn voice, began.

"Happy Birthday to you…"

Standing at the back of the ballroom, witnessing the frenzy she caused, Kevin, Freddie and Wayne were wide-eyed and dumbfounded.

"Well, I never!" exclaimed the Boy. "The girl's blooming brilliant! Anyone who can upstage Boy George is a force to be reckoned with, I tell you!"

Reacting completely out of character, Wayne was very enthusiastic and kept applauding until Kevin pulled his lover's hands apart and hissed at him, "Enough!"

Although Freddie was not a fan of Crystal's, he instinctively knew that they had all witnessed something surreal, as if time had transported them back to the Golden Years of Hollywood to glimpse the incomparable Marilyn Monroe herself.

The overall opinion of Selfridges staff and guests was that all three acts were fabulous and they noisily surrounded the performers, pushing and shoving each other in their intoxication, each wanting to be the first to have a selfie with the tribute artistes. Freddie noticed that Crystal smiled continuously under the adoration of her admirers but he also noticed that at times, her eyes had a faraway look in them, as if she would rather be somewhere else. For the life of him, Freddie could not quash the feeling of uneasiness he felt when in her presence. Camp Freddie was indeed a deeply sensitive chap.

As for Kevin, he giggled and flirted with every attractive male in the ballroom and gave his quick-witted banter back to the inebriated females who tried unsuccessfully to pull his green top hat off. How they adored him, continuously kissing him, leaving their red and pink lipstick prints on his heavily powered cheeks!

Freddie laughed to himself when several ladies surrounded Kevin and one asked in a stage whisper if he really was gay, to which the Boy retorted as only he could, "Oh course I am gay! Silly bitch! What? Do you think I only help them out when they are busy? I am as gay as a lark, ladies, gay as a lark!"

Hearing this, one of the revellers jumped up and knocked Kevin"s hat straight off his head, the bright red scarf twirling in the air as the hat floated above the crowd and crash landed on the side of Crystal's head, causing her to almost choke on her glass of Prosecco. Adoring fans caught their breath as their idol handed one of the men her glass and picking the hat up from the floor, threw it back in the direction of Kevin, just missing one of his lady admirers.

Crystal's eyes, Freddie noticed, had turned from vulnerable to flashing evil as she raised her breathy voice and murmured, in true Monroe fashion, "Yours, I believe, Boy George? No good you hanging your hat up on me, is there?"

Once more, the gathering crowds broke out in uproar. Never one to be overshadowed, Kevin, his small knowing eyes flashing in anger, retaliated. "Wouldn't dream of hanging anything up to you, bitch! Let's face it, I have no idea where you have been!"

To the loud applause from his ardent fans, Kevin swung smartly on his killer heels and begun to mix and mingle.

Seething inside but covering her feelings amicably, the only response Crystal could give after being outfoxed so cleverly was, "Touché!"

During this scenario, Freddie noticed that Wayne nervously kept his alert eyes on both male and female partygoers, always vigilant when it came to the Boy George lookalike and a drunken crowd. Luckily for Wayne, the Selfridges crowd were happy drunks.

An hour or so after the famous DJ had commenced his set and the noisy party was in full swing, Molly Rose walked over to Freddie and Wayne, explaining that she had completed her contracted hours and was about to leave. Stretching up and kissing Freddie on both cheeks, Molly Rose then turned and kissed Wayne whom she had met several times before when she and Kevin had worked together. Freddie noticed Wayne squeeze Molly's hand seductively and that she gazed lingeringly into the bodyguard's limpid eyes. This was not the first time Freddie had witnessed Wayne's interest in the opposite sex whenever Kevin was not around.

A feeling of uneasiness enveloped Freddie's mind and he tried desperately to quell it. He was very fond of both the Boy George lookalike and the unassuming Wayne, and he hoped his two friends could sort out their turbulent love life favourably.

The remainder of the evening turned out to be full of fun, although both Freddie and Wayne breathed easier when Kevin sauntered over to them just before the bewitching hour and announced that he was ready for his bed. At the same time, Crystal came wiggling up to them, three handsome young men hanging on to her arms as if she would disappear into thin air if they let go of their beautiful possession.

"Are you off now, boys?" she asked giggling as one of the handsome young men started kissing her hand.

"Yes, as a matter of fact, we are," replied Freddie glancing at the most beautiful Marilyn Monroe lookalike he had ever seen. "You can also go now, Crystal, as you have worked your contracted hours," he declared as the same disquiet feeling crept up from his stomach.

"Oh no! I shall stay to the bitter end! Having a wonderful time, aren't we, boys?" replied Crystal, glancing at her admirers in turn as they grinned back at her, longingly.

"What about you, Boy George? You're not leaving now, are you?" she queried, glancing at Kevin who had been chatting with several of his ardent fans.

"Listen, darling," came his impertinent reply, "I have been in this game for a long time. I work my arse off during my contracted hours and then I am out of there! It's been a great gig but time now for my beauty sleep. Isn't that right, ladies?" he giggled, looking directly at Freddie and Wayne, who both nodded in agreement.

"Seeing as you are a newcomer, Miss Monroe, let me give you a word of advice," he declared, bending down slightly to whisper in Crystal's ear. "Never outstay your welcome! Always leave them wanting more!"

With these words echoing in Crystal's ear, Kevin snapped his fingers at Wayne and Freddie then sauntered across the ballroom to the sounds of wolf whistles, cheers and applause, both Wayne and Freddie rushing to keep up with him. Now playing up to the cheering crowd, and in true Boy George fashion, Kevin gave them the Royal wave, causing further uproar from the inebriated revellers.

Suddenly and without warning, he slipped awkwardly, sliding on the highly polished herringbone parquet floor.

Trying desperately to keep upright on his stilettos, his long arms and legs flaying about alarmingly, there was a loud thump as Kevin landed face down on the shiny floor and slid straight out of the ballroom to the pandemonium of the enthralled spectators.

Like the resolute bodyguard that he was, Wayne, shoving people out of the way, raced quickly through the crowds to reach the lookalike.

Laughing uncontrollably at the unfolding scene being played out in front of him, Freddie murmured to himself, "Only the Boy! Only the Boy!"

Chapter 24
Christmas Abroad

It was two days before Christmas and Freddie had enjoyed a wonderful time the previous evening impersonating Liberace on his lookalike assignment at the Hilton Hotel on Park Lane. Working with some of the tribute artistes of American icons, Freddie found himself in the company of Elvis, Johnny Cash, Diana Ross, Britney Spears, Beyoncé, Justin Timberlake and Neil Diamond. This was purely a mix and mingle job where the booked artistes were hired to chat to, dance with and generally enthral the employees of the Texan oil company's Christmas party. Sinatra's Rat Pack were the chosen entertainment for the evening, before the DJ took over ensuring the party would remain in full swing into the small hours.

Freddie had met this particular Rat Pack some months before when they had arrived at Top Drawer Agency to sign a contract for a very affluent client in Paris. Freddie really liked this particular Pack and was delighted to be working alongside them on this exciting job. He quite fancied Rick, the Dean Martin impersonator, and couldn't help fluttering his dark eyelashes at the crooner whenever they were in conversation together.

When Tony, the Sinatra impersonator, noticed Freddie's antics towards his pal, he raised his voice and grinning knowingly, called out, "Hey, Liberace, you're wasting your time there, my friend! You will never convert Dino!" Poor Freddie blushed like a schoolgirl while everyone around him burst into laughter.

"I'm just admiring the eye candy, Frank! Just admiring the eye candy!" retorted Freddie, flaying his arms in the air now fluttering his eyelashes at the Chairman of the Board instead, who jokingly yelled in true Sinatra style, "Get out of here!"

Freddie was now becoming extremely excited at the prospect of seeing Claudio again. Tomorrow he would be in his lover's arms once more. Carefully wrapping the Christmas gifts he had lovingly bought, Freddie hoped they would make Claudio happy. He knew that Claudio may not appreciate the surprise visit, but he pushed this worrying thought out of his head as he began to pack his red wheeled suitcase.

Top Drawer Agency had now closed for the Christmas holidays. Dawn, together with her husband and two teenage children, had driven to the beautiful Cornish countryside where they were to spend the whole of the festive season. Belinda was due to fly to New York, and little Queenie was safe in the loving care of Big Gerty and her partner, Fanny. Freddie chuckled to himself as he imagined the two women vying for the little dog's attention, completely spoiling him.

Recalling his chat with Belinda over the telephone only a short while before, Camp Freddie hoped she would have a wonderful time in New York; she certainly sounded excited. They were kindred spirits, he and Belinda, their interests and attitudes were very similar and sadly, they both seemed to be unlucky in love. He surmised she would be at

Heathrow by now, seasonally attired in her faux fur coat and hat, ready to face the freezing New York temperatures as she joined Frank in the Big Apple. Freddie remembered Belinda telling him she would be arriving at JFK Airport close to ten o'clock in the evening New York time, where Frank was to meet her.

Hurriedly completing his packing for the following morning's flight out of Gatwick Airport, poor Freddie could not suppress a terrible feeling of foreboding that refused to disappear from his anguished mind.

As he made himself another black coffee, Freddie found he was already missing little Queenie and wished he could pop next door to see him with Big Gerty and Fanny but he knew this would be unfair to Queenie and the ladies. Instead, he decided to have a good dinner and down a few glasses of red wine, which would hopefully vanquish his feeling of disquiet.

Later that evening, before switching off his bedside light, Freddie reached for his mobile and called Big Gerty's to ask after his little dog.

"He's very content, Freddie," assured Big Gerty, her low voice letting out a sigh. "He's sound asleep on Fanny's lap at the moment. Now will you please stop fretting! As well you know, we shall spoil him rotten!" she added, sighing again.

"Yes, but I feel completely lost without him!" groaned Freddie, trying to disguise the lump in his throat.

"Freddie, go have a wonderful Christmas with Claudio and be sure to give him our best wishes!" cajoled Gerty, in response. "Smooth flight, sweetheart," she added in a half-whisper, so as not to waken little Queenie.

"Merry Christmas to both you and Fanny," murmured a melancholy Freddie. "Thank you both so much for everything," he hastily added.

Unbeknown to Big Gerty, Freddie suddenly broke down in tears; tears for leaving his little dog and tears for the foreboding feeling that wilfully came flooding back to his tormented mind...

He stood there at the barrier of the arrivals lounge, the collar of his heavy navy overcoat opened at the neck, a maroon cashmere scarf draping down the front. It was very warm in the airport after coming in from the bitter cold winter's evening.

As her searching eyes found him, Belinda's heart fluttered. She noticed he looked not so much tired but sad, as if he were carrying the problems of the whole world on his shoulders. As she walked slowly towards him, he glanced at her and those butterflies began to flutter in her tummy. She saw his dancing brown eyes spring alive.

Stepping forward quickly, he held her close to him for a full minute. She could feel both their hearts beating rapidly.

Before releasing her, he whispered, "Amore mio, mi sei mancato," *(My love, I've missed you)* then he brought his lips down to her waiting mouth as they kissed for a long time, oblivious to the amused onlookers.

Belinda knew that Frank had moved apartment buildings in the last few months and was anxious to see his new place. Continuously chatting to each other on the way back from the airport, she tingled with pleasure as Frank held her left hand throughout the whole journey while driving his navy BMW X5. His luxury apartment building was positioned at the centre of the Urban Coast, New York's most connected waterfront neighbourhood. He explained to her that Manhattan, Brooklyn and Queens all met here, at the East River.

Frank assured Belinda that he really enjoyed living in this area. There were two indoor swimming pools and a spa with a gym.

After parking his car in the underground lot, they travelled in a lift which took them close to the top of the building and to Frank's new home.

Before she could comment on the elaborate décor and mesmerising skyline views of New York, Frank had thrown off his overcoat and pulled her to him, feverishly kissing her mouth. Now desperately pulling off her faux fur coat, Belinda's body and soul screamed for his touch. Garments and lingerie were strewn over the floor as Frank masterly scooped her up in his strong, tanned arms and urgently laid her on his Italian Sharpei bed.

Only leaving on her white French knickers, Frank sucked and kissed her protruding nipples as they stood erect begging for his caress. Causing Belinda's whole body to shiver with ecstasy, his hot tongue flickered downwards, lip kissing her until he reached her creamy thighs. Pushing them apart, she could feel his fingers inside her and was conscious that a deep moan escaped his throat. Urgently positioning himself on top of her, Frank's manhood stood erect as he began to enter her trembling body. Answering his every thrust, Belinda felt as if she were on fire, toes and fingertips tingling hotly. How she adored this man, how she longed for him day and night, how she knew no other man could ever make her feel this way!

Squeals and groans of sensual passion filled the silence of the apartment as Frank's building momentum kept tempo with his lover. They stayed for hours in his bed, talking, eating, drinking wine and making erotic, uninhibited love

As dawn descended in the wintry New York sky, Belinda, wrapped in the arms of her lover, completely exhausted, but deliriously happy, snuggled down under the dark brown silk duvet. It was Christmas Eve.

Christmas Day was spent with just the two of them, wrapped up in their deep love for each other. Frank's son Mikey had decided to spend the festive season in Miami with some friends who had recently moved there. Belinda was disappointed not to meet him.

As far as Frank was concerned, there was nothing that was good enough for his lover and he had pulled out all the stops to make this a trip for her to remember forever. He wanted her to experience everything this great city had to offer. Belinda's favourite was the One World Observatory Freedom Tower, with its indescribable panoramic views of the world's most iconic city.

Belinda was completely overwhelmed with the New York she was being introduced to. Recalling her first visit there, only last year with Tanya when she had decided to surprise Frank, nothing could erase the terrible sadness that had swept over her as she watched her lover walking arm and arm with a young elegant blonde woman outside the apartment building, opposite Central Park, where he had been living at that time.

Of course, she and Tanya had presumed the worse, but his companion that day was no other than his younger sister Danielle whom Belinda and Frank were to meet for dinner on a later visit, together with her partner, Troy.

As Frank had predicted, Belinda and Danielle had instantly taken to each other, chatting and laughing as if they were long-time friends. It seemed as if the two women had a natural fondness for each other through their mutual love of Frank. Troy was a charming man and Belinda invited them both to London whenever they wished to visit.

Although she and Frank were ecstatically happy to spend time together, Belinda could not help but notice that he had lost the shimmer in his eyes. On her very last evening in the Big Apple, long after they had made sensual love and she lay completely contented in his strong arms, Belinda asked if there was anything troubling him.

Looking directly into her worried eyes, Frank quietly replied, "Darling, there are situations sometimes in life that have to be followed through, no matter how distasteful. I am forever remorseful when such situations arise."

Squeezing her hand, he assured her smiling, "It's nothing; just business. Do not worry, my love."

But the cold shiver that clawed at her heart refused to fade.

Chapter 25
Two's Company,
Three's a Crowd

"Crying is a way your eyes speak when your mouth can't explain how broken your heart is."
Anon

Although it was only the beginning of the year when Belinda's flight landed flawlessly on the runway at Heathrow, a weak winter morning sun welcomed her home. She had hardly noticed the harsh New York weather, not feeling its bitterness as her body was invariably on fire every time she was with Frank. But now, as she prepared to disembark the plane with other passengers, the loneliness she felt overwhelmed her senses as both Frank and Matt's handsome faces fleetingly swept through her mind. Fighting to hold back hot tears, she checked the overhead compartment to make sure she had retrieved everything.

Having pre-booked a black taxi, she gave the driver a quick wave after seeing her name on a plaque he was holding up in the arrivals lounge.

It was a little after eleven o'clock and a feeling of exhaustion suddenly descended upon her. Leaving Frank and New York had left Belinda crestfallen, although her lover had promised he would be back in London within the month. To her sweet surprise, he had also asked her how she would feel about living permanently in New York and with tears of joy in her eyes, she responded by throwing her arms around his manly neck and hugging him tightly. At long last, Frank had committed himself to her and she assured him she would adore living in the Big Apple, or anywhere else in the world for that matter, as long as he was by her side.

Promising to discuss further when he next arrived in London, Frank had held her close to his body and with eyes closed he had whispered, "Prendi il mio cuore con te." *(You take my heart with you.)*

It was Monday. The Top Drawer Agency was to reopen the following day, but Dawn had suggested to Belinda that she should take it easy at home and come in later during the week.

"Get over your jet lag, sweetie, then come in on Wednesday if you feel up to it," she had suggested when Belinda called her from the back of the black taxi. "Things will be very quiet here and besides, Freddie is due back tomorrow," she added as an afterthought.

"Oh yes, of course, Freddie!" declared Belinda almost to herself as if she had just remembered him. "I do hope he and Claudio had a lovely Christmas and New Year."

"I want to hear all about what you and Frank got up to in New York!" giggled Dawn. "Well, not quite everything!" she quipped giggling again.

"See you Wednesday!"

Freddie did not arrive for work on the Tuesday. He telephoned Dawn to explain how he had caught a tummy bug on the flight home. Dawn assured him she would be able to cope as it was always very quiet in the agency at the beginning of the new year.

As she replaced the receiver, she began to feel quite worried. She distinctly heard a catch, like a sob, in Freddie's voice as he bid her goodbye. Her first instinct was to call Belinda but decided against it as she would still be catching up on much needed sleep. They could discuss it the following day.

Dawn was a woman blessed. She and her husband were still ardent lovers, and she adored her two teenagers who in return adored their doting mother. The four of them had spent a marvellous Christmas with her ageing parents in Cornwall and spending time back home always gave Dawn a new lease of life. Although her own 'coupling' ran smoothly, she had great compassion for the less fortunate of those who had found only misery and heartbreak when in love. Her natural insight and sensitivity made her sympathetic towards Freddie and Belinda, concerned for them both as if they were her siblings. Dawn was a natural Earth Mother.

Upon opening the emails, her keen eye noticed two messages requesting lookalikes, immediately raising her spirits. Business had always been Dawn's pleasure and she quickly read through the text.

She chuckled as she read the first request. The High Commission of Australia in London, located in Australia House on the Strand, were prepared to pay a tidy sum for Roz Lynn, the Dame Edna Everage tribute artiste, to entertain their staff and guests for one hour at an exclusive party. Dawn silently prayed that Roz would be free on 26th

January, Australia Day. She quickly telephoned Roz and was relieved when the call was answered almost immediately. Roz assured Dawn that she would be available to accept the job, especially at such a generous fee.

"Wonderful! I shall send the contract to you imminently!" Dawn declared.

The second email was from Felipe, who owned Rocket, a famous second-hand fashion and accessories store that had begun life as a stall in Camden Market back in the eighties. Felipe had requested four Elvis lookalikes to act as serving staff to the public on 8th January, the King's birthday.

"January 8th!" screeched Dawn out loud, disrupting the soothing quietness. "Dear God, it's the bloody 7th today!" she groaned alarmingly to an empty office.

Grabbing the telephone, she called her top four Elvis lookalikes, furious with Felipe for making this last-minute request. Dawn loathed being unable to fulfil all bookings, even late ones, but this was sailing close to the wind!

Being the astute business woman that she was, within forty-five minutes, Dawn had secured her top four Elvis lookalikes, each booked and ready for action the following day. January was invariably the quietest time of year in the showbiz world and jobs were scarce. Everybody in the business was usually available during this most miserable of months.

Humming to herself, a satisfied Dawn telephoned Felipe, assuring him that Top Drawer Agency were so named because it was indeed Top Drawer! After discussing contracts and fees, Dawn confirmed that her top four Elvises would arrive no later than ten o'clock the following morning, quiffs and blue suede shoes at the ready!

Dawn noticed Belinda looked tired and a little pale as she came into the office the following morning, laden with colourful packages and gifts from New York. The two business partners kissed and hugged, both happy to see each other.

Settling down with cups of hot black coffee, Dawn coaxed Belinda to tell her everything about Christmas in the Big Apple with Frank. Assuring her friend that she and Frank were as strong as ever, Belinda mentioned to Dawn that the American had asked her if she believed she could live permanently in New York.

"Great! At last!" exclaimed Dawn loudly. "Oh! But you won't be going just yet, will you, darling?" she quickly asked, not relishing the thought of running the agency without her dear Belinda.

"No! No! Not for some time yet!" assured Belinda. "Frank is still heavily committed to his job and although I miss him terribly, I would rather be busy here in London than alone most of the time in New York!"

"That is sensible, darling," replied Dawn, relief in her voice. "You will instinctively know when you are ready to go!" she remarked, drinking the last drops of her coffee.

"Good morning, ladies," came the unusually subdued voice of Camp Freddie as he strolled quietly into the office, stopping to place little Queenie down on the carpeted floor, who immediately ran up to Belinda.

"Freddie!"

They greeted him simultaneously, rising from their chairs and rushing towards him. He lowered his head shyly so that they would not see the black and yellowish bruising around his left eye and on the side of his face which he had unsuccessfully tried to conceal.

"Oh, my God!" shrieked Belinda, causing little Queenie to whimper. Tears of frustration burnt her eyes as she peered at dear Freddie's face in disbelief.

"Freddie! What on earth happened to you?" asked Dawn, trying without success to keep the alarm out of her voice. "It was that awful Claudio who did this, wasn't it?" she stressed loudly, her voice raising into a crescendo.

Glancing into Dawn's eyes, Freddie slowly shook his weary head, before replying, "No. It was not Claudio. It was Fabrizio!"

"Fabrizio? Who the bloody hell is Fabrizio?" cried Belinda, wiping the hot tears from her eyes with a tissue.

"Ladies. Please! I am okay, truly," Freddie assured them quietly. "I am gasping for a cup of coffee then I will tell you everything!" he murmured huskily, his voice sounding emotional. Shoulders a little slouched, Freddie disappeared into the kitchenette, little Queenie following at his heel.

It was Christmas Eve, a little after one o'clock in the afternoon and an excited Freddie had arrived at Malpensa Airport. He had pre-booked a taxi to take him into Milan city centre; this was the one luxury Freddie would allow himself on this holiday. Handing the taxi driver Claudio's address, Freddie tried to relax in the quietness of the back of the taxi and imagine how his temperamental lover would react having Freddie turn up out of the blue.

As the taxi turned into a narrow side road, Freddie recognised the name of the street to be where the opera singer stayed while in Milan. Claudio had mentioned to Freddie some time ago that he was paying far too much rent for the one-bedroom apartment and eventually he would buy his own place in the sophisticated Italian city.

The taxi driver pulled up outside a rustic brick building, then opening the boot, retrieved Freddie's suitcase. Thanking the stony-faced driver then paying his fare which included a modest tip, Freddie turned and walked towards the entrance of the building. Taking the small lift up two flights to the third floor, he was aware that he was feeling both nervous and excited at the same time.

Standing outside his lover's door, he waited a full minute before pressing the doorbell. After what seemed like forever, Claudio's voice could be heard from behind the door.

"Chi e?" *(Who is it?)*

"Claudio! It is me, Freddie!" he replied, excitedly.

Abruptly, the door swung open and there stood a half-naked Claudio, a look of distaste on his attractive face. His angry eyes seemed to pierce poor Freddie's heart. He was not happy at all to be face to face with his English lover at this moment in time.

Berating poor Freddie for turning up unexpectedly, his English was broken and full of grammatical errors. Claudio did not appreciate Freddie's surprise.

"What are you doing here?" yelled Claudio. "Did I not tell you I would be busy all over the Christmas festivities and that you should not come?" his voice now breaking off.

"Yes, you did, Claudio, but I was missing you so much. I just wanted to surprise you!" mumbled an alarmed-looking Freddie in his own defence.

"Surprise me!" exclaimed Claudio. "Why surprise me? You know how I hate surprises!" he bellowed at Freddie, dark angry eyes flashing.

"Oh! I am so sorry, Claudio, but aren't you going to invite me in?" asked a confused Freddie, tears beginning to glisten in his eyes.

"Well, I have no option now, do I?" stressed Claudio, his arms flaying in the air as he irritably ushered Freddie inside.

Stepping gingerly into the apartment, Freddie was not surprised to see the lounge was cluttered with stage clothes. Claudio never was one for clearing up after himself.

Turning to face his lover, Freddie threw his arms around the Italian and hugged him, holding him silently for a long while. Did he feel the opera singer fleetingly stiffen? He could not be sure.

"I shall be as quiet as a mouse, I promise! You won't even know I am here!" enthused Freddie to a sulky Claudio. "I shall cook you wonderful meals and tidy up your mess!" he giggled, peering into Claudio's flashing eyes.

Suddenly, the same foreboding feeling crept into his heart as he tried to comprehend what the Italian was trying to say to him.

"I am sorry, Freddie, I cannot have you here," pronounced Claudio, his eyes focusing on the parquet floor, not wanting to witness whatever he might see in the Englishman's face. "I have another friend staying with me for a while. You had no right to turn up without notifying me!" he uttered, pouring two glasses of red wine and handing one to a startled Freddie.

"What?" cried Freddie, his voice rising. "What are you talking about? We are partners, Claudio! Of course I can stay here!"

Looking sheepish and quite apologetic, Claudio explained to poor Freddie that he was now in a deep relationship with another man. He had not wanted to tell Freddie before Christmas but was going to do so in the new year. His new love was a young singer and fate had thrown them together through their love of opera.

"It was as if the Gods had wished for Fabrizio and I to be soulmates!" confessed the Italian, his dark eyes expressing sorrow now for his English lover.

Freddie felt as if his whole world had fallen apart, shattering in thousands of pieces at his feet. His mind whirled. He felt dizzy; sick in fact. He could not perceive what the opera singer was saying to him. He was conscious that Claudio was speaking but he could not comprehend one single word. It was as if his ears refused to hear what they were being told.

Suddenly, the bedroom door opened and out of the dim light, a young man appeared. A very beautiful young man who instantly prompted a Greek God to come into Freddie's bewildered mind. Why was this young man almost naked?

Claudio nervously introduced the young man as Fabrizio. Freddie, head still spinning, observed that the younger man did not look him straight in the eye.

"Is this your new love?" Freddie found himself asking, as if the words had not been uttered from his own mouth.

When Claudio, eyes downcast, nodded in confirmation, a shocked Freddie exclaimed, "He must be all of eighteen years old! You are old enough to be his father!"

"Well, I am not his father!" retorted Claudio a little smugly which not only upset Freddie but infuriated him. "So now, mio amico *(my friend)*, you know everything!" Claudio declared, less complacent now.

"You have only yourself to blame. I had told you several times not to come here over Christmas. I was trying to save you from getting hurt!" he affirmed, walking over to Fabrizio, placing a protective arm around the young man's shoulders.

Fabrizio, staring at Freddie, opened his effeminate mouth and murmured sarcastically, "Questa è la vita, ne vinci un po', ne perdi un po!" *(That is life, you win some, you lose some!)*

What followed will forever remain a void in Freddie's memory. He began to scream at the top of his voice, yelling abuse at Fabrizio. Rushing towards the young man, grabbing him by his thick, dark curly hair, he pulled as hard as he could.

Completely stunned by Freddie's reaction, Claudio started to punch the Englishman in defence of his young lover. Suddenly, the wildcat side of Fabrizio erupted as he wildly clawed at the intruder's face and arms. But for Freddie, the most despicable insult was that Fabrizio spat at him several times.

This unforeseen skirmish turned into a free-for-all but the odds were against poor Freddie and he came off very badly indeed. His face was bleeding and bruised, his left eye had closed as Fabrizio's fist landed on it more than once. His new suede overcoat was ruined and ripped at the shoulder.

All of a sudden, Freddie was vaguely aware that Claudio began pulling Fabrizio off him and ordered the young man back into the bedroom.

"Go!" ordered Claudio. "Questo e sufficiente!" *(That's enough!)*

Reluctantly, the young Italian did as he was told and closed the door behind him, swearing under his breath, dark eyes glaring in anger.

Freddie was shaking; his tormented mind would not accept what had just taken place. It was as if he were a spectator looking in on another's fight. His love and passion for Claudio would not allow his heart the luxury of accepting the truth – of course Claudio loved him, he had told him many times – of course Claudio did not intend to hurt him either physically or emotionally! It was the fault of that horrid young man, Fabrizio. It was he who had enticed Claudio away from Freddie. It was he who was trying his best to separate them.

Head drooping, Freddie let out a long mournful sob as Claudio rushed into the bathroom and returning, handed his English lover a damp cloth for his swollen and bruised eye and face.

His voice shaking with emotion, a gesticulating Claudio, murmured to Freddie, "Forgive me, mio amico, but I could not help myself. As my eyes first encountered Fabrizio, so my heart was forever his!"

Placing a comforting hand on a traumatised Freddie who continued to sob, albeit quietly now, Claudio continued in a sensitive voice, "It is better if I find you a bed and breakfast close to Malpensa Airport. It is obvious you cannot stay here with me because of Fabrizio. I am truly saddened about all of this, Freddie. You know how fond of you I have become. I will also call the airline and endeavour to secure you an earlier return flight to London."

Upon hearing these words from the Italian, a devastated Freddie clung to the opera singer, pleading with him not to leave. But Claudio was deeply in love himself and as much as he hated hurting Freddie, he knew he would never sing again if Fabrizio were to go.

"Caro, Freddie," soothed Claudio. "You are a beautiful person. You will meet a wonderful lover who will adore you as I adore Fabrizio. You know better than all of us that we cannot choose with whom we fall in love. You of all people are conscious of this fact."

Walking resignedly towards the bedroom door, he opened it slightly and spoke quickly in Italian to Fabrizio, whose only response was, "Si, Si, Si," before Claudio closed the door again.

Handing Freddie another glass of red wine, which he refused, Claudio shrugged his shoulders and drank down both glasses himself. Immediately, the opera singer found alternative accommodation for Freddie, a little closer to Malpensa Airport and secured an earlier return flight. His ex-lover would be back in the UK the day after Christmas.

Watching and listening to Claudio using his magnetic charm to acquire both accommodation and flight, Freddie's very soul seemed to lose its quest for life. He quite simply adored the opera singer. For the briefest of moments, the thought of ending his now unbearable life flashed temptingly through his tortured mind.

Replacing the receiver, Claudio jumped up and, smiling at Freddie, informed him that a taxi would be arriving shortly to drive him to his newly acquired accommodation.

"I regret that you will be alone on Christmas Day, mio amcio, but I too will be alone in a way. I have two consecutive charity shows to perform which will keep me busy all day and into the evening. Fabrizio is not booked for these particular shows and so you see, I also will be alone!" he added, sheepishly.

The lady proprietor of the little hotel close to Malpensa Airport was a jolly and kind person. She insisted Freddie have dinner and from her very broken English, Freddie understood that she would bring food to his room. Poor Freddie had no appetite whatsoever but once he smelt the delicious aroma of Italian food, he ate hungrily. The lady was a friend of Claudio's and it was obvious she had been alerted about the Englishman's swollen and bruised face because she pretended not to notice it.

That night was the worst of Freddie's entire life. He lay in the dark of the cold, little room with no desire to turn on the heating. He lay there, thinking and crying, thoughts of suicide again creeping into his distressed mind, and a feeling of desperation of never being in Claudio's arms again refusing to fade. The jealousy he felt for the beautiful Fabrizio, wishing the young man harm then apologising to a silent God for his wickedness. He dallied with the idea of slitting his wrists in the bathtub but suddenly an image of little Queenie floated momentarily through his mind and Camp Freddie turned over and sobbed quietly into the soft, white pillow.

Christmas Day in Milan was quiet. The streets were quite empty apart from the odd car driving past him as he walked and walked without knowing where he was going. In the crisp cold morning air, Freddie begun to accept that his relationship with Claudio had now ended. He knew he would never truly get over the opera singer but he also knew he had to carry on. After all, he had little Queenie waiting for him and he had many good friends in London who loved and cared for him. He secretly apologised to God for his wicked thoughts of suicide but he was also sure that this heartache would be with him for a very long time to come.

As he walked and walked, lost in his private thoughts, tears began to spill down his torn face. His beloved Claudio was within reaching distance but he would not be seeing him again. Freddie prayed that once he was back on British soil, it would be easier for him to try to forget the Italian.

Belinda and Dawn sat drinking several cups of coffee, mesmerised at Freddie's revelation of how tragic his Christmas surprise visit to Claudio and Milan had been.

Both ladies, tears filling their eyes, were horrified at what they had heard, and both craved to personally horsewhip the heartless Italian opera singer and his vicious new lover, Fabrizio.

Chapter 26
Seeing Double

L ondon was now witnessing the usual procession of winter attire. Coats, hats, scarves, gloves, boots and of course, the famous umbrella. Like a grand army joining forces once again to ward off the great British winter with coughs and sneezes, the music accompanying the cold dankness. For millions of Londoners, the depressing trudge to work was somewhat eased as they turned off from reality, allowing their minds to dwell on their future summer holidays of sun, sand and sea.

Gradually as the first month came to a cold wintry close, life at Top Drawer Agency became unseasonably busy. Belinda kept a watchful eye on Freddie. Although his face showed barely a mark of the abuse he suffered on Christmas Eve in Milan, Belinda knew he still carried the scars in his heart and mind. Dawn had asked Freddie to work an extra day during the busy times and Belinda spent as much time with him as possible, dining together after work and meeting up with Tanya and occasionally Aarne at weekends. Bryanne and Simon threw a wonderfully camp party at their beautiful West London home, insisting Belinda bring Freddie along.

Although there were the good days, Freddie was often burdened with very bad days but he knew how fortunate he was to be surrounded by such warm-hearted friends. Freddie was not alone and yet he felt completely isolated without Claudio in his life.

The agency continued to tick over nicely, helping to raise the low mood which had descended upon a dark and drizzly London. Dawn could always ignore the gloominess of the first few months of the year as long as Top Drawer's services were in high demand. She smiled to herself when reflecting on the past few weeks. Although the Duke and Duchess of Sussex were no longer full-time working members of the Royal Family, together with the Duke and Duchess of Cambridge lookalikes they remained extremely popular, as were many of the Royal lookalikes. Also in great demand were the tribute artistes who flew all over the UK and Europe performing prestigious jobs.

"Oh no!" exclaimed Dawn on an unusually sunny day at the beginning of February, which caused both Belinda and Freddie to glance at her questioningly. "Our clients in Dublin are requesting two Monroes for a TV advertisement, but wait for it! They have chosen not only Crystal but also Melita!" she declared, tutting and shaking her head from side to side.

"Oh! I'm sure they will be okay," appeased Belinda. "What other characters are required?"

"None! Just the two Monroes, I'm afraid. This is exactly what I have been dreading, " she moaned, checking the contact numbers online. "If my memory serves me correctly, Melita has stipulated she would rather not work if it were just the two of them." She glanced at Belinda, frowning.

"Would you like me to call Melita and explain the situation?" offered Belinda, to which Dawn sullenly nodded her neatly bobbed hair in agreement.

"If she would rather not accept the booking, we shall replace her with either Anita or Freya. The clients must have a choice!" emphasised Dawn decisively, turning her attention to contacting Crystal for her availability.

Accepting the booking immediately, Crystal felt elated that she would have a chance to upstage her half-sister. Melita took time to mull over the concept of working closely with Crystal but the rent had to be paid, so she reluctantly accepted, assuring Belinda that for the sake of the agency, she would act in a completely professional manner while the two sisters worked together.

Clients pre-booked the airfare and hotel accommodation for all chosen lookalike and tribute artistes. Michael Fitzgerald, representative for the Dublin clients, called Top Drawer Agency, confirming flights from Gatwick for the two Monroes. Crystal and Melita were to fly to Dublin Airport, arriving at ten o'clock in the morning when they would be collected by a chauffeur assigned to drive them to their hotel.

After time for relaxation and lunch, the lookalikes were to be driven to the TV studios where they would be handed a script, detailing what was expected of them. They were also to be interviewed by Eire's top chat show host regarding their daily lives portraying the most famous icon.

Arriving at the Aer Lingus desk a little early, Melita glanced around and pretended not to notice the looks and grins from other passengers as she walked confidently up to the desk, pulling her small black wheeled suitcase behind her. Retrieving her passport from her fake fur handbag, her thoughts were rudely interrupted by the sound of loud laughter nearby. Glancing around, Melita's heart sank, immediately wishing the ground would open up and swallow her.

Some fifty metres away, looking exactly like the young Marilyn Monroe, stood her half-sister. At least seven Aer Lingus airport staff, both male and female, were surrounding Crystal as she chatting and laughed with them. Upon noticing Melita, she waved her over, confident of how her own resemblance to the icon was far greater than her half-sister's. By the expressions on the faces of the airport staff, an embarrassed Melita could tell they did not think her very much like the icon at all, not in comparison to the beautiful Crystal.

Faking a smile and walking over to the group, Melita mustered up all her courage, smiling at everyone and greeting them brightly. Politely responding to her and nodding in response, they quickly turned their attention back to the amazing reincarnation of the world's most famous legend - Crystal.

"Good morning, Marilyn," came the greetings from the cabin crew as they smiled and stared in wonder at Crystal, completely ignoring the fact that Melita was even there.

"Good morning, everybody! I am so happy to be flying with the wonderful Aer Lingus and so excited to be visiting Dublin!" replied a gushing Crystal. "My grandmother was Irish, you know!" she added, fluttering her false eyelashes at them.

"That's where you get your good looks, darling!" quipped one of the cabin crew, causing everybody to laugh, nodding their heads in full agreement.

It was obvious they would be seated next to each other but Melita thanked her lucky stars that the flight would be of short duration.

For the following hour, Crystal continued to be the centre of attention with both cabin crew and passengers. People continuously came up to their seats to chat to her. Occasionally, she spoke briefly to Melita, who in turn remained pleasant. Crystal's glibness, superficial charm and her grandiose sense of self did not escape the perceptive Melita who sat quietly, wondering how it was possible that they were sired by the same father.

Shortly after finishing breakfast, it was already time to fasten seatbelts as the pilot advised that they were now descending into a drizzly Dublin Airport.

The same excitement and enthusiasm followed Crystal and Melita from the plane into the arrivals lounge. Heads turning as eyes scrutinised and compared the two lookalikes, some blatantly pointing to Crystal, silently intimating that she was the best. A strutting Crystal waved and blew Monroe kisses to the crowds who, in turn, applauded her.

Unbeknown to her younger sister, Melita had been in these situations many times before, hardening herself to accepting the fact that she would always be second best. She had worked many times with Kay Carney, the foremost Monroe who was still in great demand around the world. Ironically, Melita and Kay worked well together and although Kay knew that she was the very best, she never once tried to belittle the less fortunate Melita.

Noticing both their names printed on one of the signs held high above the waiting crowd, Melita trotted quickly over to Crystal, who was still throwing kisses to the crowds, alerting the younger woman that their chauffeur was waiting for them. To loud wolf whistles and cheers, the two of them were escorted out of the airport and into the back of a charcoal-grey limousine.

Arriving at the Shelbourne Dublin hotel, close to St. Stephen's Green, the chauffeur explained that this area was one of the best in the whole of Dublin for attractions, shopping and dining.

"Pity!" exclaimed Crystal, flirting outrageously with the handsome black-haired, grey-eyed Irishman. "We're only here until tomorrow morning!" she said, pouting her full lips.

"Yes, I know that. I shall be driving you both back to the airport," came his husky voice in reply, glancing at his glamorous passengers through his driving mirror, winking at a beaming Crystal.

The Shelbourne Dublin was even more impressive than expected. They were given double rooms adjacent to each other which was one of the stipulations written into Top Drawer Agency's contracts, that all female lookalikes and tribute artistes should be accommodated on the same floor.

Idling in the foyer, chatting and flirting with the chauffeur, whose name they learned was Shamus, Crystal seemed in no hurry to leave his company. Melita went straight to her room and unpacked the clothes and lingerie she would require for the advertisement.

Laying her expensive make-up out in the beautifully decorated bathroom, she was elated to see the lights were very bright which would enable her to transport herself into Marilyn more easily. They had been advised that lunch would be served in their rooms at noon after which the chauffeur would collect them at precisely two o'clock for the short drive to the TV studios.

Sometime later, as Melita was relaxing on the comfortable king-sized bed, she heard Crystal entering her own room. To her dismay, she could hear her half-sister whispering and giggling. She was in no doubt that the cause for Crystal's schoolgirl antics was the handsome Shamus.

The drive to the TV studios was no more than twenty minutes and Melita spent most of the time looking out of the window as Crystal and Shamus laughed and chatted to each other. Every now and then, peering at her through the driver's mirror, Shamus would bring Melita into the conversation and she pleasantly reciprocated. She had a feeling her quietness made him feel uncomfortable and was relieved when the limousine pulled up outside the studios.

For Melita, the day was full of uncertainty. If it had not been for one of the junior directors taking a liking to her, she was quite sure the rest of the crew would not have noticed her at all. Unnecessary as it was, Crystal tried every trick in the book to upstage Melita, including accidentally standing a little in front of her when they were asked to be photographed together at the end of the programme. Melita tried not to notice when two of the cameramen whispered together about the two Marilyns. She did not have to hear what they were saying to each other; it was obvious by the expressions on their faces that they were only interested in Crystal, as they focused their eyes and cameras on the amazing Marilyn Monroe impersonator.

Darragh Claffey, the chat show host, was a pleasant-looking, friendly, young man who made no exceptions between the two lookalikes sitting in front of him. He was a young man of astute insight and immediately picked up on Crystal's narcissistic personality, which for some reason angered him. Unlike most of the world, Darragh took an instant dislike to Crystal and tried to bring Melita more into the conversation, asking her questions about her hobbies and lifestyle. To Darragh's dismay, Crystal actually answered for Melita on several occasions and he even found himself being upstaged by her!

As the day and filming came to an end, Melita was much more convinced after witnessing her half-sister's antics, that she definitely had sociopath traits. Melita was certain that Crystal was unable to empathise with the pain of her victim, having only contempt for others' feelings of distress and readily taking advantage of them. She noticed also that Crystal possessed an impulsive nature, that she could blow hot or cold, alternating with small expressions of sweetness and approval, producing an addictive cycle for abuser and abused, as well as creating hopelessness in the victim.

Arriving at the TV studios to escort the two Monroe lookalikes to dinner at one of Dublin's finest restaurants, Michael Fitzgerald, the rep for the Dublin client, made himself known to them. To Crystal's disappointment Shamus was now off-duty. Their host was a short, slim young man with doleful brown eyes, cropped blonde hair and large ears that looked like he was ready for take-off!

Laughing to herself, Melita watched as Crystal tried to dominate the whole conversation during dinner but could not quite match Michael Fitzgerald. God had indeed bestowed the gift of the gab upon him and he chatted non-stop for the remainder of the evening. Trying her utmost to keep from laughing out loud, Melita could see how infuriated Crystal was becoming with Michael's insistent chatter.

"Now, ladies, I do hope we have wined and dined you in the manner to which you must have become accustomed," he remarked, as he signalled for the waiter to bring the bill.

"You've been very quiet throughout dinner, Crystal!" he remarked, a glint in his mocking eyes.

"Really?" she responded sarcastically, then glancing at Melita, raised her eyes to the ceiling.

"Thank you very much, Michael. It was most entertaining and the food was delicious," responded Melita quickly, feeling uncomfortable by Crystal's rudeness.

"You are very welcome, Melita. We have loved having you beautiful ladies here in Dublin and hope to bring you back again some time!" replied Michael, smiling across the table at her as he accepted the bill from the waiter. Turning his attention to Crystal, he asked whimsically, "Would you like that, Crystal?"

Stiffening noticeably in her dining chair, Crystal focused her eyes on the rep and murmured sarcastically in the famous breathy Monroe voice, "Can't wait!"

Both tired now and ready for their beauty sleep, the half-sisters walked towards their individual hotel rooms. Melita tried to explain to Crystal that she should be more respectful towards the clients' representatives and that being sarcastic and offish to one of them could jeopardise the good name of Top Drawer Agency.

"Whatever!" came Crystal's response unconcernedly as she swiped the card allowing her entrance into her room. "Good night!" she called as the door closed behind her.

Before allowing herself the luxury of sleep, Melita had decided that she would speak to Belinda about Crystal's attitude towards Michael Fitzgerald. Making up her mind that it was better to resolve this problem sooner rather than later, she closed her eyes and drifted away in slumber.

Chapter 27
A Catch-22 State of Affairs

It was a Sunday in February and bitterly cold in New York City. Frank checked the time on his nineteenth-century gilded bronze Ormolu mantel clock, and decided he would call Sergie in London for a quick catch-up. Although they often spoke, today he felt somehow detached and needed to talk to his good friend, hoping this would lift his low mood.

It was almost one o'clock in the afternoon and knowing it was close to six in the evening in London, he hoped Sergie would be home.

Allowing the telephone to ring for some time, he was about to replace the receiver when the line in London was picked up.

"Yeah?" asked a groggy-sounding voice.

"Is that you, Sergie?"

"Yeah, it is. Oh! Hi, Frank, just got up, paesano. Had a late night!" he yawned down the mouthpiece.

"Sorry, my friend, wouldn't have called had I known you'd had a late one!" joked Frank, wondering whether Sergie was alone or not.

"Just wanted to catch-up, that is all. Listen, Sergie, I will call another time," he added quickly, aware that his melancholy was returning.

"No way, Frank! Now is good! I am fully awake, paesano!" replied Sergie, yawning again.

"You alone?" asked a sullen Frank.

"Yeah. The little lady took off in a black taxi more than an hour ago," laughed Sergie.

Now also laughing, Frank asked after Joey and was pleased with what Sergie had told him, that both he and Joey were doing great.

"When you back over here, Frank?" asked Sergie, stifling yet another yawn.

"Not sure yet. Waiting to hear," then changing the subject, Frank continued. "As you are aware, Sergie, my business with Aldo in Vegas was brought to a satisfactory conclusion for The Society before the Christmas holidays."

"Yeah. Great detective work, paesano," praised Sergie. "You are without a doubt Capitano Numero Uno," he added, rubbing his blurry eyes.

"Obviously, I cannot divulge the names of the perpetrators but these are two young guys, still wet behind the ears. I cannot seem to shift this feeling of devastation," disclosed Frank. "I know I can trust you, Sergie. Just wanted to get it off my chest."

"Frank! Frank! I know how you feel," cajoled Sergie. "You had a job to do with Aldo and you did it, paesano. These guys, young or old, knew the consequences from the moment they were initiated into the Society. Draw a line under it, otherwise it will drive you crazy," advised Sergie, fully awake now.

"Thanks, Sergie. Of course, I know you are right. I must be getting soft in my old age!" quipped Frank, aware that his mood had now lightened somewhat.

"Listen, Frank. Any time you want to chat, call me! No matter what time!" replied Sergie, inhaling deeply on his second cigarette.

Later that evening, Frank was pleased he had not divulged to Sergie, even in confidence, that there was in fact a third culprit who was involved with the two young perpetrators. The third person's identity was still unknown but once he was unearthed, he too would join the two young men on the Society's hit list.

Frank knew the culprits would have no idea that they had been discovered and as usual would go about their daily duties for their bosses. They would continue to skim off thousands of dollars of the Society's money before transferring it into a New York bank account. Frank and Aldo were under no illusion that the culprits – Vinny Messina and Lukey Amato – were not working alone. Somebody was responsible for moving the money from the bank account in New York to places unknown, possibly anywhere in the world.

The hierarchy of the Society had spoken to Frank regarding his opinion of whether the Pellini brothers, Dino and Marco, should be given the contract to deal with the culprits in Las Vegas. Frank did not agree with the Pellini tactics used regarding interrogations, but try as he may to dissuade the hierarchy not to use them, his concerns fell on deaf ears. This added to his present anxiety and left him now feeling he was losing his Midas touch.

Frank had known Dino and Marco Pellini for many years, watching them grow into elegant, ambitious young men albeit with a fetish for cruelty, especially Marco. Frank recalled how gentle they both were with animals and yet they could cause so much pain and suffering to their own species.

The brothers relied on each other for friendship and kept themselves to themselves socially. Frank had known their father, Carlo Pellini, now deceased. He had been first cousin to Mikey Paponi, the notorious gangster from the early sixties. Everyone was aware that Marco Pellini was most like his father's infamous cousin in that he had a tendency to get off on the cruelty he dealt out to the unfortunates whose names appeared on the Society's hit list.

The Pellini boys were born some thirty plus years ago in Elizabeth, New Jersey to Domenica and Carlo Pellini. There were no other siblings. Their childhood and upbringing were privileged and both fared well in high school, although neither went to college or university, preferring to enter their father's olive oil business, both working their way quickly through the ranks to directorship status.

Following in their father's footsteps some ten years earlier, Dino and Marco became made men for the Society. Like many of the New Jersey Mafioso, they had carried out most of their work in New York.

Now Las Vegas beckoned, and the brothers were honoured to be awarded the coveted contract which would in turn enlarge their bank accounts tremendously. Within the following few weeks, they would arrive in Sin City and carry out, in fine detail, the task of interrogating the two perpetrators until the name of the third loser involved was known to them.

Dino and Marco Pellini, both tall, handsome and self-opinionated, were not only harsh, but cruel in their dealings with those who had the effrontery to skim from their bosses' businesses. Dino, the eldest by one year, was fanciful and loved the ladies who appeared to prefer his younger brother with the darker side to his character. Dino thrived on keeping three lovers on the go at one time, cunningly dividing his time between them all without causing any suspicion of where he was when not with them.

Marco, on the other hand, appeared to prefer to sustain one relationship at a time. If and when he had enough of his current lover, Marco would buy the lady concerned a very generous gift and send her on her way, thus giving him his invaluable freedom to move on to another lover without the ugliness of being caught out as a cheater. Marco was the more complex character of the two brothers and the more sadistic in his treatment of any fellow human who was unlucky enough to be interrogated by him and his brother.

Lost in thoughts, sitting alone in his plush New York penthouse apartment, a glass of red wine languishing in his hand, Frank allowed the unexpected hot tears to flow from his sad eyes down his anguished face. Dusk had now settled over the bitterly cold city. Slowly rising from his navy leather armchair, Frank picked up the phone and called another London number, emotionally waiting for Belinda to answer.

Chapter 28
Mr President – Tough Guy

It was a chilly Monday morning as Belinda opened Top Drawer Agency ready for another busy week. She could not compress her melancholy mood, nor her concern for Frank. When speaking to him yesterday, he assured her he was fine; she felt he was trying to appease her. He had mentioned that he would hopefully be in London soon, but as yet, could not give a definite date. They chatted for over an hour, expressing their love for each other.

When Frank again mentioned her moving permanently to New York, Belinda found herself evading the subject. Promising him that she would give it more serious thought, she felt both elated and pressured when he admitted he now knew that without her, he could never be truly happy. Belinda loved New York but she was a born and bred Londoner. As much as she loved Frank Lanzo, missing him every second of every day, Belinda could not comprehend leaving her native city, her wonderful job, and her close family and friends to live in New York, even if it was to be with the love of her life.

Maybe he had committed himself to her too late? A year ago, she would have left everything and everyone behind in order to be by Frank's side and although she loved him as much or more now, something was holding her back. It was as if she had resigned herself after all this time to their long-distance relationship. Toying with the idea of asking Frank to move to London instead, Belinda turned on her computer.

"Morning, Belinda, darling," came the familiar voice of Freddie as he sauntered into the office, little Queenie in his arms.

"You sound happier, Freddie," she remarked, glancing up and smiling at him.

"Not really, but I am trying, sweet pea," he answered, lowering the little dog onto the carpeted floor. "I must tell you though, I met a really cute guy last night at Big Gerty and Fanny's dinner party," he added, grinning at her then walking into the kitchenette.

"Oh! That is good news, Freddie!" exclaimed Belinda.

"Have only just met him but I am willing to give it a go!" he announced, walking back into the office, a hot cup of coffee in each hand. Handing one to a mesmerised Belinda, he continued, "He is very handsome, very cute and very young. Yes! I really took to him!"

"Not too young, I hope!" commented a concerned Belinda. "He is of legal age, I suppose?"

"Yes, of course he is!" replied Freddie, tutting as he patted little Queenie who had made himself comfortable in his doggy bed.

"Big Gerty told me he had just turned twenty-one," he said, walking over to his desk and picking up the post.

"What is his name then?"

"Boss-eyed Syd!" declared a very serious Freddie, to which Belinda almost choked on her hot coffee.

After composing herself as quickly as possible and genuinely looking bewildered, she exclaimed, "Boss-eyed? I thought you said he was handsome!"

Dropping the post on the desk, an indignant Freddie responded to her last remark.

"Yes! He is handsome, sweet pea! Syd is not really boss-eyed, more cross-eyed! He has a visible cast in his left eye, that is all, darling!" sniffed a very offended-looking Camp Freddie."Besides, I think he is handsome and so he is!" Freddie added defiantly. "After a while, the cast is hardly noticeable!"

"Better get on, Freddie!" Belinda remarked after a while. "Remember, Dawn is taking the day off and we have a busy week ahead."

From then on, the day passed smoothly. Belinda noticed Freddie had the spring back in his step as he hummed quietly to himself while ploughing through the weekend post and emails.

"The Royals are in demand again, sweet pea!" he announced, glancing up from the computer and raising his blue eyes to Belinda for a response.

"An enquiry here for the Duke and Duchess of Sussex for a corporate event in Windsor and one for the Prince of Wales and Duke of Cambridge to attend a dinner party regarding environmentalism in Luxembourg," said Freddie wistfully, wishing he had looked like one of the Royal Family instead of Liberace.

"Excellent! Would you please call Spencer Carlisle and Jason Armstrong to make sure they are available for Luxembourg? I'll call Max and Ada myself."

By the end of the day, Belinda was delighted to have booked the Prince of Wales and Duke of Cambridge for the Luxembourg job. The two were to fly out the following Friday morning in order to attend a dinner party of a prominent member of the government that same evening. As the Prince of Wales, a well-known environmentalist, Spencer Carlisle was expected to give a relevant speech on this topic as if he really were the future king.

Belinda was always confident when booking Spencer; he had been portraying the Prince of Wales for several years now and was an accomplished speaker on environment issues. Jason Armstrong as the Duke of Cambridge was Top Drawer Agency's most sought-after Prince William, having the most uncanny resemblance to the second in line to the throne.

Just before the end of the working day, soon after Belinda had left for the evening, leaving Freddie to lock up, a knock was heard. Interrupting Queenie's cosy snooze, the little dog started to bark as loudly as he could.

Rushing out of the kitchenette where he liked to tidy up, Camp Freddie hurried towards the door and peered through the peephole. Giggling to himself upon recognising the late visitor, Freddie swung open the heavy oak door and curtsied as Bernard Shaftoe, the agency's foremost President Trump lookalike, strolled into the agency as if he owned the place.

"Hi, Freddie, I was just passing so decided to pop in to sign the contract for my Charing Cross job and to say hello to you all, " he exclaimed, looking around the office for Dawn and Belinda.

"What, all alone?" he asked, checking the time on his wristwatch.

"Afraid so, Mr President. It is almost six o'clock, you know," reminded Freddie, walking over to Belinda's desk and opening the top drawer in order to retrieve the aforementioned contract for Bernard to sign.

"Yes, I am a little late, I guess, but glad that I caught you!" grinned Bernard, in his best fake New York accent.

"No problem, Mr President!" responded Freddie sarcastically, laying the contract on Dawn's desk and pointing to three places marked with an 'X' ready for Bernard's signature.

"Good work, Freddie!" exclaimed Bernard, now reverting back to his native North of England accent.

"Any time, Mr President, any time at all!" replied Camp Freddie, clipping the red leather lead onto Queenie's diamanté collar.

Walking over to Freddie, Bernard pursed his lips and with the famous finger and thumb circle gesture customary of the real President Trump, winked at Freddie. Then, turning on his heel, he waved and disappeared out of the door, causing little Queenie to bark ferociously.

Freddie liked Bernard. Even though his phoney New York accent was extremely irritating, he found the American president lookalike very amusing. Freddie had an uncanny feeling that Bernard was neither straight nor gay, and probably batted for both sides.

Bernard Shaftoe was a born and bred Geordie from Newcastle-upon-Tyne. A tough guy, calling a spade a spade, not only did Bernard have an uncanny resemblance to President Trump but he was also tall and well-built. He wore a blonde toupee covering his balding pate to complete his portrayal of the fiery American president.

The one thing where Bernard differed from President Trump was that he possessed large hands, but this was a minor concern for Top Drawer Agency since Bernard was always a great success. The clients were always overwhelmed with this particular President Trump lookalike. Dawn found she had a soft spot for Bernard herself which she decided was probably because she somehow fancied the real forty-fifth American president...

Being a divorcee, Bernard had moved down to London several years earlier but visited his place of birth as often as he could. He had only been married for a short while and there were no children from this brief union. Since becoming a highly successful lookalike, he found many of his weekends taken up with presidential lookalike work and the duration between his trips to his beloved Newcastle-upon-Tyne was becoming ever greater.

For Bernard, life could not be sweeter. Awarded a high fee for every job he undertook, the more in demand his character became, the more his bank account grew. President Trump, the Royals, along with Boris Johnson, were in very high demand. This he accepted readily with the knowledge that if and when President Trump were ever toppled from office, then his career as a lookalike would also topple. He knew that if and when this exciting new career of his came to an end, he could always become a car salesman again. Pushing these negative thoughts from his mind, Bernard's new adage was to "make hay while the sun shines".

Freddie was not entirely wrong about Bernard. Although he had been briefly married to a young woman some years earlier, he did in fact dally in the homosexual world. Many of Bernard's friends were gay and he found he could relax and talk more openly with them, so much easier than any heterosexual friend he had. Bernard was indeed batting for both sides – he was bisexual.

Bernard was looking forward to being guest of honour at Pathway To Paradise nightclub in Charing Cross. This was one of London's most famous gay cabaret show bars with a different crowd-pulling theme every night and he was to be guest of honour at the owner's birthday party the following Thursday evening.

Because of Bernard's strong resemblance to the real president, Dawn decided to send a bodyguard along with him but Bernard refused her offer, explaining he preferred to work alone and that she should not concern herself about him. After all, he was a Geordie and could take care of himself! If and when Bernard had found some of the public were anti-Trump, he would imitate the president's voice and mannerisms for them, never failing to turn their frowns into laughter.

Bernard Shaftoe was indeed a class act.

Chapter 29
Royal Titles Lost

"Birth is the Start of Life, Beauty is the Art of Life
Love is the Part of Life, But Friendship is the Heart of Life."
Prasanti Mandal

It was the middle of February and as expected in London, temperatures struggled to get above freezing. It was cold. Freddie turned on the central heating as soon as he and little Queenie entered the agency. Keeping his thick Boden wool pea coat on until the office warmed up, he scurried about filling the kettle for tea and coffee, ready for the ladies when they arrived from their daunting early morning journeys into work.

Dawn was the first to arrive, smiling as she removed her gloves and blew on her cold fingertips.

"My God! It must be minus today. It is too cold to snow!" she exclaimed, gratefully accepting the cup of hot coffee from Freddie.

She was extremely relieved and thankful that even with the breaking news revealing Prince Harry and Meghan Markle would be leaving the UK for the cold but private shores of Vancouver and that they had been stripped of the privilege of using the Sussex titles, they continued to be in great demand worldwide simply as Harry and Meghan.

She and Freddie were enjoying a cup of coffee as Belinda came rushing through the door, her faux fur coat buttoned up to her chin. After the usual morning formalities, the three settled down to deal with the many incoming emails and telephone calls. Dawn was in high spirits. Business was good, especially for the time of year.

Freddie went to the post office taking little Queenie with him for a brisk walk. The little dog wagged his furry tail as Freddie pulled on his red wool coat before attaching his lead to his diamanté collar. Queenie seemed much calmer these days which the ladies knew was due to the fact that Camp Freddie appeared to be somewhat happier since meeting boss-eyed Syd. For the moment, the new lovers appeared to be besotted with each other, although Belinda was certain it would take Freddie a long, long time to completely get over Claudio, if ever.

Glancing up over her Cartier glasses, Dawn asked Belinda to call Max Rushton and Ada Demir, referred to now as simply Harry and Meghan, informing them that their latest contracts would be imminently emailed to them for signature.

The two were booked as guests of honour for a 'rounding off' birthday party of a local resident in Windsor, at the charming Boatman pub, nestled below Windsor Castle beside the River Thames. Both Max and Ada were available and thrilled to accept this very exciting job. Obviously, both felt alive to be working together again.

They had now been lovers for some months, desperately trying to find ways of meeting up without causing suspicion. Lying not only to Mehmet, but to her whole family, Ada could not suppress the feelings of guilt she suffered but she was deeply in love with Max and knew she had to be with him, no matter what the consequences.

Recently, there had been a couple of instances where Ada was booked to work with the Duchess of Cambridge lookalike instead of the now ex-Duke of Sussex. This made her terribly forlorn. A concerned Max continuously assured her that he would find a way for them to be together. Ada had tried to explain to him time and again that both her and Mehmet's family honour would come into question and that it may be impossible for her to ever break away.

Ada had tried speaking to her mother about the fact that she did not feel ready to get married to Mehmet just yet and she was definitely not ready to start a family with him. Ada's mother remembered her own feelings of foreboding when she was betrothed as a young woman to Ada's father, but she assured her daughter that these feelings would pass with time and that Ada should remember her own forthcoming marriage to Mehmet had been traditionally arranged with Ada's consent. As she tried to explain to her mother that she had come to change her mind about the marriage, the older woman held her index finger to her daughter's lips and insisted that Ada must try to accept that this was the way of life for Muslim women and everything that was prearranged must come to fruition. There could be no question about that. Ada and Mehmet would soon marry and raise a large, healthy family.

When Ada mentioned to Mehmet that she was booked on another job with the ex-Duke of Sussex as guests of honour at a high-class birthday party, Mehmet made a quick decision. He would drive Ada to Windsor, wait until her job had finished and then drive her home again. There would be no need for her to stay overnight. Remembering with consternation every word that Archie Barnes had insinuated about seeing Ada on the platform in Brighton with a male companion, Mehmet's jealousy overwhelmed him to think that his beautiful fiancée may have lied to him about who she had worked with in the popular coastal resort.

'There is no smoke without fire' was Mehmet's philosophy of life and he had promised himself to keep his eyes wide open.

Both Ada and Max were devastated to learn that Mehmet was to accompany her to Windsor and back. Presuming she would be staying overnight with him, Max had pre-booked a double room in a four-star bed and breakfast close to The Boatman. With sadness, Max now visualised himself alone, without his lover.

"I am so sorry, Max," murmured a tearful Ada over the telephone. "For some reason, Mehmet has insisted on accompanying me on this job and I can do nothing to dissuade him," she added, catching her breath.

"Yes, darling, I know. Hopefully, we will be able to meet at my place one evening instead or perhaps during the day," encouraged Max, trying to sound cheerful.

"It would be better if I came over during the day," suggested an unhappy Ada. "I'll ask my friend Ekrem to cover for me, but I cannot promise," she added, despondently.

"I understand, darling. Do not worry. We will find a way to be together, I promise you!" came Max's optimistic reply, which belied his pessimistic feelings.

The drive down from London was alarmingly clear of traffic although Mehmet drove slower than usual. It had been another cold winter's day and he told Ada that many people would not venture out at this dark depressing time of year once the weak wintry sun had slid down from the sky, giving way to the black starless evening skies. In addition, the roads were becoming icy again which could prove unsafe for driving.

Mehmet and Ada arrived at The Boatman one hour earlier than scheduled, giving Ada time to change her clothes and retouch her make-up. Mehmet parked his white Alfa Romeo Giulia in the station car park adjacent to The Boatman and walked round to open the passenger door for his fiancée.

Climbing out, Ada walked around to the roomy boot to collect her small wheeled cabin case containing her outfit, shoes and make-up for the evening's lookalike job. With her heart racing at the prospect of seeing Max again, she smiled as Mehmet took the case, then protectively placing one arm around her shoulders, walked alongside her into the famous Boatman. As the young couple walked into the foyer every head turned with excitement, staring at Ada Demir.

"Darling, they think you are the real Meghan!" whispered an amused Mehmet, as they reached the reception desk.

"Hello, you must be Ada. I am Clara, the clients' rep. I hope you had a good journey?" she enquired, smiling, her accent cultured and very English. "I must say, Ada, you are extremely authentic. I thought you were the real Duchess, sorry, Meghan!"

Eyes shining, Ada answered very demurely, "Yes, thank you. We had a very smooth journey. The roads were unusually quiet this evening."

Turning to introduce Mehmet as her fiancé and driver, Ada tried unsuccessfully to quieten her racing heart when Clara informed them that the "Duke, sorry, Harry!" had arrived ahead of them.

There he stood in the centre of the large Green Room, chatting to an elderly gentleman, completely oblivious to the attractive waitresses scurrying around him as they rushed to make sure their purple and gold costumes were perfect and their stockings straight. In and out of the Green Room they trotted, eyes shining, with smiling red lips revealing white veneered teeth as they carried sparkling wine glasses into the adjacent room, ready for the birthday party.

Ada's heart skipped a beat as her searching eyes beheld him. How much like the real Prince Harry he looked in his dark navy suit and white linen shirt, she mused, trying unsuccessfully to quieten her beating heart.

Suddenly Max glanced towards the open Green Room door and seeing Ada and Mehmet, waved over to them as casually as any acquaintance would. Making his excuses to the elderly gentleman, the pounding inside his chest increased as he walked over to the couple and bending down briefly, brushed a quick kiss on Ada's cheek, before turning to Mehmet smiling as he held out his hand in greeting.

Max was not looking forward to meeting his lover's fiancé but he knew he had no choice but to appear nonchalant. He had tried to instil into Ada that they had to be very careful not to give any reason for Mehmet to become suspicious of them.

Accepting Max's hand in greeting, Mehmet smiled at the Harry lookalike but his black eyes showed only coldness.

"How was your journey?" enquired Max looking directly at Mehmet.

"Actually, it was very good. Found the traffic unusually quiet this afternoon," replied Mehmet, his cultured English accent belying his dark Mediterranean looks. "And you?" he asked, making polite conversation, although not at all interested.

"Clear for the most part but I have decided to stay over tonight. The roads could ice up somewhat, I think," replied

Max, turning and smiling at Ada, whose heart sank after hearing he would be staying in Windsor.

An unhappy Ada had noticed many of the attractive waitresses giggling and chatting about Max as they scurried about their duties. Clara, after speaking with some young waiters on the other side of the Green Room, walked over to the lookalikes and asked them to be ready in thirty minutes to meet and greet the first of the party guests.

Turning to Mehmet, Clara explained that he was welcome to stay in the Green Room until the lookalikes' contracted hours were finished. Thanking the representative but refusing her offer, Mehmet smiled at Clara charmingly, and advised that he would be leaving to find a restaurant for dinner then return to the Green Room to wait until Ada was ready for the drive home.

The dispirited lovers found some time in which to talk, agreeing that Ada should ask her dearest and most trusted friend, Ekrem, to give her an alibi so that Ada could visit Max very soon at his flat without causing any concern or suspicion. It was decided that Ada and Ekrem would ascertain that they were meeting for a girlie chat, coffee and shopping spree, something they occasionally did. This was the safest option to the lovers' predicament.

"I will ask her tomorrow and then call you with a convenient day that will suit all three of us," whispered Ada to Max as the many guests vied to have their photographs taken with the lookalikes, some of them becoming boisterous with excitement and far too many glasses of wine.

Clara was extremely satisfied with Top Drawer Agency's Harry and Meghan, complimenting herself on her excellent choice of lookalikes. She would definitely use Max and Ada again in the future, Harry and Meghan's popularity permitting, of course!

Like many of the pretty waitresses, Clara was quite smitten with Max Rushton and had no qualms about letting the unsuspecting ex-Duke of Sussex know that she was very interested in getting to know him better. Although Max was oblivious to the situation unfolding in front of him, Ada was not and she became quite dismayed as she watched the tall, leggy blonde flirt unashamedly with him. The fact that she could do nothing about it made her all the more unhappy. Instantly, she promised herself she would do everything in her power to break off her engagement to Mehmet. Her heart belonged to another man and she would fight with her dying breath to be with Max, the man she now knew to be her soulmate.

Arriving back at the Green Room almost an hour before the lookalikes' contracted hours had been completed, Mehmet sat patiently, mobile in hand as he concentrated on the tiny screen coming to life before him.

Suddenly, they appeared together at the entrance of the Green Room, smiling and waving back at the party guests in the banqueting hall. Mehmet studied them closely. To his suspicious mind, they both looked starry-eyed. Would that be because of the exciting evening they had shared as special guests at the party, or could it be because they enjoyed each other's company too much? Mehmet was not sure but he knew deep down, he was not happy with Ada working with this particular Prince Harry impersonator. His intuition, his sixth sense, had never failed him in the past and seeing them together now, holding hands with eyes shining, he was deeply troubled.

He stood up from the comfortable chair as they entered the room. Upon seeing her fiancé, Ada rushed over to greet him, her heart aching at the thought of having to leave Max behind with so many pretty women. Barely smiling at his adored betrothed, Mehmet asked her if she had enjoyed the assignment to which Ada nodded enthusiastically.

"You off now?" came Max's voice as he tried desperately to sound casual.

"Yes, as soon as Ada has changed," replied Mehmet not smiling at the other man. "I must have some private time alone with my beautiful fiancée," he added, directing his gaze at Max.

Max was eaten up with jealousy. He had come to loath Mehmet almost as much as the other man loathed him. Even with Ada out of the situation, these two young men would never have been bosom friends. Their instant dislike for each other was mutual, making it all the more unpleasant for Ada.

"What excuse will you give to Mehmet?" asked a worried-sounding Ekrem.

"I will think of something. Please try not to worry," replied Ada, trying with difficulty to pacify her best friend.

"Please listen, Ada!" stressed a troubled Ekrem. "I hope you know what you are doing! If this ever gets out, Max, you and me will have to emigrate!" she added, causing Ada to burst out laughing.

"Oh, please!" exclaimed a now sober Ada. "I hate to ask of you such a risky favour, especially as it could have adverse consequences but I must push this unsavoury thought out of my mind or I shall never have the courage to find the happiness I desperately need. I really could not live without Max now."

Dropping her childish voice to a whisper, Ekrem, her face full of concern, replied, "I am deeply troubled, my friend, but because you are like a sister to me, I shall help you."

Wrapping her arms around her pretty friend and moved by emotion, Ava could only hug Ekrem, whispering in response, "Thank you from the bottom of my heart, my dearest sister."

Chapter 30
Mickey Finns All Around

It was early Thursday evening. For the past few days, the cold February rain had been relentless. Bernard Shaftoe, pulling his navy coat collar around his neck, jumped jovially out of the black taxi after paying the chatty cab driver. He was happy to be away from the young man who continually talked throughout the whole journey. Bernard was always at his most positive when he was portraying the controversial American president. He felt very important as he stood on the wet pavement, the lights outside the Pathway To Paradise nightclub glistening in the puddles causing them to shimmer and wobble. Checking his reflection in the club's shiny windows, Bernard walked towards the entrance and took a deep breath. Several passers-by turned in unison as they thought they had witnessed President Trump disappear through the door of the traditional gay boozer situated halfway between Soho and Paradise!

Never having visited this famous London club before, Bernard was pleasantly surprised how warm it was as the door closed behind him. As it was still quite early in the evening, a little more than a dozen people sitting at the long bar glanced his way and kept their curious eyes on him. He stood upright in the doorway basking in their attention, a hint of a smile playing on his pursed lips. He was becoming familiar with this feeling of power that came over him as he stood questioningly glancing around the room.

"Mr President!" came an excited musical voice, as a very tall, heavily made-up woman came rushing towards him, grinning from ear to ear, her white veneered teeth dazzling in the bar's lights. Bernard knew instantly that this was a drag queen of the highest calibre. Apart from her extreme height, she had a voluptuous figure and possessed large breasts. The wig she wore could also be described as voluptuous; it was deep red and reminded Bernard of a lion's mane.

"Hello, Mr President. So wonderful that you could grace us mere mortals with your presence on this cold and wet evening," she gushed, as she touched her hand to Bernard's, then pirouetted and made a bow. Before the lookalike could answer her, she fluttered her long fake eyelashes at Bernard then hastily added, "I am Rose Garden, your special host for this evening. The boss lady will be along later, so in the meantime, Mr President, your every wish is my command!"

To Bernard's amusement, the drag queen then winked seductively at him.

"I am honoured, dear lady, to have you at my beck and call!" joked Bernard, wondering whether or not Rose Garden did in fact now have a rose garden or not! He chuckled to himself as this thought flashed through his devious mind.

Slipping her arm possessively through Bernard's, Rose exclaimed excitedly, "Wonderful, Mr President! Come with me and I will introduce you to some of the other lovely ladies who will be performing downstairs this evening in our centre stage bar. You are in for a real treat, sir!"

Against Top Drawer Agency's policy of no alcohol while working, Bernard nevertheless decided to have one small glass of Champagne, just to unwind and relax, he tried to convince himself as he accepted a glass from one of the lovely drag queens standing nearby, a silver tray laden with the famous French bubbly held carefully in her velvet gloved hands. Bernard winked at the young drag queen who fluttered her enormous fake eyelashes at him as she smiled coquettishly.

"Yes, sir!" she remarked, in a half whisper. "I think I am going to enjoy myself this evening!" and with that, Rose Garden whisked him downstairs to the famous cabaret bar and into the wonderfully camp world of the highly talented drag queen artistes.

Within the next hour, Pathway to Paradise became quite full and Bernard loved the attention the beautiful drag queens gave him throughout the evening. He had to admit to himself more than once that there were at least three of these queens whom he quite fancied. Bernard could swing both ways and if he had a yearning for someone, whether male or female, then he would invariably satisfy this yearning.

The evening was a great success for the President Trump lookalike. Many inebriated people wanted to have their photographs taken with him. Bernard noticed that several straight couples were amongst the revellers enjoying the entertainment and cabaret put on by the inimitable talents of the drag queens. A rowdy group of effeminate men sitting together on a round table close to Bernard and Rose Garden would occasionally hold up their glasses and jokingly toast the fake American president. Bernard was in his element, nodding his head and giving the spectators the famous thumb and index finger gesture, causing an uproar from the boisterous party revellers.

Of course, the lookalike had to deal with segments of confrontational people as well, one calling him a choice name which would have made a lesser, more sensitive person cringe. Not so Bernard; he brazenly grinned through the insults as the real American president would, turning a deaf ear to the negative remarks, while acknowledging only the positive.

Refusing a second glass of Champagne from Rose Garden, Bernard requested instead a tonic water, advising his bemused companion of Top Drawer Agency's no alcohol policy.

"Well, hello, Mr President!" came an alto-sounding male voice, causing Bernard to gulp on his tonic water as his amused eyes took in yet another apparition of fake female beauty.

Lilly Pond, the boss lady, resplendent in a floor-length red evening gown, stood smiling down at her special guest, her right hand encrusted with diamanté rings extended to the American president impersonator as she waited for him to kiss it. Ever the gentleman, Bernard rose immediately to his remarkably large feet and seductively kissed the boss lady's hand as he looked up into twinkling violet eyes which brought images of Elizabeth Taylor flashing through his mind. Bernard wished Lilly Pond a "very happy birthday".

"Simply marvellous to have you in our midst this evening, Mr President! You have made my birthday even more special!" purred the boss lady. "I trust Rose is keeping you amused and wanting for nothing?" continued Lilly Pond, noticing with intrigue, the strong resemblance between her hired lookalike and the real president of the United States.

Still standing out of courtesy, Bernard assured the boss lady that he simply could not have wished for a more attentive host than Rose Garden. He thanked Lilly Pond for her hospitality and for booking him as her guest of honour for her birthday celebrations.

"I'm so happy, Mr President, that you are enjoying our special little part of Paradise," gushed the boss lady, her dazzling smile outshining her twinkling violet eyes.

"Please ask for anything that takes your fancy during the evening. Rose Garden is here to pander to your every whim!" she added with a throaty giggle. Bending down, she whispered something in Rose's ear, causing the other drag queen to squeal with laughter. Lilly Pond then sauntered across the room, her buttocks swaying from side to side. Upon reaching the exit to the centre stage bar, black curly wig bobbing around her slim shoulders as it caught the multicoloured lights, Lilly Pond turned back and blew Bernard a seductive kiss.

"Now that's one beautiful lady!" remarked Bernard to Rose Garden as he watched the boss lady disappear out of view.

"Yes, she is and she has a beautiful heart too" responded Rose nodding, her eyes glowing in the dimmed lights.

"All you ladies are beautiful, especially you, Honey," remarked Bernard, remembering to keep up his American accent and not to slip back to his natural Geordie tongue.

Rose Garden's response to Bernard was to giggle to herself, fluttering her spider-like false eyelashes at the American president impersonator.

If Dawn had been a fly on the wall that evening in the centre stage bar, she would have instantly ripped up Bernard Shaftoe's contract with Top Drawer Agency. Dawn ran a very tight ship and she expected full cooperation from all her lookalike and tribute artistes to act accordingly. Accepting even one alcoholic drink whilst working was prohibited until the contracted hours had been satisfactorily completed.

Bernard was fully aware of the no alcohol policy and yet this evening he had immediately accepted Champagne. As far as Dawn was concerned, accepting the first drink was fatal, since it would invariably lead to others.

It was now blatantly obvious to the effeminate young men occupying the nearby table that the American president lookalike was becoming very touchy-feely with the drag queens. This in turn convinced them to arrive at the unanimous decision that the Trump impersonator was indeed bisexual. Staring now long and hard at Bernard, it appeared as if their turned-up smiles had suddenly become turned downward and their brows became furrowed. The five young men then hatched up a plan which had them giggling and sniggering as they excitedly discussed it among themselves.

After a short while, another gorgeous drag queen walked over to Bernard and Rose Garden's table. From her silver tray, she picked up a glass of Champagne in her bejewelled left hand and placed it in front of Rose Garden then smiling demurely, placed a dark brown drink in a whisky tumbler on the table in front of the American president lookalike.

Reacting quickly, a smiling Bernard begun to push the tumbler away from himself, explaining that he was only drinking tonic water. Tutting quietly under her breath, the drag queen bent down and whispered to Bernard that the gentlemen on the table close by had very kindly sent the drinks over and it would be in very poor taste to refuse their generosity. Rose Garden assured the lookalike that she completely agreed with the waitress and they should accept the young gentlemen's drinks graciously.

"Well, maybe just this once, but I will be in hot water if my agents get wind of this!" declared Bernard, picking up the tumbler then raising his right arm, thanked the effeminate young men sitting on the table close by. Grinning and leaning over the arm of his chair, one of the group insisted that Bernard drink the concoction down in one go to get the most marvellous affect. Smiling and pouting, President Trump threw back his head and in one gulp, drank down the thick liquid, causing the effeminate young men to clap and stamp their feet under the table.

"Thank you, guys," said Bernard in his very best Trump accent. "I have no idea what the hell that drink was but it was real good!" he hiccuped. As an encore, the young men erupted in laughter, clapping and nudging each other as their mischievous eyes focused on the lookalike as he clumsily sat back into his gold-coloured chair.

Although he didn't drink another alcoholic drink for the remainder of the evening, Bernard was quite sure the young gentlemen's generous mysterious drink had well and truly been a Mickey Finn and laced with something. He tried desperately to hide the fact that he was now blissfully intoxicated. With his arm linked to Rose Garden to steady him, he cautiously swanned around the centre stage bar, having his photograph taken by the other revellers, their mobile cameras flashing in his face as they excitedly jostled to get his attention.

Bernard had been thoroughly entertained and amused by the wonderful female impersonator cabaret artistes. His particular fancy was Kitty Kat, being drawn to her slight build and enormous breasts. The lookalike was desperate to feel them in his large hands. Chuckling to himself as these thoughts filled his fuddled brain, Bernard held out his arms in greeting as Lilly Pond sauntered over to the table where he and Rose Garden had unsteadily returned to. It was now well past the end of the American president impersonator's contracted hours.

"You have been simply amazing, Mr President!" exclaimed Lilly Pond, pecking him flamboyantly on both cheeks. "It is well past the midnight hour and your carriage awaits, sir!" she added, curtseying to him.

Bending down, she whispered in Rose Garden's ear, who immediately stood up muttering, "But of course, Lilly. I shall be delighted to accompany the President to his waiting carriage!"

Lilly Pond was well aware that the lookalike had had one too many but as far as she was concerned, this all added to the fun of the evening for her guests and customers alike. However, she had no idea that Bernard had been given a psychoactive drug, a Mickey Finn but nevertheless, she had already decided not to mention his drunken state to the Top Drawer Agency when they would follow up his appearance with a telephone call to enquire whether the American president lookalike had lived up to expectations and behaved in a professional manner.

"My dear lady," slurred Bernard, his American accent completely forgotten, as he slipped drunkenly back into Geordie. "I have had the very best time! Thank you for your wonderful hospitality and thank you too, Rose Garden," he added, turning and slurring as he tried unsuccessfully to kiss the amused female imposter's hand. "I shall return to see you lovely ladies again and again and again!" His last words were chaperoned by hiccups.

Before Rose Garden could accompany a staggering Bernard to the exit, the effeminate young men at the adjacent table had gathered round and offered to walk the American president to where the Uber was patiently waiting.

"Why, thank you, boys," enthused Lilly Pond. "Be sure President Trump gets safely into his waiting carriage," she giggled, offering her evening gloved hand to Bernard, who swayed and chuckled as he tried to kiss it without success.

"Oh! Do not worry, Miss Lilly! We will take great care of the President!" answered one of the effeminate young men. With that, the five of them surrounded Bernard and ushered him out of Pathway to Paradise nightclub and onto the cold, drizzly and empty London streets.

Walking over to the waiting Uber, Douglas, the ringleader of the group, pulled a £10 note out of his trouser pocket and leaning into the open window of the car, handed the money to the driver after explaining that his services were now no longer required.

As the Uber drove away in the opposite direction, Douglas returned to his fellow revellers who were talking and laughing with a now roaring drunk Bernard.

Hustling the President Trump lookalike towards a desolate Trafalgar Square while still keeping his spirits high, the effeminate young men listened intently as Douglas instructed them to remove their ties. Taking his own tie from the pocket of his black leather coat, Douglas handed it to Harvey, his current partner, and told him to knot the five multicoloured ties together very securely.

Douglas and the other young men had earlier devised their cunning plan for the fake American president although one or two of them did not realise Douglas was determined to go ahead with it.

"I need your belts as well, boys!" instructed a now serious Douglas. "The ties alone will definitely not hold such a bulky body now, will they?" he quipped, walking round the others and holding out his hands for their belts.

"You are really going ahead with this then?" enquired a frowning Raymond, the newest member of the group.

"Oh course we are, darling!" giggled Douglas. "You will learn that when I say I am going to do something, I always do it! Isn't that right, boys?" he queried, turning and bowing to the rest of the group who were still trying to keep the fake American president upright. Unanimously, they all agreed and laughed with excitement as they reached the centre of Trafalgar Square.

What happened next did not faze Bernard Shaftoe. His brain had taken on a 'devil may care' attitude and he roared with laughter as the young men cleverly and swiftly removed his trousers. They had stopped beside a beautiful Victorian lamp post just a few yards from one of the four Landseer Lion statues protecting Nelson's Column.

Removing the lookalike's thick overcoat, Harvey placed it neatly on the damp paving stones, ready for the most famous American derrière to sit on. Leaving Bernard's shirt, underpants and suit jacket on, the young men coaxed Bernard to sit down on his navy coat with them and he happily did so, enjoying the fun he was having. His mind was seeing everything in a very amusing light and he giggled hysterically as his newfound friends pulled his long arms round his back and tied them around the lamp post.

With a black marker, Douglas had written the following on the back of one of Pathway to Paradise's wine lists: 'TAKE ME IMMEDIATELY, IF NOT BEFORE, TO NO. 10 DOWNING STREET!' Handing this to a giggling Bernard, he sniggered as the lookalike tried unsuccessfully to read the message.

"Okay, President Trump, we are off now! Do not do anything we would not do!" announced the ringleader and with those parting words, the five young men, still giggling, scurried quickly away just in time before the excited media and reporters arrived for the exclusive scoop they were promised by Douglas earlier over the telephone.

As the various reporters reached their destination, one or two late-night revellers wandered across Trafalgar

Square, blinking as their unbelieving eyes focused on the apparition tied to the lamp post. They watched in disbelieve as the reporters flashed their cameras at 'President Trump', who by now was fast asleep and snoring loudly. Chunky bare legs sprawled out ungentlemanly for all the world to see, his underpants unsuccessfully covering his modesty.

"I can see why they say he is cocky!" quipped one of the reporters, setting everybody laughing as they stared in fascination at the well-endowed president.

Bernard slept in oblivion to the scene unfolding around him. A sharp-eyed reporter noticed the handwritten message and immediately placed it strategically on the sleeping president's body so that it could be read easily in the picture he was about to take. Like unexpected lightning, the cameras flashed, seriously thinking they had been handed an exclusive scoop.

Deciding at last to alert the police, the reporters were somewhat surprised to see two patrol cars pull up speedily outside the National Gallery just minutes after their call. Six uniformed officers sprung from the shiny black police car and ran swiftly towards the huddled figure tied to the lamp post.

What a night this had turned out to be for the media! They had taken several amazing photographs of President Donald Trump in the most undignified position of his political career and this exclusive scoop had been handed to them free of charge by an unknown informer...

It was some time before the reporters and police realised that the sleeping president was in fact only a lookalike. At first, they were all astonished to witness the opinionated American president in such an appalling state and without his bodyguards. The police were not even aware that the President was in the UK. An urgent call to Scotland Yard checked with MI5 and MI6 and assured them that President Trump was not in the UK at all, but safe and sound in the White House!

Bernard Shaftoe did not awaken from his drunken stupor. The Mickey Finn was indeed dangerously potent. The remainder of the night was spent in St Thomas' Hospital.

He slept soundly; his loud snoring, resounding around his solitary private room into the adjacent ward, had the night shift nurses giggling amongst themselves. They were all fascinated at the uncanny resemblance between the snoring patient and the President of the United States.

Chapter 31
Sweet Grapes for the President

"**A**re you ladies sitting down?" asked Freddie, full of concern. "Take a look at these!" he exclaimed, rushing over to Dawn and Belinda as they chatted together over cups of hot coffee.

Placing the open newspapers on Belinda's desk, he pointed out several photographs. Both agents frowned at each other. Hurriedly putting on their glasses, they looked at the headlines in despair.

"What?!" screeched Dawn, bending down closer to the newspaper and studying the photographs of Bernard Shaftoe, half naked and tied to a lamp post.

"Oh, my God!" exclaimed Belinda, glancing up at Freddie. "Is he alright? Was he drunk?" she asked, stumbling on the word drunk.

"Well if he was sober, sweet pea, he deserves an Oscar!" quipped Freddie, sauntering into the kitchenette and pouring himself a cup of coffee.

"For heaven's sake!" exclaimed Dawn. "It says here that Bernard had been given a Mickey Finn which caused him to be so inebriated." Then trying to make sense of the newspaper's account, she retorted, "Surely, he must have known the Mickey Finn was alcoholic when he began to drink it!"

"Exactly!" agreed Freddie, taking a sip of the hot coffee before placing a saucer of water down for little Queenie.

"Surely he smelt the alcohol, so why did he drink it?" queried Belinda, shaking her head and raising an eyebrow knowingly at both Dawn and Freddie. "And why did he continue to drink it?" she asked, looking from one to the other.

"It is obvious he was very drunk indeed to allow somebody to tie him up and remove his trousers!" fumed Dawn, walking angrily around the warm office, little Queenie following behind her.

As if on cue, Freddie, arms and legs flaying about flamboyantly, began to sing in an inferior Scottish accent:

"Let the wind blow high, Let the wind blow low,
Through the trees in ma kilt I go,
All the lassies say 'hello',
Donald, where's yer troosers?"

Sensing his master's joviality, little Queenie raced over to Freddie and began to jump up and down. Laughing loudly, Belinda reached for the little dog to try to calm him down.

"Freddie!" screamed Dawn. "This is not funny! I assure you both, Bernard Shaftoe will be struck off Top Drawer's books imminently!"

"Oh! Whoops! Sorry, Dawn," apologised Freddie, sauntering to the kitchenette. "But you must admit, the song is so appropriate for the situation," he added sheepishly, glancing at an angry-looking Dawn.

"Yes! Yes! Very appropriate!" she remonstrated, waving her hand disapprovingly. "I am appalled to see my foremost President Trump ridiculed all over the papers! This will do Top Drawer Agency no good, no good at all!" she complained, a nervous twitch playing at the corner of her mouth.

Walking into Dawn's office, Belinda turned on the TV. The others quickly followed her. As Piers Morgan's apparition appeared on screen, everyone caught their breath. The co-presenter of ITV's *Good Morning Britain* was discussing the weird incident that had occurred in Trafalgar Square the previous evening.

Piers Morgan explained to the nation that the sleeping, half naked figure of a man tied to a lamp post was not the President of the United States, but a gentleman called Bernard Shaftoe, a much sought-after lookalike for the American president. To both Dawn and Belinda's horror, Piers' words cut through them like a knife,

"Mr Bernard Shaftoe is the number one President Trump lookalike with Top Drawer Agency, owned by two lady partners, Dawn Jarvis and Belinda Flynn."

Camp Freddie could see how worried and upset both of his friends were, so in an attempt to shine some kind of light on this highly embarrassing situation, he quickly announced, "Ladies! Ladies! Let us look at this in a more positive way, shall we? Although Bernard was drunk on the job, his foolishness has just given this agency some publicity, and let's face it, ladies... bad press is far better than no press!"

Dawn's eyes glazed as she turned to glance at Camp Freddie and murmured, "Maybe so, but I am very disappointed in Bernard ignoring our no alcohol policy and bringing Top Drawer Agency into disrepute."

A shocked Belinda could say nothing but nod her auburn head in agreement with her partner.

"But, ladies!" exclaimed Freddie. "If Top Drawer Agency is being discussed because of Bernard's antics, whether good or bad, then surely that could be beneficial. It will bring the agency to the whole world's attention!"

Jumping up from her chair, Dawn's expression changed from concern to mindfulness,

"Actually, Freddie, you may just be right! Call all the newspapers and television stations and inform them that I, as agent for the lookalike in question, wish to put the record straight regarding our wonderful, albeit unfortunate, President Trump impersonator."

"What have you got in mind?" asked a bewildered Belinda, relieved that Dawn's anger had now subsided and was replaced by her tenacity to make sure Top Drawer Agency was shown in the best possible light.

"I shall make up some sob story about Bernard being in a terrible accident as a young man which left him with no sense of smell or taste whatsoever!" replied Dawn, triumphantly. "That way, Bernard cannot be accused of drinking the Mickey Finn when he was supposed to be on a no alcohol contract," she concluded satisfactorily, a victorious smile lingering on her rose-coloured lips.

"Belinda, darling, would you please call the hospital and enquire about poor Bernard," she urged. "I shall help Freddie with the newspaper and television stations."

Sometime close to eleven o'clock, across town Bernard Shaftoe came groggily out of his inebriated state. During the early hours of the morning, he had been meticulously

monitored by the prudent nurses and doctors, his heart rate and blood pressure taken every hour. Luckily for the lookalike, he had been treated as soon as he had arrived at St Thomas' Hospital the night before. There was a police presence waiting to interview him; the whole incident was being treated as highly suspicious.

Bernard was shocked to learn that he was the talk of the town on that blustery sunny February Friday.

A little later, once he had eaten a hearty breakfast and while the police were interviewing him, one of the nurses informed him that his agents were on their way to the hospital to see him. Poor Bernard tried to explain to the police exactly what happened the previous evening but he really could not remember much after he had drunk the Mickey Finn. He informed the police that the drink had been sent over to him by a group of young men in the night club sitting at a nearby table. Unfortunately, he could not remember their faces nor what they were wearing.

In order to throw some light on this very worrying prank which could have easily ended tragically, the Sergeant sent two of his men to Pathway to Paradise night club.

Although Lilly Pond, Rose Garden and Kitty Kat had been interviewed by the police and all three had been extremely cooperative to the boys in blue, not one of them could remember, or so they said, who had sent the Mickey Finn over to the President Trump lookalike. The boss lady, Lilly Pond, knowing full well who the culprits were, bent the truth by stating that it was impossible for any of her girls to keep a check on exactly who sent which drinks to the many tables during the evening.

"After all," she remonstrated to the police officers, a sly smile playing on her ruby lips, "several hundred partygoers were here last night especially for my birthday celebrations!"

Briefly forgetting the three beautiful night club hostesses were indeed female impersonators, the two young policemen, upon leaving the night club, gentlemanly nodded to the 'ladies', then Frank Cullen, the more self-assured of the two, actually held Lilly Pond's gloved hand gently when she extended it to him.

Seeing the formidable figure of Bernard lying in the pure, white-sheeted hospital bed brought a lump to Belinda's throat. Slowly, she walked towards him.

Glancing down, she was somewhat relieved when he grinned up at her and, his voice, huskier than usual, uttered weakly in his finest American accent, "Well, hello, my beauty! What brings you here?"

For all his joviality, Belinda noticed a vaguely pained expression in Bernard's eyes as she gently replied. "Oh, Bernard, what happened to you? We are all so worried. Are you feeling better now?"

Propping himself up in the bed, Bernard solemnly reverted back to his native Geordie accent and revealed to her everything he could possibly remember up until he had drunk the fated Mickey Finn. Expressing his sadness at causing the agency such embarrassment, Belinda noticed a dark shadow flutter across Bernard's pale blue eyes and quickly replied encouragingly.

"No! No! Please do not worry about the agency, Bernard. All Dawn, Freddie and I want is for our favourite President Trump to recuperate speedily and get back to work!"

Upon hearing these words, Bernard reached over and took Belinda's small hand, gracing her with a very weak smile.

'Oh! He's good' she thought to herself, reminding herself how charming this person could be.

"But seriously, there is just one thing, Bernard. Why on earth did you accept and drink the Mickey Finn when you knew of Top Drawer's no alcohol policy on all contracted jobs?" she asked, her expressive eyes flashing fleetingly with indignation.

A flicker of a blush swept over Bernard's features as he realised he had been caught out not adhering to the agency's policy. In an attempt to redeem his actions, he murmured quietly that he had only had one small glass of Champagne just to be 'sociable' for the boss lady's birthday celebrations, but that he did not realise until he had drunk the Mickey Finn that it was in fact alcoholic, and then, of course, it was too late.

After listening courteously, Belinda explained to Bernard that the agency had decided to keep him on their books as long as he agreed to confirm Dawn's suggested excuses to the media – that due to a terrible accident as a young man, he had tragically lost his sense of taste and smell and therefore had no idea he had drunk a destructive alcoholic drink in the club. Belinda then explained that Dawn had already used this synopsis to the media, all of whom were carrying the breaking news regarding the foremost British lookalike of the American president.

Looking straight into Bernard's eyes, Belinda explained to him, in no uncertain terms, that if he were ever to be caught again drinking while on a contracted job, Top Drawer Agency would have no other option but to strike him off their books permanently. There would be no way back whatsoever.

Nodding his head in agreement, Bernard fought to hold back the tears that threatened to spill down his sad face.

Regaining his composure, he said with deliberation, "I am so sorry, Belinda, please believe me. You have my word that I will never again touch a drop of the hard stuff whilst working on contracted jobs. Please convey to Dawn that I will corroborate her story for the good of Top Drawer Agency and for my personal career."

As she walked sprightly out of the hospital, a gust of wind tugged at Belinda's ankle-length overcoat, giving an extra chill to the sunny but crisp February afternoon. She found her thoughts now lingered on Frank causing, as always, an excited stir deep down in her tummy. Just a day or two earlier, he had telephoned her from New York relaying that he had been called to a meeting in Las Vegas, but that he would only be in Sin City briefly, after which he hoped to visit London.

Reaching the agency, Belinda was told by a very excited and exuberant Dawn that the telephones had not stopped ringing regarding the amazing President Trump lookalike.

"In fact," announced Dawn, a satisfied grin on her pretty face, "I have just finished speaking to the producers of *A Very Good Morning* who have invited Bernard on the ITV breakfast programme as soon as he is well enough to appear!" Her eyes sparkling brighter than the small overhead chandelier.

Smugly preening himself at his desk, fully aware that his prognosis regarding the final outcome of the President Trump saga was unerring in that both the agency and Bernard Shaftoe would now be in greater demand than ever, Camp Freddie, displaying his hands in open gesture, glanced over at Dawn and Belinda.

"Well, ladies, didn't I tell you this would be a blessing in disguise?"

Chapter 32
The Third Deadly Sin

*"Greed makes man blind and foolish,
and makes him an easy prey for death."*
Rumi

Both Vinny Messina and Lukey Amato were a little puzzled after receiving an invitation to attend the Society's Las Vegas headquarters, ensconced on the twenty-fifth floor of Caesars Palace for a meeting on 10th March. Neither young man had any idea why this meeting was called at such short notice and that they would be the star attractions. They had no inkling that their skimming of the Society's profits had been discovered by the Capitano Numero Uno, Frank Lanzo, and his right-hand man, Aldo Lamarina.

The hierarchy of the Society had decided to give the two young men a chance to redeem themselves before they were handed over to the notorious Pellini brothers, Dino and Marco. Not that admitting to their guilt would help them out of trouble, but the Society thought that at least these two low lives would keep some dignity if they had the strength of character to hold up their hands. And strength of character, as far as the hierarchy were concerned, was the confidence to be confronted, the self-assuredness to know what was important, and the logic to do the right thing, even at one's own expense.

March 10th was barely one week away. Vinny and Lukey chatted together speculating on the forthcoming meeting. They wondered whether any of the other employees of the Society knew the answer. Vinny asked Aldo when he saw the older man having coffee one morning in the Venetian Hotel, but Aldo was evasive, replying that he too had been invited and that it was probably just a yearly catch-up meeting for all of the Society's Las Vegas employees. This explanation appeased both young men.

In the blink of an eye, the date arrived, along with the United Airlines plane carrying Frank from New York's JFK Airport. Frank looked concerned as he waited for the Society's limousine at McCarran Airport to drive him direct to Caesars Palace where he had arranged to meet Aldo Lamarina for breakfast.

"Good to see you, paesano," came Aldo's husky voice as he hugged Frank in brotherly affection when they met outside the Cascata restaurant inside Caesars Palace.

Stepping back, Frank whistled and remarked to his friend, "Wow, paesano! You're looking good! How much weight did you lose since I was last here?"

Smiling broadly, Aldo answered self-consciously, "A little, Frank. Just a little."

"A little, he tells me!" retorted Frank, kidding his friend. "You are slimlined! Slimlined, I tell you!" and with that the two Capitanos strode into Cascata for a hearty breakfast and serious discussions regarding the Society's imminent meeting.

Aldo cautioned Frank to remember that once the meeting began, all eyes would be focused on the two of them. After all, it was they who had unearthed the underhand dealings of the culprits who had been skimming thousands of dollars off the Society's businesses in Las Vegas for months. The identity of the perpetrators was known only to Frank, Aldo and the hierarchy of the Society, but before the conclusion of the meeting, everybody in attendance and beyond would know who they were.

Leaning closer to Frank as they took their seats at a square table for two in the plush restaurant, Aldo whispered to his friend, "You'll have to appear impassive about all this, Frank! Do not give the big shots reason to believe we may be involved because you look so despondent. Remember, there is a third culprit and we do not want them to think it is one of us!"

Frank's only answer was a nod of his aching head and a pat on Aldo's back, indicating that he understood and was in full agreement with his right-hand man. Frank's heart was indeed heavy.

"Okay then, paesano!" declared Aldo, picking up the breakfast menu and handing it to his friend.

It seemed as though the whole world had turned up for the Society's conference. Frank and Aldo were surprised to see such a large crowd busily taking their seats. Several hierarchy walked over to Frank and Aldo, wishing to shake their hands. Not wanting to come face to face with Vinny Messina and Lukey Amato, try as he might, Frank could not help gazing around the spacious hall to catch a glimpse of the two young men. He spotted them close to the back row of seats. He thought them anxious-looking, although they were chatting with other employees. Frank's heart sunk but he was conscious he had to muster up all the strength within him to prove to the hierarchy and the world that his position as Capitano Numero Uno was justified and that he was proud to bring to justice anyone who 'sputare nel piatto dove si mangia.' *(spits in the plate they eat from)*

Taking their seats on the top table along with the hierarchy and a couple of invited 'made men' from the East Coast, Frank was surprised not to see the Pellini brothers at the meeting. He was fully aware that they had been awarded the contract from the Society to interrogate from Vinny and Lukey the third person involved in their deceptive skimming ring.

As the meeting began, Aldo moved uncomfortably in his chair as he glanced towards Frank with a knowing look. Frank slightly nodded his head then turned his full attention to the speaker, recognising him as Romelo Catalano, the husband of one of the hierarchy's daughters.

After complimenting both the Capitano Numero Uno and his Uomo Destrorso *(right-hand man)* for exposing the names of the perpetrators, Romelo became very serious as he opened his stocky arms wide. Addressing the awestruck audience, he invited the guilty ones to come forward and to at least save their dignity.

"You know who you are and more importantly, we know who you are," came the high-pitched voice of Romelo, his slender lips pursing as his expressive brown eyes searched the many rows of packed seats.

An unruly uproar broke out as the entire assembly began to look around the large hall, muttering to each other and fidgeting uncomfortably in their comfortable seats.

Frank found he could not look towards the back of the hall but he knew deep in his heart that both Vinny Messina and Lukey Amato would be desperately trying to appear calm while perspiration through fear would make this impossible for them. Frank knew that terror would be blazing in the eyes of the two young men.

A final invitation to the silent culprits from Romelo to come forward and show strength of character, to know what was important to them and the logic to do the right thing, even at their own expense, fell on deaf ears.

"This saddens me!" exclaimed Romelo, looking disappointed and shaking his head.

Suddenly, the gathering fell deathly quiet. There was no movement or sound from the entire assembly.

Stepping down from the podium, Romelo Catalano moved his bulky physique stealthy towards the back of the room, slowly, deliberately. Suddenly, there was a commotion as both Vinny and Lukey pushed their way out of the row of occupied seats seemingly to make for the main door. Crew (soldiers) were situated outside and as they tried desperately to escape the crowded hall, two heavily-built soldiers grabbed them and held them in vice-like grips.

Vinny Messina and Lukey Amato felt as if they were living a nightmare. Sadly for the two young men, this was not a nightmare but real life, and they were indeed living it. Romelo, together with other made men, kept the huge doors closed and the meeting's invitees in their seats as Frank, Aldo and the hierarchy joined the Society's soldiers and the two culprits outside.

For Frank, this was one of the most tragic days of his entire life. The fear in the two young men's eyes would haunt him, he knew, until his dying day. He had tried desperately but without success, to change the Society's decision to award the Pellini brothers the contract to interrogate Vinny and Lukey in order to find out the name of their accomplice. Frank had no time for Marco Pellini and little more for his brother, Dino. As far as Frank was concerned, Marco was a psychopath who enjoyed killing or inflicting violence and suffering on his fellow humans.

A member of the hierarchy was talking to the soldiers, instructing them to take Vinny and Lukey into one of the smaller rooms on the floor. There they should wait until the Pellini brothers arrived to collect the 'trash'.

Frank opened his mouth to say something but Aldo squeezed his arm and instead Frank turned and walked back into the large hall with Aldo close behind. They had done their job. They had brought the bad guys to justice. They were the Capitano Numero Uno and his Uomo Destrorso.

As they entered the large hall, several men gathered around them, then several more, slapping them on their backs and calling out "Congratulazioni!"

Mustering up all his power and strength, Frank, faking a broad smile, accepted his accolades, as did Aldo, but both men could not help feeling compassion towards Lukey and Vinny, who were gullible enough to imagine they could outsmart their bosses and the Mafioso.

Chapter 33
A Bombshell from LA

The howling wind was doing its utmost to disrupt Londoners' sleep but it had not disturbed Belinda. It was the insistent ringing of her mobile phone, laying on the night table close to her large double bed that had woken her.

Her heart leapt.

"Frank! Darling! It is three-fifteen here! Where are you? Are you alright? Are you ill?" she blurted out to her lover.

"Hi, babe, still here in LA!" echoed Frank's voice into the phone. "Don't worry. I am good but needed to speak to you. Sorry to have spoiled your sleep, my darling!" he added, his voice becoming husky with emotion.

"Frank! Sometimes you worry me! As long as you are alright!" she replied quickly.

There was a long silence.

"I sense a melancholy mood, darling!" remarked Belinda. "Are you sure you are alright?" she asked, rubbing her sleepy eyes as she propped herself up in her comfortable, spacious bed.

Although a deep sadness had overwhelmed Frank for Vinny and Lukey, he tried to make his answer sound cheerful.

"I am just tired, il mio amore. But good news! I hope to fly to London in the next few weeks! How great is that?" he added, the anticipation of their sensual lovemaking filling his senses and exciting his manhood.

"Oh! Wonderful!" squealed Belinda "It has been so long! I long to see you, my love," she whispered, feeling the butterflies fluttering deep down, bringing to mind his caress, his talented lips and his manly body.

Laying back on her bed, Belinda found it difficult to recapture sleep. Her mind continuously recalled the other telephone call that she had received only yesterday. Belinda knew Frank would be troubled had she mentioned it to him but she also knew he would have to be told eventually. The caller was Frank's closest friend but she had nothing to hide and neither did Count Luigi Boggia.

The Count had reached Belinda at the agency the previous day. He had explained in his inimitable charming Italian accent that he had been thinking about her and so decided to call and say hello. Revealing that he was aware Frank had been dealing with urgent business in the Gambling Capital of the World for some time now, he would try and visit Frank in New York as soon as his friend returned home to the Big Apple.

Try as she may to push the thoughts out of her head, Belinda knew she felt some attraction for Count Luigi Boggia. Although an older gentleman, he was still extremely handsome, elegant and charismatic. Of course, her heart belonged to Frank and she adored him but, guiltily, she would often imagine herself in a sexual relationship with the Count and how his Italian eyes would make her feel sensual. She was astonished at how these thoughts of another man could cause the very same butterflies in her tummy to stir and her face to flush.

March brings breezes loud and shrill, stirs the golden daffodil. This particular March morning found a troubled Belinda daydreaming about the following few weeks. Although thrilled she would soon be back in the strong tanned arms of Frank, she was becoming anxious about telling him of Count Luigi's telephone call. Belinda was deeply in love with Frank but she was beginning to realise it was indeed possible to be attracted to two people at the same time. She remembered with dismay how Frank had shown intense jealousy when he had learned that the Count had sent flowers to her some time ago.

"Morning, darling!" The greeting cut sharply through her unsettling thoughts as Camp Freddie sauntered flamboyantly into the office, little Queenie trotting happily behind his master.

"Oh! Good morning, Freddie," replied Belinda, snapping out of her melancholy mood.

"Everything okay, sweet pea?" asked Freddie as he ostentatiously threw off his mid-calf brown leather overcoat and hung it neatly on the coat stand.

Belinda tried to appear as casual as possible but Camp Freddie could instinctively tell there was something on her mind.

"Hey, Belinda! Please! Pulling the wool over my eyes! You know I can always read you like an open book! Come on, sweet pea! I am all ears!" coaxed Freddie, sauntering into the kitchenette to pour them both a cup of coffee.

Without hesitation, Belinda recounted all her worries to Freddie who listened intently as he slowly sipped his hot coffee.

They eventually agreed that it would be best if Belinda told Frank about Count Luigi's telephone call.

"After all," announced Freddie, swallowing down the last drops of his coffee, "it is worth remembering that the devil makes the pot, but not the lid!"

"Meaning?" enquired Belinda, looking at him a little confused.

"Meaning, sweet pea, that sooner or later, the truth will come out, which would cause Frank to become very suspicious indeed!" Freddie warned, opening his computer then glancing at Belinda anticipating her reaction.

She did not respond so he continued. "If you withhold this information, Frank will obviously be sceptical, sweet pea! You really must mention it to him, darling girl!"

Certain that Freddie was undoubtedly right with his advice, Belinda agreed she would mention it to Frank when he was back in London.

The sudden ringing of Dawn's telephone made Belinda rush into her partner's office. Although it had just turned eight-thirty, a representative of Top Drawer Agency's paramount German client was enquiring about several lookalikes possibly required for a star-studded evening scheduled to take place in Düsseldorf early in May.

After making a note of the requested lookalikes, Belinda asked Freddie to telephone all the names on the list and check their availability. Hopeful blue eyes scrutinised the sheet, but Freddie was yet again discouraged to see that Liberace had been overlooked.

Seeing his disappointment, Belinda cajoled, "Freddie, darling! La Collins is not on the list either!"

Slouching his shoulders, Camp Freddie sullenly replied. "Yes. I noticed, sweet pea, but it has been a long time since my last lookalike job!"

"Me too, Freddie!" emphasised Belinda. "Remember, business is now perking up! You and I will be in high demand. Just you wait and see!"

"I wish!" came Freddie's unconvinced reply as he brought up the relevant file, listing contact details of all lookalike and tribute artistes.

"Oh! I see Pamela Anderson is on the client's list," Freddie called out to Belinda who was making a fuss of little Queenie in the middle of the room.

"Yes, I spotted that. Tanya will be so pleased!" she replied, walking back to her paper-strewn desk.

"On reflection, Freddie, don't bother to call Tanya, I will do that a little later. I know how she likes to sleep late!" she added, giggling to herself, recalling how her friend was rarely on time and would probably be late for her own funeral.

Later on, and lost in thought after her call to Tanya, regarding her availability for the forthcoming job in Düsseldorf, Belinda felt perturbed. Tanya had never been nonchalant about her lookalike career and was always so enthusiastic about portraying the iconic Pamela Anderson, regularly calling the agency to enquire whether there had been any enquiries for her character.

Admittedly, pondered Belinda, work for some of the lookalikes, herself included, had been rather slack of late, but all professional impersonators were aware of the ups and downs of this precarious business. She was mindful of how unsettling and disappointing it could be for the morale when one was continuously left off clients' lists and how some artistes could possibly loss interest and even worse, confidence, especially if they had not worked for some time. However, Belinda sensed that this was not the reason for Tanya's lack of fervour. Deciding not to mention this to Dawn for the time being, she made a decision to meet Tanya, hopefully shedding some light on this clandestine situation. She was certain something, or possibly someone, was having a very negative effect on her close friend's well-being.

"Good morning, all," greeted Dawn as she walked into the office, fair hair windswept courtesy of the angry March winds.

"Coffee for you, Dawn?" asked Freddie, alighting from his chair and sauntering into the kitchenette again, already knowing her answer.

"Yes, please. Thank you, Freddie!" replied a smiling Dawn, walking over to Belinda where she divulged in a stage whisper, "I had a weird voice message left on my mobile from Kay Carney. She urged me to make sure I buy the morning papers! Unfortunately, I have only just listened to her message so haven't bought any!"

Rushing out of the kitchenette, surprisingly not spilling a drop of coffee, Freddie handed Dawn the cup of hot liquid then announced excitedly, "Oh! Queenie and I will go get them! By the way, did Ms Carney say which ones to get?" he asked on a more serious note.

"Unfortunately, no. Be a darling, Freddie, and pick up what you can, please. Knowing Kay Carney, I am sure she has a starring role in all of today's news headlines, otherwise she wouldn't bother to alert us!" she added sarcastically.

"Very true!" agreed Belinda turning on her computer. "I wonder what this is all about?"

Dawn replied by rolling her eyes to the ceiling.

As he reached the door, turning, arms flaying buoyantly, a tutting Freddie exclaimed, "My knicker elastic will break if I have to wait any longer to find out what Ms Carney has been up to! I'm off! Toodle pip!" then he swept out of the door, little Queenie following closely at his feet.

Mouths dropping open in disbelief and helpless with laughter, Belinda and Dawn almost collapsed in a heap at the inimitable Camp Freddie's temerity.

Only his high-combed black hair could be seen behind the pile of newspapers as Freddie and little Queenie arrived back at the agency. It appeared as if Freddie had bought up every paper he could get his hands on.

"Take a look at these, ladies!" urged a smug-looking Freddie as he lay a dozen newspapers on Dawn's desk.

"You are not going to believe what Ms Carney has been up to these last few months!" he smirked, as he unclipped Queenie's red leather lead.

Immediately picking up the *Morning Star*, Belinda's searching eyes swept quickly over the section featuring both Kay and Zac Lewis. Finally coming to the end of the report, her eyes full of bewilderment, she glanced up at Freddie for his reaction.

Dawn kept muttering, "I don't believe it!" over and over as her startled eyes read the breaking news regarding Kay Carney, the glamorous Marilyn Monroe impersonator, and Zac Lewis, the iconic star and multimillionaire.

"What did I tell you?" declared Freddie triumphantly, walking over to Dawn's desk and picking up one of the newspapers.

"She has practically caused World War III in Beverly Hills!" he declared dramatically, glancing over to where Dawn, now unusually quiet, had stopped muttering and was staring into space.

"Ladies, I think we all need a nice hot cup of sweet tea for the shock!" he announced, sauntering into the kitchenette.

"Kay Carney, pregnant!" murmured Dawn almost to herself.

"Yes indeed!" replied Freddie popping his head out of the kitchenette, "And the father is reported to be none other than Zac Lewis himself!"

"Goodness gracious!" moaned Belinda, disbelief written all over her face. "The whole world knows that Zac Lewis is gay!" she exclaimed, now looking confused.

"Well! He obviously is not as gay as he thinks he is, sweet pea!" retorted Camp Freddie from the kitchenette.

Looking up over her glasses, Dawn began to shake her head, scepticism crossing her features as she mused, "Kay Carney pregnant by a world-famous multimillionaire! Did I not tell you she would go far?"

"Well! If you ask me, she has gone too blooming far this time!" exclaimed a pursed lipped Freddie, exiting the kitchenette carrying a tray laden with three cups of hot sweet tea.

"Let's call Kay later and see what she has to say for herself," suggested Belinda, getting up from her chair and taking a cup of hot tea from the tray.

"It will have to be much later, sweet pea!" alerted Freddie returning the now empty tray to the kitchenette. "Don't forget the big time difference between London and Los Angeles!"

"Yes, of course," acknowledged Belinda.

Turning to Dawn, she asked, "Do you think we should call her?"

"Oh, most definitely, Belinda!" replied Dawn, scrutinising the other newspapers scattered over her desk. "After all, she did leave me a voice message. I shall stay here in the office a little later today so that I can have a word with our dearest Kay," she added thoughtfully, a secret smile dancing briefly across her mouth.

"Well, there you are, ladies!" exclaimed Camp Freddie later that day, as a thoughtful looking Dawn replaced the receiver after speaking at length with Kay.

All three had been listening silently on the conference phone as Kay explained to Dawn how she had suddenly fallen deeply in love with Zac Lewis.

"Suddenly fallen deeply in love with his bank accounts more like!" exclaimed a smug Freddie, glancing from Belinda to Dawn, who both chose to ignore his flippant remark.

"You now have it from the horse's mouth!" declared Freddie, his perfectly shaped eyebrows raised enquiringly.

"Yes, we certainly do!" agreed Belinda, a look of amazement sweeping over her face.

Walking over to the large window and surveying the darkening sky outside, Dawn turned back slowly. Directing her words to her audience of two, she declared, "Have I not told you often that darling Kay would do well for herself?"

"Do well for herself?" queried Freddie, eyes widening in disbelief. "She certainly has done that! I dare say she will receive a nice tidy sum from Zac Lewis to keep her and the child in positive luxury!" he remarked, sarcastically.

"Good for her!" exclaimed Dawn. "He is the father and should pay up! Do you agree, Belinda?" she asked, glancing at her business partner.

"Yes, of course I do, Dawn!" replied a pensive Belinda. "If Zac is the father of Kay's child, then of course, he must take responsibility. The fact that he is an extremely wealthy and famous man is neither here nor there!" she added earnestly.

"Exactly!" came Dawn's response.

"Well, ladies, I'm off! I have a heavy date with scrumptious Syd!" announced an elated Freddie as he and little Queenie hurried towards the door.

Immediately stopping Freddie in his tracks, a jesting Dawn pertinently asked, "Would that be boss-eyed Syd or cross-eyed Syd?"

Whirling around, blue eyes blazing and effeminate lips set in a sulky pout, Camp Freddie pertly retorted, "That would be both, Madam! I bid you ladies goodnight!" and with that, he and little Queenie flounced out of the office.

Lifting her head and peering directly at Dawn, Belinda urged her mockingly, "You really must stop teasing poor Freddie about Syd." Sounding in earnest, she continued, "I feel dear Freddie is finally getting over that ghastly Italian opera singer and it is all thanks to boss-eyed, or possibly cross-eyed, Syd!"

"Or possibly both of them!" giggled Dawn.

Moments before closing down her computer for the evening, an email appeared in Belinda's inbox.

"Great stuff!" she called out to Dawn who responded by poking her head out of her office, a look of supposition on her face.

"A nice enquiry just in from our clients, Red Roof Promotions, regarding a commercial for ITV," announced Belinda, glancing up at Dawn who by now had reached the desk and, leaning over her business partner, began to read the email for herself.

"Excellent! This could be an exemplary job for Top Drawer Agency!" exclaimed a joyous Dawn.

"Could you possibly deal with this before you go, Belinda?" she asked placidly. "Come in later tomorrow to compensate," she suggested, before disappearing out of the door.

Conscious of how precarious the lookalike and tribute artistes industry could be, Belinda knew it made sense to strike while the iron was hot. Agreeing to compile all the relevant photos and videos ready to forward onto the client without delay, her eyes flickered quickly down the list of celebrities asked for. Robert De Niro, Lady Gaga, Daniel Craig as 007, HRH Prince Charles and President Trump. She smiled to herself recalling how often Bernard Shaftoe's name appeared on the clients' lists, especially since his escapade in Trafalgar Square some weeks before had dominated the media.

Checking the online file for current confirmed jobs, Belinda noticed that Bernard had already been booked in for three other clients, two of the jobs being back to back. Although the agency had four other acceptable President Trump impersonators on their books, the clients invariably requested Bernard. Red Roof Promotions had not given a precise date for when the TV commercial would be filmed but affirmed in their email that it would, in all probability, be some time at the end of June. Fortunately, Belinda noted, Bernard had nothing else confirmed as yet at that time.

Later that evening, as Belinda settled down in front of the TV, the sudden ringing of her mobile phone broke her train of thought. Quickly reaching for it, she quietly answered but before the caller had spoken, the quivers in her body assured her that Frank Lanzo was on the other end.

Chapter 34
The Awakening of Zac Lewis

Although he had cleverly hidden his emotions completely when he observed Kay standing half-naked in the ballroom of his château the evening of his birthday party all those months ago, Zac Lewis was acutely aware at the time that his brain was relaying thoughts and feelings to him that he had never ever felt for a woman. He was stunned.

As he tried to keep his eyes away from Kay's dishevelled appearance, the torn dress revealing her magnificent body every bit as breathtakingly beautiful as the real Marilyn Monroe, Zac could feel his manhood stirring.

Aside from being a well-loved music legend, if his performance that evening was anything to go by he was also an extremely accomplished actor. Had Oscars been awarded that night, he would most definitely have won. The way he had apathetically walked in on the 'after fight' between his lovely Kay and the spiteful Ajlal woman, nobody would have guessed what was really going on in his mind and loins as he took full control of the embarrassing situation.

Instantly dismissing Rex the stagehand and his fiery girlfriend Ajlal for completely disrupting his birthday extravaganza, Zac then fussed over his special guest artiste, Kay Carney, asking the two lady singers, Jess and Lola, to look after her while she returned to her quarters to recover from her terrible ordeal, and to freshen up and change her ruined evening dress.

Although outwardly Kay appeared to have recovered quickly from the trauma she had been through, inside she was extremely shaken. Never before had such an awful thing happened to her. Usually she got along well with other women, even though most of them envied her looks and lifestyle. There was something childlike about Kay that invariably appealed to the mother instinct in most other women, young or old.

Sometime later when Zac escorted Kay back to the party, now in full swing, the revellers stopped dancing one by one, quietened down and began to applaud loudly. They were mesmerised at how beautiful the Marilyn Monroe impersonator looked after her earlier ordeal and showed their admiration by clapping and whistling for a long time. It was quite an ovation.

From that surreal display of support for Kay, everything went smoothly for the remainder of the party. Poor Kay's feet were on fire by the end of the evening, having danced with practically every red-blooded male in the room as well as several of the besotted females! Revelling in all the glory and flirting outrageously, she had not noticed that one pair of eyes in particular had not left sight of her.

As night slowly dressed for dawn, the highly-spirited, inebriated guests reluctantly took their leave from the opulence of Zac's château and glorious party. Not one of them was aware that their music legend host had discovered he had strong sexual feelings towards a woman and that woman was none other than the delectable Monroe impersonator.

Unable to bear the thought of Kay leaving the following day to return to London and her glamorous life and career, Zac almost begged her to join him and Daniel at his Beverly Hills mansion. Kay Carney was over the moon.

"Oh! Zac, darling!" she squealed, eyes shining. "Of course I would love to join you, but I have an outstanding contracted work commitment in London in a couple of days' time for one of my most prestigious clients." Staring into Zac's disappointed face, she squeezed him coquettishly.

"Of course, my precious one," replied Zac smiling down at her. "But you must promise me that you will join us as soon as you have completed your commitment," he gently added, pulling her close to him as his stirring manhood ascertained that he was becoming besotted with this amazing woman.

The astute Kay was now amusingly aware that her famous friend, whom the whole world knew was homosexual, had developed strong sensual feelings for her. She would most certainly join him and his partner at their Beverly Hills mansion as soon as she was able.

Having worked in Los Angeles several times in her illustrious career, Kay felt quite at home as George, Zac's chauffeur, stood in the waiting crowd to collect her as she passed through customs. She recognised her name written on a large white card held high in the chauffeur's hands as his almond shaped eyes searched the faces of the arriving passengers. Waving and smiling, she walked swiftly to where he stood and introduced herself to him.

"Pleased you meet you, Miss Carney, or should I say, Miss Monroe?" he asked, slightly bowing to an amused Kay.

She thought he was almost as beautiful as Daniel, Zac's partner, but she was certain George was not homosexual. Nestling comfortably in the plush red leather seats in the back of the black Bentley Continental GT3, Kay felt excitement flutter in her tummy as she surveyed the passing views from the windows. She remembered the palm tree lined streets, the white buildings glistening in the late afternoon sun, the open green spaces, the tall trees swaying in the light breeze outside walled houses.

"Here we are, Miss Carney!" exclaimed George, coming to a stop outside a double-gated walled complex.

Peering out of the window, Kay was elated. It was like arriving in paradise. After all, not only were the neighbours here in Beverly Hills world-famous icons, her host was one of the most famous of all, and as George drove the Bentley slowly up the driveway to the double-fronted fortress-like door, she could see that Zac's Californian home and grounds were breathtakingly beautiful and palatial.

Before George had a chance to open the back door of the Bentley for her to alight, Daniel, looking like a Greek God in yellow swimming trunks, two golden retrievers at his heel, came rushing up to the car.

Excitedly pulling the door open, he proceeded to help Kay out of the car, kissing her in greeting. She thought him quite exquisite.

"Marilyn, darling!" came a loud cry from the open door. Turning in the direction of the emotional cry, Kay's heart skipped a beat, as her shining eyes focused on Zac waving to her. She noticed how his expensive porcelain teeth glimmered in the afternoon sunlight, and as she hurried towards him, he immediately opened his short muscular arms for her to enter. She nestled fleetingly in his protection, conscious yet again that his body reacted to her closeness. Looking up into his rugged face, she realised he was crying and smiling at the same time. Tears of joy! He held her at arm's length, studying every part of her. Resting his dark grey eyes on her beautifully made-up face, he nodded his head in approval, gently pulling her close to his body again. She could feel his hardness.

Although Kay adored Zac, she adored more so the beautiful home and lifestyle he shared with Daniel in Beverly Hills, not to mention St. Tropez, Rome, New York and London, where he owned other amazing palatial properties.

While sunbathing after an enjoyable morning swim, Kay fantasied about being as rich as Zac and how she would fly from one home to the other whenever the fancy took her, spending Christmas in London with her family and friends, then leaving for the sunnier climes of St. Tropez.

Noticing that the divine Daniel frequently had his younger set of friends over for pool parties, Kay also noticed that he would sometimes leave with them, arriving back the following day. One morning, joining Zac for breakfast, she asked the music legend if he was really happy with his life.

Glancing at her, then reaching across the table for another slice of hot toast, he let out a sarcastic tut before answering her question.

"Happy? My darling Kay, who is really happy? Surely happiness has a different meaning to each of us?" His curt words caused Kay to blush uncharacteristically. She was aware that Zac could be terse at times but she quickly realised that his abruptness this morning was caused by the absence once again of Daniel.

Without noticing her awkwardness, he continued, "Daniel and I are good for each other if that is what you mean. We get along well and he makes himself available to me when I need him. I realise he is much younger than I, and so I turn a blind eye to his little indiscretions."

"Oh! I am sorry, Zac. Please forgive me for being too inquisitive," fibbed Kay. "As long as you are happy, then I am happy!" she added demurely, glancing at him sheepishly.

As Zac took Kay's hand across the table, she could see tenderness in those dark grey eyes as they focused on her.

"Forgive you, my darling Kay? Nonsense! Having you here is bringing me more happiness than I ever thought possible!" he declared, his mood becoming less subdued.

Giggling girlishly, Kay hugged him tightly, feeling again his excitement at her closeness.

Zac's mood changes could be quite overwhelming for both himself and others. Undoubtedly, this temperament was expected and accepted of such a highly talented artiste but to Zac, it often felt like a demented whirlwind, ensuring peace and tranquillity eluded him.

"Let us go for a lovely long drive today, darling! We'll stop and have lunch at Ocean Prime on Wilshire Boulevard," he suggested, getting up from his chair and stroking his two retrievers who reciprocated by pressing themselves affectionately against his legs.

"Juan, my valet, will walk Goldie and Sunny today," he murmured mostly to himself as he rubbed the adoring dogs' ears.

It had been a long time since Kay had felt so ecstatic with life. Her black silk chiffon scarf fluttered in the light breeze which accompanied the perfect warm sunny day as Zac's Aston Martin Valkyrie headed smoothly towards Santa Monica beach.

The two friends strolled barefoot in the sand along the water's edge, Kay playfully splashing the music icon who quickly retaliated before restraining her in his arms, instantly aware that he was enlivened by the rapture he was feeling for this woman.

With its sophisticated décor, Ocean Prime lived up to its name and reputation. The pair had a sumptuous seafood lunch, chatting relentlessly, while Kay enjoyed the choice of wine ordered by Zac, who favoured iced water for himself.

"Must not drink and drive, darling!" he muttered partly to himself, finishing the last refreshing drop of water in his glass. "Mind you, sweetie," he continued, winking devilishly at a smiling Kay, "I will make up for it once we arrive home! You and I, my beauty, will continue the party there. What do you say to that?"

Grinning widely, her red lipstick imprinted on her porcelain front teeth, a slightly tipsy Kay Carney squealed in response.

"I say yes, yes, yes!" causing not only Zac, but the other diners to giggle and laugh at this mesmerising couple, the famous music legend and his companion, the replica of the icon that was Marilyn Monroe.

It was late afternoon as Zac pulled into the driveway. Stopping the car outside the fortress-like front entrance, Juan was waiting, ready to drive the Aston Martin safely back to its garage. There was no sign of Daniel or his wild young group of friends.

"Looks like it's just us for dinner this evening, my darling," declared Zac matter-of-factly, helping Kay out of the passenger's seat. She noticed the disappointment and sadness in his grey eyes.

"Will Daniel be late again?" she enquired, feeling concern for Zac.

"Very late, I imagine, darling! Probably will not return until late tomorrow," he replied. "Not to worry, my sweet. You and I can get nicely sloshed!" he quipped, grinning at her.

"Now go rest before dinner, my angel, then we shall drink each other under the table!"

Giggling and hiccuping at the same time, Kay sauntered slowly towards the winding staircase which lead to her en suite rooms. Turning, she pursed her pouting lips, blowing her besotted host a perfect Marilyn Monroe kiss.

Kay often reminisced of how easy it had been for her to entice and seduce the music legend that was Zac Lewis. Although the world knew he was homosexual who indeed lived with a younger man, the world was not aware that somehow deep down inside, a light had been switched on, creating sensual and sexual longings towards one woman; the world's foremost Marilyn Monroe impersonator.

Smirking to herself, Kay recalled every detail of that fateful night, with Daniel conveniently out of the way until the following morning, ignorant of the fact that he had bestowed on her the precious time she needed to change her life forever.

She shimmied seductively down the winding staircase, looking stunningly gorgeous in her red satin evening gown. He let out a long low whistle as his adoring eyes took in her every beguiling movement. As his manhood began to stiffen in his black satin trousers, Zac knew without a shadow of a doubt that he had to have this beautiful creature, desperate to kiss every inch of her breathtakingly beautiful body. He was astounded how, as a gay man, he was totally enticed sexually by this one woman. She kept her eyes fixated on him as he held out his left hand to escort her into the dining room where, he told her, they would be tasting the delights from the highly talented hands of one of the world's top chefs.

Smiling sweetly up at him, Kay had determined then and there that she would do everything in her power to permit her to live this wealthy and affluent lifestyle forever. As a smiling Zac held out the gold-seated cushion dining chair for her, she demurely slid into place, suddenly conscious of the butterflies that excitedly fluttered about inside her tummy, as if they too sensed that an amazing experience was waiting for her.

They danced closely under the glittering crystal chandeliers that adorned the vast ceiling in the beautiful Art Deco dining room. Dinner for just the two of them was both joyful and special as their glowing eyes focused on each other over the highly polished traditional table. Kay had never tested such exquisite food in all her life. Zac Lewis certainly knew how to live!

"I am beginning to think you are quite decadent, Zac!" she muttered to him tipsily before brazenly placing her hand on his thigh and squeezing seductively. Feeling his body shudder under her touch gave her a feeling of power and excitement.

"Come. Let us dance, darling!" he suggested, getting up from his chair and holding out his hand to her, his alert grey eyes watching closely. Giggling girlishly as she almost lost her balance, Kay stood up and slowly walked towards him. They had each drunk several large glasses of wine and as the nectar of the Gods spun its magic through their veins, they danced to enchanting love songs from the spellbinding voice of Frank Sinatra.

Tenderly escorting her from the dance floor, Zac, his red gold inlaid tailcoat jacket accentuating his grey eyes, led Kay, now smouldering with sexuality, up the long winding staircase to her boudoir. She leant against him quietly humming to herself until they both disappeared through the white and gold door, protecting them from the prying eyes of the world.

Zac desperately wanted to express his feelings for this amazing woman who now lay on the large king-sized bed, her creamy, bare arms stretched out towards him as he fell gently onto her, the pink silk sheets feeling sensual to the touch.

To Kay's astonishment, Zac took full control of their lovemaking. Later she recalled he had been playful yet passionate, making her feel not only sexy, but cherished. She loved his confidence and the fact that he was not afraid to be vulnerable. Zac was probably the most sensual lover she had ever known and there had been many.

As a gay man, he had been adventurous and willing to experiment with her, and for Kay she sensed they were not just having sex but making love. He had taken delight in exploring her body, mind, and soul, wanting to share an intimate connection with her. Sometime later they slept lightly in each other's arms, both oblivious to the fact that through their surreal sexual connection, a new precious life had begun.

Chapter 35
Düsseldorf Delights

"Well, that is all the contracts returned, signed and dated!" announced Camp Freddie, stretching languidly in his office chair and yawning loudly, causing little Queenie to stare up at his master quizzically.

"Well done, Freddie!" came Dawn's response from her office. "Not a minute too soon either, seeing as the lookalikes are flying the day after tomorrow!"

"I am green with envy! Wish I was going!" groaned Freddie, stroking little Queenie then yawning again before continuing. "They will have such a great time. The Germans, as the Italians, certainly know how to pull out all of the stops!"

Appearing at the entrance to her office, Dawn smiled encouragingly at Freddie before predicting optimistically, "Freddie, dear, your character will be in demand again soon; I am confident about that. Remember, there is talk of another film in the offing regarding Liberace's turbulent love life. Apparently, he had secret affairs with several other famous prominent Americans!" she reminded him.

"Oh! Yes, so there is," pondered Freddie. "You know, Dawn, I was reading about that probability in a magazine only last week," he added, his melancholy mood lifting somewhat.

"Well, there you are then!" declared Dawn. "Now, please stop fretting and think positively," she urged, before disappearing back into her office.

It was almost lunchtime before Belinda arrived at the agency, hurriedly taking off her dark green wool jacket and hanging it on a peg, little Queenie jumping up to greet her.

"Good morning all, or should I say good afternoon?" she quipped, walking over to her desk, little Queenie still at her heel.

Blowing her a kiss, Freddie sauntered into the kitchenette to make coffee.

Spectacles placed on the top of her head, Dawn wittingly responded, "You should say afternoon! But better late than never, Belinda, darling!"

"Sorry, full moon last night. No sleep at all!" replied Belinda, turning on her computer.

"You are not a werewolf, are you?" enquired Dawn jokingly, causing Belinda to laugh.

"Who's a werewolf?" came the dulcet tones of Freddie's voice as he appeared from the kitchenette, three cups of hot coffee strategically placed on the silver tray.

"I suppose I must be," responded Belinda, grinning widely.

"Are you now?" queried Freddie, handing her a cup of coffee. "I hear the full moon strongly affects you lot!" declared Freddie, walking towards Dawn and playfully winking at her.

"You sound as if you are an authority on werewolves, Freddie!" remarked Belinda, glancing over to Dawn and raising her eyes to the skies.

"Well, I used to be a werewolf, but I am alright nowwwwwwwwwwwwwww!" came Freddie's shrill remark.

The thunderous laughter from the two ladies set little Queenie barking excitedly.

Sometime later, walking over to the large window and glancing down at the busy street below, Dawn asked Belinda, "By the way, did you have a good evening with Tanya? I hope she has everything organised for the Düsseldorf job?"

"Yes, she is ready and is excited to be working with her lookalike friends again," replied Belinda. "We had a lovely time and chatted for hours. Tanya is thrilled to be portraying Pamela Anderson again!" she added, feeling guilty for lying to her business partner.

"I just hope she arrives at the airport before the flight takes off!" came Dawn's sarcastic remark. "We all know what a terrible timekeeper our lovely Tanya is!"

"Dawn, she promised me she would be the first to arrive at Gatwick Airport and I am sure she wouldn't let the agency or us down!" exclaimed Belinda, hoping to appease her.

"Well, I hope you are right, Belinda. As you are aware, Top Drawer Agency must always be exactly what the names suggests – Top Drawer!"

Not entirely believing her own words, a concerned Belinda replied, "I have complete faith in Tanya to carry out an excellent job for the agency as she always has done. She will not let us down!"

Pausing at the entrance to her office, turning back, Dawn replied, "Excellent! I will trust your judgement. Now I must call Crystal to reiterate that at all times Top Drawer's artistes must have impeccable manners. I have not forgotten how upset Melita was at Crystal's belittlement of Michael Fitzgerald, our client's representative in Dublin!"

"Yes, I think a little word in her ear before she leaves for Düsseldorf would be beneficial," agreed Belinda, taking a banana from her large brown handbag and peeling it.

"It is a pity that Melita was not chosen for this job instead of Crystal!" exclaimed Freddie glancing at Belinda, then quietly muttering under his breath, he added, "She is trouble, that one! Mark my words!"

"I appreciate what you say, Freddie, but the clients adore her and if they want Crystal and she is available, then we cannot disappoint them," Belinda reasoned, finishing her late breakfast, wrapping the banana skin in a tissue before walking into the kitchenette to dispose of it. "As Dawn suggests, all we can do is remind Crystal about the politeness policy of Top Drawer Agency," she declared, returning to her desk.

"Yes, I suppose so," agreed Freddie sulkily. "But believe me, that little madam is trouble!"

"I am certain Crystal will behave herself" stressed Belinda in the lookalike's defence. "After all, HM Queen Elizabeth II is also on the Düsseldorf job and we all know how Marina Greenslade expects everyone to conduct themselves in an orderly manner!"

Letting out a quick laugh at Belinda's sardonic remark regarding Marina Greenslade, Dawn remarked, "Yes, of course! Dear Marina will clip her wings if necessary. Have no doubt about that!"

True to her word, Tanya arrived at London Gatwick Airport before any of the other artistes. Dawn had stipulated that all of the lookalikes should meet at the check-in desk whether or not they had already checked in online. This way, she reasoned, they could all stay together before the flight, making sure no one would be left behind.

Neil Patterson was the first to arrive shortly after Tanya. She noticed how heads turned to stare in disbelief at the gorgeous George Clooney lookalike as he made his way towards her. Neil was a confident young man who enjoyed losing his native Scottish accent to mimic the husky voiced American superstar.

Tanya had worked with Neil several times before and found him quite charming. She smiled and waved to him. As they kissed each other in friendly greeting, they were impolitely interrupted by a childlike voice.

"Where is my kiss, Georgie Porgie?"

Looking up quickly, they encountered the vision of the icon known as Marilyn Monroe. Tanya was instantly taken aback at how Crystal was dressed totally in character for the flight to Germany. Now feeling rather insecure in her jeans and cropped jacket, Tanya regretted not choosing a more glamorous outfit in which to travel.

Of course, Neil needed no further encouragement to kiss the beautiful Crystal. Turning debonairly from Tanya, he walked purposefully up to the vision of Marilyn Monroe, took her masterfully in his arms then, bending his head down, kissed the seductive icon tenderly on her red-painted lips which seemed to linger on and on. It was obvious to Tanya the pair seemed to be completely lost in each other.

As she was about to tap Neil on his shoulder, Elvis lookalike Rob, his jet-black quiff glowing under the airport lights, called out in an unmistakable Memphis accent, causing amused passengers nearby to gasp in wonder.

"Who's this son of a bitch making out with my woman?"

Instantly Neil and Crystal broke away from each other, a look of shock on their flushed faces before they began to laugh out loud upon seeing Rob, waving his fist in the air, faking anger at them.

Crossing over to the Elvis lookalike, Neil, still laughing, shook the other man's hand in friendship.

"Hey, man, you got lipstick all over your kisser!" blurted out Rob, now grinning at the George Clooney impersonator.

"Oh no!" moaned Neil, pulling a white handkerchief from his jacket pocket. Turning to an awkward-looking Tanya, he asked, "Have you got a mirror handy, Pammy?" His hand outstretched towards her.

Before Tanya could respond, the provocative Crystal had wiggled up to Gorgeous George and, looking up at him flirtatiously under her spider-like fake eyelashes, handed him a silver-plated handbag mirror, which he accepted graciously. Glancing into it, he began to vigorously clean the telltale signs of lipstick from his mouth and chin.

Tanya and Rob had worked together several times before and she always enjoyed the company of this particular Elvis lookalike and tribute artiste. Not only was Rob the very best Elvis, but he had a light-hearted sense of humour that never failed to keep everyone in the group laughing and feeling relaxed. He greeted her with a bear hug which almost winded the petite Tanya. Sweeping her up swiftly, he swung her around, much to the amusement of the other passengers waiting in line at the check-in desk.

The only two lookalikes in the group who had never worked together in the past were Rob and Crystal. Rob had worked many times with the delectable Kay Carney and had flirted outrageously with her but this was the first time he had met Top Drawer's newly crowned Marilyn Monroe and he, like the rest of the male population, was eager to make the acquaintance of such an alluring woman.

As Tanya was about to introduce Rob to Crystal, Marina Greenslade arrived at the check-in desk by way of an electric cart. Waving at the other lookalikes, she tipped the driver who, after helping her to her feet, appeared to bow to her as if she were indeed HM Queen Elizabeth II. The uproar from the growing queue of waiting passengers as their eyes focused on their beloved sovereign was surreal indeed and the fact that Marina Greenslade was known worldwide as the foremost Queen impersonator did not stop the passengers treating her as if she were Queen Elizabeth II herself.

Those who dwell in the copycat world of lookalike and tribute artistes become accustomed to the rest of the world's fascination with them. Just a handful of these everyday people really look remarkably like some very famous faces and it is those who become the finest in their field. Marina was the foremost, the principal, the pre-eminent lookalike, and over the years had become extremely distinguished in her portrayal of HM Queen Elizabeth II. The world had long ago accepted Marina Greenslade as the 'other Queen'.

Acknowledging the boisterous passengers with the royal wave which overexcited them, Marina then greeted her fellow lookalikes before gently taking Tanya to one side for a quick catch-up. Having both worked together many times before, all over Europe and the UK, the two women were completely comfortable in each other's company.

Since Kay's departure from Top Drawer Agency, Marina had only worked once with Crystal; however, as she confided to Dawn and Belinda afterwards, she much preferred Melita to her half-sister, whom she felt was rather forceful and full of herself. She did, however, agree that Crystal had an uncanny resemblance to the real icon, even more so than Kay and definitely more so than Melita.

In fact, mused Marina, Kay and Crystal looked more like sisters than the real sisters did.

The flight to Düsseldorf proved pleasant enough. Marina sat beside Tanya and Neil, changing places with Neil for his aisle seat just before take-off, permitting her to have a comfort break whenever necessary without disrupting the others. Neil, ever the debonair, readily occupied Marina's window seat instead. Everybody loved Neil Patterson; he had manners, wit, style and dashing looks, and was almost as handsome as his film star doppelgänger, George Clooney.

Tanya, happy to listen while Marina consistently chatted throughout the short flight, noticed how well Crystal and Rob were getting along. Seated just two rows in front of them and across the aisle, Tanya could see the Elvis lookalike bending over backwards to amuse Crystal, who giggled at everything 'The King' said. Tanya had also worked with Crystal once before and although she thought the newcomer had an amazing resemblance to the real icon, she, like many of the other lookalikes and tribute artistes, much preferred to work with Crystal's half-sister, Melita. Even the ostentatious Kay, with all her artificiality, proved to be favoured more than Crystal.

Like a cosmic eagle, the silver British Airways plane, soaring high in the air, suddenly begun to descend as the Captain informed his excited passengers they were now descending into Düsseldorf International Airport. Expertly, the aeroplane was brought to a smooth stop.

As the passengers were about to disembark, Marina leant over and whispered in Tanya's ear, "Look at her! What a narcissistic personality she is!"

Rising from her seat to retrieve her hand luggage in the overhead compartment, Tanya casually glanced towards Crystal who was nonchalantly blocking the aisle posing for photographs with some of the captivated passengers.

Lost in her element, giggling and blowing kisses to everyone, Crystal was not impressed when Marina shouted at her. "Stop showing off and move along so that we can leave the aircraft before midnight!"

Haughtily, Crystal shrugged her delicate shoulders, blew further Monroe kisses at the awestruck spectators then taking hold of her red wheeled trolley, slowly and deliberately in true Monroe-style, she wiggled out of the aeroplane and into the welcoming German sunshine, pausing as she carefully took each step down onto German soil.

With his iconic dyed black quiff catching the brightness of the sun, Elvis lookalike Rob awkwardly dragged his silver wheeled trolley behind him as he rushed to fall into step with the femme fatale as she wiggled towards the waiting shuttle bus. Walking behind, Tanya, Marina and Neil found the bizarre situation unfolding in front of them quite surreal as if they were witnessing a scene from a comedy.

Momentarily losing his balance as he stumbled to retrieve his footing, Elvis the Pelvis appeared to suddenly take off, before landing heavily on his back, long thin legs with feet encased in blue suede shoes suspended high in the air, his wheeled trolley crashing into the side of the shuttle bus.

Curiously glancing out of the windows, several pairs of eyes stared in amusement as they witnessed the icon known as The King sprawled ungentlemanly over the runway.

Rushing to assist his friend, Neil tried to help Rob up but, being of slight build himself, fell clumsily on top of him. There they lay entangled, the foremost George Clooney and Elvis Presley impersonators, laughing uncontrollably over their mishap. Commotion could be heard from inside the bus as bemused passengers instantly and right on cue began clicking with their phones as they focused on the dishevelled pair unsuccessfully trying to get back on their feet and restore a little decorum.

"For God's sake!" hissed Marina, the articulate Royal accent fleetingly forgotten. "I will have something to say to Dawn about this masquerade!" she threatened loudly, glaring at Gorgeous George and The King, who were still laughing hysterically as they brushed dust off each other's clothes. Poor Tanya, unable to answer, tears of laughter tumbling down her face, could only nod in agreement with an infuriated-looking Marina.

As Neil and Rob climbed self-consciously onto the shuttle, they were greeted by the sound of clapping from the smiling passengers in appreciation apparently for keeping everyone entertained. Feigning a bow to his amused audience, Rob's eyes searched the bus until they found Crystal. She sat in one of the few seats at the back looking through the messages on her mobile, quite oblivious to Rob and Neil's misadventure. Tanya and Marina stepped on board just as the doors were about to close.

Marina Greenslade lived her life as if she were indeed HM Queen Elizabeth II. Everyone who knew her personally was aware of this fact and also that Marina did not suffer fools lightly. For a person born and bred in East London, it was most unusual that she had hardly any sense of humour at all. Finding her posh accent once again, the 'other Queen' wasted no time in berating Rob, blaming him for not looking where he was going in his urgency to catch the attention of the Marilyn Monroe lookalike.

Conscious not to ruffle Her Majesty's feathers any further, Rob ingeniously replied, "Yes, Ma'am... yes, Ma'am..." in his finest Memphis accent, causing Marina to oblige him with a nod of her head and a long, hard stare.

While the passengers alighted noisily from the shuttle bus upon reaching the airport, hurrying up to Tanya and Marina, Neil insisted on pulling Marina's trolley for her. As all five lookalikes hastened through the airport, Tanya grinned to herself, noticing heads turning in astonishment as stunned passengers and airport staff alike focused on the apparition in front of them.

They hurried through customs and into the waiting limousine that was waiting for them to drive them direct to the five-star Capella Breidenbacher Hof Hotel, where the clients had booked their individual rooms.

The star-studded evening was every bit as amazing as Camp Freddie had predicted, with the Germans being almost as proficient as the Italians when it came to panache.

Marilyn Monroe, the most revered icon of all, received much of the attention from not only the gentlemen guests, but also the ladies.

Looking very like Pamela Anderson, Tanya also had her share of admirers. Several young men vied for her attention, pushing each other to stay close to the sexy lookalike. Deep in her heart, Tanya knew this was due partly to the scarlet *Baywatch* bathing suit and matching calf-length silk cloak she had decided to wear for the charity gala ball that evening. The red bathing suit invariably ensured everybody instantly recognised the character she was portraying.

Reflecting back to the earliest memories of her career as a lookalike, Tanya remembered how terribly anxious she would become if a member of the public blatantly asked her who she was supposed to be, suggesting that her resemblance to the American actress was not inevitable. Tanya knew she was not the only lookalike who had ever been asked this very perturbing question but she soon realised that some of the artistes who portrayed the top icons, past and present, need only wear a certain dress or outfit, and style their hair a particular way, for the world to immediately recognise who they were impersonating, even if they did not look exactly the same.

Over the years, Tanya had met many aspiring impersonators of Marilyn Monroe, Elvis and Charlie Chaplin who, without the iconic dress, hairstyle or hat and cane, would never have been recognised as the icon they were emulating. Nevertheless, this category of impersonators have always been necessary as back-ups for the elite list of lookalikes who do strongly resemble some of the worlds most famous faces. Today, Tanya mused, to herself satisfactorily, the German clients had chosen the finest of each character from Top Drawer Agency and, she, as the principal Pamela Anderson lookalike in the UK, was among that illustrious group.

Halfway through the exciting evening with the Great Gatsby Swing Band making it almost impossible for the guests to remain seated, Neil and Rob were causing excitement among the ladies. Catching sight of Elvis together with the replica of George Clooney as the two lookalikes strolled leisurely around the busy dance floor, mixing and mingling with the dancing guests, caused many of the ladies to squeal and swoon.

Suddenly, Rob and Neil were surrounded by an unruly throng of females of all ages, pushing and jostling each other to get to their idols, many shouting rather coarsely that they wanted to have their photographs taken with the lookalikes.

Realising that the situation could become explosive, Rob, his lip curling in true Elvis fashion, announced in his perfected Memphis accent, "Hey, ladies! Steady on there! Let us keep this nice and civilised, shall we?"

This immediately caused the inebriated horde of female guests to squeal ever louder.

The whole ballroom appeared to be watching in awe as The King and Gorgeous George tried unsuccessfully to escape the amorous clutches of the so-called fairer sex.

Surrendering now to the boisterous requests for selfies as the ladies clamoured to be the first in line, the two lookalikes posed as elegantly as possible under the pressure of female arms flailing about their necks, as red-painted lips ardently kissed them all over their amused faces.

Suddenly, a hush filled the ballroom as the Great Gatsby Swing Band, halfway through the Beatles' *Can't Buy Me Love*, stopped playing abruptly. The unruly group of amorous females, still surrounding Elvis and George, continued to squeal and giggle oblivious to the instantaneous silence.

"Girls! Girls! Please!" came the booming voice of a burly security officer as he and three other brawny bouncers swiftly rushed towards the crush of tipsy ladies who were noisily shoving each other out of the way in their woozy attempts to grab hold of the startled lookalikes.

"That is enough! Please give Elvis and George space to breath, otherwise we will have to ask you all to leave!" he bellowed as he and his team began pulling the enamoured females away from the astonished lookalikes, as two of the tipsy ladies proceeded to pinch Elvis' neat little buttocks.

From where she stood laughing with several awestruck young men, Tanya now nervously peered across the ballroom, her eyes squinting from the dazzling chandeliers as they appeared to dance above the joviality below. Searching the crowds for a sight of Marina, Tanya was dismayed to see HM Queen Elizabeth II sullen faced as she stood scrutinising the cause of the commotion that had disrupted her evening and that of the overwhelmed party guests that had surrounded her.

"Oh! I should have known!" seethed Marina in an elevated angry voice almost to herself as Elvis and George were hurriedly rushed away from the rowdy intoxicated fairer sex by the two muscular bouncers, as the enraged security officer reprimanded the giggling women.

Gratified that the Great Gatsby Swing Band began to play again and the revellers had taken to the dance floor once more, Tanya made her way gingerly to where Marina was still holding court, as she continued grumbling about the disturbance to anyone who would listen.

Noticing the Pam Anderson lookalike, Marina excused herself from her besotted fans. Motioning Tanya to one side, she whispered, "I am furious with those two and so will Dawn be when I speak to her. They have been a complete nightmare on this job, especially Elvis!"

Responding quickly and knowing she must humour the elder woman, Tanya replied cautiously, "Marina, I really do not think it is fair to blame Rob and Neil. Those women were very tipsy by the time the boys came across them this evening. After all, they are being paid to be charming to everybody, aren't they?"

Seeing the concerned look on Tanya's pretty face, Marina, being fond of the younger woman, conceded, "Hmmm, maybe so, but I am bitterly disappointed nevertheless!"

Detecting a soft note in Marina's haughty voice, Tanya smiled sweetly and whispered, "Thank you, Your Majesty! You are the very best!" and with that, the incident was largely forgotten by the world's most famous lookalike.

The remainder of the evening was a great success, with no further drunken disturbances. Elvis and George mixed and mingled, causing great squeals of excitement from the ladies and envious glances from the gentlemen. The security officer had authorised one of the bouncers to chaperone the lookalikes, making sure there would be no further frenzied outbreaks from intoxicated females.

Wiggling her way from table to table, Crystal smiled jubilantly as enchanted guests vied for her to join their individual groups, the women slyly watching their partners' reaction, forced smiles frozen on overpainted faces as the amazing Crystal flirted and cosied up to their menfolk, cameras flashing, capturing the elation on the gentlemen's smitten faces.

Settled back at her table once again, surrounded by Royalist enthusiasts, Marina picked up the conversation from where she had left off, charming her admirers as they listened in wonderment to her words of wisdom.

Graciously dancing with every member of the opposite sex who plucked up the courage to ask her, Tanya's wide smile and sparkling eyes belied the torment that was escalating in her head, threatening to spoil the rest of the evening for her. As she whirled in the arms of besotted young men, the scarlet silk cloak draped over the scarlet bathing suit wrapped itself sensually around her stunning figure, making her all the more desirable.

All too soon, the Great Gatsby Swing Band began to strike up with Sinatra's *New York, New York*, indicating the end of a most successful evening for the guests, the clients and a triumph for Top Drawer Agency. Much to Marina's displeasure, Crystal, Rob and Neil had decided to have a nightcap in the hotel's luxurious and elegant lounge bar, eager to keep the excitement of the evening alive for as long as possible, even though they had an early morning flight back to London.

As soon as her weary head lay on the white down pillow, blonde hair hanging untidily around her shoulders,

Tanya found with dismay that she could not fall asleep, even though she was totally exhausted. Aarne's square, serious-looking face flickered fleetingly through her mind, causing her to shudder.

Aarne Virtanen, her live-in lover, whom she had met barely six months earlier, had charmed her into bed quicker than any other man. Aarne – sometimes amusing, sometimes confrontational, sometimes caring, sometimes spiteful, but always dominant – had become almost unbearable lately to be with. From the first day they had met at a mutual Finnish friend's birthday gathering, this strong-minded countryman of Tanya's understood fully that she had a successful lookalike career as Pamela Anderson. In the beginning, he was impressed with his new girlfriend's celebrity status and would boast constantly to his group of male friends, most of whom were from his own country.

For the first two or three months of their relationship, everything was wonderful and although she had always valued her independence and freedom, Tanya began to think seriously about settling down with him.

Now tossing and turning trying desperately to sleep, an exhausted Tanya arose from the comfortable king-sized bed and trotted towards the minibar on the opposite side of the room, retrieving a small bottle of German Riesling, which she proceeded to drink in one go. Returning to the warm bed, Tanya prayed the sweet wine would help her sleep so that her tormented mind would not ponder on her crumbling relationship, and how in her anguished and deepest thoughts, she hopelessly sought a safe way of finishing it.

The final deciding factor for Tanya to end their association was when Aarne forbade her to accept the job in Düsseldorf. That evening, she had argued with him fervently that the contract for this latest job had already been signed, thus making her responsible for all costs incurred by the client if she did not honour her commitment. Reluctantly, Aarne had agreed that under the circumstances she should go, but that this must be her last job as a lookalike.

Alone the following morning at Top Drawer Agency, Belinda sat daydreaming, lost completely in her thoughts. This time, they were not of Frank, but of her close friend and fellow lookalike, Tanya Christensen, who had called her an hour earlier once she and the others had arrived back in London.

Belinda was relieved to hear that everything went so wonderfully well in Düsseldorf and that the German clients had, as always, treated the English lookalikes as if they were the real stars.

It is usual practice that most lookalike and tribute artistes report back to their agent as soon as possible after completing a contracted job, whether it had been in the UK, Europe or further afield. This way the agent learns first-hand how the artistes were treated by the clients and whether or not some changes should be implemented in order to protect their people at all times. In turn, clients also telephone the agents giving their opinion and assessments of the impersonators they had paid highly for.

Although Frank was due in London the following evening, Belinda could not shake the disquiet she was feeling with regards to Tanya. When the two had met recently for a chat, she felt her close friend had not been completely truthful with her. It was as if Tanya was holding something back from her, some secret that she could not even trust her dearest friend with.

This saddened Belinda because they had always confided in each other in the past. Making her mind up to cautiously approach this subject face to face with Tanya as soon as possible, Belinda switched on her laptop as images of Frank swept into her mind causing her to catch her breath.

Chapter 36
London Liaisons

Unbeknown to Belinda, Frank Lanzo had arrived at Heathrow Airport two days earlier. There was no other possible way of making sure Belinda would never learn that her deceased husband Matt Flynn had been an Associate Member of the Society and that the two men in her life had become close friends.

It had been a while since Frank last visited London and a shudder passed through his body as he stepped from the plane onto the airstair, guardedly following the other passengers as they descended down and onto the waiting shuttle bus. Sergie had arranged to meet him in Arrivals. Although Frank thought of London as his second home and was thrilled at the prospect of seeing Belinda again, he was apprehensive to be back at the Soho betting office which still held sad memories for him of Matt's untimely and unjust demise.

"Hey, Frank, over here!" came the baritone voice of Sergie Belladoni, as he waved fervently from behind the crowded barrier in the arrivals lounge. Frank laughed to himself; good old solid Sergie; always reliable, always punctual and always wearing that boyish grin which had a way of calming Frank's demons.

He walked quickly over to his paesano. Although neither were born in the old country, they were by blood and heritage fellow countrymen – fellow Italians.

"Come diavolo sei?" *(How the devil are you?)* asked Frank as the two men hugged each other fondly.

"Facendo del bene," *(Doing good)* came a grinning Sergie's reply. "Let's have some lunch at the airport and you can tell me what has been going down in Vegas," he suggested, slapping Frank jovially on the back.

They ate heartily at one of the more exclusive restaurants. Frank reminded his paesano that while in London he should, as always, be known by his pseudonym of Gene Capalti. Frank had decided on the flight over that he would bring Sergie into his confidence regarding the fate of Vinny Messina and Lukey Amato, his lip curling in distaste when he mentioned the infamous Pellini brothers.

Listening intently as the Capitano Numero Uno divulged privileged information to him, Sergie, his head slowly shaking from side to side, tutted as Frank described how Vinny and Lukey had tried to escape the Las Vegas meeting, only to be detained by the Society's soldiers.

"I presume the brothers have dealt with Messina and Amato by now?" asked Sergie, noticing a sudden look of sadness had covered Frank's face.

Turning his eyes to Sergie, Frank slowly nodded, his face sullen as his tortured mind tried to erase the images of what had been left of the two young culprits after the Pellini boys had completed their interrogation.

Placing his right hand on his heart, Frank, lowering his voice, remarked, "I tell you this in confidence, Sergie; those monsters carried out a sadistic inquisition in order to find out the name of the third culprit. I swear the Pellini brothers are the devil's spawn!"

Curiosity filling his senses, Sergie cautiously asked, "Did they succeed? Do they have the name of the indiscernible culprit?"

"Who knows?" replied Frank fidgeting in his chair. "For now, the Society is playing this one close to its chest, although I have been informed that both myself and Aldo will shortly be advised of the aftermath," he added, lifting his wine glass and drinking slowly, savouring the nectar.

Placing the empty glass back on the table, allowing the attentive waiter to refill it, Frank focused his brown eyes on Sergie and cautioned, "This conversation stays between us, capisce? Even Joey must hear nothing about this until I inform you otherwise."

Stretching his arm across the green, white and red-coloured tablecloth, Sergie placed his right hand on Frank's left arm, and looking his esteemed mentor in the eyes, replied, "Capisce."

For the following two days together with Sergie, Frank was kept busy carrying out a huge audit of accounts and financial documents, not only in regards to the Soho betting office but for the Society's other two offices in Victoria and Maida Vale. Annoyingly for Frank, the visibility in the back room of the office was becoming quite dense due to Sergie's chain-smoking.

Suddenly, getting up from his executive chair and stretching his legs, Frank opened the windows then berated Sergie for not giving up the filthy habit as he had promised many times.

The employees were very happy to have Gene Capalti back with them after so long and chatted with him intermittently during the course of the day, making sure he had everything he wanted during his short visit. They had always respected their American bosses, finding them solicitous and generous.

It was good to see Joey Franzini looking so well. As Frank and Sergie entered the Soho betting office, the young American glanced up and hurried from behind the large counter, his arms outstretched in welcome, the smile on his beautiful childlike face completely genuine.

"Gene!" came his loud exclamation as he reached Frank and threw his arms around his revered mentor. "It's great to see you again!" Turning then to his staff, he bellowed, "Hey, guys! Gene Capalti is back!" causing the employees to whistle and yell their greetings noisily at Frank. Customers glancing up fleetingly from studying the form, curiosity showing on their faces, wondering who this person was that generated such elation.

The two Americans hugged each other warmly, Joey looking somewhat overwhelmed at having his mentor back albeit for just a short stay.

"Dinner on me this evening!" he declared, ushering Frank towards the back room as Sergie chatted with some of the customers, explaining who the stranger was.

By the end of the day, Frank was beginning to feel at home once again in this vibrant city which held bittersweet memories for him. He found himself wondering about Joey. Although the young New Yorker appeared carefree, Frank sensed an edginess in Joey's demeanour of which he had never noticed before.

As soon as Joey was out of earshot dealing with one of the punters, Frank took the opportunity of taking Sergie to one side enquiring whether he had noticed Joey's uncharacteristic edginess.

Frowning as he took time to reflect on Frank's question, Sergie replied, "Joey's good, Frank, though recently he had a bust up with his latest lover. A female, this time!"

"Sorry to hear that," responded Frank, walking across to the window and glancing out onto the busy Soho streets. "Possibly that is causing his uneasiness?" he suggested.

"Yeah! I guess that must be it, but between you and me, paesano, I know Joey is not over James Swift!"

Turning immediately from the window, his voice rising somewhat in anger, Frank instructed, "Do me a favour, Sergie. Do not mention that lowlife to me!"

"Hey, buddy! Okay! Just saying, that's all!" replied Sergie in his own defence. Rising suddenly from his chair and walking over to Frank, the big man continued, "I have wet-nursed Joey through his traumatic grief then watched him crawl back slowly from the dark place until he was completely over it, or so I thought! Joey has plenty of company, both male and female, but often I see the deep sadness in those hazel eyes and I know where his mind's at."

"Okay, Sergie. Excuse me for the outburst but you know I will always blame James Swift for causing Matt's tragic death," replied Frank, apologetically.

Playfully slapping Frank on the back, Sergie walked over to the tall maroon coloured refrigerator and suggested, "How about a nice cold beer, paesano. A great idea, don't you think?"

"Now that, paesano, really is a great idea!" agreed Frank as the two friends settled down, completing the six-monthly audit just as the Soho betting office was about to close after another busy day.

For Joey Franzini, apart from his beloved father Paulo, Frank was the man he held in the highest esteem. Frank had always believed in Joey, constantly building the younger man's confidence from the moment he commenced his career with The Society some years before. Frank thought Joey most courageous as he flew back and forth to New York and London, brazenly carrying millions of pounds sterling of dirty money through British customs, always undetected.

It was as it the gods smiled on Joey Franzini.

Shuddering, Frank recalled his own hazardous predicament in Venice, how he was framed by Pietro Gabrini, Manager of Airport Security. Since his release from the notorious Venetian prison, successfully orchestrated by the Society, Frank had never been instructed to carry dirty money for his employers again. The hierarchy of the Society consisted of mature wise businessmen who had indisputably decided that due to the Capitano Numero Uno's traumatic situation which saw him incarcerated in an Italian prison, it was no longer in their interest to order Frank Lanzo to carry dirty money in and out of the many countries in which they operated. He was far too valuable to them on the outside.

The evening arranged by Joey was completely uplifting for Frank. The three Americans hailed a black taxi from outside the Soho betting office to Gordon Ramsay's Modern French fine dining restaurant, Pétrus in Knightsbridge. Neither Sergie nor Frank had visited this Ramsay restaurant before, but both were highly impressed.

"Thought we should go French for a change," declared Joey. "Trust you guys won't be disappointed!"

"Disappointed?" echoed Sergie, as he scrutinised the restaurant's centrepiece glass-encased wine room. "I love it!"

"Frank?" asked Joey, leaning across the table and grinning at him, "what is your opinion?"

"Well now, guys," replied Frank, grinning back at Joey, his dancing brown eyes taking in the round tables covered by the whitest tablecloths and napkins he had ever seen, the amazing decor of pearlescent pink and dusky grey, bringing burlesque to mind. "If the food and wine is half as mesmerising as the decor, then we are in for a hell of a night!" he quipped, swallowing down one of the finest French wines chosen from the menu of the high-profile legendary British chef.

"I will second that!" declared Sergie, picking up the pearlescent pink menu, frowning as he found it difficult to decide on just one appetizer, main course and dessert, coveting to sample them all.

The evening was one of cross-cultural New York/Italian humour as the conversation flowed easily. Sergie was always eager to hear how things were doing in their native city.

"How did you find it when you flew over a couple of months back, Joey?" asked Frank, his head cocked slightly to one side as he waited for Joey's response to his question.

Wiping his mouth with a pure white napkin, the young American hesitated before replying. "Last time I flew over to collect the merchandise was about six weeks back but it was a whistle-stop trip, so I had no time to check out how my neighbourhood was doing, nor visit my family."

"That reminds me, guys!" intervened Sergie, his eyes clouding over thoughtfully. "Must take a trip as soon as and go see my mom and kid sister in Jersey. It has been a while!"

As if on cue, a French waiter walked around the table refilling the Americans' glasses, in an orderly and systematic manner. Without uttering a word, he placed the bottle of wine in the casket at the centre of the table before nodding his head in Frank's direction, then weaving his way through the large restaurant, disappeared from view.

Frank turned to speak to Sergie, agreeing that his paesano should take a couple of weeks' break and fly home. After all, Sergie was entitled to his vacation and Joey was more than competent to run the Soho betting office without him for a couple of weeks.

"Ain't that so, Joey?" asked Frank, looking directly at a now slightly tipsy Joey, his cherub face flushed from several glasses of wine he had consumed during dinner.

"Yeah! Of course! Go ahead, Sergie! I got plenty of support at the office," came Joey's swift response, a smile spreading across his face.

"That's settled then!" chirped in Frank. "Time to visit your mama, paesano. She ain't getting any younger!"

"She and me both!" retorted Sergie, prompting loud laughter from his two companions.

By the end of a most enjoyable evening of fine wines and lavish cuisine, the East Coast boys had this time decided against visiting Sergie's favourite London casino. It had been an exceptionally long and draining day for Frank after flying in from the Big Apple earlier that morning.

As usual, he had booked himself into the Sherlock Holmes Hotel close to Regent's Park and was trying to explain to a very persistent Joey that he was desperate for sleep and would be going nowhere apart from his desired bed. It was well past midnight as the three stood outside the Michelin-starred restaurant in a chilly Knightsbridge, Frank's right arm extended above his head as his weary eyes searched the roads for a black taxi.

"Me? I am with you, Frank!" announced Sergie, slightly swaying while having difficulty lighting a cigarette as the breeze refused to allow the flame to burn. "I have had a great evening but I am now deadbeat!" he added, turning to Joey as the young American groaned and tutted with disappointment.

"Listen, buddy, we have an early start tomorrow!" declared Sergie then turning to Frank for support, he asked, "Ain't that right, Frank?"

"Yeah! That is right!" replied Frank. "Business before pleasure!" he quickly added, glancing towards a sulking Joey who reluctantly agreed that maybe it would be better to visit the casino the following evening instead.

Hailing a black taxi, Frank quietly directed the driver to drop his two companions at their individual addresses before taking him on to Regent's Park and sleep.

As he lay his aching head on the soft down pillow, gratefully drifting into a slumber, an image of Belinda swept through his weary mind causing a smile to appear on his mouth.

Frank was somewhat surprised to see both Sergie and Joey busy in the Soho betting office when he arrived at eight-thirty the following morning. He was feeling full of energy and excitement; in fact, quite exuberant at the prospect of being with Belinda later that day. They had been apart for quite some time and Frank had astonished himself that he had not even looked at another woman. For many months now, he was conscious of the fact that he would never be truly happy without Belinda permanently in his life.

"I am impressed, guys!" quipped Frank walking over to where Sergie was chatting to one of his employees while Joey examined the form of the horses on a computer.

"Hey, Frank!" came Sergie's baritone voice. "You had a good sleep?" he asked grinning at the Capitano Numero Uno.

"Never better, paesano! Never better!" replied Frank, grinning back at Sergie.

"Coffee, Frank?" asked Joey, getting up from his chair and walking towards his mentor.

"Great idea. Thanks!" he said, walking into the back room, Sergie following behind.

When Joey entered the room, handing cups of hot coffee to his mentors, Frank asked him to take a seat for a second. Doing as he was asked, Joey looked up enquiringly at the Capitano Numero Uno.

"Joey!" said Frank, his voice catching slightly. "I appreciate you are in work nice and early this morning after our rather alcohol-fuelled evening but, I tell you, it bothers me a great deal about leaving you in sole charge of this betting office if Sergie were to fly home for a quick visit."

Irritated, Joey rose from his chair and proceeded to query Frank's remarks. Walking agitatedly up and down the room, he spent the following five minutes defending himself and why his mentor had no cause for concern.

"Listen to me, Joey!" came Frank's voice dropping menacingly. "If anything goes wrong over here while Sergie is away, there will be all hell to pay!"

"Frank! Frank!" wailed the younger American. "Did you or did you not mentor me?"

The dancing brown eyes glared at Joey.

"What the hell does that have to do with your excessive drinking?" yelled Frank, becoming exasperated.

Trying to calm his two paesanos, Sergie walked in between Frank and Joey hoping to defuse the ensuing argument.

"Hey guys! Come on! Joey! Listen to what Frank is saying. I totally agree with him. You have been drinking a hell of a lot lately!"

Without saying another word, Joey held up his hands in surrender and apologised to Frank, knowing he could not possibly deny his heavy drinking.

"Frank! You saw today that I was on the shop floor early. As you are aware, I have hollow legs and can hold my alcohol. Ask Sergie… I have never let my social life get in the way of my career. Ain't that correct?" he added, turning to Sergie for support.

Before Frank could reply, Sergie cut in.

"Yeah, Joey! That is correct but, I gotta say, just lately your drinking has been getting out of hand! I guess it is due to the recent split with your lady friend?"

Walking over to Joey, a frustrated Frank quickly broke in. "What the hell! Split or no split! That is of no importance! What is important is how the Society's London businesses will run without Sergie at the helm!"

Joey became increasingly disturbed that he had angered Frank. Attempting to calm things down just as Sergie had tried to do, he fervently assured his revered mentor that he would never do anything to jeopardise the trust that Frank and the Society's hierarchy had placed in him.

"You know as well as I, Frank," reasoned Joey, an anxious look appearing briefly in his hazel eyes, "that we are fortunate enough to have trusted employees here who will completely support me in Sergie's absence."

"Then, Joey, I suggest you quit the booze as of now, otherwise I will have no alternative but to recommend the Society replace Sergie while he takes that break. Capisce?" snapped Frank, replacing his empty coffee cup on the highly polished table.

"Hey, Frank! Joey understands! Ain't that right, Joey?" interrupted Sergie, walking over to the younger man who had sat back down on his chair once again, a forlorn look playing on his face. "Ain't that right, Joey?" he repeated.

His voice dropping to a near whisper, Joey rose from his chair and holding out his hand in a show of unison to the Capitano Numero Uno, he murmured, "You have my word, Frank, as a Man of Honour."

Accepting the outstretched hand of his prodigy, Frank declared, "Accetto." *(I accept.)*

Chapter 37
Lovers Entwined

The semi-detached Edwardian house stood silently, its carved features common of that very short era between 1901 and 1910. As Frank climbed out of the black taxi outside the well-constructed property, he was conscious that the adrenalin surging through his body was causing his heart rate to increase; it was now racing. He noticed with alarm that his legs were trembling slightly and his breathing shallow.

"Goodnight, Governor!" shouted the taxi driver, carrying out an 'about face' as the front wheels turned sixty-three degrees, courtesy of the turning circle, the party piece of the famous black London taxi.

Without turning his head, Frank raised his right arm above his head and gave the thumbs up gesture in reply.

His emotions filling his senses, Frank walked unsteadily towards the pretty entrance of his lover's house. He wondered why he felt so apprehensive. He had been to this lovely home several times before and for months had been yearning to hold Belinda in his arms. Deciding his anxiety was due to their long separation, he walked through the Edwardian arch and continued up the winding path to the blue stained-glass front door.

Before he could raise his hand to lift the lion head brass knocker, the door opened slowly framing her in the evening light, tears glistening in her eyes. Suddenly catching his breath, Frank stood rooted to the spot with fear and amazement, unable to move forward as she came towards him, gently taking his arm and ushering him inside.

Their passion and deep love for each other erupted as they clung together listening to their racing hearts. Before they had reached the spacious, beautifully furnished lounge, a surge of energy swept wildly through Frank's body. Sweeping his lover up into his arms, he carried her zestfully into the beckoning bedroom.

Barely noticing Belinda had nothing on under her red silk kimono apart from a pair of black lacy crotchless panties, he urgently yet artfully pulled off all of his own clothes, his tanned physique as strong and masterful-looking as ever. She let out a muffled groan as her eyes focused on his erect manhood, standing up ready to pleasure her. Slickly climbing onto the large bed, Frank's body covered Belinda's. Laying deftly on top of her, his lips fervently kissing hers as she felt his tongue flicking swiftly in and out of her mouth, tongues entwined sensually. She could feel his hardened manhood now pressing against her stomach as his talented tongue licked her lips, neck and breasts as her body quivered, yearning for him to enter her.

Feverishly, he reached down to her vagina, then slipping his middle finger inside her crotchless panties, he caressed her as she let out a long sensual groan, lost in paradise as her love juices flowed. As her hunger for Frank reached ecstasy, she pushed her quivering body up to him as he swiftly entered her, his swelling throbbing manhood thrusting and thrusting deep inside, bringing them both to sexual abandonment as they climaxed together, filling the bedroom with sounds of passion.

"Ti adoro e ti amo, mia cara," *(I adore and love you my darling)* whispered Frank, his face pressed in her untidy hair as she lay, body glistening, in his strong tanned arms, the smile on her lips silently divulging to him that she adored and loved him more than ever.

For Belinda, having Frank back in London for even a few days was bittersweet. The guilt she felt for having deceived Matt stubbornly refusing to go away, saddening her. Of course, she knew her wayward husband had had affairs with other women but ever since his untimely death in the tragic car crash almost two years earlier, she had carried the burden of guilt in her heart. Although she was deeply in love with Frank and when apart, missed him terribly, yet when together, whether in New York, London or elsewhere in the world, guilt would come flooding back accusingly into her mind. She had consulted her GP who explained in no uncertain terms that guilt shared a lot of symptoms with depression and he had warned her, his brown eyes holding her gaze, that depression could develop within someone with severe guilt issues. He had offered her antidepressants but Belinda politely refused. She had known several friends who had taken unnecessary advantage of the wonder drug only to become, at best, more depressed as well as paranoid.

They spent the remainder of the evening eating, drinking, talking and fulfilling their sexual desires for each other. Eyes sparkling with the deep love she felt in her heart and soul for this man, Belinda coquettishly flirted with him, giggling girlishly at his entertaining little stories about his life over the last few months.

While she chatted and laughed happily with Frank, she momentarily forgot about the telephone call she had received from Count Luigi Boggia a short time ago and the fact that she had no other option but to disclose this to her lover before he flew back home to New York.

As Frank, his head laying on her ample breasts, began to snore quietly, Belinda stared up at the high, elaborate Edwardian ceiling, the chandelier dimmed for their lovemaking. Again, she began to worry how Frank would take the news about Count Luigi's telephone call. Although she was certain the Count was simply being polite and friendly, he had suggested she should fly to the Floating City, the 'Queen of the Adriatic', and spend some time in the enchantment of Venice.

"Of course, my dear," his charming Italian accent inducing Belinda's schoolgirl blushes, "bring a girlfriend with you if you wish," he added as an afterthought before ending the call.

Remembering the confusion and sadness she felt at Frank's unreasonable jealousy when she had innocently mentioned to him the first time the Count had telephoned her, Belinda was now becoming apprehensive, quite fearful to tell her lover again. Making a decision not to mention it until the very last minute, Belinda pulled the cream coloured silk sheet over Frank's slumbering tanned body and closed her shining eyes.

For Belinda, the three days spent solely with Frank had been incredible. Sensual sexual lovemaking appeared to be their greatest pleasure. They occasionally ventured out into the busy London thoroughfare for long walks across the sweeping Clapham Common, idyllic at any time of year but during the long hot summer days, all-embracing.

Frank realised, as they strolled leisurely hand in hand, that he would be extremely content and happy to make London his home from home. Over the last few months, he had gradually become more flexible about where he should live. He had spoken at length to one of the Society's hierarchy who assured him that there was no reason why he should not relocate to the UK and continue his committed career with the Society from London, unless, of course, the Boss and Underboss felt differently.

Opening her sleepy eyes, Belinda viewed Frank's last day with trepidation, mindful that the silver-winged aeroplane would carry her lover far away, leaving her desolate and melancholy yet again.

The night before, as they lay together breathing deeply, their passions having been spent, Frank had pressed his lips to her ear and whispered, "Non voglio vivere senza di te, mia cara." *(I do not want to live without you, my darling)*

He stirred in the darkness of the bedroom as the dawn moved gently away from the ensuing sunrise. Belinda glanced at Frank, now snoring softly. She noticed the slightly parted lips seemed to be smiling at something that was solely for his delight in the secrecy of dreams. How she adored this very sensual yet sensitive man, ever since their fated meeting in Venice.

"Venice!" she exclaimed unintentionally into the early morning light of the bedroom, remembering with aghast that she still had not mentioned Count Luigi's telephone call. In that instant, Belinda made a final decision about revealing this to Frank. They had been deliriously happy during the past few days and as deceitful as it may appear, she had no intentions now of completely ruining their precious time together. The most sensible thing was to say nothing to Frank until after he had arrived back in the United States. She would then confess that she had completely forgotten to mention the call to him.

"Un penny per i tuoi pensieri?" *(A penny for your thoughts?)* whispered Frank, causing Belinda to jump in surprise. He was watching her closely as his sleepy eyes became accustomed to the morning light streaming into the casement windows, a feeling of foreboding suddenly overwhelming his senses.

Chapter 38
The Spirit of Dawn

When Belinda arrived at the agency the following day, the pleasurable smell of hot coffee greeted her. She noticed Freddie bending down in the kitchenette as he placed a saucer of water on the parquet floor for little Queenie.

"Sweet pea!" called out Freddie excitedly as he saw Belinda standing quietly smiling at him. Rushing towards his dear friend, he hugged her close before kissing her on both cheeks. Belinda's desolation lifted immediately as Freddie and the little dog made it quite clear that they were delighted to see her.

After handing Belinda a hot cup of coffee before Dawn arrived, Freddie, eyes full of curiosity asked, "Well? How did it go? Tell Freddie everything!"

There was no answer. He knew instantly from Belinda's silence as well as the look of guilt on her flushed face that she had not mentioned Count Luigi's telephone call to Frank after all.

"Oh, my God!" exclaimed an astounded Freddie, hands flaying in the air as he walked around in circles, little Queenie following close at his heels.

Placing her coffee cup down on her desk, Belinda assured Freddie she tried many times to tell Frank but could not find it in her heart to destroy their remarkable time spent together over the last few days.

"It would have ruined everything, Freddie! We were deliriously happy. Frank would have been so disheartened and I really could not cause him such anxiety!" she blurted out, hoping he would understand her reasons.

Walking over to Belinda, Freddie shook his head dolefully as his eyes, full of concern, looked into her troubled face, the intonation of his voice dropping dramatically.

"But, sweet pea! How many times have I told you? The devil makes the pot but not the lid! You know as well as I that sooner or later, Frank will find out!"

Rising from her chair, Belinda carried her coffee cup into the kitchenette and began to refill the kettle. Walking back into the office, she admitted to a perturbed Freddie that she agreed with him completely but that she just could not find the right time in the last few days to mention the call to Frank for fear of upsetting him.

"Well, sweet pea!" remarked Freddie, concern clouding his dark blue eyes, "if you do not mention it to Frank, he will presume you and the Count have something to hide!"

"Yes, Freddie, I know this, and I will definitely broach the subject when he calls me this evening," came her quick response, fidgeting guiltily in her chair.

"Make sure you do, darling girl!" encouraged Freddie, sauntering towards Dawn's office as the telephone rang, signalling an end to their sensitive discussion.

Lifting the receiver, Freddie listened quietly to the voice on the other end of the telephone.

"Yes, of course, sir! One of the agents is right here. I will put you on to her straightaway," he assured the caller. "One moment, please, sir!" he said, signalling for Belinda to take the receiver.

As she did so, Freddie, pouting knowingly, whispered to her, "A potential new client from South Africa no less!"

Eyes raised in surprise, Belinda introduced herself and Top Drawer Agency to the gentleman on the other end of the telephone, secretly wishing Dawn had been available. Although Belinda had grown considerably in confidence as a partner and agent, it was the resourceful Dawn who, with the gift of the gab and professional expertise, secured and clinched most of the foreign deals, especially those from new potential clients.

As the call ended on a very positive note, Belinda's mood brightened once more and replacing the receiver, she smiled satisfactorily at Freddie.

"Who are the new clients interested in?" queried Freddie, knowing without a shadow of a doubt that it would not be Liberace.

"Meghan and Harry. Just those two!" Belinda called out from Dawn's office dialling her business partner's number.

"That is a shame!" tutted Freddie disappointedly. "I was going to suggest perhaps I could portray President Nelson Mandela if he were on the list!"

"Oh, Freddie!" giggled Belinda. "You are incorrigible! You look nothing like Mandela! You know Alvin Ebete is our finest President Mandela!"

"Ah well! One can only live in hope, sweet pea!" replied a sulky Freddie, concentrating once again on the pile of unopened envelopes sprawled across his desk.

The remainder of the day passed by smoothly. Freddie becoming despondent when two new enquiries came in requesting several tribute artistes and lookalikes. Sadly, he noticed that Liberace was missing from both lists. Studying the names of those that were enquired about, Freddie noticed that Dame Joan Collins was down for one of the potential jobs.

"Are you available for a photo shoot with Liz Taylor, Audrey Hepburn and Marilyn Monroe, sweet pea?" he called to Belinda.

Looking up from her computer screen, Belinda answered him with an inquisitive look.

"Photo shoot, darling! In London, portraying some of the most prominent female movie star icons of the Golden Age of Hollywood of which La Collins is one, is she not?" he announced, gesturing theatrically with his hands as he grinned at Belinda.

"Excellent! The Dorchester Hotel no less!" she exclaimed, reading through the request. "It has been a while since I adorned myself as Dame Joan!" she added as an afterthought, turning towards the mirrored wall emulating the actress' pout.

"Freddie, would you please call the others listed for the photo shoot and I will deal with the Hollywood-themed evening enquiry," she requested gently, noticing the disappointment on his face. Conscious of how desperate Freddie was to portray Liberace again, Belinda's heart went out to him.

"Things will look up for your character, Freddie! You'll see!" she mollified, hoping to reassure her dear friend that a job would come in for him soon.

"Actually, I am thinking of dying my hair blonde and becoming a lookalike for Leonardo DiCaprio!" declared Freddie, prancing around the office, bringing to mind Beau Brummell, rather than the iconic American actor.

"Who? Leonardo Da Vinci?" came Belinda's piercing remark, almost choking on her coffee.

"Oh, please! I said DiCaprio, sweet pea!" was Freddie's self-assured reply, studying his reflection in the walled mirror.

"Oh! Freddie, darling!" appeased an amused Belinda, trying not to upset him. "Where is your resemblance to Leonardo DiCaprio?"

"Well, we are both Scorpions!"

By the end of the working day, all selected lookalikes and tribute artistes had been contacted and provisionally booked. Belinda had notified both Max Rushton and Ada Demir and was delighted to tentatively book them for the South African job scheduled for five days' filming in the famous Sun City Resort and Casino at the end of July.

That same evening, as Belinda prepared to have a long luxurious bath, her mobile began to ring impatiently. Rushing to answer its intrusion into her secret thoughts, she was conscious of those butterflies building up in her tummy as Frank's husky voice greeted her.

After the usual niceties and whispered promises of how much they missed and loved each other, Belinda was startled when Frank, dismay now prevalent in his voice, asked, "Why didn't you tell me that Luigi had telephoned you?"

Becoming flustered, and anxious to defend herself, she admitted to Frank that she thought it best not to mention the call to him because she knew he would become frustrated and angry as he had done in the past.

"I am sorry, darling, but I did not want to spoil our wonderful time together," she remonstrated to him, hoping he would understand.

His reply made her blood run cold.

"It rips my heart out that you deceive me, Belinda."

Suddenly shaking inside, Belinda tried to console Frank. She was conscious of her voice trembling slightly as she accused him of being unnecessarily jealous and suspicious.

"Why does it anger you so much that your closest friend, who is like a brother to you, telephoned me out of politeness?" she asked, before continuing without waiting for his answer. "You seem to forget that he has always been there for you. I assure you, Frank, Count Luigi has never been anything but a friend and gentleman to me."

"Maybe so, mio caro, but as fond as I am of Luigi, he is a tough act to follow!" replied Frank, dismay still lingering in his voice.

"Frank! Frank!" cried Belinda, her voice faltering with emotion. "Please do not be like this! You know how much I love and adore you. As far as I am concerned, you are the toughest act to follow, not the Count!" she emphasised, tears forming in her eyes.

"Forgive me, il mio amore, I guess I will always be jealous of another man's attention to you," admitted Frank, dismally. "Especially a man like Luigi!"

For a long time into the evening, they chatted endlessly, neither one wanting to be the first to say goodbye. Frank revealed to Belinda how Count Luigi had telephoned him from Venice earlier that day to discuss a future project, then casually mentioned to Frank he had called Belinda to ask after her welfare and hoped Frank would not object to him telephoning her. Facetiously, Frank had warned Count Luigi Boggia off his woman, but a disturbing feeling deep in the American's soul prompted him to be very vigilant nonetheless.

When at last they finally whispered their goodbyes and undying love for each other, Belinda, walking slowly towards her bathroom, realised she must never allow Frank to learn that the Count had asked her on more than once occasion to join him in Venice.

Sometime later that evening, alone in his plush New York penthouse, Frank, his heart full of despondency, remembered how troubled he had become when Luigi informed him during their telephone conversation that Belgium's specialised Diamond Police had reopened the mysterious unsolved diamond heist case that took place in Antwerp's Diamond Centre the previous year. He shuddered as he recalled how perilous it was for them to leave Belgium and of how the Count's talented bodyguard and chauffeur, Alessandro Longo, sped expertly towards Italy and safety, carrying the distinguished diamond thieves and their red-hot merchandise.

The following day saw a refreshed looking Dawn back in control. She and Belinda spent the best part of the morning making sure the contracts from the new South African client were flawless and exact. As always, Belinda never ceased to marvel at her partner's business prowess and proficiency and after a telephone call direct to Johannesburg, Dawn had professionally manipulated the new clients to acceding to all her terms and conditions regarding Top Drawer Agency's acclaimed lookalikes.

A little later as the two lady agents were finishing for the day, a knock was heard at the door.

"I'll get it!" announced Belinda, rushing towards the oak door and opening it.

"Good evening, ladies! Just driving by so decided to stop to say hello!" came the dulcet tones of Lady Denise Ava as she strode into the office, smiling and glancing around. A look of disappointment showing on her face and she exclaimed, "What! No Camp Freddie?" before walking over to Dawn and kissing her agent on both cheeks in greeting.

Turning to Belinda, she remarked, "You look lovely, darling!" sitting down and crossing her slim legs, the close-fitting yellow two-piece accentuating her feminine shape.

"Well! To what tittle-tattle do we owe this great pleasure?" jested Dawn playfully, winking at their foremost Madonna tribute artiste, fully aware that if there was any gossip worth listening to, Lady Denise Ava would be the first to pass it on!

Choosing to ignore her agent's sarcasm, the Lady, displaying the famous gap in her Hollywood smile, grinned good-naturedly.

"Driving past so thought I would say hello and see how business is doing," she offered, placing her black leather handbag down onto the thick grey carpet before accepting a cup of coffee from Belinda.

"What happened to Freddie and Queenie?" she asked glancing around again as if they would suddenly appear.

"Nothing at all, my dear!" replied Dawn, offering her visitor a chocolate biscuit. "Freddie left early for a change, that's all."

"Aww, sorry to have missed them! Say hello for me, will you?" requested the Lady.

"Yes, of course we will," replied the agents simultaneously.

After interesting gossip about one of the other lookalikes, Lady Denise Ava, upon finishing her coffee, leant over to place the empty cup on Belinda's desk then asked whether there had been any enquiries for her.

"I must be losing it!" she tutted irritably when Belinda shock her head apologetically. "It has been a while since this agency last booked me!" she exclaimed, pouting as she glanced from one agent to the other. "I was wondering why that would be?" she said, raising her eyebrows quizzically.

Both Dawn and Belinda spent the following half hour explaining to their concerned Madonna that admittedly, work had been a little slow of late but was now picking up nicely again. Unfortunately, there had not been any enquiries for a Madonna, but stressed in their defence they were continuously recommending all their artistes, the Lady included, to both their established and new clients.

Becoming a little tetchy, Dawn assured the Lady that Madonna had always been one of the foremost artistes to be nominated to their clients. In her professional opinion as a leading agent, she could guarantee that when the festive season came around, Madonna together with other tribute artistes would be in great demand.

"After all this time on our books and throughout your successful career with this agency, I am amazed you felt you had to question us!" declared Dawn, holding the gaze of the embarrassed Madonna impersonator.

"Oh! No! No! I apologise profusely if I offended either of you," responded an anxious-looking Lady Denise Ava, not relishing the thought of upsetting an indignant-looking Dawn Jarvis. "It is just that I heard through the grapevine that Lady Gaga lookalike is booked on the TV commercial for Red Roof Promotions," she stuttered, somewhat embarrassed.

"And?" queried Dawn, her eyes penetrating her foremost Madonna.

"And I am a little surprised really because I have worked for Ref Roof Promotions in the past," explained the Lady, hunching her shoulders.

Belinda and Dawn glanced at each other before Belinda decided to answer the Lady, hoping to appease her. "Lady Denise," she uttered gently, "we are all familiar with the nature of this business. One day you are in, and the next you are out. Lucky for you, Madonna will always be in. Lady Gaga is in high demand these days along with Queen Elizabeth, President Trump, 007, Marilyn Monroe and Elvis. These are currently our A-team, although as you are quite aware, our A-team can also change. It all depends on who is topical at the time!"

Watching the Madonna tribute artiste closely, her head nodding in agreement with her business partner, Dawn quickly interposed, "The rest of our artistes, as professional and authentic as they may be, are currently part of our B-team but we are fully aware that this agency would not flourish without both teams working alongside each other!"

Dawn, managing a weak smile, continued, "But, it is our A-team that are our crème de la crème!"

"Yes. Yes, of course!" replied a humbled Lady Denise Ava. "I know this is the finest agency and I really do appreciate all you ladies do for me. I just hope some work comes in for Madonna soon."

"I am quite confident it shall, my dear Madge!" encouraged Dawn. "Whatever would the world be like without you, Your Majesty!" she added sarcastically before offering the crestfallen Lady Denise Ava another chocolate biscuit.

Chapter 39
The Risk Takers

When Ada Demir replaced the receiver after speaking to Belinda, an emotional conflict of feelings overwhelmed her senses. The first was of elation, that she would be alone with Max for five days and nights inasmuch as the South African job would be confirmed. The second was of trepidation, that Mehmet may not agree to her accepting this very prestigious lookalike job, since it would entail her being thousands of miles away from him. Although this particular job offered an extraordinarily high fee, Ada was concerned that Mehmet may oppose to her signing the contract.

Ever since the wonderful Windsor job some months earlier when Mehmet insisted on driving her all the way there and back home again the same evening, Ada had been planning and plotting ways to meet Max without Mehmet's knowledge. Ekrem, her dearest friend, had been crucial to Ada's plans being a success, making sure she gave Ada all the alibis she needed in which to spend time with her lover. Ada was conscious of hot flushes suffocating her whenever she recalled the Windsor job and the many pretty waitresses flirting with Max as they vied for his attention.

Max and Ada were now more in love than either of them ever dreamt possible. Without Ekrem's friendship, they both knew it would have been impossible for them to meet at Max's London flat.

Over the past few weeks, they had kept the same rendezvous every second Tuesday, the one day in the week that Mehmet was busy all day with company meetings. Ada had cunningly mentioned to her besotted fiancé that the Prince Harry lookalike had met a girl who was now living with him. She deviously relayed to an uninterested Mehmet that Max had met his new love interest the night of the birthday party in Windsor.

"Ada!" came Mehmet's annoyed response. "I have no wish whatsoever to know anything at all about your lookalike friend or his new girlfriend. Please do not spoil my evening!"

Knowing how easy it was for her to charm and tempt an angry Mehmet, she had by the end of the evening made sure her fiancé was in no doubt that Max was deeply in love with his new girlfriend, inventing not only the girl, but also her name.

With the seeds of her deceit embedded firmly in Mehmet's mind, Ada hoped he would no longer think of Max as a threat.

Recently, Ada began to feel her betrothed seemed less controlling. He had even encouraged her to meet occasionally with Ekrem and have a nice time with her closest friend whilst he was busy working. Only last Tuesday evening, after she had spent the whole day in bed with Max, did Mehmet show any interest to where she had been that day. As always, Ada clarified that she and Ekrem had met for a coffee and bite to eat before spending the remainder of the rainy day shopping.

She recalled the strange way he had looked at her before asking, "Did Ekrem stay with you all day, Ada?" to which she replied a little too defensively, "Yes, of course, she did; why do you ask?"

"No reason, my love," soothed Mehmet, hugging her to him. "It is just that as a mere man, I find it mystifying how you women can spend all day shopping and still arrive home empty-handed!" he exclaimed smiling down at her. Did his eyes really catch a look of sudden surprise that swept fleetingly across her beautiful face? He was quite certain they did.

Ada was not only astute but she was also gifted with sharp wit. Nuzzling up close to her fiancé, she demurely responded, "Mehmet, darling! That's because we women are fastidious when choosing the finest of costumes for ourselves, just as we are when choosing the finest of husbands!"

Her pleasing remark caused an ordinarily surly Mehmet to throw back his head in laughter then tilting her chin up towards him, he proceeded to part her lips with his hungry tongue, almost causing Ada to retch.

Sometime later that evening, Ada retrieved her secret mobile phone from its hiding place in the surrounds of her beautiful en suite bedroom upstairs in her family's double-fronted house. She dialled Max's number.

Impatiently drumming her slim fingers on her French Château white dressing table, she was about to end the call when her lover finally answered.

"Hi, darling," she whispered "What took you so long?"

"Was just shoving a TV dinner in the microwave, my beauty" declared Max, before adding jokingly "Now you know how Royalty really lives!"

The two discussed their latest provisionally booked job in Sun City, sometimes referred to as the Lost City.

"I checked it out," announced an excited Max. "Apparently it is situated in the North West Province of South Africa, about 140 km from Johannesburg."

"I just hope Mehmet will agree to me going," said Ada, her voice full of disquiet.

"Why wouldn't he agree?" queried Max, a feeling of anger sweeping his senses as he thought about the dominance Ada's fiancé had over her. Before she could answer, Max quickly continued, "You have told him that I am all loved up with a new girlfriend?" he questioned, his voice taking on an irritable tone.

"Yes! I did, Max, but if I know Mehmet, he will try to find something else to put in my way!" she answered, lowering her voice when she heard footsteps descending the staircase outside her bedroom.

"Oh! I doubt that very much!" replied Max assuredly. "The fee is amazing and if I know anything about mercenary people, he will agree to you signing that contract, especially now that he thinks I am no longer a threat," added Max, sniggering.

Arranging to meet at Max's flat the following Tuesday, the lovers finally whispered goodnight to each other before ending their secret call.

Ada found it very difficult to sleep that night. Although Mehmet appeared to be more relaxed and less controlling these days, a strong feeling of despondency seemed to be suffocating her.

At long last, as the darkest night sky paved the way for the anticipated lightness of dawn, Ada buried her face in the soft pillows and gratefully drifted into slumber.

Just a few miles away, sipping slowly from a tumbler of whisky held in his right hand, a troubled Mehmet, alone in his flat, ended his call to Zehab, an acquaintance of Mirac, his brother. Swallowing the remainder of the sharp, brown liquid down in one gulp, Mehmet was stunned when Zehab confirmed to him that Ekrem had not been with Ada the previous Tuesday. He had trailed her from her home to The Mall in Wood Green where she had met with two young women, but neither of them Ada.

Zehab assured Mehmet he had kept Ekrem in his sights without her knowledge for most of that day and Ada did not arrive at any time whatsoever.

Mehmet was completely satisfied that Zehab, who had come highly recommended as the most prominent pursuer in the Turkish Muslim community in London, had carried out his sleuth investigation thoroughly.

"I have all the evidence you need, Mr Tekin, right here on my Canon 5D Mark III," boasted a confident sounding Zehab. "Ask your brother Mirac why they refer to me as the Invisible Stalker" he urged, letting out a gruff laugh.

"Yes, Zehab, I have heard why," came Mehmet's impartial reply. "I will have another job for you within a week or so. Can we meet beforehand to discuss this please?" he enquired of the other man, his voice sounding hoarse.

"But, of course, Mr Tekin. Just decide when and where you would like us to meet and I will be there!" assured Zehab assertively. "I could then also personally hand you the video confirming how the young lady Ekrem spent last Tuesday."

After requesting that Zehab merely call him Mehmet, the two men bid each other lyi geceler *(goodnight)* before the connection was terminated.

For a very long time, Mehmet sat silently staring into space as he wrestled with his inner demons. His tormented mind tried unsuccessfully to ignore the tenacious voices in his head vilifying Ada. One thought kept recurring in his distressed mind. Why had Ada lied to him without batting an eyelid, assuring him that Ekrem had been with her all day on Tuesday? The insistent vindication whispered by his voices kept repeating over and over. "Wake up, you idiot! It is obviously another man!"

Much to Ada's astonishment, a few days later when she mentioned to Mehmet that the agency had asked for her availability regarding a prominent job in South Africa, he agreed instantly to her accepting the contract. Even when she disclosed that it would be five days duration and that Max was also pencilled in to portray Prince Harry, Mehmet consented to her going.

"After all, my love," whispered Mehmet to his beautiful fiancée, "apart from the sizeable fee, I am confident that your lookalike friend is no longer a threat so I insist you accept without delay!"

Ada was mystified. Her betrothed was such a controlling jealous man and ever since she had been asked for her availability for the job, she had been dreading having to broach the subject to him.

"Oh, Mehmet!" she squealed before throwing her arms around his strong bull-like neck. "Are you sure you are happy for me to accept this job?" she asked, peering up into his dark eyes before nuzzling her nose against his left ear.

"Yes, of course I am. We cannot let another Meghan Markle lookalike steal your crown, can we?" he reassured, drawing her close to himself where she felt his manhood stiffen at her nearness.

"Oh! Thank you, darling!" she gasped, easing herself gently away from his grip.

"That is settled then!" announced a smiling Mehmet. "Now let us enjoy the rest of the evening, my love," he encouraged, pulling her close again. She prayed he could not feel the tenseness in her body at his nearness.

"What did I tell you?" came Max's rather smug remark when Ada had called him disclosing the good news. "We will have five long days and nights together! I am over the moon!" blurted out a joyful Max, smiling widely when he heard Ada giggling.

"Yes! I cannot wait, my love!" declared Ada, her voice dropping automatically for fear she could be overhead from within her beautiful en suite bedroom. "Roll on July and Sun City!"

"Yes," giggled Max. "And sin we shall!"

Mehmet was anxious to appear his usual efficient and methodical self, although the inner voices in his head seemed to be ever present these days. He had spoken at length with his therapist, Mr Havers in Wimpole Street, who strongly recommended that Mehmet start a new course of medication which he was happy to prescribe immediately.

Apart from his close family, nobody knew of Mehmet's bipolar disorder, not even Ada nor her family. Over the years he had managed it well with prescribed medications and monthly visits to his therapist but lately he had noticed that when he was depressed or anxious, those malicious whisperings would begin to torment him.

Mr Havers had stressed to Mehmet many times that he was not mentally unwell and that auditory hallucinations could be suffered by people with bipolar. However, Mehmet refrained from informing him that, although the talking therapies were essential in improving his capacity for coping with the highs and lows of life, the forceful voices were becoming more frenzied and more malign.

It was Thursday and a troubled Mehmet had just arranged to meet with Zehab the following day. They agreed upon The Barrowboy & Banker in London Bridge. Mehmet had strongly recommended this grand split-level pub, feeling he could breathe easier here because of its very large windows and double height ceiling. He also enjoyed the impressionable gallery with its winding staircase that seemed to disappear into the rafters.

"How will I know you?" he asked Zehab before terminating the call.

"No problem, Mr Tekin... I mean Mehmet... I shall know you, sir. Mirac tells me you and he are like twins, only he is better looking!" came Zehab's jesting reply.

Choosing to ignore Zehab's last remark, Mehmet bid the other man goodnight.

"That is excellent!" exclaimed Dawn as she replaced the receiver. "Ada Demir has just confirmed that she is available for the South African film and will scan the signed contract over immediately," she declared, looking up from her computer and breaking into a satisfied smile.

"That is wonderful!" agreed Belinda. "Max and Ada are now set to go!"

"Oh, how fabulous!" came Camp Freddie's voice from the kitchenette. "How I would love to visit Sun City with all those suntanned male bodies running around everywhere!" he remarked appearing now in the doorway, a sulky pout displayed on his mouth.

"Me too!" giggled Belinda. Turning to Dawn, she asked light-heartedly, "Do you think Freddie and I should chaperone them?"

Throwing back her head and letting out a loud laugh, Dawn, appreciating her partner's jesting declared flippantly, "Chaperone indeed! Whatever do you mean? I would have to send a chaperone to chaperone you two gooseberries!"

"No! No!" interrupted Freddie, twirling around the office. "Let me play gooseberry, please!" causing Belinda and Dawn to burst into laughter.

"Why would you want to go, Freddie? I thought you were not keen on Ada," queried Belinda playfully, watching her friend as he studied his handsome face in the walled mirror.

"Who said anything about Ada Demir?" replied Freddie, admiring his own reflection. "I could chaperone Max!" he added, sauntering back to his desk, little Queenie watching his every move.

"You could, but you will not!" declared Dawn still grinning widely. "No chaperones on this job, I am afraid. Our new clients have paid handsomely for our foremost Meghan and Harry and we do not want to upset the apple cart, do we?" she urged, drinking down the last of her now cold coffee.

"Oh, by the way, ladies," announced Freddie, pottered back into the kitchenette to refill the kettle for tea, his voice elevating, "I am throwing a surprise birthday party Saturday week for Syd. Big Gerty and Fanny are happy for us to use their place as it is so much bigger than mine. Obviously, you are both invited and please bring whomever you wish, within reason, of course!" he added nonchalantly.

"Belinda!" he called popping his head out of the kitchenette. "Please extend the invitation to Bryanne and

Simon; they are such fun!" he giggled, before turning his attention to Dawn. "Do bring Maurice and the teenagers. I would love to meet them all," he suggested, before urging Belinda to ask Tanya and her bloke as well.

"How lovely!" remarked Belinda, looking up from her computer and smiling sweetly at Freddie. "What a nice thing to do for Syd's birthday. I will call Bryanne and Simon later and, Tanya, of course."

"Yes, it is a lovely thing to do," agreed Dawn. "Thank you for the invite Freddie. I shall have a word with Maurice this evening."

Just before the end of the busy working day, Dawn decided to go to the post office before making her way home a little earlier than usual and asked Camp Freddie if he would answer the few remaining emails that she had left unopened in her inbox.

Belinda was busy tying up any loose ends regarding contracts for Red Rooftop Promotions for their imminent television commercial concerning a new competitive network provider. She had carried out the final checks over the telephone with all lookalikes involved but became anxious when she could not contact Bernard Shaftoe.

When Bernard finally answered his mobile, the President Trump lookalike explained that he had been at Man About Town salon in Mayfair having a hair trim, facial and manicure.

"Gotta look the part, honey!" he quipped to a relieved Belinda. "After all, I am one of the richest guys on the planet!" he joked before informing his agent that he was ready and excited for the television cameras the following day.

"Have a good one!" she told him before terminating the call, but Belinda was conscious of that unsettling feeling that seemed to flood her senses whenever Bernard Shaftoe was booked on a job. Although he was their principal President Trump, mishaps seemed to follow him like a shadow. She recalled how Marina Greenslade had disclosed to Dawn and Belinda that Bernard had been a complete menace on their last job. Of course, the whole industry knew how scathing Marina could be, but when she had finished telling them, they both felt an overwhelming feeling of disquiet.

"I know I drive a hard bargain, ladies," admitted Marina glancing at both of her agents simultaneously, "but your Trump fellow was literally stalking a handsome young man for a good part of the evening!" The last word was lost in her deep intake of exasperated breath.

"There he was, President Trump! Flirting outrageously with the same handsome young man in a corner of the ballroom, his right hand on the young man's shoulder which prompted one of the organisers to walk over to him requesting he join me and the photographer immediately, which of course he did."

Frowning now, she looked directly at Dawn and asked, "I didn't realise Bernard was homosexual, did you?"

"Homosexual?" echoed a startled Dawn. "Oh! I doubt he is homosexual. He loves the ladies far too much!" she proclaimed, tutting whilst she shook her head.

"What do you think about him?" Marina asked, turning her steely grey eyes on Belinda, her eyebrows raised, waiting for an answer.

"Well personally, I suppose he could be bisexual," offered Belinda. "Many men and women are these days, you know," she added as an afterthought.

Waving her hand in an irritable manner, Marina, tutting loudly, replied, "No! I do not know what people get up to these days and have no wish to know either! Very soon we will have no idea whether to call one he or she! As far as I am concerned, the world has gone completely and utterly bonkers!"

Interrupting the discussion between Belinda and Marina, Dawn quickly added, "Please be assured, Marina, that I shall have a very serious talk with Mr Shaftoe. Have no fear, my dear. I shall read him the Riot Act in no uncertain terms!"

Dawn was true to her word and did in fact have a serious face-to-face chat with the American President lookalike.

Chapter 40
The Invisible Stalker

It was a little after five o'clock on Friday evening as Mehmet Tekin made his way into the imposing entrance of The Barrowboy & Banker public house in London Bridge. It had been an extremely hot day and he carried the jacket of his cashmere grey suit over his left arm as he surveyed the familiar surrounds of his favourite public house.

It was already becoming busy with customers. Several groups of noisy officer workers were enjoying the end of the working week, some of them downing too many glasses of beer to quench their thirst from the heat of the day. London, like all big cities, was most uncomfortable during the hot summer months and this year's unusually high temperatures had already broken all known records.

Walking purposefully towards the beautifully carved wooden bar, he pulled a white handkerchief from his trouser pocket and wiped his perspiring forehead.

"Mr Tekin?"

Mehmet turned towards the direction of the voice and looked directly into the face of a fellow Turk.

"Zehab?" he enquired, the faintest flutter of a smile at the sides of his mouth.

"At your service, Mr Tekin, sorry, Mehmet!" replied the other man, holding out his right hand in greeting. "Yes indeed! I would have known you anywhere, Mr Tekin. You and Mirac are very alike, I must say!" remarked a grinning Zehab, ushering Mehmet towards a table close to the bar.

"What is your poison, Mr Tekin?" he asked, walking towards the bartender.

Mehmet was already feeling irritable in the stranger's company. Although his looks were typical Mediterranean with black shiny eyes that missed nothing and a grin as wide as any he had ever seen, he spoke like a Londoner, even using London expressions.

As Zehab turned his attention to the bartender, the voices in Mehmet's head started hissing and jabbering together, making no sense at all. He coughed forcefully in order to try to suppress them from his mind but they had decided to stay around to unsettle him.

Walking back to the table, Zehab handed Mehmet a large glass of red wine then, taking a gulp of his beer, stated, "Serefe," *(Cheers)* to which Mehmet reciprocated with a sullen expression on his face, only mouthing the word.

What irritated Mehmet most about this person who referred to himself as the 'Invisible Stalker' was that Zehab allowed everything to go over his head. Nothing seemed to bother him in the slightest and it was this smug attitude that caused Mehmet's great intolerance towards the other Turk.

It was while watching with distaste, as Zehab sat down opposite him at the table, successfully slipping his long slim legs out of the way, that Mehmet suddenly remembered how desperately he needed this man's assistance if he were to find out the truth about Ada's whereabouts on Tuesday.

Mustering up enough tenacity enabling him to shut out the prattle and babble of the voices, Mehmet took centre stage and opened the seriously problematic discussion of exactly what he would ask of Zehab with regards his beloved Ada.

Sometime later, the two men shook hands civilly. Satisfied that every aspect of Mehmet's plan would be followed through professionally, Zehab walked towards the exit of the now crowded public house, turned and grinned conspiratorially at Mehmet, before disappearing out of view.

The following Tuesday was dull and downcast, a far cry from the beautiful warm days Londoners had enjoyed in the last few weeks. Ada hardly noticed the change in weather; she was far too excited at the prospect of spending the entire day with Max, deceiving Mehmet yet again, assuring him that she and Ekrem would be shopping and spending their usual girlie time together. She recalled he had asked her to buy something pretty for herself this time instead of just window shopping. To appease him, she had promised she would do so.

It was just after ten o'clock when Ada called out goodbye to her mother, Afet, as she walked briskly down the wide pathway of her parents' beautiful house in Haringey, North London. In terms of weather, it was a disappointing day and she shivered as she zipped up her dark green wool jacket. It was not cold exactly, just dismal, but somehow her feelings of excitement at being with Max again seemed to change into melancholy.

"Be careful, darling!" her mother called after her from the open door. "Do not be late, Ada. We are eating at seven."

Without turning back to her mother, Ada raised her right hand in the air and waved in answer.

Reaching Bounds Green Underground Station, she made her way down the stairs and onto the waiting tube train, noticing how few passengers were in her carriage.

When eventually arriving at East Finchley Station, Ada was conscious that her mood had become one of excitement again, clearly at the prospect of being in Max's arms very soon.

Queuing at the nearest bus stop, she boarded the 102, choosing one of the many vacant seats on the lower deck. Within minutes, she had reached her destination and carefully alighted the bus.

Walking quickly now, her heat beating with elation, she turned a corner into a pleasant leafy cul-de-sac where the trees appeared to compliment the rows of attractive two-storey houses either side. Ada stopped outside number 11, glanced up at the windows, catching the morning sunlight, then walked towards the navy-blue front door.

Before she had a chance to ring the bell, a tall young man, wearing nothing but white boxer shorts together with a beaming smile, stood there. He reached out for Ada who rushed lovingly into his arms. Raising her face up to the young man, he bent his head down to appease her waiting lips.

Secluded by a large weeping willow tree some distance away opposite number 11, a Canon 5D Mark III was expertly videoing down to the very slightest detail, every passionate embrace between the pretty fiancée of Mehmet Tekin and, to Zehab's amusement, a ginger haired man who had an uncanny resemblance to Prince Harry.

Lingering for no more than two hours, satisfying himself that the lovebirds had no intentions of leaving the little house, Zehab walked out from the shadow of the accommodating tree and back to the main thoroughfare where he spent a good part of the day drinking espressos in Starbucks and making telephone calls on his mobile.

As the Invisible Stalker had anticipated, it was almost four-thirty when the navy-blue door, proudly wearing number 11, reopened for the first time that day since the besotted couple had shut it closed behind them earlier. Zehab's camera was ready to record the parting of the ways of the lovers.

Sniggering to himself as he captured their amorous farewell, Zehab wondered how the unlikeable Mr Tekin would react once he had the proof, in black and white, of his fiancée's duplicity.

Chapter 41
Violet Eyes

Before the Dorchester Hotel photo shoot had been awarded to Top Drawer Agency, it had been a while since Belinda had been booked by a client to portray Dame Joan Collins. Being a sensitive woman, Belinda often thought about giving up her lookalike career but with Dawn and Camp Freddie's encouragement, she managed with some difficulty to push her insecurities out of her mind, remonstrating with herself that she was the principal Dame Joan Collins impersonator in the UK.

"Seems like I am not the only sensitive girlie in this jungle!" came Freddie's voice, slightly mocking Belinda for her own timidity regarding their precarious careers.

"Freddie, you know quite well that most of us in this copycat world are very insecure, me included!" replied Belinda, tutting as she shook her head in wariness.

"At least La Collins does get booked occasionally!" declared a sulky-looking Freddie. "Liberace has not tickled the ivories for ages!" he moaned.

"Oh, Freddie! Let's not go over this again! None of us have been busy lately, apart from our A-team. I am sure Liberace will be asked for soon!"

Taking in a deep breath and suddenly regaining his usual positive attitude, Freddie twirled around the room throwing his head back, and glancing up to the high ceiling, announced in his very best theatrical voice, "Dear Universe, I am still waiting for you to shine your light on me! I am waiting! I am waiting! Can you hear me? I am waiting!"

Laughing and applauding her friend's sudden change of mood, Belinda returned her attention to reading through the many emails.

It was Friday and the tantalising sun had decided to revisit grateful Londoners, lifting the city's mood in anticipation of a fine weekend. Although only the clients' second choice, both Dawn and Belinda were pleased that Melita Morgan was to portray Marilyn Monroe on the photo shoot at the Dorchester Hotel scheduled for the following Monday. Luckily for Melita, her estranged half-sister Crystal had been previously booked on that day to perform the icon's famous songs on a show produced by one of the Agency's more prominent clients in the north of England.

"I am so looking forward to working with Melita again after all this time!" remarked Belinda as she began shutting down her computer for the evening. "I called her earlier and she is thrilled to be on the photo shoot and loves the cerise *Diamonds* dress the wardrobe mistress had fitted her for."

Looking up over her new Cartier glasses, Dawn, nodding her head in agreement, replied, "Yes, it will be much nicer for all of you to have Melita on the shoot instead of Crystal. At least everything will run in a professional manner and tantrum-free!"

"Exactly!" declared a smiling Belinda, taking her black linen jacket off the coat stand. Turning, she asked, "Shall I call you Monday evening to let you know how it went?"

"No need, sweetie," replied Dawn. "You can tell me everything over a cup of coffee on Tuesday!" she suggested, blowing the younger woman a kiss.

"Break a leg!" she called after Belinda as La Collins' lookalike disappeared out of the door.

How grand and imposing the Dorchester Hotel looked, mused Belinda, as the Uber pulled up outside the main entrance on Park Lane. The stunning gardens at the front of the five-star hotel were full of colour and positively breathtaking as the weak morning sun crept arduously from under the fluffy grey clouds.

Her driver, wanting to appear professional, leapt out of his seat to open her door. The doorman, adorned in the recognisable green and gold uniform of the hotel, smiled as she walked up to him. Directing Belinda to the lifts and up to the fourth floor, he assured her that this area was assigned for the photo shoot and that a woman with a resemblance to Elizabeth Taylor had already gone up.

Thanking him for his assistance, Belinda suddenly caught her breath as Vicky Sutton's beautiful face flashed across her mind, reminding her that she would never forget her friend whose life had ended so tragically on a deserted dirt road in West Africa.

As she reached her floor destination, Belinda recalled how she had enjoyed her dress fitting afternoon with the wardrobe mistress and her talented team of seamstresses in regards to the photo shoot. Black and silver were to be the colours in which to adorn La Collins and Belinda adored the long tapering satin evening gown the wardrobe mistress skilfully fitted on her. Stealthily glancing at the beauty staring out at her in the full-length mirror, Belinda allowed herself a tiny smile of satisfaction as she 'became' Dame Joan Collins, her blue/green eyes sparking in rivalry with her diamanté necklace and earrings.

Belinda began to feel excited about the forthcoming photo shoot and how it could enhance the careers of all four lookalikes.

Stephanie Jones, now the agency's foremost Elizabeth Taylor lookalike, was sitting cross-legged on the carpeted floor chatting to a cameraman when Belinda walked into the changing area. Turning and getting up as soon as she saw her agent arrive, Stephanie Jones walked confidently over to Belinda and kissed her in greeting. This was not the first time the two women had worked together, but try as she may, Belinda could not push Vicky Sutton's image out of her mind whenever she worked with Stephanie.

As far as Dawn and Belinda were concerned, Stephanie did not quite have Elizabeth Taylor's expression in her eyes but nevertheless, she was successful in her career as a lookalike for the violet-eyed actress and if the clients were happy with her, then so was Top Drawer Agency.

Some five minutes later, Grace Simmons, bearing a strong resemblance to Audrey Hepburn, arrived chatting and giggling with Melita Morgan, who smiled and waved to Belinda. The lookalikes were offered beverages before having their make-up done, which they readily accepted. Due to the early morning call time, breakfast had also been laid on for the crew together with anyone else who did not have time to eat before leaving home.

Stephanie was not happy. During their break earlier, three different people involved with the photo shoot, approached the lookalikes giving their unasked for opinions on who looked the most authentic. Each time prying eyes turned towards Stephanie.

"Are you supposed to be Elizabeth Taylor?"

This caused her great humiliation. Stephanie felt so crushed. Being asked this question in front of her fellow artistes and her agent! An embarrassed-looking Belinda tried unsuccessfully to change the subject but the last inquisitor, a cameraman, seemed to take pleasure in criticising Stephanie's authenticity.

"Where are your violet eyes? If it wasn't for your black hair and short legs, I would never have known who you were meant to be!" he said, a mocking grin on his mouth as he stood looking down at her.

Feeling for Stephanie, an angry Melita rudely interrupted. "Then why did you ask her if she was supposed to be Elizabeth Taylor? She obviously brought the actress to your mind!" she snapped, keeping her angry eyes on the intruder.

"Just my opinion, darling!" came the reply from the insensitive cameraman. Turning his gaze on Belinda, he added, " I have to say, Joan, that you and Audrey over there have the closest resemblance to your characters!" Turning to snigger in Melita's direction, he then walked back to his waiting crew.

"We have been in this business long enough to know that as lookalikes we occasionally have to listen to unkind remarks, but we refuse to take notice or acknowledge those comments. Do you understand?" Belinda stressed to an embarrassed-looking Melita.

Blushing now as tears threatened to flood her perfectly made-up eyes, Melita, head bowed, nodded at Belinda in agreement as Grace and Stephanie patted their friend's shoulders in a comforting way.

Being aware that Melita had only reacted the way she herself had done in the past, Belinda then put her arm around the distraught girl and said encouragingly, "Now, ladies, let us forget this whole nasty incident. Let's show the mockers of this world just how fabulous we Top Drawer lookalikes really are!"

All in all, the photo shoot was a great success. After hours of posing for the cameras, the director called a wrap and everybody sighed simultaneously.

The directors had singled Belinda out as the agent and complimented her and the other lookalikes on a top-class job.

The four women, high heels kicked off from aching feet, gratefully returned to the changing area where they began to take off their costumes for their outdoor attire. Belinda had agreed to give Melita a lift to Victoria Station for her onward journey. Stephanie had already ordered an Uber for herself and Grace's boyfriend was to collect her at the hotel. Melita had spoken privately with Belinda and was thankful that she had promised not to mention her outburst with the cameraman to Dawn.

"Personally, I would have expected this from Crystal, but not you! Is everything alright?" she asked, peering into the other woman's secretive eyes.

Relieved to take Belinda into her confidence, Melita quietly relayed just how horrid Crystal had been to her lately. As they drove towards Victoria, Belinda listened quietly as Melita revealed to her.

"She makes a point of calling and gloating every time she is chosen for a job over me and as you know, that is every single time!" stressed Melita, pulling a white tissue out of her red handbag as the tears threatened yet again to spill over. Sniffing quietly, she continued, "I know she makes fun of me behind my back. I have been told about this by other lookalikes. Apparently, she refers to me as her understudy, which in a way, I suppose I am!"

Turning to a distraught Melita as they had stopped at the traffic lights, Belinda tried to console the other woman.

"Both Dawn and I believe you have been very unlucky where the Marilyn Monroe crown is concerned, but you really must try your hardest to ignore Crystal's nasty remarks."

"I do try, Belinda," replied a forlorn Melita. "You really have no idea how nasty my little half-sister can be!" she groaned, dabbing at her tear-filled eyes.

Stopping the car in a parking bay outside Victoria Station and sighing deeply, Belinda asked, "Shall I speak to Crystal for you? This immature behaviour of hers has to stop!"

"Oh no! Please, Belinda!" came Melita's adamant reply. "If Crystal knows I have spoken to you, she will be completely insufferable!" she reasoned, her voice trailing off in despair.

"Well it cannot go on! Let me know if you change your mind," Belinda emphasised, as Melita climbed out of the car.

Belinda was fuming with Crystal. As far as she was concerned, this young woman had no right to treat her half-sister in such a dreadful way, no matter what family feuds existed between them.

Chapter 42
A Birthday Party

It was Friday, the day before Camp Freddie's surprise birthday party for his young lover, Syd. Dawn had previously agreed that Freddie could take the day off, allowing him plenty of time to make sure everything ran smoothly the following evening. Dawn was proposing to attend the party albeit now briefly, as her teenage son, Ellis, had suddenly developed a sore throat and could hardly whisper his needs. Maurice had decided to work from home ensuring that if the boy's condition worsened, he would be on hand to cope with the situation. This in turn permitted Dawn to work in the agency that day after driving her daughter, Rebecca, to school.

Deep in thought regarding the warring half-sisters, Melita and Crystal, Dawn glanced up and smiled as Belinda, dark auburn hair in disarray, compliment of the unexpectedly strong winds, swept into the agency, her purple wool jacket emphasising the colour of her eyes. She greeted her business partner warmly, pecking Dawn affectionately on the cheek.

Explaining to Belinda about Ellis' sore throat and the fact that she would only be making a flying visit to Syd's birthday party, Belinda understood Dawn's dilemma perfectly. She herself had passed on Freddie's invite to

Bryanne, Simon, Tanya, Aarne and Eileen, her friend from the Old Tyme Music Hall group who had met Freddie several times. Everyone had accepted Freddie's kind invitation except Tanya, who had explained to Belinda that Aarne was working on Saturday and that he would be too exhausted to attend a party that evening.

"Why can't she come alone?" asked Dawn, peering over her glasses at Belinda.

"That is exactly what I asked," replied a thoughtful-looking Belinda.

"And?" queried Dawn.

"And she assured me she could not attend the party without Aarne because it would be unfair to him," replied Belinda, her eyes raising heavenward in disbelief.

"You are kidding!" exclaimed Dawn, eyes widening in incredulity.

"Nope! That is exactly what she told me! Personally, I am beginning to think Tanya is afraid to upset Aarne in any way whatsoever."

Dawn tutted as she stood up and walked into the kitchenette. "Maybe you could have another word with her, Belinda," she called out. "Try to get to the bottom of this relationship of hers. If we are not careful, we shall lose her altogether!"

It suddenly occurred to Belinda she had been worrying about Tanya and her relationship with Aarne for quite some time now.

"Yes, I most definitely will. In fact, I shall make arrangements to meet her sometime next week," she assured a worried-looking Dawn.

Big Gerty, her double chin appearing cumbersome, along with Fanny and Freddie, pulled out all the stops to make cross-eyed Syd's twenty-second birthday party a night to remember. Freddie had saved his money, sparing no expense in supplying delicious food and goodies together with a well-stocked bar consisting of almost every alcoholic beverage known to man. Big Gerty had volunteered to perform as barmaid for the evening and dear Fanny spent two whole days tarting up their two-bedroomed flat to make it bright and colourful for the guests. There were balloons and flowers in every colour imaginable embellishing the high ceiling and walls. Fanny had painstakingly fashioned a large pink silk banner embroidered with the words '*Happy Birthday Darling Syd*' in silver thread.

All in all, this would be a beautiful surprise for the unsuspecting birthday boy, who had been told he and Freddie had been invited for dinner by Big Gerty and Fanny.

Belinda had arrived at the party a little early, ensuring she was already there when Bryanne, Simon, Eileen and Dawn appeared. Choosing a full-length, figure-hugging, dark green dress for the occasion, everybody whistled, Big Gerty included, as Belinda walked into the bedecked spacious living room.

Freddie, little Queenie at his heel, rushed over and hugged her closely while the little dog chased his furry tail excitedly.

Whilst being introduced to Syd, Big Gerty and Fanny, Belinda accepted a tall glass of Champagne from Freddie, who gushingly stressed that she looked more like La Collins than La Collins, which caused everybody to burst out laughing!

Instantly, Belinda warmed to Syd. In fact, she thought one hardly noticed his cross-eye because the remainder of his face was quite beautiful, immediately bringing to mind a Botticelli cherub. She noticed his hair had been peroxided, giving his creamy skin a flattering glow.

Holding out his hand in greeting to Belinda, Syd shyly smiled and she noticed that although his teeth were quite white, one of his front incisors was chipped creating his vulnerable appearance.

As Syd and Belinda were chatting fondly about Freddie, a loud knock was heard at the front door and upon answering it, Fanny entered the living room followed by the delectable Bryanne and Simon, each carrying a bottle of Champagne. The smiles on their handsome faces brightening up the already colourful venue.

Circling the room several times, Bryanne, his famous white quiff bouncing about his head, asked for the birthday boy. Rushing to introduce Syd to these magnificent guests, both exquisitely attired in lavender and pink, Camp Freddie tripped and landed face down at Bryanne's feet adorned in white suede slip-ons.

Stepping back instantly and glancing down at his embarrassed-looking host, Bryanne playfully declared, "I know I am irresistible, Freddie dear, but this is not the time nor place!" Everybody roared with laughter.

Eventually Bryanne and Simon were introduced to everyone including Syd. They had decided that they liked the birthday boy very much and thought him a perfect partner for dearest Camp Freddie.

Another knock was heard. Dawn had arrived to wish Syd a happy birthday. She had brought her young daughter Rebecca with her, explaining to Camp Freddie why Maurice and Ellis could not make it.

Encouraged by her assertive mother, Rebecca handed Syd a large box beautifully wrapped in red and gold paper as she shyly wished him a happy birthday.

More guests arrived, attractive young men accompanied by other attractive young men, until Simon had to have a quick word with Bryanne who began to flirt outrageously with most of them.

"Spoilt for choice, are we, darling?" remarked Freddie, as he sidled up to a flushed-looking Bryanne.

"Oh! Freddie, darling!" came Bryanne's surprised response. "Just window-shopping, sweetheart, just window-shopping!"

Giggling loudly and giving a knowing wink to Simon, Freddie bent towards a smiling Bryanne and playfully remarked, "You will be exhausted, dear; so many windows to peer into!" before sauntering off towards the bar and Big Gerty.

All in all, the surprise birthday party was very gay indeed. Big Gerty and Fanny had invited some of their lesbian friends and the ladies mixed and mingled with the beautiful young men dancing, drinking and making merry.

Dawn, who looked very classical in a little black dress, danced and danced, thoroughly enjoying herself and quite forgetting she was only making a flying visit! Rebecca, sitting chatting with Syd and another young man, occasionally glanced towards her mother and cringed openly at some of Dawn's dance moves.

Roars of laughter could be heard wherever Bryanne happened to be. Simon dancing with Belinda, grinned down at her. His eyes shining from the effects of several glasses of Champagne, he commented, "Never a dull moment when my dear husband is about. Always the life and soul!"

"He is amazing!" exclaimed a relaxed Belinda. "An impossible act to follow!"

"He certainly is that!" exclaimed Simon, becoming ambitious with his dance moves as he excitedly twirled Belinda around the floor, accidentally bumping into Dawn who appeared deeply engrossed with her own interpretation of the music as she clung on tightly to a rather feminine-looking young man. Stopping briefly to hug each other tightly, Belinda and Dawn giggled then went back to their respective dance partners.

At first, nobody heard the gentle knock at Big Gerty and Fanny's front door. The second knock was louder and Camp Freddie moved quickly, weaving his way through the gyrating dancers to answer it. He guessed it was Eileen who had told Belinda two days earlier that she would be attending the party albeit a little later.

"Eileen, sweet pea! So glad you could make it!" declared a happy Freddie, opening the door wide and enveloping his late guest in his arms.

Camp Freddie was fond of Eileen. Ever since he had first been introduced to her by Belinda, he found this mature Thespian lady not only highly talented on stage, but also a very amusing and funny person offstage.

Taking her light brown coat and announcing her arrival at the top of his voice to the revelling guests, Freddie scanned the crowded room for Belinda. Immediately jostling her way over to Eileen, Belinda greeted her dear friend with a hug then endeavoured to introduce her to everybody all at once.

With elegant short, recently peroxided hair and long shapely legs accentuating her slim figure, Eileen Hobbs belied her true age. Belinda always loved being in the company of her friend and she thought the older woman looked charming in a knee-length purple dress matched with black patent ankle boots. Taking Eileen by the arm, Belinda walked her towards the bar and asked Big Gerty for Champagne. Looking over the bar, Belinda noticed little Queenie had settled down in his doggy basket and was curled up fast asleep, completely oblivious to the noise.

A little later during the evening found Freddie dancing with Bryanne. The whole party were in uproar as Bryanne, impersonating a female, fluttered his long eyelashes at a giggling Freddie as they whirled and twirled around the floor, both trying to out manoeuvre the other.

Somebody had asked the Alexa device to play a Scottish reel purely to see Bryanne's reaction as a Scotsman or Scotswoman! They were not disappointed. When Bryanne's ears picked up the reel, immediately he turned away from a bemused Freddie, throwing himself into the Highland fling, arms stretched towards the beautifully decorated ceiling, his white suede shoes pointed perfectly. On and on he danced, back-stepping, toe-and-heel, rocking, second back-stepping, cross-over, shake and turn until the mesmerised guests squealed, whistled and screamed for more.

A further knock at the front door was heard by no one except little Queenie who barked and barked as he made his way from the comfort of his little doggy bed through the applauding spectators. An exhausted middle-aged Bryanne finished his rendition of the Highland fling and was downing a bottle of cold water, basking in the cheers and compliments from the other party guests. Big Gerty, following the little dog, reached the door first, an inquisitive Syd by her side.

He stood there, the bright lights from the doorway shining in his dark eyes. His smile was captivating in his handsome face. The clothes he wore so stylishly were expensive. Big Gerty raised her eyes enquiringly and boss-eyed Syd, standing close behind her, wondered who this stranger could be.

"Yes? Can I help you?" asked Big Gerty, her flushed face likening her to the Babushka dolls.

"I hope you can, my dear. I am looking for Freddie Lawlor. He is a good friend of mine. I have knocked at his place but there was no reply," replied an amused Claudio.

"And who might you be?" enquired Big Gerty, turning to glance at Syd who was still standing close beside her, peering intently at the newcomer.

"I am the world-famous opera singer, Claudio de Domenico! Is Signor Lawlor there, please?" he asked, his thick Italian accent betraying a feeling of superiority.

"Who?" screeched Big Gerty. "Are you telling me you are that bloody Italian who beat up our adorable Freddie?" and upon hearing these words, boss-eyed Syd sprung at Claudio with such force that the two men fell heavily to the ground, clawing, biting and punching the singer.

The whole neighbourhood could hear Big Gerty's screams. Syd was in a frenzy until he felt strong arms pulling him off Claudio, who was completely shocked and caught off guard by the attack. His black fedora and elegant suit were quite ruined.

Now several of the party guests jostled at the open door, curious to see who or what had the audacity to disrupt their wonderful evening. Dawn and Belinda pushed their way to the front, eyes widening as they recognised the unfortunate person laying on the ground.

Catching his breath as he looked down at the crumpled heap on Big Gerty's doorstep, Freddie found it difficult to comprehend the surreal imagery of the situation. It felt as if his brain had suddenly died. It was not instructing him what to do. Could it be true? Was that indeed Claudio lying on his back, blood oozing from above his left eyebrow, his clothes ripped and torn, his fedora completely flattened?

Big Gerty watched with a smirk on her rotund face as boss-eyed Syd kicked the limp figure on the ground.

Deep in his heart, Camp Freddie still adored the Italian. Screaming loudly, he pushed an agitated Syd to one side.

"Syd!" he yelled, "What the hell do you think you are doing? Stop this insanity. Now!"

Angry at his lover's distraught command, boss-eyed Syd began to argue with Freddie but Fanny had rushed forward and placed her hand gently over Syd's mouth at the same time, ushering the birthday boy back to his curious guests.

"This has nothing to do with you. Let Freddie deal with this, please!" she emphasised to a seething Syd.

Belinda, Dawn and Eileen surrounded their dear friend, satisfying themselves that he was not in any danger. Once assured, they too returned to the swinging party leaving Freddie, Big Gerty and little Queenie with Claudio. Although Big Gerty was not at all happy to assist the Italian, she made a prompt decision not to leave Freddie alone with him, agreeing to help her darling friend. Simon, without the inebriated Bryanne in tow, joined Freddie and Big Gerty on the doorstep and helped to get a befuddled Claudio to his feet.

Syd was not happy. He had heard all about the opera singer and now felt threatened, being fully aware that Freddie had once been deeply in love with the handsome Italian. Because of the amount of wine boss-eyed Syd had consumed during the evening, he returned to the doorstep full of bravado, insisting that Freddie throw Claudio off the doorstep and go back into the party. Simon gently spoke to Syd, assuring him that Big Gerty had already called an Uber to take the Italian back to his hotel in Victoria. A grumbling Syd tutted then turned and walked slowly back into the house.

Poor Freddie was beside himself with grief and emotion. Although Claudio and Fabrizio had beaten him up badly in Italy on Christmas Eve, causing him so much sadness and distress that he had seriously contemplated suicide, he could not find it in his heart to hate his ex-lover. Seeing the Italian laying on the ground hurt and helpless made Freddie realise that he would love Claudio de Domenico until his dying day.

Freddie knew he must never admit his true feelings to any of his friends and certainly not to Syd, for they could never comprehend why, after all he had suffered at the hands of the opera singer, his heart still burned with a never-ending passion for Claudio.

When the Uber driver pulled up in the street outside the small block of flats, Big Gerty and Fanny were there to greet him. Simon and Freddie, with little Queenie trotting closely behind, helped walk a sobbing Claudio to the waiting car, who then frantically grabbed Freddie's arm and begged, his usual strong voice toned down to almost a whisper.

"Freddie, mia cara, please come with me. I have to talk to you. I have finished with Fabrizio because I found I still love you, mia cara."

With a heavy heart, Freddie wrenched himself free from Claudio's grasp then peering at the forlorn Italian now crumpled in the back of the car, replied soulfully, "Claudio, in Italy you shattered my heart and it lay on the ground in a million pieces. I would have died for your love but it is now too late. Please do not contact me ever again," and with those words, he closed the back door of the car and signalled for the driver to go. Big Gerty, Fanny and Simon wrapped their arms around a tearful Freddie, while little Queenie whimpered softly at his master's obvious misery.

Little more than a week after boss-eyed Syd's birthday party, a surprised Freddie received a text message from Claudio who had returned to his native Italy. The opera singer had opened his heart to Freddie as he had never done before. Claudio admitted he had been a careless lover. His admiration for himself as not only a handsome and charismatic man, but also an acclaimed world-class opera singer, accustomed to adulation from others, had convinced him he was indestructible.

The Italian confessed to Freddie that he now realised albeit too late, no matter how many beautiful boys came into his life, there would only ever be one Freddie Lawlor, the big-hearted Englishman whom he would miss and carry in his heart forever.

Poor Freddie was both devastated and elated. Once he had read Claudio's heart-rendering and pitiful words of lost love, he realised that no matter how happy he was with Syd, the Italian would always be a poignant reminder of Freddie's most cherished love.

Gradually life regained its steady momentum, as the enquiries for lookalikes trickled unwaveringly through to the agency, which in turn kept many iconic names working. It appeared that President Trump was one of the highest sought-after impersonators of all time but Dawn often worried that this newfound fame would have an adverse effect on Bernard's disposition. Rumours and gossip stubbornly surrounded him within the lookalike world.

The agents were no longer shocked when they heard furtively from other lookalikes, who were booked on the same job, about the antics President Trump had been getting up to. Dawn had in fact spoken at length to Bernard, who assured her that most of the tittle-tattle going around about his exuberant behaviour should be ignored. He put this down to the little green-eyed monster, simply because he was constantly in demand, placing him in the A-team which would obviously cause jealousy amongst the B-team. Dawn was not convinced.

Bernard's mindset was beginning to mirror the real American President's.

Dawn was completely dumbstruck when Bernard decided to take her into his confidence, the ever-present twinkle in his eye, as he disclosed that he was now happily settled with a new partner, a mature woman whom he had met very recently.

"Not only is she gorgeous, rich and generous, but lively in the sack for a woman of her age!" boosted a grinning Bernard, emulating the American president's accent. "Yes, ma'am!" he gushed. "I guess you could say I am now completely satisfied both spiritually and sexually!"

Poor Dawn! This had been far too much information for her, yet she would often chuckle to herself remembering how she almost choked on her coffee at the president's brazenness.

Belinda kept herself busy both at the agency and within her social life. The pain of living so far away from Frank would often cause her sleepless nights. On other occasions she found herself stretching out an arm to touch him only to awaken and find she was quite alone. Knowing she now had the choice of moving permanently to New York to be with her lover, something she had always dreamed of since their fateful meeting in Venice, somehow something was holding her back. She was reluctant to leave behind her extremely satisfying life in the London she loved. Although appreciating that she would be only a seven hour flight away if resident in New York, the thought of not seeing her family and friends as often and having to leave her exciting career and job behind, made Belinda subconsciously push this decision out of her head. She was playing for time.

Frank had at last committed himself to Belinda, even mentioning marriage, which made her glow with happiness. In that instant, Belinda had felt a sense of youthful exuberance simply because she adored and loved Frank Lanzo so much – he was her soulmate. Frank had asked her to seriously think about his offer of love and marriage but that he did not want to wait too long for her answer.

That was some months ago now and although they had spent a wonderful time together recently in London, Frank had not mentioned her moving to New York on that visit. Being a middle-aged widow, Belinda felt that such a move at her age would be a very daunting step indeed and yet she also felt that if she wanted Frank in her future, then there would be no other way of securing him than to take that daunting step.

Chapter 43
A Seed is Sowed

The voices were talking to him all at once. He could not make out exactly what they were saying. He moved quickly in circles around his large master bedroom holding his head in his hands, desperate to drown out the things they were screaming at him. His heart racing, he could feel the blood rushing to his head. Mehmet Tekin had just been handed the proof he so desperately wanted from Zehab, the renowned Invisible Stalker. Now that the evidence was in his hand, he still could not, would not, believe that his beautiful Ada had betrayed him with another man.

He groaned loudly to shut out the cacophony of voices, vilifying and disparaging his betrothed. He made his way downstairs to the living room, heading straight for the drinks cabinet where he poured himself a large whisky and soda. Drinking down the sharp brown liquid in one gulp, he poured another.

Now the voices were subsiding, becoming much quieter and calmer, allowing Mehmet to sit and think carefully about the discriminating evidence Zehab had placed in his hands regarding Ada and that obnoxious ginger-haired Prince Harry impersonator. She had lied to him, his Ada, assuring him that Max Rushton had become besotted with a new lover, when all the time it was she who was the object of the Englishman's desire.

"She lied! She lied! She lied!" screamed the voices, suddenly becoming agitated and completely audible again.

"She mocked you behind your back with her lover!" they shrieked simultaneously.

"She has made you a laughing stock!" they screeched at poor Mehmet, before breaking out in a tirade of terrifying laughter, then suddenly every one of them fell deathly silent.

During the course of the evening, although tormented, he kept watching the video over and over, trying to find a way in which to excuse his beloved Ada. Mehmet would never blame her, convincing himself in his persecuted mind that Max had bewitched her somehow.

Intending to call Ada, he reached for his mobile but changed his mind instantly as the voices began to besiege him again. It seemed to Mehmet that every time he thought of Ada, the voices would berate and reprimand him. He felt trapped and alone. He had watched in horror and disbelief as his betrothed had knocked quietly at a dark blue door bearing the number 11, and upon the door being opened, she had reached up and placed her arms around Max's neck, kissing him passionately for a very long time. Smiling and gazing up at him, Ada giggled sensually as Max placed his hand possessively on her private parts and fondled her before, arms around each other, they disappeared into the house.

Mehmet, his eyes and heart full of hate for Max, could not accept that his Ada had willingly deceived him. He now knew what he had to do. Pouring himself another large whisky and soda and sipping the liquid thoughtfully, he studied the contact numbers on his mobile. Finding the one he had been searching for, he quickly dialled it, the voices in his head quite silent now as if they approved of his intentions.

When the call had ended, Mehmet became desperate to speak to Ada, yet he knew that he must appear as normal as possible. His body and soul yearned for her but he had been drinking far too heavily and was now in no fit state to drive to her parents' home. This evening, he would have to be content with hearing her melodic voice over the telephone.

Max Rushton had been one of the most sought-after lookalikes of late. His character was often requested without a Meghan Markle. Many hospitality organisations would book just one artiste and Prince Harry was proving as popular as he had been long before he had married.

This particular week had begun on a quiet note for most of the lookalike industry, including the Prince Harry impersonator who, finding time on his hands, had arranged to meet his closest friend, Josh Roberts. They had known each other since their teenage years when they had played for the same amateur football team.

Josh, unlike Max, was of average height but thick set, his hair dark and always unruly. He had commanded many of their football games as an impressive striker. Although Max's heart was never really into sports, he enjoyed the camaraderie and played to the best of his ability, proving he could become, with dedication and determination, a fine goalkeeper. For Max, his heart beat as a Thespian and the bright lights of the show business world had always beckoned him.

Instantly noticing that the name of the public house they entered was The Windsor Castle, Josh jokingly remarked to Max that he could not have chosen a more appropriately named venue.

The two friends spent the following hour enjoying the excellent beer and atmosphere of the charming pub.

Exchanging snippets of news and gossip from their lives, remembering and reminding each other about the boys they used to play football with, Max and Josh vowed to meet up more often in the future.

Suddenly, a voice interrupted their conversation.

"Well, I never! I could have sworn you were the real thing!"

Josh was the first to glance up as a young, short, balding man wearing dark glasses walked over to their secluded table. Glancing up slowly, Max politely nodded his head to the stranger hoping he would go away, but the intruder stood looking down at him grinning. Josh peaked across to Max raising his left eyebrow.

"I have to say this, mate, but you are the spitting image of Prince Harry, even down to the ginger hair!" remarked the man shaking his head in disbelief.

Before Max could say anything, Josh replied, "He is the top Prince Harry lookalike. Great, isn't he?" to which the stranger nodded his head in agreement, still studying Max behind his disconcerting dark glasses.

"Do you have a card, mate?" he asked, speaking directly to Max and ignoring Josh who had detected a slight stammer in the man's speech. "I might be able to put a bit of business your way!" he advised, his London accent revealing that he was probably from the south of the river.

Max, along with other A-team lookalikes, were often asked for business cards from strangers, especially when on contracted jobs. Very few artistes remained true to their agents, occasionally accepting private work.

Something made Max Rushton hesitate, although he was aware that his right hand had automatically moved towards the inside breast pocket of his Ted Baker funnel neck jacket where he carried just two business cards for this very reason.

Noticing Max's fleeting hesitation, the intruder quickly declared, "Look, mate, let me explain. My name is Tom Pike and I have a very good friend called Lee MacNamara who served in Iraq."

Turning, he pointed over to the corner of the pub where he had been standing earlier with a group of noisy men. He then continued, "All us blokes here know what happened to Lee out there in that hellhole. He is now a bilateral amputee. Thing is, he will be celebrating his thirtieth birthday on Wednesday next week."

Pausing, he made a gesture of open hands to Max, who understood immediately what this man was asking of him.

"And you want me to attend as Prince Harry?"

Clicking his fingers, Tom Pike replied enthusiastically, "Yes please, mate! That would be brilliant! Just a flying visit to brighten Lee's birthday. Let me know your asking price."

Pulling out one of his business cards and handing it to Tom Pike, Max said, "Here are my details. Call me and I will see what I can do. I am pretty sure Wednesday is free."

Max could not see Tom Pike's eyes properly behind those dark glasses, but he assumed they were gleaming with satisfaction.

"Oh! By the way! Where can I check this Lee MacNamara out?" he queried, keeping his eyes firmly on the other man. "As a professional, I like to make sure I know who the birthday boy is and what he looks like," he quickly added, feeling a sense of superiority.

Josh, sitting quietly just watching and listening, could not be sure but he had the distinct impression that the bloke's shoulders stiffened briefly at Max's last remark.

"No problem, mate!" came Tom Pike's swift reply. "You can find him on social media. I will call you tomorrow evening with all the necessary details," he added, grinning broadly before turning on his heel and rejoining the group of rowdy men on the other side of the room.

"Will you take the job?" queried Josh, looking across at Max before drinking down the last drops of Guinness in his glass.

Rising from his comfortable chair in order to buy another round of drinks, Max replied in a half whisper, "Yes, Josh, I think I will, but only because this solder boy did his duty for Queen and country and is now sadly a bilateral amputee!"

"That's a good enough reason! Good on you!" replied his friend, nodding his head and grinning at Max, although for the rest of the evening, Josh could not suppress the uncanny feelings of uneasiness.

Ever since Crystal had received, some days earlier, a telephone call from Freddie informing her that Dawn was asking the A-team artistes to attend individual meetings at the agency's offices, she had been curious. Try as she may to find out more information from Freddie, her questions fell on deaf ears.

"Sorry, Crystal," came Freddie's adamant response. "All I know is that I have been asked to set a date and time with you to attend a meeting here sometime this week."

A sulky Crystal finally stopped pushing Freddie for answers and reluctantly agreed to be at the agency the following Monday afternoon.

Both Dawn and Belinda had agreed it was about time to speak seriously with their principal Marilyn Monroe. They'd had further upsetting reports from at least three other lookalikes who had recently been contracted on the same jobs as Crystal. She had been very disparaging about Melita again.

To Dawn, her artistes were her extended children, and how she enjoyed the role of mother hen! It had not escaped her notice that most of them, whether in the A or B-team, somehow found it easier and less daunting to search out Belinda if they felt they had a problem or needed some sound advice. This did not faze Dawn in the slightest; after all, she was the founder and senior partner of Top Drawer Agency and as far as she was concerned, it was feasible that she should not be too approachable. Unlike Belinda, she had never worked as a lookalike herself, so it was easily perceived that the artistes could relate more comfortably with her junior partner. All Dawn insisted on, was that through Belinda, she should learn every detail of every one of their personal concerns.

Noticing how impersonal Freddie was towards her as he answered her knock, Crystal knew instinctively that the imminent meeting arranged with both Dawn and Belinda was not going to be a particularly pleasant one for her.

Completely ignoring Queenie, who uncharacteristically remained where he had been lying, Crystal smiled sweetly at Freddie, who politely offered her refreshments.

"I would love a black coffee, please, Freddie," she replied. "May I sit down while I am waiting?" she asked demurely.

Becoming irritated by her act of modesty and with a solemn expression on his face, Freddie flamboyantly waved his arms around the large empty room declaring, "Of course! Take your pick, Crystal. The choice is yours. The ladies will be with you in a few minutes."

Freddie then disappeared into the kitchenette with little Queenie close at his heels.

Carefully carrying three cups of hot coffee on a round tray into Dawn's office, Freddie felt he could cut the atmosphere with a knife. Excusing himself for the interruption, he lay the tray carefully down on Dawn's desk, observing she sat upright on her executive leather chair, a stern look on her usually pleasant face. Not glancing up, Belinda sat beside her. Sitting cross-legged opposite her agents, Crystal glimpsed at Freddie and smiled, but he chose to ignore her insincerity. Even after all his unsuccessful love affairs, Freddie prided himself on his excellent judge of character and he had never taken to this lookalike with just one name.

After some time, a very haughty Marilyn Monroe lookalike quickly said her goodbyes and left the agency.

Freddie learned later that Dawn had severely reprimanded a shocked Crystal, who seemed to be completely clueless about the complaints the agents had received from other lookalikes of how belittling she had been about Melita and her new boyfriend. Of course, a very devious Crystal defended herself shrewdly, bringing up the age-old family feud encircling Melita and herself.

Suddenly becoming uncomfortable with her agents' probing, Crystal had admitted that she may have mentioned something about Melita to a couple of the other lookalikes; but then went on to explain to a serious-looking Dawn that it was hardly her fault Melita's new boyfriend had made a pass at her when he had arrived to collect her half-sister from a mix and mingle job they had been contracted on together.

Dawn was a very astute woman; she had a special gift of accurately assessing situations and people. Instinctively, she knew that the true story was that Crystal had thrown herself at the handsome young man, even though she knew he was dating Melita.

Now sitting up very straight in her chair, eyes flashing, Crystal focused them on her agitated agents simultaneously before declaring assertively, "I am sorry to disillusion you both but I would not touch Melita's boyfriend with a barge pole! So please do not concern yourselves with that, ladies!"

Abruptly rising from her chair, her beautiful face contorting suddenly, she continued, her voice rasping, "Poor little Melita is welcome to him! Besides, they suit each other. A real couple of losers!"

Unable to tear their eyes away from Crystal, Dawn and Belinda were mesmerised at how this self-asserting young woman could change from damsel in distress to femme fatale in the blink of an eye.

Now slipping her black jacket back on before sitting down briefly again, Crystal bestowed one of her most beguiling smiles on her captivated audience, before murmuring in her finest Monroe voice, "I apologise if what I had said about Melita was significantly falsified when reported back to you both, but that is hardly my fault now, is it?"

At this point, she fluttered her thick eyelashes and pouted sulkily. Before waiting for an answer, she persisted, still perfectly imitating the voice of the world's greatest icon.

"I assure you, ladies, that Melita is of no interest to me whatsoever and if I may reassure you even further, her name will not pass my lips again to anyone!"

Taking a deep breath, Dawn, her eyes focusing on the beautiful lookalike as she replaced her empty coffee cup on its saucer, stressed, "We are very happy to hear that, Crystal. Both Belinda and I have always aspired to running a happy haven here for all our artistes and we will not tolerate anything or anyone rocking the boat! Is that understood?"

Rising again from her chair then nodding her head in agreement, Crystal replied indignantly, "Understood perfectly, ladies!" Her loathing for her half-sister had increased twofold.

Chapter 44
Vengeance Unleashed

It was Wednesday evening and a feeling of satisfaction and positiveness descended upon Max Rushton as he climbed into the back of the Uber that had arrived on time outside his house. Surprisingly, Tom Pike had been true to his word contacting Max the day after their chance meeting at The Windsor Castle. After agreeing on a fee plus expenses for the lookalike's appearance at the young soldier's birthday celebration, Tom had suggested that Max book an Uber to drive him to the venue located close to The Spaniards Inn, the famous sixteenth-century pub on the edge of Hampstead Heath.

Before ending the call, Tom Pike had asked the lookalike to make sure the driver drop him at the back entrance of the venue via the small service road, so that he would not be seen by any of the party guests gathering at the main entrance to the Trinity Rooms. Tom had arranged to meet Max outside the back entrance at precisely nine o'clock.

Max had telephoned Ada just before he left for the evening expressing his love and devotion for her. She was genuinely pleased that Prince Harry was in such great demand, with or without her. To Ada, every contracted job they could win together or separately meant their elopement became ever closer. Soon there would be enough money for them to slip away, but lately Ada found she was living under the shadow of apprehension and uneasiness. Try as she might, these feelings remained with her every waking moment and invaded her dreams, causing a disquieted Ada to awake in the middle of the secretive night, fear clutching at her heart.

When the Uber driver eventually pulled around the back of the Trinity Rooms at precisely nine o'clock, he found he had to turn on his full beam headlights due to the darkness in the small service road. Somebody was standing smoking outside the back entrance and waved as the car came to a stop. It was Tom Pike.

Handing the driver a twenty-pound note, Max muttered something to him before getting out of the car and walking towards the lone figure, his hand held out in greeting. Max was surprised to notice that Tom Pike was still wearing dark glasses. Probably had an eye infection of some kind, Max reasoned.

"Good of you to do this for Lee," declared Tom, accepting Max's hand and shaking it before adding. "You will make his thirtieth birthday very special, very special indeed!"

Smiling, still relishing the warm feeling of satisfaction, Max shook his head, replying modestly, "It is nothing really. This is what I do, especially for someone like your friend Lee. After all, he is one of our soldier boy heroes!"

Slapping the lookalike on the back in friendly response, Tom Pike turned towards the entrance asking Max to wait for a few minutes while he went into the Trinity Rooms, making sure everything was set for the 'grand entrance'.

"Got to make sure the photographer is ready to capture the expression on Lee's face when Prince Harry walks in!" he called back over his shoulder, grinning at Max before disappearing behind the large double doors.

Barely five minutes had passed when the doors creaked slowly open again. Looking up from his mobile, Max was surprised to see two strangers appear. Assuming they were workers leaving for the evening, he looked away and glanced again at his mobile, hoping Tom would not be much longer. It was beginning to turn a little chilly.

What transpired next would have no bearing on Max's memory. Everything happened so quickly, yet left lifelong devastation in its aftermath.

One of the men walked over to him enquiring if he was the Prince Harry lookalike. Instantly, Max noticed the person's foreign accent and dark Mediterranean appearance.

The stranger's question was never answered. Without warning, Max was viciously hit on the head from behind with a heavy object and with such force that he was rendered completely unconscious, feeling nothing of the near-fatal beating he endured at the hands of the two Turkish hit men.

Not only was Max's future career hanging in the balance but so was his life. He lay motionless on the ground, the dampness of the summer evening surrounding his crumpled body, blood seeping freely from his crushed head, his legs smashed and broken under his lifeless body.

Suddenly, the back doors swung open again as Tom Pike stepped out into the night, removing his dark glasses as he nodded for the two men to leave. He stood for a few seconds staring down at the pathetic heap on the ground before replacing his dark glasses again.

Quickly, his hands rummaged into Max's jacket and trouser pockets, taking the lookalike's mobile phone, bank cards and money. Glancing up to ensure the small service road was still deserted, he walked briskly away from the motionless body as he disappeared into the chilly summer evening, shrouded by the watching darkness.

Marius Bogdan was satisfied with his new life in the United Kingdom. He prided himself on the fact that his command of the English language was far superior than most of the other Uber drivers he became acquainted with in London. Marius had worked hard in his native Romania, enabling him to come to the UK and begin a new life there with his long-term partner, Alina. Although for the present time he drove people from one destination to another, Marius had his sights set on acquiring a position as an IT consultant. He had always been technically minded and had studied earnestly to achieve his ambition as soon as possible. He enjoyed living and working in London, finding it to be a vibrant multicultural place in which to raise the family that he and Alina would hopefully have in the near future.

Checking the time on his dashboard, Marius Bogdan decided to make his way back slowly to the Trinity Rooms so that he would be ready and waiting outside the back entrance of the service road where his client, Max Rushton, had arranged to meet him at ten-thirty, ready to be driven home again.

Driving past the main entrance of the Trinity Rooms before turning into the small service road at the back, Marius was surprised to see that everything appeared so quiet. Suddenly remembering to turn on his main head beams, he drove cautiously towards the back entrance's double doors.

At first glimpse, Marius assumed somebody had dumped a large bag of rubbish in the middle of the dark, deserted road. Becoming curious, he stopped the car, pulling on the handbrake carefully, climbed out of the driver's seat and tutting to himself, walked over to the heap on the damp ground.

Early life in Romania had not been a sheltered one for Marius. This not only made him aware of the cruelties of human beings, but also gave him the resilience he now needed to deal calmly with the horrific scene he was about to encounter.

Noticing the ginger hair now matted with dark red blood, Marius instinctively knew that this pitiful lifeless figure was indeed Max Rushton, the Prince Harry lookalike he had dropped off little more than an hour before. A feeling of deep sadness swept over his body for the friendly young man who appeared full of the zest of life.

Kneeling down beside Max's twisted body, Marius felt for a pulse. His shaking hands could only feel the weakest ticking of life. Beginning to sweat, he fumbled desperately in his jacket pocket for his mobile, then called for an emergency ambulance before notifying the police.

Now standing alone, silently, a feeling of melancholy swept over Marius. He had watched without really seeing as one of the young police officers searched Max Rushton's clothes, finding nothing apart from one of the lookalike's business cards in his breast pocket.

"Looks like a violent mugging to me!" declared the young officer, standing up again and shaking his head.

"Why is that, George?" queried his Sergeant, walking over to survey Max's body again.

"There is nothing on him, Sarge. No credit card! No money! No mobile! Definitely a brutal mugging, if you ask me," he responded.

"Yeah! You are probably right! Well spotted, son!" encouraged his Sergeant.

When questioned, Marius explained to the police in broken English, that when he dropped the victim off earlier, he recalled the figure of a man could be seen waiting outside the back entrance of the Trinity Rooms, the light from his cigarette burning brightly. Marius assured them that it would be impossible for him to identify this man because he had driven away once Max had got out to greet the shadowy figure who incidentally, Marius added, his Romanian accent clipping his words, was wearing sunglasses in the darkness!

It was quickly decided an air ambulance be called because of the severity and intensity of Max's wounds together with his slow weak pulse. The noise of the air ambulance landing on the Heath saw several people running from a nearby pub, curiosity filling their eyes and minds as they gathered as close to the air ambulance as possible, alerting others passing by to join the throng.

Quickly and with much patience, the police dispersed the growing gossiping crowd who objected to having their curiosity unfulfilled.

A team of specialised doctors and paramedics provided life-saving surgery on the Heath before Max's motionless body was airlifted to the Royal London Hospital in Whitechapel. Marius was amazed to learn that this specialised team of doctors and paramedics performed medical procedures at the roadside that are normally only carried out in hospital emergency departments. Marius was impressed.

After taking down his details, the police eventually allowed Marius Bogdan to leave. Finding his usual optimistic outlook on life had completely deserted him, a sorrowful Marius pointed his car in the direction of his home in Archway and the loving care of Alina.

Chapter 45
Every Cloud

B ad news travels fast and it made no exception in spreading, like wildfire, the shocking and unbelievable tragedy encountered by the highly popular Prince Harry lookalike. Max's family and close friends were of the same mind that he had been the innocent victim of a random, yet violent mugging. The police nevertheless were doing their utmost to find the perpetrators.

Top Drawer Agency was in deep shock as Dawn mourned for one of her extended family. The charming Max Rushton lay lifeless in Intensive Care clasping on to his young life as his grip slowly weakened. The surgeons were to be celebrated for saving his life – but what life? A memory that no longer remembered, athletic legs that had been smashed so badly they would never walk again, let alone run.

The only life the surgeons could offer the dashing Max was a life reliant on a wheelchair, a life needing assistance for his every personal need, a life where severe loss of memory imprisoned him in darkness and nothingness, a life that had ended on that fateful evening on Hampstead Heath, although its heart continued to beat.

Lookalikes and tribute artistes who had worked with Max over the years telephoned each other, trying unsuccessfully to make some sense of how this tragedy could befall such a lovely fella. The incident had been handed over to the Regional Serious Crime Squad who were being extremely thorough in their handling of this heartbreaking case.

Although to all appearances Max was the victim of a brutal mugging, the Serious Crime Squad were not fully convinced and were using all the resources at their disposal to find the person or persons responsible.

Many people had already been interviewed and interrogated, amongst them Max's good friend, Josh.

After giving a lengthy written statement to the Serious Crime Squad, Josh Roberts stressed that he suspected a stranger he and Max had met a week earlier in The Windsor Castle. Uncannily, everything Josh had noticed about Tom Pike was cemented in his memory, even down to the slightest of stammers and the fact that he wore dark glasses indoors.

Before the Serious Crime Squad terminated the interview, they showed Josh a book with dozens of photographs of known criminals in the hope that he would recognise the stranger.

After carefully studying the faces that had even the slightest resemblance to Tom Pike, Josh could not be completely sure if he would ever be able to identify this person, simply because his eyes were hidden at all times.

Before taking his leave, Josh suddenly remembered that apart from the slight stammer, he had detected a South London accent as soon as the stranger began speaking to Max. The Crime Squad had noted down every detail he had given them.

Ever since he had been notified of the horrific beating endured by his closest friend, Josh had been unable to sleep. Guilt was beginning to suffocate him as he berated himself for failing to ask Max at the time whether he should accompany him to the hero soldier's birthday party. Why had he not taken note of his gut feeling regarding Tom Pike instead of brushing off his insistent sense of apprehension and ignoring it?

Josh was in unusually low spirits and the sadness he felt for Max was overwhelming. As he walked towards his parked car, the warm summer wind playing with his unruly hair, a devastated Josh made a silent pledge to himself to find the eerie and unnerving stranger.

Sadly, life for Max Rushton was, in every sense of the word, over. No more would he confidently carry out his prestigious Prince Harry lookalike contracts to the praise of everyone. No more would he enjoy a couple of beers in his local pub with Josh and other friends. No more would he feel the rapture of making sensual love with Ada Demir, the woman he adored. Max's heartbroken family had been advised by his surgeons not to hope for even the slightest of improvement in his present condition as this would be futile.

For nine days and nights, Ada did not leave her bed, did not eat, did not sleep, for her life now held nothing. No meaning, no future, no love.

Her alarmed parents and close family gathered around trying unsuccessfully to bring her out of her deep foreboding and distress which descended upon her after receiving the tragic news of her secret lover and fellow lookalike. Her mother could not understand why her daughter had taken the tragic news so very painfully and personally. Of course, she knew that Ada had always been a very loving and passionate young woman who cared fervently for her friends and family, but Ada taking to her bed and refusing to eat the slightest morsel of food for days was alarming and frightening for Afet and for all of the family.

Try as he might, Mehmet failed miserably in trying to coax his beloved Ada from her bed. Ever since Max's terrible beating, the voices in Mehmet's head were constantly chatting to him simultaneously; foolish, excitable and confusing chatter. He found to his consternation that the voices never seemed to leave him these days, even after taking his prescribed medication.

Walking up and down in his large living room, shaking his head violently to be rid of the exasperating torment, Mehmet went over and over in his mind every detail that Tom Pike had relayed to him regarding Max's attack. His sick mind became exhilarated as he tried desperately to picture the beating that had been heartlessly bestowed on the lookalike. How he wished he could have been there as a hidden eyewitness to savour every blow that crushed the hated Max Rushton. But what to do about Ada? He knew deep in his heart he would forgive her because he would never be able to live without her.

Now, as the voices began to screech at him loudly, disparaging his betrothed, Mehmet, his head feeling as if it were about to explode, poured himself a large whisky and soda and drank it down swiftly.

His manic-depressive state of mind began to feel hatred towards Ekrem, Ada's closest friend. He remembered how Ekrem had assured him, when he had furtively telephoned her one evening, that she and Ada had been out together several times when in fact he knew she was lying. Now the voices were screaming at him again "She lied! She lied!" Mehmet's tortured mind was sad, hopeless and terribly sluggish.

Pouring another large whiskey and soda, this time allowing the soothing liquid to slide slowly down his dry throat, Mehmet tried desperately to ignore the menacing reproachful voices as his mood suddenly became more energised as the alcohol deceivingly offered him a false sense of positiveness which he desperately desired.

Somewhere in his tormented mind, he began to think again about Ekrem and how close she was to his beloved Ada. Unexpectedly now, he began to forgive the young woman. After all, she had only proved to be a sincere and caring friend to Ada and no matter what she had conspired to do against him, he had now made up his mind to allow Ekrem to continue supporting and caring for the distraught Ada.

Unfortunately for her agents, Ada had now become quite unwell and a complete reclusive, only allowing her mother, father and Ekrem near her – even Mehmet had no option but to abide by her distraught parents' wishes that he should stop visiting for a little while, enabling her to rest and get over her deep despair. Everything possible was done to encourage and coax Ada out of her low-spiritedness but nothing seemed to help, although she had now begun to take the occasional mouthful of soup spooned carefully to her by her dearest friend.

Afet called a family meeting intimating that she and Ada's father were seriously considering taking Ada back home to Turkey for a few months, hopefully allowing their beloved daughter to recuperate fully.

The Top Drawer Agency were in turmoil. The life-changing injuries suffered by Max saddened everyone, causing an air of despair all around. The prestigious South African job for Prince Harry and Meghan Markle was of the utmost importance. The new clients had explicitly booked Ada Demir and Max Rushton for five days' filming in the glamorous Sun City. The clients were extremely explicit with their choice of lookalikes and were not at all impressed when Dawn had telephoned their representatives in Johannesburg, explaining why she had no option but to replace Ada and Max.

Being extremely proficient at her role as senior partner of the leading lookalike agency throughout the UK and Europe, Dawn nevertheless breathed a huge sigh of relief as she replaced the receiver.

"Thank God!" she shouted, causing Belinda and Camp Freddie to rush into her office. "The clients have gone for Jeff Williams and the new girl, Louise Clarke," she announced, the worried look on her face disappearing.

"Louise Clarke?" queried Belinda. "I thought perhaps Charlotte or Amanda would have been chosen," she remarked, turning to Freddie who held out his hands and hunched his shoulders.

"Well! There you are, my dear! The clients have the choice and they have chosen Louise," replied a smiling Dawn. "Be a darling, would you, Belinda, and call Louise to make sure she is available."

Walking over to the large window, she glanced out at the overcast and very still sky that usually had a daunting effect on her sensitiveness, but not today. For Dawn, today was one of positiveness.

"Freddie, dear, would you please call Jeff Williams to reaffirm that he has indeed been booked in for the Sun City job," urged Dawn, turning from the dismal day and walking back into her office, a feeling of relief, allowing a small smile of satisfaction to play at the corners of her mouth.

"Will do! Straightaway, Boss!" Freddie called out loudly, causing little Queenie to open one sleepy eye as his master's voice suddenly disturbed his afternoon nap.

Chapter 46
The Italian Count

ount Luigi Francesco Umberto Boggia, who did not have to prove to the world that he was indeed a real titled Count, had arrived in New York from his palatial home in Venice. He had accepted Frank Lanzo's invitation to stay with him in Frank's latest plush New York penthouse on the East River, instead of one of the luxurious hotels owned by the Society.

Although the Count was used to extreme luxury, he was nevertheless highly impressed with his dear friend's new home. The elaborate decor showed class and taste and the mesmerising skyline caused the Italian aristocrat to catch his breath every time he glanced out of the large windows. The Count, accustomed to flying all over the world for both business and pleasure, was under no illusion that this would be a week of high-powered meetings with the Society's hierarchy, together with Frank.

Because of his Italian notability, Count Luigi dallied with families and individuals who were recognised by sovereigns, as members of an upper class who officially enjoy hereditary privileges, which distinguished them from others. Count Luigi Boggia romanced and entertained only the most beautiful and highest bred of women. Yet with all of these luxurious birth rights, his besotted heart continued to desire Belinda, the love interest of his closest friend.

For Frank, it was always great to be in the company of Count Luigi. They did not see as much of each other as they used to before Frank's close call with the Italian authorities. Ever since then, the Society had ceased sending their Capitano Numero Uno to Venice for the foreseeable future. Although he had been wrongly accused and indeed set up by Pietro Gabrini, the Security Manager at Marco Polo Airport, it had taken the greatest expertise and an immense amount of money to win the Italians over in agreeing to release Frank without charge.

Sadly for the American, he had always looked forward to visiting Venice, Queen of the Adriatic, and working with Count Luigi who lavished such luxury and culture on him. Over many years, through their association with the Society, the two men had become close. Often marvelling at Frank's hidden class, the Count admired the American's taste in so many things: food, wine, books and most importantly, women. Although coming from two completely different backgrounds, the Count knew they were two of a kind.

Unbeknown to Frank, Count Luigi had always admired and envied his dear friend, often admitting to himself that he would probably lay down his life for Frank Lanzo, his patriot, his fellow esteemed diamond thief – his brother.

The following days passed far too quickly for both Count Luigi and Frank. Although having visited and worked in New York many times, the Count invariably discovered something new and amazing about the Big Apple each and every time he visited.

Hearing that the expected high-pressure meetings with the Society's hierarchy would take little more than a couple of days, this was indeed excellent news for the two friends, enabling them to spend some bonding time together. Frank was happy to pull out all the stops to ensure his dear friend would enjoy some wonderful days, dining in the most elaborate of restaurants that New York had to offer, seeing the finest of shows on Broadway and shopping on Fifth Avenue, probably the most famous shopping street in the world.

The Society's meetings covered almost every aspect of their businesses in the United States and around the world where their powerful enterprises continued to flourish – gambling, real estate, restaurants including pizzerias, bars, pornography, music recording and many others.

Immediately after the last meeting came to an end, an Associate, Frankie Mazzarini, dark eyes alert as he walked over to Frank and Count Luigi, whispered quietly in Frank's ear.

Nodding and shaking Frankie Mazzarini's hand, Frank relayed the whispered message to the Count. Silently, the two men made their way towards the back of the now empty auditorium where they were greeted warmly by three of the Society's hierarchy. Standing some distance away stood three soldiers, their eyes never wavering from their bosses.

When the five were seated at a round marble table, the Count was asked by Leonardo Agosti, the Underboss, to relay to them the details of his telephone conversation with Maurice Englert. Maurice was the Society's Associate Jewish jeweller in Antwerp who had also participated in the mysterious unsolved diamond heist little more than a year ago.

Nodding then glancing briefly at three sets of steely eyes steadily focusing on him, the Count explained in his enchanting Italian accent, word for word, the brief conversation between himself and Maurice Englert.

"Of course, you understand, gentlemen," came Count Luigi's velvety thick-accented voice, "Maurice and I could only stay briefly on the line with such delicate information". Clearing his throat, he continued, "Apparently, Belgium's Diamond Police have fresh evidence regarding the heist which has caused the case to be reopened. Evidently, this is the latest rumour within the Diamond Centre, Maurice tells me."

Tapping the Count on the arm, Leonardo Agosti declared, "Thank you, Count Luigi, for bringing this to our attention. The Society will also make sure Maurice Englert is compensated for his diligence and that he is well protected. We have already set this in place via our Associates throughout Europe."

Clasping his perfectly manicured hands together, the Count declared, "I thank you, Leonardo. Of course, Maurice, being in the thick of it, will continue to be our eyes and ears regarding future information from the Diamond Centre."

"That is settled then!" announced the older man, drumming his short, thick fingers on the table top. "Like Maurice, our chosen Associates in Antwerp will be watching every move those specialised Diamond Police make!"

Frank did his utmost to dispel the constant imaginings in his tormented mind of Vinny and Lukey after the sadistic Pellini brothers had interrogated the two young men for the name of the third perpetrator. Apart from the two inquisitors, the Society's highest-ranking hierarchy were the only ones to have been privileged to learn the clandestine name. Even Frank and Aldo Lamarina, as Uno Capitano and Uomo Destrorso, were not entitled to know this strictly kept secret. Frank was assured that in time, he would be informed but felt this was unlikely until his bosses contracted him to make sure, beyond any reasonable doubt, that the name uttered to the Pellini brothers by Vinny and Lukey, muttering inaudibly as their young lives ebbed away from them, was indeed the correct one.

Chapter 47
A Stranger Arrives

It was Wednesday and the sun bestowed its warm golden rays generously on an enthusiastic London. Although the magical sun greatly raised her spirits, Belinda was nevertheless feeling a little apprehensive. She had spoken to Frank the previous evening and realised he had not mentioned again her moving to New York. It was as if he had never asked her all those months before. Deep in her heart, Belinda knew she would have to give him an answer soon but for her this decision would be the most important one of her entire life.

As her troubled mind pondered on Frank's coolness regarding this situation, the phone on her desk suddenly interrupted her despondency.

"Good morning, Belinda, it's Tanya."

Fleetingly forgetting her own problems, Belinda was elated that the Pam Anderson lookalike had returned her call so promptly.

"Good morning, Tanya, thank you for coming back so quickly. You sound bright and breezy, I must say!" replied Belinda, completely forgetting about Frank and the fact that she would have to make a very complex decision very soon.

Before Tanya could answer, Belinda quickly asked her close friend if she would meet her the following evening for a catch-up. Sensing a sharp intake of breath at the other end of the receiver, Belinda became anxious again for Tanya who agreed to meet but explained that she could not stay long because Aarne expected his dinner ready and waiting when he arrived home from work.

Belinda could hardly believe that this was the same feisty Tanya who had been her close friend and ally for so long. Not wanting to cause any upset, Belinda chose not to discuss anything further over the telephone but would wait until the following evening when the two of them were face to face.

Although the beautiful Tanya smiled and giggled as she hugged her closest friend in sincere greeting when they met outside the popular Italian coffee shop, Belinda instantly noticed that Tanya had lost quite a lot of weight and crows' feet marked the corners of her sad-looking eyes.

After the pair had chatted and downed several cups of coffee, summing up courage, she remarked to Tanya that she and Dawn were extremely worried about her relationship with Aarne.

Instantly becoming angry and indignant, the Pam Anderson lookalike began to defend her live-in lover. In her heart of hearts, she knew it was no use her trying to convince Belinda that she and Aarne were getting along well and that their relationship was running smoothly.

"Tanya, darling!" exclaimed a distraught Belinda. "This is me you are talking to! Please do not tell me you and Aarne are fine!" she stressed, her voice almost inaudible with emotion as she reached across the square table, affectionately touching her friend's arm.

Suddenly, Belinda's heart filled with sadness as tears began to run swiftly down Tanya's distressed-looking face. Quickly pulling paper hankies from her black leather handbag and handing them to her weeping friend, Belinda hugged her as Tanya's racked body shuddered, desperately trying to suppress her sobs.

Surveying them from behind a marble counter, the coffee shop proprietor walked slowly over to their table and asked Belinda if there was anything he could do. Finding it difficult to muster a smile for the olive-skinned, grey-haired older gentleman, Belinda shook her head and whispered to him that her friend had received some very upsetting news and she would be taking her home shortly.

The few customers, enjoying a late cup of coffee on their way home from work, glanced over to Belinda and Tanya's table, inquisitive eyes curious, speculating on the relationship between these two women and why one of them was sobbing in despair. Perhaps they were lovers having a tiff or maybe their romance had come to an end, which would account for the uncontrollable tears.

Glancing quickly around the little coffee shop, avoiding the intrusive eyes of other customers, Belinda listened attentively as a now dishevelled Tanya disclosed, in the faintest of murmurs, the truth about her relationship and life with Aarne. The man she fell in love with, one of her own countrymen, had over time proved again and again that he was a control freak.

Catching a sharp intake of breath at Tanya's revelation, Belinda was horrified. Suppressing her rising anger, she handed Tanya more paper tissues, patted the younger woman's hand and told her quietly that if she was serious about leaving Aarne, then both Belinda and Dawn would come up with a safe plan.

❧

It was still bright and sunny when Belinda and Tanya kissed goodbye, making sure that Tanya would arrive home some time before her abusive lover. They had arranged for Tanya to call Belinda at the agency the following day once Aarne had left for work.

That evening, before she retired to bed, Belinda had already decided on the plan of action they should take in order to keep Tanya safe once she had finally left her controlling partner.

As soon as it was safe to do so the following day, Tanya telephoned Belinda at the agency.

"It sounds good, Belinda," replied a worried Tanya after listening to her friend's plan of action, "but I am not sure I can really involve you in my troubles. If Aarne finds out where I am staying, all hell will break loose!" she exclaimed, her voice trailing off with despair.

Reacting quickly, Belinda assertively replied, "Listen to me, Tanya! You are my closest friend and I will be involved in not only the highs of your life, but also the lows!"

"But, Belinda, I—"

Before Tanya could finish, Belinda interrupted her fervently, causing little Queenie to grumble in his sleep.

"No arguments, my friend! You will be moving in with me as soon as possible! He has no idea where I live so you will be safe!"

Tanya had stayed at Belinda and Matt's beautiful three-bedroomed home many times in the past and always felt lighthearted when in the affluent vicinity of Old Town, Clapham Common.

"You will have to move little by little, Tanya, to make sure he does not become suspicious," advised Belinda, constantly referring to Aarne as 'he' because using his name gave her a bad taste in her mouth.

"But, Belinda!" declared a worried Tanya. "Remember, the flat is in my name! How can I leave?" she groaned pessimistically.

"Yes, of course, I know the flat is your responsibility," replied Belinda, sipping her hot black coffee placed on her desk by Freddie, who gave her the thumbs up sign, showing he fully agreed with her advice. "You telephone your landlord today and give him notice," suggested Belinda, winking at Freddie who in turn gave her the thumbs up sign again.

"What about Aarne?" asked Tanya apprehensively. "Where will he go?"

After the despicable way he had behaved, Belinda was astonished at Tanya's question.

Controlling her fiery temper she gently advised, "Well, he can take over the rent or find somewhere else to live!" Inhaling deeply, she continued, "Tanya, you must be one hundred percent sure that you no longer want to be in this relationship before you make your move. Okay?"

Swiftly and with conviction, Tanya replied, "Oh! Believe me, Belinda, I am more than one hundred percent sure! I have to get away from him, no matter what. I want my life and freedom back more than anything!"

"Good girl! Let me know when it will be convenient for me to collect some of your belongings," offered Belinda, a feeling of elation sweeping over her.

It was now a little after one o'clock and as Dawn had taken the day off, Belinda and Freddie had decided to go for lunch at the little Greek restaurant around the corner which they both liked so much. They sat outside on the charming blue and white chairs, little Queenie laying at his beloved master's feet as the summer sun bathed them in its warmth. Endlessly, they chatted about Tanya's disastrous situation, hoping that Aarne would accept the fact that she had at last decided to leave him.

Strolling leisurely arm in arm back to the agency, little Queenie sniffing his way along the pavement, Belinda and Freddie were giggling at something he had said as they turned the corner and saw her. She stood there on the top step outside the agency's main door studying the nameplates. Neither of them recognised her, although she looked very familiar.

Freddie was the first to speak.

"Hello! Can I help you, please?" He noticed that the woman was quite tall and comely. As soon as she turned to face him, a wide boyish grin spread across his face. He did not wait for her reply.

"WOW!" he exclaimed, "You look exactly like Diana Dors! I adore Diana Dors! No wonder we thought you looked familiar!" he rattled on, excitedly.

The woman let out a nervous giggle.

By this time, Belinda had joined Freddie and the woman, little Queenie making his own investigation as he sniffed the visitor's brown kitten-heeled shoes.

"You guessed! That is why I have come along – to see if I am good enough to join your agency as a lookalike!"

"Well, you are in luck!" replied Freddie still grinning like a schoolboy. "This is Mrs Belinda Flynn, one of our agents," he declared, turning to Belinda who smiled pleasantly at the woman. "By the way, what is your name?" asked Freddie as an afterthought, still smiling.

"Ruby Clement," she replied.

At this point, Belinda took over the conversation. "Hello Ruby. I take it you are a Diana Dors lookalike?" she asked, watching the woman closely, who smiled and nodded her head. Her long, bleached hair, the replica of the golden screen goddess, fell about her shoulders.

"Well, yes, I suppose I am. Everybody tells me I look like her," replied Ruby shyly. She had a London accent and her voice was low and quiet.

Being impressed with the newcomer's resemblance to the 1950's popular screen goddess, Belinda asked Ruby to join them where Freddie would take some details from her.

Smiling from ear to ear, Ruby willing agreed and hurriedly followed them through the heavy door and into Top Drawer Agency's waiting area.

Belinda filled the kettle for coffee while Freddie, making sure Ruby was comfortably seated, chatted easily to her, asking whether she had brought a portfolio along.

"Actually, I have, but I am not sure whether any of the photographs will be acceptable to this agency," stuttered Ruby, digging into her large tan coloured handbag and retrieving a medium-sized album which she held out to Freddie.

"Oh! I am sure they are amazing because you look so much like her!" appeased Freddie, flicking through the album, smiling appreciatively.

Carrying a silver tray laden with three cups of coffee and a milk jug, Belinda handed one to Ruby. Gazing up shyly at Belinda, she thanked her and smiled, noticing how extremely attractive the agent was.

After a long discussion regarding Ruby's personal commitments and whether these would jeopardise her availability for any future work, Belinda learned that although Ruby had a two-year-old son, she in fact lived with her widowed mother who was more than happy and capable of caring for little Mattie when Ruby was working or out for the evening with friends.

Belinda was impressed with the new Diana Dors lookalike and although they already had Sandy Jenkins on their books, Belinda thought Ruby had an exceptionally strong resemblance to the 1950's screen siren and was quite sure that Dawn would immediately place the newcomer into the A-team. Although Marilyn was the most sought-after icon of all time, there was still plenty of interest in Diana Dors, whom some called the British Marilyn, with her curvy figure, long blonde hair and undeniable sex appeal.

"Freddie, dear, take half a dozen shots of Ruby, would you, please?" Belinda called out to him as she studied a long list of emails that had arrived in Dawn's inbox.

"I thought you would never ask, sweet pea!" came Freddie's cheery reply as he appeared in the doorway of Dawn's office, arms flamboyantly waving about, setting both Ruby and Belinda giggling while little Queenie began to bark at his interrupted snooze.

"This way, please, Ruby, or should I say Miss Dors?" quipped Freddie, holding his hand out to the bemused newcomer who, still giggling, followed him into an adjacent room where he took some fabulous photographs of her.

Before Ruby's interview had come to an end, she had mentioned to Belinda that she would be more than happy to help out in the agency if they ever found themselves short of staff. Looking a little embarrassed, she continued, explaining to her new agent that as a barmaid she was able to change her shifts with any one of the other girls if necessary. Belinda assured Ruby that she would keep her offer in mind.

As Ruby left, Freddie kissed her jovially on both cheeks as he escorted her out. He rushed back to Belinda, "She will be amazing!" he gushed, parading around the office, glancing admiringly at his reflection in the mirror.

"Yes, I do believe she will be," agreed a thoughtful Belinda. "Dawn will be very impressed with Ms Ruby Clement, I am sure."

Dawn was indeed impressed with the newly recruited Diana Dors lookalike, very impressed indeed.

"Make sure Ruby is on the A-team Artistes List when the ads go out to our clients, please, Freddie," came Dawn's request the following day, as she studied Ruby's photographs, a satisfied smile playing on her lips.

"Consider it done!" replied Freddie, swanning around the office. Little Queenie's head cocked to one side as he watched his beloved master flouncing about.

Rudely dragging her attention away from Ruby's impressive photographs, Dawn's mobile rang shrilly. Dawn was delighted to hear the chirpy voice of Kay Carney, all the way from California.

"How are you, darling? How is that pregnancy of yours?" she asked her favourite ex-lookalike.

"All wonderful! Thank you, Dawn. I had a scan last week. Zac and I are over the moon!" declared an excitable Kay. "It is a boy!" she squealed, her voice full of happiness and laughter.

"Wow!" exclaimed a thrilled Dawn. "What fabulous news, darling girl! Thank you so much for letting us know. When will little Zac be with us?" she asked, tears of emotion appearing in her bright eyes.

"End of November or early December apparently," replied a thoughtful Kay. "The doctors estimate that I am about twenty-two weeks now," she added, before assuring Dawn that she was feeling extremely well and happy and that Zac was not only spoiling her but was more in love with her then ever.

"What does the boyfriend have to say?" asked an inquisitive Dawn, before glancing up at two sets of eyes steadily focusing on her as Belinda and Freddie held on to every word. She winked at them both as she continued her conversation.

"Oh! That is good! I was a little concerned that he may have caused some trouble for you. I am really pleased to hear that he understands and gives his blessing!"

"Yes, thank God!" replied Kay. "Daniel has requested to continue to live with us after the baby is born. Says he cannot wait to be an adoring uncle!" she added, a nervous laugh escaping from her throat.

"That is nice," remarked Dawn believing that Zac's ex-fiancé Daniel would indeed hate to give up such a lavish lifestyle, even for the green-eyed monster.

"Besides," reflected Kay, "Daniel has always had his own friends and interests outside of his relationship with Zac."

Not wanting to sound rude, Dawn nevertheless could not help replying, "Yes! I did rather pick that up from our chats over the last few months, dear."

"Poor Zac was more like a sugar daddy to Daniel and still is!" retorted Kay, her tone of voice belying her sudden giggle.

"Oh! I see!" replied a pensive Dawn. "Well, at least all's well that ends well, darling," she remarked glancing at her enthralled audience and raising her eyes.

For some time, they discussed the terrible tragedy that had befallen Max Rushton. Kay mentioned that she had telephoned Max's sister just days before to enquire after her good friend. Sadly, there had been very little progress in his condition but that his family were ever hopeful. Kay's sorrow for the Prince Harry lookalike was evident to Dawn.

"Oh, by the way! Before I forget!" declared Kay suddenly becoming brighter. "I have managed to locate Luke Cohen here at Universal Studios. Zac and I have seen quite a lot of him lately. Zac thinks he is an amazing Charlie Chaplin impersonator and an extremely talented actor!"

"Oh! How lovely!" exclaimed Dawn, squealing. "Please give Luke our fondest wishes when next you speak to him!"

"Yes, of course I will," assured Kay "His career, not only as a Chaplin impersonator but as an actor in the LA theatre land, has really taken off over here. You were quite right, Dawn, in predicting that Luke would one day make it in Hollywood."

Giggling, Dawn replied, "But, of course. Aren't I always right?"

"Yes, I guess you are, madame!" quipped Kay, the slightest touch of an American accent now evident as she quickly added, "Okay. Got to go! Stay safe. Love to all. Will call again soon. Love you!"

And with those last words, the connection from sunny California was ended.

Chapter 48
Tomb of Tears

They arrived by sleek black limousines at the county's oldest Catholic church, the historic Madonna Church and Mausoleum in Newark, New Jersey. Old and young solemn faced men, their attire showing the world they were men of affluence. Eyes focusing ahead, dark angry eyes as they walked beside and supported their women. Glamorous women of Italian heritage, eyes wet with heartbreak. These were the sorrowful families and friends attending the tragic double burial of two young men, young men who had gone through kindergarten, high school and college together, before their natural initiation into the dark and secret world of the Society.

As the two high-gloss cherry veneer caskets, each carried by six male coffin bearers, were carefully carried from the flower-laden hearses into the Madonna Church, a large, twelve-foot statue of Jesus, located outside the beautiful arched entrance, gazed down at the flock of mourners, compassion lighting his sad eyes.

Amongst close family mourners attending this most tragic of funerals were several members of the Society. Leonardo Agosti, the sotto il capo *(Underboss)*, together with Ronaldo Trapani, the Consigliere *(Adviser)* stood with Frank and Aldo Lamarina.

Standing several metres behind them was a group of capos and soldiers, each wearing black suits and dark sunglasses. Frank's heart was heavy as he slowly surveyed the sorrowfulness of the grief-stricken families and friends of the deceased. He watched as Leonardo Agosti nodded to several of the male mourners in recognition, who respectfully nodded back, then quickly diverted their eyes from Underboss.

The piteous, lifeless young bodies of Vinny Messina and Lukey Amato had been discovered exactly one month earlier after the Pellini brothers had tortured and murdered them, ordering their bodies to be wrapped in durable plastic sheets then dumped in Nelson, a ghost town just forty-five miles outside of Las Vegas. The town, littered with the ruins of buildings and vehicles, was, as far as the Pellini brothers were concerned, the perfect dumping ground for the ragazzi saggi *(wise guys)* who were under a foolish illusion they could outsmart the Society.

The Las Vegas Met Police Department attributed the discovery of Vinny and Lukey's remains to two male passengers on a tourist coach trip to the Nelson ghost town. The young Australian backpackers were travelling around the West Coast before flying to the East Coast and the excitement of the Big Apple.

It had been a very hot airless day and a quiet one for the Oasis Coach Company. The two Australians, Jack and Shane, found themselves surveying the desert landscape with a handful of other tourists, as their cream-coloured coach travelled from Las Vegas to the ghost town.

It was a little over an hour later, as the Australians were taking photographs of the amazing view of the Colorado

River flowing peacefully through the Eldorado Canyon from the Nelson Overlook, when Shane suddenly tagged on Jack's shirt sleeve, a frown descending on his perspiring forehead as he quickly removed his Ray-Ban sunglasses, wiping his eyes with a large, red handkerchief.

Turning towards his friend, Jack's eyes followed Shane's finger, which was pointing some fifty metres away where a fall of earth ran down the side of the hill. The young men were curious; they could see that there was something out there, possibly another old relic from the ghost town, and their curiosity had to be satisfied.

What unfolded next was totally unexpected. Upon reaching the spot, they discovered plastic-wrapped bundles. Shane immediately began to tear at the covering with his penknife as Jack knelt down beside his friend pulling and ripping the wrapper apart. Immediately, the putrid and offending smell caused them to cough and choke.

Suddenly, Shane screamed and jumped back as a human arm, covered in burn marks, flopped onto his knees. Only a thumb remained intact on the lifeless hand; all fingers were missing. They appeared to have been cut off with a sharp instrument.

On hearing his friend's piercing scream and the sight of the arm, Jack swore several times as he too jumped to his feet, shouting "Oh, my God! Oh, my God! Oh, my God!"

Then came the Las Vegas Metropolitan Police and medical team, three cars taking little more than half an hour to reach Nelson ghost town, their sirens shattering the peaceful eeriness of the desert. The medics carefully tended the two distraught Australians, who had become quite ashen-looking, still shaky after their shocking discovery.

They then turned their attention to the coach driver and the other few tourists who were all astonished and upset to hear what their fellow passengers had uncovered. The medics worked quickly, making sure everyone had been taken care of satisfactorily before returning to the city.

Shane and Jack were driven to Las Vegas Metropolitan Police Station to make a full written statement of exactly how they stumbled across what looked like a mob killing to the vigilant police.

Some weeks before, at the Society's Las Vegas headquarters in Caesars Palace, where Vinny Messina and Lukey Amato were handed over to Dino and Marco Pellini for questioning, was the beginning of the worst day of their young lives; not just their worst day but also their last. Everybody who had even the slightest connection with the Society knew about the notorious Pellini brothers. Their infamous reputations clung to them like cheap eau de toilette. Even the most cynical endeavoured to stay out of their way and reach.

Arriving at the Society's Las Vegas headquarters together, being driven by one of their bosses' elite chauffeurs, Dino and Marco Pellini walked purposely into the room where half a dozen Mafia soldiers were waiting to hand over a terrified Vinny and Lukey.

Marco was the first to speak, his thin unattractive voice belying his toned svelte physique and swarthy good looks. He clicked his long fingers arrogantly as he demanded loudly, "Okay! Okay! Hand over the trash!"

Every eye in the room turned to Marco Pellini, who appeared jumpy yet excitable.

Two short thick-set soldiers, both unable to disguise their Sicilian heritage, frog-marched Vinny and Lukey over to where Marco and Dino were waiting and watching. The brothers stood back scrutinising the two young offenders;

a small scar on Dino's left cheek, caused by his younger brother some years earlier, appeared to change colour as if he were trying to control the hatred he was feeling towards the pair. At the age of thirty-two, Dino was one year older than his brother and a couple of inches taller. He too possessed a toned svelte physique, visiting the gym every day assuring he was every bit as macho as his younger sibling.

Directing his focus on the two soldiers, Dino instructed, "Okay, guys! Let's go!" In contrast to Marco, his voice sounded deep and throaty as he pushed a falling lock of his chestnut brown hair out of his large hazel eyes.

"Yeah! You heard him. Let's go!" demanded a scowling Marco, glaring at both Vinny and Lukey simultaneously.

As the soldiers pushed the two young culprits in the back with their Thompson submachine guns, Vinny and Lukey moved forward quickly out of the room. The Pellini brothers, whispering together, followed close behind.

Marco jumped quickly into the sleek black limousine alongside the chauffeur, leaving Dino to sit in the back with the two submachine carrying soldiers and the 'trash.'

It seemed as if they had driven for a long time when, blindfolded and handcuffed, Vinny and Lukey were bundled out of the limousine. They could hear the chauffeur receiving instructions to wait until he was called for. They were then frog-marched, still handcuffed and blindfolded, into a small solitary building in the grounds of one of the Society's palatial properties. Once again, they could hear orders being given, this time to the two soldiers to position themselves outside the building until they too were called for.

Lukey Amato and Vinny Messina were petrified. They knew only too well they had to answer for their misdemeanours towards the Society, but nevertheless, they both prayed that something or someone would come along to save them from a fate worse than death.

Lukey begun to sob like a baby, begging the Pellini brothers for mercy, as warm urine ran down his legs, saturating his navy cotton slacks. Vinny was talking rapidly, babbling excitedly that he and Lukey were remorseful and guilt-ridden for their violation of the Society's code and that they would give every last dollar back. They would work for nothing until they had repaid everything to their bosses.

"What?" screeched an irate Marco. "Too late, you snivelling load of trash!" he screamed. "We want the name of your accomplice and the sooner you give it over, the easier you die."

These words caused Lukey to howl in desperation until Marco walked over and slapped him in the mouth, causing blood to seep from his lower lip and cascade down his white tee shirt.

"Now shut the fuck up!" yelled Marco loudly, still appearing extremely jumpy.

Dino Pellini had seen his brother like this many times before. As far back as he could remember, Marco had always psyched himself up for the imminent interrogation. Dino despaired of his brother's fetish with inflicting agonising pain on his fellow humans, even if they had been proven without a shadow of a doubt that they were guilty and deserved every torment that was coming to them.

A soft tap on the door interrupted and irritated the brothers, but they relaxed when Antonio Bruni, the Society's Supremo Electrocutioner, entered. He was a short, slim man, possessing olive skin and fine brown hair that was beginning to recede. His eyes took in everything within seconds, including the 'trash'.

Looking up, Marco smiled at the newcomer, walked over to him and shook his hand, declaring, "There you are, Antonio. We have been waiting for you!"

Antonio noticed that Marco Pellini used the top-handed shake, holding his own hand in a horizontal position making sure it was on top above Antonio's hand. Of course, the Supremo Electrocutioner was fully aware that this meant the infamous Marco Pellini was feeling superior towards him.

Dino then joined his brother and greeted Antonio warmly, slapping him on the back jovially. They had met Antonio socially on a few occasions but had never worked with him before, until today.

Although Antonio despised both Pellinis, he would gladly take Dino every day of the week as opposed to Marco. This, of course, was the general consensus within the secret world of the Society. Only the adoring opposite sex flocked around the younger Pellini, vying for his attention.

Antonio Bruni had earned his supremo reputation by carrying out more successful electrocutions than any other member of the Society. He carried out his craft quickly, cleanly and with as little pain as possible to the unfortunates. His inquisitions were that of a true artiste. He had been somewhat surprised and a little uneasy to have been called in by the Pellini brothers to demonstrate some of his more extreme electrocuting methods during their interrogation of Vinny and Lukey. Even such a person as Antonio Bruni found Marco Pellini gave him a nasty taste in his mouth, and because of this, he had decided to show the brothers only selected methods of his elite prowess during electrocution.

By this time, Lukey, whimpering in the corner of the concrete floored room, had completely soiled his cotton slacks. Both he and Vinny tried desperately to see under their blindfolds but it was impossible. Vinny sat close to his childhood friend and, although completely petrified, tried unsuccessfully to encourage Lukey to stop the noise as it would anger the interrogators even more.

Too late! Dino Pellini had opened the door, calling to the two waiting soldiers outside to enter, commanding them to bring the 'trash' over to the centre of the room where two black dentist-type chairs were rooted into the concrete floor.

Grabbing a quivering Vinny and Lukey, the soldiers taped their mouths with cross-weave reinforced tape then, pushing the young culprits roughly in their backs with the submarine guns, frogmarched them to the middle of the cold room and the feared black chairs.

Feet and arms fastened with thick leather straps, mouths secured with tape and still heavily blindfolded, Lukey and Vinny were terrified as they awaited their fate. They could hear the soldiers being ordered to return to the outside of the building and wait for further instructions.

Antonio's loathing for Marco Pellini before the interrogation became twofold when it was over. He had never been so repulsed by any other human being than he was when watching Marco, eyes blazing, as he inflicted such cruelty on the two young culprits. It appeared as if by just watching their anguish and suffering, he was becoming aroused. Antonio was repelled when Vinny and Lukey's arms and bodies were burned as the Pellini brothers pressed lighted cigarettes on to them each time the young men shook their heads in defiance when asked the name of the third perpetrator.

Turning away, then walking slowly to the back of the room, Antonio Bruni stood, his aching head becoming more intense. He kept his eyes focused on the concrete floor and tried unsuccessfully to dispel the overwhelming disgust he felt not only for Marco and Dino Pellini, but also for himself. Although still only middle-aged, Antonio's eyes were those of a very tired old man since they had witnessed terrifying cruelty over the years. From where he stood, his headache now pounding, he glanced towards the two black chairs and could see Marco slowly cutting off one of the culprit's fingers with a large hunting knife then, moving towards the other culprit, proceeded to cut off his index finger.

Blood flowed freely, running down the victims' legs and into pools on the concrete floor. A string of expletives escaped Marco's mouth as he kept demanding, over and over, for the name of the third perpetrator.

Dino was also becoming agitated as he continued to press the tips of burning cigarettes into Vinny and Lukey's severely scarred arms, his throaty voice breaking as he too demanded the name.

Glimpsing the large gold crucifix hanging hypocritically around Dino's strong neck, Antonio stared, as though hypnotised, as it glittered and shone in the eerie light of the single overhead light bulb. Fleetingly, he wondered if Jesus Christ would ever forgive the wickedness of the Pellini brothers. He somehow doubted it.

Although Vinny and Lukey were both in agony, they continued to refuse to give their torturers a name. It was as if they had suffered so much pain that they could no longer feel, as if a spiritual presence had taken over their bodies, bestowing them a power which miraculously gave them both the high tolerance to bear whatever was inflicted upon them. The Pellini brothers knew they could not overdo their interrogations for fear their victims should die before revealing the coveted name.

Glancing over to where Antonio stood silently, a jittery Marco waved him over.

Demonstrating the quickest and most humane way of electrocuting a person in order to retrieve desired information, Antonio noticed that Dino Pellini had hesitated when he gave him the first offer to try it out. However, Marco, eyes full of hatred, swiftly shoved his brother aside and, snatching the appliance from Antonio, proceeded to electrocute the young offenders, who shook like rag dolls as they writhed in agony, their bodies twisting and squirming.

"Are you crazy?" yelled Antonio, grabbing the electrocuting device and pushing a furious Marco out of the way. "You will kill them!"

Faltering on his feet, Marco yelled back, "Yeah! That is the general idea!"

"I thought you guys needed information from these two?" shouted Antonio, pointing to Vinny and Lukey, both now simpering like wounded animals, the blood continuing to drip onto the cold floor where their fingers lay scattered and discarded.

"Yeah! We do!" yelled Marco, his thin voice now croaking.

"Then let me show Dino the correct way," suggested Antonio calmly. "His temperament is more suited to this line of work," he added, glancing at Dino and cocking his head for the elder Pellini brother to join him.

Knowing he had gone too far too soon, a now troubled Marco stepped back, allowing his brother to carry out the electrocutions together with the Supremo.

It was Lukey, failing rapidly, who first nodded his head. Vinny followed him almost immediately, prompting Antonio and Dino to stop the persecution.

As the cruel appliances were downed, Marco rushed over and instructed Antonio to leave the room pronto because only he and his brother were permitted to hear, in secrecy, the name from the dying 'trash' before they met their maker.

Vinny Messina and Lukey Amato's caskets were lowered into the double plot of ground next to each other. Their families had decided it was befitting that their beloved sons, who had grown up together and were like brothers, should rest in eternal peace alongside each other. That is how they would have wanted it, sobbed their heartbroken mothers.

As the funeral party walked slowly away from the forlorn graveside, an anguished wail escaping from the very soul of Mrs Amato caused a cold shudder to shoot through the bodies of everyone present, including the Society's hierarchy.

Turning suddenly to Frank, Leonardo Agosti placed his hand on the revered Capitano's arm and ushered him slowly away from listening ears, including those of Aldo Lamarina.

Frank was shocked and dazed. He felt dizzy, as though he would collapse. It was as if his mind could not take in what Leonardo had discreetly revealed to him, there at the graveside of the two tragic young men.

His ears were buzzing, yet he could hear the low dark voice of Leonardo, as he continued.

"What I need from you, Frank, is your adept opinion. Use whatever it takes, your power, talents and flair, to ascertain that we have indeed the correct name of the third perpetrator."

"Consider it done, Leonardo," replied Frank, focusing his brown eyes on the Underboss, his confident attitude belying the turmoil inside.

"In the meantime, Frank, take a well-earned break. You deserve it!" Leonardo Agosti was saying, his smile the smile of a kindly old uncle. "Go lighten up and pamper yourself ready for your next triumph!" suggested Leonardo, slapping Frank on the back, before signalling for his chauffeur to prepare to drive himself and the Consigliere, Ronaldo Trapani, to Newark International Airport for the long flight back to Las Vegas.

The name given to Frank in a low whisper by the Society's Underboss kept swimming around in his head. He glanced over to where Aldo was standing, chatting to a couple of the Capos, then, turning, he shook Leonardo's held out hand. For a few minutes, they spoke briefly in Italian before the Underboss took his leave, nodding occasionally to certain Capos as he weaved his way carefully among the peaceful dead and their stones of remembrance.

Assuring an enquiring Aldo that he was feeling okay, Frank knew that Aldo would be disappointed not to have been privy to the information that had been passed on to the Uno Capitano. The two men made small talk, not mentioning Society business as they said their goodbyes. Both men were well acquainted with the unwritten law that the decisions of the Society's hierarchy are never questioned.

Although it was a warm July day and the sun shone powerfully, Frank suddenly shuddered as a feeling of deep despair enveloped his very being.

Undoubtedly, he knew that he had to be with Belinda again as soon as possible.

Chapter 49
Out for Fair Play

It was Tuesday and the sun bestowed its warm rays on a vibrant London as people took advantage of its generosity. Poor Freddie was feeling terribly downhearted and remorseful. He and little Queenie had arrived at the agency earlier than usual. He had to get out of the flat to be on his own so that he could think things over quietly. Boss-eyed Syd was proving to be very possessive and Freddie was finding this stifling.

After filling up the kettle, he took his mobile from his navy lightweight jacket pocket and read again the text message from Claudio.

"Good morning, Freddie!" The lively greeting from Dawn caused Freddie to jump as she rushed into the office, pulling off her linen jacket and hanging it neatly on the ornate coat stand.

"Oh! Good morning, Dawn" came Freddie's response, clicking off his mobile. "Er, coffee?" he asked, a little flustered.

"Yes, please" replied Dawn, walking over and stroking little Queenie who had made himself cosy on his little round doggy bed beside Freddie's desk.

Shortly afterwards, Belinda arrived.

Dawn noticed she appeared deep in thought.

"Come and have coffee with me, Belinda," she called out from her office. "Let us have a quick catch-up, shall we?" she suggested, light-heartedly.

Entering the senior partner's office, Belinda's worried expression caused Dawn to enquire if there was anything worrying her, to which Belinda, hunching her shoulders, declared, "We both know what life is like, Dawn. It never rains but pours!"

"Oh! I see! Then please tell me about it before you get saturated, my girl!" she joked, smiling affectionately at Belinda.

Over coffee the two women chatted about Belinda's concerns. How she was helping Tanya to move her belongings little by little out of her flat, making sure Aarne was either at work or out with 'the boys'.

"I am so worried for Tanya," confessed Belinda to an attentive Dawn. "I realise how sneaky this looks, but I am sure this is the only way for her to leave him safely." A deep sigh escaped from her throat.

"Yes, I completely agree," remarked Dawn, finishing the last drops of her second cup of coffee. "Be discreet but be careful!" she encouraged. "As long as this person has no idea where Tanya is staying, then things should be okay."

Belinda looked perturbed as she lay her empty coffee cup down on Dawn's mahogany desk.

"He has no idea that Tanya will be leaving him!" proclaimed Belinda, assuredly.

"Okay, good! I presume he has no idea where you live, by any chance?" came Dawn's next question, a frown farrowing her forehead.

Glancing up quickly, Belinda replied, "Not as far as I know." Suddenly she let out a whispered curse as realisation set in.

"Damn! Of course, Tanya may have mentioned to him that I live in Clapham Old Town, I suppose."

"Well, you had better check with her before you bring trouble to your own doorstep, my girl!" advised Dawn, tutting and shaking her head in disbelief.

"Yes. Of course. I will call her shortly," assured Belinda, picking up the two empty coffee cups and returning them to the kitchenette. The prospect of Aarne knowing where she lived sent a shiver through her body.

Noticing Freddie working quietly at his desk, Belinda walked over to him.

"Freddie! How are you, darling?" Little Queenie yelped as he bounded over to greet her.

Glancing up, Freddie replied in a half-whisper, "I will tell you later!" He wanted to keep his predicament a secret between just the two of them for now.

"Oh, okay!" she mouthed back at him, wondering why Freddie was being so secretive. All of a sudden, she began to worry that Freddie's love affair with boss-eyed Syd may be cooling off, as so many of his relationships had done in the past. Suddenly, she felt downhearted not just for Tanya and Freddie but also for herself.

"We will have lunch together today. Is that alright with you, Freddie?"

"Yes, please, sweet pea! That would be lovely!" replied Freddie, a weak smile fleetingly touching his lips. Belinda noticed his eyes were full of sadness.

The morning proved to be a busy one, bringing excitement with new enquiries for many lookalike and tribute artistes. For the first time ever, Freddie was relieved that Liberace's character had not been asked for. At the moment, he was not in the proper frame of mind to prance around as the flamboyant piano-playing genius.

During lunch, Freddie took Belinda into his confidence and disclosed to her that Claudio had been texting him for some weeks now, with the devastating news that he had a terminal illness. Claudio had recently been given the tragic verdict from his Italian doctors that he had stage IV throat cancer. The tumour was large and had affected multiple lymph nodes, also spreading to his lungs. Claudio was dying; his beautiful operatic voice would be silenced forever by a cruel disease. He had begged Freddie to visit him now that he had been transferred to a hospice where he would lie in wait for the inevitable end of his illustrious life.

As the hot tears filled Freddie's dark blue eyes, he quietly told Belinda that Claudio had begged his forgiveness for the terrible pain he and Fabrizio had caused the genteel Londoner.

Belinda was overcome with sadness. Her own troubles seemed so insignificant now. Gently, she reached across the small oval shaped table and held Freddie's slightly shaking hand as she herself fought back threatening tears.

Glancing at her and nodding his head in gratitude, Freddie, in silent answer, squeezed her hand.

Dabbing at his blue eyes with a black silk handkerchief, Freddie confessed to Belinda that he still had the deepest feelings for Claudio and had made up his mind to fly to Milan for a few days to bid farewell to the greatest love of his life, and grant his forgiveness to the dying opera singer.

When Dawn was informed of the terrible situation, she agreed that Freddie should be allowed to take leave from work whenever he felt it was time for him to visit Claudio. The opera singer's consultants had given him no more than three to four months before the inescapable tragic end.

Although neither Dawn nor Belinda cared for the Italian, they were overwhelmed with sorrow for their dear friend Freddie.

When Freddie had revealed Claudio's tragic diagnosis to Big Gerty and Fanny, he had implored them not to mention anything to boss-eyed Syd. Lately, Freddie found he could not cope with his young lover's extreme possessiveness and jealousy. Big Gerty, being a warm-hearted woman, was always ready to help anyone in distress, especially Camp Freddie. As far as she and Fanny were concerned, Freddie was the brother neither of them had. He was family, and for family, both women would bend over backwards. Of course they would take care of little Queenie when the time came for Freddie to fly to Milan. The two women had suggested that he tell boss-eyed Syd he had a potential lookalike job in Italy, which would mean he would be away for a few days.

Although Freddie knew his lover would question where in Italy he would be working, he nonetheless felt less stressed now that he had an excellent alibi for returning to Claudio's country.

His voice sounded husky and full of desolation when he greeted her on the telephone. She asked him gently what was causing him such anguish but he let out a false laugh, assuring her that he was fine, just a little tired.

Belinda knew Frank was concealing how he was really feeling and she sadly wondered why he could not confide in her like he used to.

She was pleased to hear his contract in Las Vegas went well and that he was taking a few days off before returning to his offices in the Society's New York headquarters.

They talked for a long time about their love and need for each other, before Frank disclosed that he would hopefully be returning to London sometime in August to attend crucial business meetings for his bosses. Belinda's spirits immediately rose, her insides tingled with the memory of his muscular body lying beside her, on top of her, the elation as he entered her.

Since Tanya would probably still be staying at Clapham Old Town in August, Belinda became concerned about also having Frank there. Although there were three large en suite bedrooms, space was not the issue as far as Belinda was concerned. Realising Tanya would feel extremely lost and saddened once she had finally left Aarne, Belinda had assured Tanya that they would spend as much time as possible together to make sure her friend was coping.

Now with the news that Frank would be arriving shortly, Belinda's overwhelming need for him, along with his passionate and sensual lovemaking, would completely take over her senses.

When she mentioned her anguish to Tanya, she was relieved that her friend understood her predicament perfectly.

"Belinda," came Tanya's quiet voice, the English attractively clipped with her native Finnish. "You have done so much for me, and I will always be grateful. Of course, Frank must stay with you. I love Frank, you know that!" she added, a girlish giggle escaping from her throat.

"Besides," she continued, "I have been meaning to visit my cousin Veera and her family in Worthing, so that is what I shall do while Frank is here. And furthermore, I do not want to play raspberry!" she exclaimed, an indignant expression crossing her perfect features.

Belinda burst into laughter at her friend, then playfully corrected her, "You mean you do not want to play gooseberry!"

"Yes, those as well!" replied a grinning Tanya.

The following days saw Tanya move many of her possessions into Belinda's home. This was to be a safe haven for her and one that Aarne did not know about. Tanya had assured her that she had never mentioned exactly where the Joan Collins lookalike lived, other than it was in South West London.

Little by little, Tanya had collected her belongings together and packed them neatly into Belinda's silver Peugeot 508 hatchback. Aarne was none the wiser, and it was made easier by the fact that Tanya kept most of her clothes and possessions in a small spare room adjacent to their master bedroom. When not rushing out to work, Aarne was playing pool or darts with his fellow Finns in one public house or another. He had not noticed Tanya's perfumes and cosmetics gradually dwindling in the bathroom.

Life for Aarne Virtanen was good. He adored Tanya and was much calmer now that he had managed to stop her working for the agency. Aarne was not only a possessive man but also a controlling one, having no intention of allowing his woman to parade around the world dressed in skimpy costumes pretending to be some has-been American actress. No matter how much money Tanya made or how much publicity she received from the media, it did not impress him.

Of course, he knew that Tanya was indeed a professional lookalike when they first met, but from the beginning it had not been his intention to permit her to continue in her chosen field much farther. Now that she was no longer flying around the UK and Europe for Top Drawer Agency, he found he could control his beautiful countrywoman more easily, noticing over the last few weeks that Tanya was somewhat more passive and even-tempered. He liked that change in her and he intended to keep her that way.

He did not appreciate the influence the people at the agency had had on her, especially one of the partners, Belinda, whom he had socialised with on the odd occasion together with Tanya and other friends. He was much more relaxed with his all these days and intended to start a nice little family with Tanya as soon as possible.

It was a pleasantly warm July morning. Alone in Top Drawer Agency, Dawn was feeling low, having just received a telephone call from Ada Demir's mother, Afet.

Ada and her parents were leaving for Turkey the following day. Afet had assured Dawn that Ada was recovering slowly but sadly, still appeared to have lost the will to live. The agent listened attentively as Afet explained that Ada's proposed marriage to her fiancé Mehmet Tekin would be postponed for the foreseeable future and would not be discussed again until their daughter had fully recovered. Ada's closest friend, Ekrem, would also fly to Turkey, staying for a few weeks to support her friend.

Solemnly, Afet revealed to Dawn that nothing appeared to make Ada smile these days. It seemed as if her heart had simply died since learning that for the remainder of his life, Max would be in a vegetative state, shut away in his own secretive world.

The beautiful young man that was Max Rushton was now brain dead and his exciting future cruelly ended.

For Mehmet, his whole life had been turned upside down. Without seeing or touching his beloved Ada, he was finding it impossible to carry on. He had never been a patient man and found it unbearable to wait for his heart's desire. Now he knew he may never possess the beautiful Ada, she may never be his blushing bride and the mother of his children. How confusing it was for him to understand why she had taken Max's mugging so personally?

The voices in his aching head were not helping at all. When alone, they sneered at him and vilified his beloved Ada throughout the long nights as the empty darkness watched him pacing his bedroom floor, a man full of agony.

Their families had met for lengthy discussions, talking continuously into the early hours, speculating about what the future may hold for Ada and, in turn, for Mehmet. How he hated being the subject of such scrutiny with so many people, even though they were all members of the two Turkish families.

He managed to drag himself into his place of work every weekday morning, trying desperately to keep a low profile. Although his work colleagues were kind and understanding about the fact that his betrothed had become mysteriously unwell and their forthcoming wedding delayed for the time being, Mehmet knew they were gossiping behind his back.

Apparently, some weeks earlier, whilst reading in a reputable daily newspaper about the tragic news regarding the Prince Harry lookalike and the repercussions this seemingly had on the Meghan Markle lookalike, Archie Barnes had broadcast all over the office that Mehmet's fiancée often worked with the said Prince Harry impersonator, so it was hardly surprising that this dreadful news would have upset her enormously.

"To react the way she did only shows how close the two of them were!" insinuated Archie, ignoring the distasteful look directed at him from Danny Jones.

Later that day, when the other employees had left for the evening, Danny walked up to Archie and told him exactly what he thought about his nasty little jibe regarding the tragic lookalikes.

"It was unnecessary and well below the belt, even for you!" declared an angry Danny, eyes flashing as his voice rose into a crescendo.

"Oh, come off it, mate!" retaliated an arrogant Archie. "It would not surprise me at all if that smug bastard had something to do with that poor bloke's beating!" he added, nodding his head in defiance.

Quick as a flash, Danny replied. "Well if he has, eventually it will all come out but I do admit the devil is in the detail!"

"Who needs the devil when we have Mehmet Tekin?!" retorted a sulky Archie. Then, playfully slapping his friend on the back, he proclaimed, "Come on, Boyo, I've got the devil of a thirst!"

ॐ

Almost relentlessly, ever since Max had suffered the savage mugging some weeks before, Josh Roberts was determined to search for Tom Pike, if that was indeed his real name. As soon as he had returned home to East Finchley from his job in the City, he would make it his business to wander into the Windsor Castle public house, casually order a pint of Guinness, then find an empty seat where he could survey the comings and goings of the patrons.

He had asked everyone he came in contact with if they knew of a short balding man who tended to wear dark glasses indoors, but they each in turn shook their heads.

He also spoke again to the police who were responsible for the investigation regarding Max's case. Much to Josh's exasperation, the police were of the opinion that the case would be closed as it was now unequivocally clear that

Max Rushton was, in truth, the victim of a random savage mugging.

Josh felt otherwise and although his dear friend's case could very likely be closed and added to the pile of Unsolved Crimes collecting dust in the Metropolitan Police archives, Josh silently made a further promise to Max that he would continue in his search for the one known as Tom Pike, no matter how futile it may appear.

Chapter 50
Tanya's Distress

D awn sprung back to life as Freddie and Belinda arrived together, both a little late. She was pleased to have their company. Afet's telephone call had brought the senior partner's usually positive mood quite down this morning and she mentioned it to Belinda as soon as she could.

Her junior partner, as always, was very sympathetic and assured Dawn that there was light at the end of the tunnel for dear Ada and that some months in the beautiful warm climes of Turkey would help the foremost Meghan Markle lookalike to recuperate more quickly.

"Ada will be back in the A-team before you know it!" encouraged Belinda, smiling fondly at Dawn. "But in the meantime, we must continue to pray for darling Max," she added, her eyes clouding over with sadness.

"Yes, of course, we must," replied Dawn, nodding her head solemnly in agreement.

The morning passed by quickly, seeing Dawn now having a good day as the enquiries for lookalikes and tribute artistes came flowing in steadily.

Suddenly, cutting through the soothing silence, Freddie let out a loud whistle, causing little Queenie to bark as he jumped out of his deep sleep, his little furry ears twitching in confusion.

"Wow! Tom Cruise, La Loren and La Collins are being summoned to the Film Festival on the island of the Lido in the Venice Lagoon!" exclaimed an excited Freddie.

Instantly jumping up, Belinda rushed over to Freddie's desk, eager to read the email.

"September! Excellent!" she declared, reading quickly through the email.

"Yes, from the 1st to the 5th apparently," stated Freddie, glancing up and winking at her. "A nice little earner!" he added grinning.

"Life is good!" exclaimed a delighted Dawn, rising from her chair and walking over to read the email for herself. "Belinda!" she exclaimed excitedly "You could also be wined and dined by the Count!"

"Oh! The Count! Yes, that would be nice!" replied Belinda, the colour in her cheeks flushing pink, which did not escape Dawn's attention.

"Yes! That would be very nice indeed!" agreed Freddie, interrupting. "You must introduce him to the beautiful Elaine, our fabulous Sophia Loren!" he suggested buoyantly. "I am sure the Count would love her!"

"Oh, I am sure he would!" agreed Belinda smiling graciously but she was somewhat surprised at how the little green-eyed monster raised its jealous head.

Sometime during the late morning, Dawn had suddenly decided to take the afternoon off. It was her son Ellis' birthday and she wanted to buy him a special gift.

Before leaving, she had asked Belinda to call Elaine Catina and Charlie Fox for their availability for the Lido job. I have checked all future bookings up to the end of September," she informed Belinda. "It appears that both Elaine and Charlie are free on those dates, although Charlie is very busy throughout August and again from the middle of September onwards. Let us hope neither of them have anything else going on during those dates. Best to contact them right away, Belinda," suggested Dawn as she disappeared out of the door.

The Italian clients were delighted with their British lookalikes. Elaine Catina, as Sophia Loren, was wonderful. Not only did she bear a strong resemblance to Italy's revered film actress, but she was also tall and elegant as La Loren herself. Belinda Flynn, as Dame Joan Collins, again had an uncanny resemblance to the English actress and her powerful walk and mannerisms were faultless. These clients had worked with Belinda several times in the past and were delighted that she was available for them again.

As for Charlie Fox impersonating Tom Cruise, the Italian clients could see no differences at all between the lookalike from London and the real American actor. Charlie was the most authentic lookalike they had ever encountered. He was very aware of this and the fact that he could pass himself off as the actor whenever and wherever he wished.

That evening before falling asleep, Belinda's worrying thought was how Frank would take the news that it was highly likely she could run into Count Luigi in a few weeks' time at the Film Festival in Lido di Venezia. Of course, she reasoned with herself, she did not have to notify the Count that she would be working in his city, but Belinda knew he would almost certainly be attending the Palazzo del Cinema for the Film Festival and that they were bound to cross paths.

Once again, Belinda had decided not to mention anything to her lover until he was again in London.

It was now eight days since Tanya had walked out of her flat for the last time, away from Aarne. She was sure that if her lover had been less controlling and less bullying, they would still be together. Tanya had been her own woman for a long time, and although she fell deeply in love with Aarne at the beginning of their relationship, his archaic attitude made her very unhappy, causing any feelings for him to disappear.

Settling quickly into one of the large en suite bedrooms, situated alongside others on the vast upper landing of Belinda's beautiful home, Tanya Christianssen felt sad, albeit safe and free.

On that wet Wednesday afternoon, a little more than a week ago, it had been traumatic for her as she picked up her few remaining possessions from the flat, left a letter on the side table addressed to Aarne, then closed the door behind her.

Eyes filling with hot tears, she climbed quickly into the passenger seat of Belinda's car, who turned towards her and whispered encouragingly that everything was going to be alright.

Over the last days, Tanya sadly often wondered how Aarne was doing.

Evidently, he had already contacted Top Drawer Agency early one morning, searching for her. Freddie had answered the call and assured Aarne that as Tanya no longer worked for the agency, nobody had seen or heard from her. Aarne was not convinced. He cross-examined poor Freddie, seeking information and requesting Belinda's address until Freddie became irritable and explained explicitly to the Finn that it was strict company policy not to give out any information whatsoever concerning Top Drawer Agency's employees.

Begrudgingly, Aarne slammed the receiver down as yet again his anger got the better of him. He had to find Tanya and speak with her. He had to win her back. He also had a strong suspicion that she was possibly staying with Belinda. If he could find out where Belinda lived, then he was certain he would discover the whereabouts of his beloved Tanya.

When Belinda and Dawn had arrived at the agency, Freddie, his face solemn, informed them about Aarne's telephone call.

Over coffee, the three of them chatted about the worrying situation and all agreed to ensure Aarne would never learn where Tanya was staying for the foreseeable future.

Later that morning, during a call with one of Top Drawer Agency's most prominent British clients, Dawn found herself apologising profusely after the client's representative had called to complain about Sammy Trent, the agency's foremost Adele lookalike and tribute artiste. Although the clients were overwhelmed by Sammy's amazing voice and personality, they were somewhat surprised that the impersonator was much larger than her photographs and videos implicated. In fact, Sammy Trent was quite obese. The representative quickly reminded Dawn that, for some time now, the acclaimed singer known as Adele had lost a lot of weight and they were extremely disappointed that Top Drawer Agency had not ascertained that their lookalike had followed suit.

As the call ended, Dawn, looking peevish, glanced up and gazed over her glasses at Belinda and Freddie.

"Right! With post-haste, we must send emails to all our lookalikes and tribute artistes," she pronounced. "I want up-to-date photographs and videos of every last one of them, and I mean bang up-to-date!" she demanded.

Before Belinda or Freddie could answer, Dawn continued. "Top Drawer Agency is the finest in Europe, and I intend to keep it that way!" she added defiantly. "I want the message to be abundantly clear," she said, a look of determination sweeping across her pretty face, "that those who want to remain on our books should check their appearance regularly, making sure they look as close as possible to the icon they are portraying, and that includes their weight!"

Chapter 51
Concerns for Joey

The sun shone throughout the long balmy August days, bringing a wonderful feeling of light-heartedness to Londoners. At long last, after enduring weeks of dreary cold and rainy weather, came the much awaited and longed for warmth of summer, filling the late evening skies with brightness. The high-flying planes left a silver thread trailing behind them as they soared through the fluffy white clouds, disappearing into the azure sky.

His heart skipped a beat as he knocked lightly on her door. Almost instantly, she appeared as it opened widely, the soft yellow kaftan opening at her left thigh. As his manhood stirred excitedly, he thought her the most beautiful woman he had ever seen. They stood there in the friendliness of the fading sun, eyes locked together as their individual emotions erupted deep within, causing their hearts to shudder with dizzy anticipation. She moved back slowly, allowing him to step over the threshold, neither of them able to glance away from the other.

Reaching out and gently pulling her to him, Frank kissed her so passionately that Belinda felt as if she would collapse with desire.

His hungry mouth now close to her ear, she was conscious of him uttering "Mia amore" over and over, causing her whole body to tremble with longing. Urgently, she took his hand and steered him into her large beautiful bedroom, the super-king bed adorned with ivory silk sheets.

Fervently she helped to take off his clothes as perspiration glistened on his muscular tanned body, the grey chest hair adding to his manliness. Deftly, he threw her back on the bed before climbing on top of her. She was conscious of a sensual moan escaping from her throat and then another as he kissed and gently bit her protruding nipples, causing her ample bosoms to heave. His strong head, the greying hair wiry and coarse, rubbed against her stomach as he lick-kissed the inside of her thighs, his tantalising tongue sensually flicking in and out of her honey pot until she let out a shuddering moan as her quivering burning body craved for him.

Masterfully, he entered her and she eagerly answered his every thrust as his manhood, throbbing and erect, brought them together in a surrendering climax of ecstasy.

For Frank, being with Belinda brought real contentment and joyfulness, more than any other person had done, apart from his son, Mikey. He had fallen deeply in love with this beautiful Englishwoman almost as soon as she had glanced in his direction as he sat at the end of the bar in the Venetian Hotel Splendor.

During their long-distance relationship, he had often asked Belinda to move into his plush New York penthouse so they could always be together, but of late he found her quite reticent about giving him a straight answer. He knew, of course, that she adored her career as a lookalike and enjoyed being a partner at Top Drawer Agency. Belinda, Frank realised, would be saddened to leave her family and friends but, as he had often reassured her, New York was merely a few hours' flight from London.

The following days of pleasant sunny climes glimpsed the lovers deliriously lost in their own secret world of love and lust. To dispel Frank's doubts, Belinda repeatedly promised him that by spring the following year, she expected to be in a more favourable position for her to leave London and join him permanently in New York.

As the lovers held each other tightly just before Frank's departure back to New York, he raised Belinda's spirits by assuring her that he understood completely how moving home was an arduous and traumatic task, especially when one was moving both home and country. However, he also stressed that he could not wait much longer for her answer and she must decide soon what it was she really wanted.

Frank's parting words caused a lightning shiver deep within her as he murmured quietly, "I love you, Belinda, but even I cannot wait forever. Capisci?"

Frank's patience were wearing thin.

Unbeknown to Belinda, Frank had arrived in London three days earlier. Although he hated himself for deceiving her, Frank knew she must never learn about his close friendship with her deceased husband, Matt. Letting out a sigh of relief when he caught sight of Sergie Belladoni waiting in the arrivals lounge at Heathrow, Frank waved ardently in his direction. Striding swiftly up to his grinning paesano, the two friends hugged each other fondly.

For the first three days of his visit, it had been arranged for Frank to stay at The Sherlock Holmes Hotel, situated close to Regent's Park, with its tree-lined pathways and exquisite gardens. This hotel had always been one of Frank's favourite places to stay in London, primarily because of the wonderful times he had spent there with his beloved Belinda.

It was almost closing time at the Soho betting office as Sergie and Frank walked through the entrance.

"Gene, you old devil!" came the excited voice of a smiling Joey Franzini, as he slid quickly from behind the long counter where he had been in discussions with one of the staff.

Walking over to the new arrivals, Joey hugged Frank who whispered quietly to him, "Glad you remembered my pseudonym, Joey!"

Whispering back to his revered mentor, Joey replied, a wide grin spreading across his cherubic face, "How could I forget? In London, you become Gene Capalti!"

"Attaboy!" exclaimed Frank slapping the younger man on his back and the three Americans laughed out loud at their little secret.

It was Friday evening and although the following day was the busiest of the whole week in the bookmaking world, Joey and Sergie had arranged to take Frank to The Ritz Club in St James's, not only for the amazing food, but for the gambling. Frank had spent many wonderful evenings at this stunning London club and he was delighted to re-experience the jaw-dropping opulence of its cuisine and surroundings.

"If you want to feel like a millionaire, The Ritz is where to do it!" declared a winking Sergie as he ushered Frank and Joey through the grand entrance of the club.

To Frank's surprise, both Joey and Sergie were already busy at the Soho betting office when he walked through the door out of the wind the following morning. All three of them had spent a pleasant Friday evening at The Ritz Club, with Sergie leaving £500 richer after a good gambling session.

The Soho staff greeted Frank with stamping of feet and loud wolf whistles, expressing their continued belief that he was a "Diamond geezer". Frank spent some time chatting to the employees he knew and being introduced to the newcomers, then it was down to business. He and Sergie retired to the back room where Sergie handed Frank a double espresso. The files, invoices and accounts where brought over from the Maida Vale and Victoria Betting offices by specialised couriers, alerting Frank and Sergie that this was going to be a hell of a busy session for them.

Surveying the boxes lined up to be reviewed, Sergie, taking a mouthful of coffee, remarked, "This is why Joey and I decided to wine and dine you last night, Frank. Looking at this lot, I think we should have brought our sleeping bags with us!" to which Frank, threw back his strong head and laughed out loud.

The sleeping bags would have been a good idea, because it was close to eleven o'clock that night by the time they had checked every file and invoice from all three offices. They had drunk a large glass of wine each as they neared the end of the long session, when Frank questioned Sergie about Joey.

"Joey's good, Frank," came Sergie's reply, in defence of the younger American. "Don't concern yourself about Joey! He is doing great! Stop worrying about him; he is a big boy now!" he added, anxiety shadowing his face.

Frank gave Sergie a weak smile in reply. He still had paramount business to deal with while in London and was determined to have this sorted by the end of the following day – Sunday.

By Monday, he would be desperate to take Belinda in his arms.

Chapter 52
Queen of the Adriatic

W alking quickly through a bustling Heathrow Airport towards the Alitalia check-in desk for the early morning flight to Marco Polo Airport in Venice, Belinda became quite nostalgic as her memory fleetingly brought back her first meeting with Frank Lanzo some two years earlier. Belinda had spoken to Frank several times since he had returned to New York after his recent visit to London, but she had not mentioned her imminent lookalike job at the oldest Film Festival in the world. Deciding to keep this secret from her lover, Belinda hated herself for deceiving him, but she knew how jealous and suspicious Frank could be, especially if she did happen to encounter Count Luigi in Lido di Venezia.

Belinda had suggested the lookalikes all meet up at the Alitalia check-in desk. As she placed her boarding pass back into her deep-green leather handbag, Elaine Catina came walking up to her, a smile spreading across her beautiful full mouth, instantly bringing Sophia Loren to mind.

Chatting happily together, the two lookalikes were causing quite a stir amongst other passengers who were rushing about the airport. Some smiled at the impersonators, while others called out "Joannie!" or "Sophie!"

Enjoying the attention, Belinda and Elaine giggled as a group of twenty-something men came rushing over to them, their mobiles pointing at the bemused lookalikes as the flashes came rapidly, causing both of them to blink.

"I could get used to this!" giggled Elaine, her green catlike eyes glowing with amusement.

"Oh, I am sure you could!" assured a smiling Belinda, "There's no doubt about that!"

Yelling at the top of their voices, suddenly, the group of young men began to run in the opposite direction. Looking surprised at each other, Belinda and Elaine glanced ahead and there he was, Charlie Fox, looking more like Tom Cruise than Tom Cruise! He walked in that slow, calm manner, mimicking to perfection the iconic American actor. The famous flashing smile perpetually on his handsome face as he waved at his gawking audience as they nudged one another in awe.

Shouting with excitement, the group of young men swiftly surrounded him, their mobiles flashing incessantly at an amused Charlie.

"Oh, my God!" exclaimed Elaine, her beautiful eyes wide with astonishment. "He is amazing!"

Smiling as she waved the Tom Cruise lookalike over to the check-in desk, Belinda quietly agreed, "He certainly is."

Airport security were urgently called to quieten the now rather disorderly group of youngsters, and to usher all three lookalikes quickly through to the appropriate gate where they boarded their plane for their flight into Italy.

Elaine Catina and Charlie Fox had never worked together before and so Belinda was delighted to see them chatting easily. Although Elaine had been with Top Drawer Agency for little more than six months, she was proving to be a real contender for the La Loren crown. There were two other Sophia Loren impersonators on the agency's books but Elaine was undeniably the bee's knees. Belinda found herself wondering whether the Count would fall in love with Elaine. After all, not only was she elegantly beautiful, she had an uncanny resemblance to an Italian goddess. Surely all Italians were a little in love with their goddesses?

Belinda caught her breath as they started their descent into Marco Polo Airport. It was very warm as she wiped the window quickly with her hand, searching for her first glimpse of Venice in such a long time.

As if on cue, the fluffy white clouds drifted apart and there she was, Regina dell' Adriatico *(Queen of the Adriatic)* – Venice! How Belinda adored the iconic Italian city as it flirted temptingly with its crowds of wide-eyed tourists all craving to absorb her culture and beauty.

"Welcome to the city of love!" came the pilot's heavily accented voice over the tannoy as he expertly brought the silver-winged aeroplane to a near-perfect stop on Italian soil. "Enjoy your stay in our beautiful city which oozes love and charm and is often considered the most romantic city in Europe," he continued. "Remember, Signore e Signori, it is a city that you are bound to fall in love with!"

A warm feeling of excitement flooded her senses as Belinda collected her purple-wheeled trolley from the overhead cabin. Following the other passengers out of the aircraft and through the jet bridge, she quickly caught up with Elaine and Charlie, still chatting and laughing together.

After collecting their suitcases at the baggage carousel, the three of them made their way through customs then out into the arrivals lounge where they were met by Giovanni Bianchi, a charming young representative of Top Drawer Agency's most prestigious Italian client, La Bella Vita Promotions. He asked them in his attractive broken English to call him Giovanni. He was tall and tanned with the sleekest of blonde hair, a lock of which constantly fell into his ice-blue eyes. He brazenly surveyed the three lookalikes, a wide smile swiftly spreading across his handsome face.

"You are all wonderful!" he exclaimed, clapping his hands in appreciation. "Especially you, Tom Cruise! You surely must be the real Tom Cruise, no?" he asked Charlie.

Charlie laughed out loud before replying, "Sorry, Giovanni. Unfortunately not!"

Feigning a disappointed look, the young Italian then declared, "Ah! Not to worry, my friend. You look more like Tom Cruise than Tom Cruise!" which caused them all to burst out laughing.

Gallantly, insisting he would push the luggage cart containing all three lookalikes' suitcases, Giovanni explained to Belinda that he had arrived with one of the client's chauffeur-driven limousines to drive them to Venice's Tronchetto parking island, where they would then travel by ferry to San Nicolò, the landing port on the Lido.

Barely an hour later, Paolo, the chauffeur, chatting with Giovanni, drove his elite passengers out of San Nicolò, turned sharp left, then made his way towards the centre of Lido di Venezia and the many exquisite and exclusive hotels.

Belinda had never visited the Lido before and was very excited that the lookalikes were booked into Hotel Excelsior. The hotel was just a few steps from the Palazzo del Cinema where the Film Festival was held and where on four of the following five days, La Loren, La Collins and Tom Cruise were booked to mingle among the upper-classes of Venice and international celebrities, causing excitement and, hopefully, some fun-filled confusion for the hordes of intrigued tourists.

Hotel Excelsior certainly lived up to expectations. It was both extensive and exquisitely beautiful. Elaine squealed when she saw the rows of sunbeds and white umbrellas lined up on the hotel's private beach. She squealed again when her eyes took in the enchanting interior courtyard and the breathtakingly beautiful colour of the many flourishing plants and trees.

The lookalikes' en suite bedrooms – spacious, airy and extremely elaborate – were all on the second floor of the hotel. The two ladies were adjacent to each other while Charlie's was situated further down the hallway.

"I must be in paradise!" exclaimed Elaine, taking off her wide-brimmed ivory hat and shaking her head as the bellboy, smartly attired in purple and gold, unlocked her room before bashfully handing her the key card.

"You and me both!" quipped Charlie, blowing kisses to her as he followed the bellboy down the hallway towards his own room.

"Glad you approve!" declared Belinda before entering her own room. "Our clients, La Bella Vita Promotions, are famed for treating lookalikes and tribute artists as if we were the real thing!" she remarked, more or less to herself.

After a work-free first day, which found the three lookalikes enjoying themselves and relaxing on the beach, the following two days found Belinda, Elaine and Charlie earnestly throwing themselves into their celebrity lookalike personas, easily misleading the masses of tourists from all over the globe attending the Film Festival.

As the three impersonators swanned around, graciously agreeing to be photographed with the world and his wife, panic broke out in the middle of a very large crowd of noisy Tom Cruise fans. Things became quite scary when a jumbled assortment of people, many of them gay, surrounded Charlie Fox and closed in on him.

"Tom! Tom! We love you, Tom!" they yelled at the top of their voices, now becoming hoarse through constant shouting. Charlie could not be seen in the mass of revellers, causing Belinda to panic. She noticed Elaine had stopped talking with an admirer as she stared open-mouthed at the group of unruly pleasure seekers, a look of fear showing in her beautiful almond-shaped eyes.

Walking over to Elaine, Belinda took her arm and quickly ushered the stunned girl away from the chaotic crowd.

"Stay here, Elaine! Don't move! I have to find Giovanni!" she stressed.

No sooner had Belinda finished speaking, Giovanni Bianchi rushed up, together with four burly security guards, who ran towards the disorderly crowd shouting orders above the commotion in both Italian and English for the masses to disperse immediately. They worked quickly and competently, pulling one excitable fan after another away from the throng of perspiring bodies of both sexes as they chanted for their hero.

"Jack Reacher! Jerry Maguire! Ethan Hunt! *Mission Impossible*! *Top Gun*!"

Suddenly, as the rowdy crowd began to scatter, Giovanni punched the air in triumph as Charlie suddenly appeared from the centre of the hordes, safely tucked between two of the security guards, his clothes and hair askew, face covered with imprints of kisses in the brightest of reds and pinks.

Blinking at the deep blue Venetian skies, he beamed the classic Tom Cruise smile to the watching world as the sun shining on his perfectly veneered white teeth made them appear to flash.

Both Belinda and Elaine rushed towards the awry lookalike, concern showing on their expertly made-up faces as they fussed over him, making sure he was unhurt.

"There are 1-List actors, and then there is Tom Cruise!" mused Giovanni to whoever was listening.

Charlie took a deep breath, the twinkle in his eyes showing mischievousness as he murmured, "They think I am the real McCoy! Now why is that, do you suppose?"

La Collins, La Loren and Giovanni stared at him in disbelief, before all four of them dissolved into laughter.

For the remainder of the contracted days, Giovanni ordered the burly security guards to stay close to all three lookalikes, especially keeping a watchful eye on the Tom Cruise impersonator. This was due to the attendance of a huge number of excitable fans of the real Tom Cruise, who was reputed to be attending the Film Festival himself this year.

"Remember our British lookalike is the exact double of Tom Cruise!" Giovanni reiterated to the security guards again for clarity. "Undoubtedly, the people will be fooled! You must keep your eyes on Charlie Fox at all times!"

The fourth day proved even more chaotic than the previous two for Charlie. It appeared as if almost everybody attending the Film Festival were wearing Tom Cruise inspired tee shirts and hats, emblazoned with his handsome face. Many wore the iconic Ray-Ban Aviator Classic sunglasses, emulating the actor in *Top Gun*.

Charlie loved the attention given to him from the animated crowd as he strolled nonchalantly passed the hordes of yelling fans calling out to him. All four security guards, whose dark eyes were rapidly surveying the masses, moved in closer to the lookalike, fleetingly forgetting La Collins and La Loren. While the throng were only interested in their hero, Tom Cruise, they practically ignored the two widely-acclaimed actresses.

Unexpectedly, several young Italian men approached Elaine, jockeying to have their photographs taken with La Loren. The lookalike raised her beautiful eyes and smiled coquettishly at each of them in turn before posing like a prima donna for the photographers.

Suddenly one of the young men rushed over to Belinda, grabbed her by the hand, and pulled her into the line of the flashing cameras, where the other young men then began vying for La Collins to have photographs taken with them.

They quickly surrounded the two apprehensive lookalikes. They spoke quickly in Italian, making it difficult for Belinda to understand exactly what they were saying. She could hear the word "toy boy" being referred to and was not surprised when one of the young Italians asked her, in broken English, if he could please be her new toy boy.

Laughing and giggling together with Elaine, Belinda was shocked when a voice she thought she recognised suddenly loudly commanded, "Va bene, questo e abbastanza, signori." *(Okay, that's enough gentlemen.)*

Glancing up and seemingly recognising the intruder, the noisy young men suddenly moved away from Belinda and Elaine, one of them bowing respectfully to the handsome encroacher, apologising profusely in broken English, "Excuse us, Count. We meant no harm."

"I am happy to hear it, young man," replied Count Luigi Boggia, his classically handsome face slowly breaking out into a breathtakingly beautiful smile, the bright sunlight dancing on his even, white teeth.

"Thank you, Count Luigi. Have a lovely day," replied the young embarrassed-looking Italian as he waved for his group of friends to leave with him.

"Arrivederci," called out the Count as the young men weaved their way expertly through the crowds, one of them turning back to blow kisses at La Loren and La Collins.

Belinda was completely awestruck as the pale blue-grey eyes focused on her, as if they were penetrating her very soul.

"Belinda!" he uttered, his breath catching with emotion. "Why did you not alert me that you were attending the Film Festival?" he asked, his Van Dyke goatee concealing his lips pouting in disappointment.

"Count Luigi!" she stammered nervously. "It is so good to see you again!" She was trying desperately to sound natural but the blush on her face gave her embarrassment away.

"You disappoint me, mio caro," he murmured in a half-whisper.

Regaining her composure, Belinda explained to the Count that she was working at the Film Festival for only a few days and had no idea whether he was in Venice, Milan or maybe farther afield.

"You are my very good friend, mio caro," came Count Luigi's solemn reply. "It would have made me very happy if you had telephoned to say that you and your friends would be spending time in my home city," he continued, his sad eyes focusing on her, as he shook his head despondently.

Turning quickly, Belinda introduced Elaine to the Italian aristocrat who showed his admiration for the Sophia Loren lookalike in his appreciative glances. Taking the bemused Elaine's hand gently, Count Luigi proceeded to kiss it, causing her to giggle girlishly.

"Are you a real count?" Elaine asked, noticing how extraordinarily handsome he was. His body belied his age.

"Yes, I am," he replied. "Has Dame Joan Collins never mentioned me to you?" he asked, gazing now at a disconcerted-looking Belinda.

"No, she has not, and I can understand why!" replied Elaine, her almond-shaped eyes seductively scrutinising the distinguished Italian.

"You must dine with me this evening!" declared the Count enthusiastically, his mood suddenly changing as he became less serious.

"Oh! Sorry. Not this evening, Count," declared Elaine. "We are being taken out by a rich American oil magnate, courtesy of our Tom Cruise lookalike!" she added, turning towards Belinda who nodded her head in confirmation. "You see, the oil magnate will not accept the fact that Charlie Fox, our Tom Cruise lookalike, is British and not the real American actor. He and his wife have insisted they take all three of us for dinner this evening on their luxury yacht!"

"A luxury yacht?" queried the Count, his eyes twinkling at her.

"Yes," interrupted Elaine. "Charlie says we should accept the invitation and enjoy the hospitality from the rich guy. If he has set his heart on the fact that Charlie is the real deal, then Charlie is happy to go along with it for the evening!" she revealed, retrieving a black lace fan from her red leather handbag and waving it vigorously in her face as a means of cooling herself.

"Oh, that is a great pity!" proclaimed the Count "Although, I am sure Belinda will not allow me to dine alone this evening. Isn't that so, mio caro?" he stressed, turning and focusing his eyes once again upon her.

Before Belinda could reply, the Count placed his expertly manicured hands on her shoulders and declared, "That is settled then! For old times' sake, I shall insist my chauffeur and trusted bodyguard, Alessandro Longo, collect you this evening at your hotel seven-thirty sharp, then drive you to my luxury yacht, where you shall be wined and dined like the princess you are!"

A puzzled-looking Elaine remarked, "Oh! You also have a yacht, Count Luigi?"

To which, eyes shining, he replied, "Yes, mio caro. I am a very privileged and blessed man!"

Chapter 53
Like a Moth to the Flame

Glancing at her appearance in the gold ornate mirror hanging in her hotel room, Belinda applied another touch of blusher to her fine cheekbones. La Collins was overcome with worry, glancing every few seconds at the elaborate gold ornate clock which matched the mirror perfectly. Charlie and Elaine had come to see her before they were whisked off by the excitable rich Americans for an evening to remember.

Charlie was somewhat disappointed that Belinda would not be joining them. Being aware of how strong his resemblance to Tom Cruise was, Charlie wanted to impress his agent. After all, most lookalikes were what the word suggested – 'lookalikes' – but when it came to a double deception, then there were barely a handful of impersonators worldwide who could claim this accolade, and Charlie Fox was at the top of that short list.

"You both look amazing!" complimented Belinda as Elaine, shimmering in a yellow organza midi dress, and Charlie, white teeth glowing in competition with the open-necked white shirt he wore so seductively, his tan bringing to life the emeralds in his green eyes, turned to leave Belinda's hotel room.

"Remember, we are working tomorrow before our evening flight back to London," she reminded them gently.

"Oh! Please do not worry about us!" remarked Elaine watching her closely. "There is safety in numbers so you are the one who should be careful!" which caused Belinda to blush profusely.

As they disappeared out of the heavy oak door, Elaine, giggling, called out rather loudly, "Don't do anything I wouldn't do!"

Poor Belinda jumped when the telephone jangled loudly on the bedside table. Moving quickly to answer the insistent ringing, Belinda took a deep breath before answering. It was the evening receptionist advising that Count Luigi Boggia's chauffeur had arrived to collect her.

Glancing with satisfaction at her reflection in the full-length mirror, Belinda felt confident with the way she looked. It had been very hot in Venice so she had chosen a purple silk dress which flowed beautifully with her every movement. Her feet were encased in red kitten-heeled sandals and she matched these with a small red leather clutch bag which contained her lipstick and perfume, a white handkerchief and her hotel room's key card.

Her mind was racing as she took the lift down to the foyer. How was she to explain to Frank that she had ran, purely by chance, into his closest friend at the Film Festival? Belinda knew Frank so well. She adored him but he was a very jealous man. Frank would never believe that she had innocently ran into Count Luigi.

As these troublesome notions filled her weary mind, a heavily accented voice cut through her thoughts.

"Belinda Flynn?"

She glanced quickly towards the inquisitor.

He was of short and of stocky build. Definitely more Sicilian than Italian, she thought.

He was smiling as he walked slowly towards her. She noticed the size of his massive hands and tried to pull her eyes away from them in case of causing any embarrassment.

"You are Belinda Flynn?" he asked, dark brown eyes focusing on her.

"Yes, yes, I am Belinda," she replied a little nervously, finding it difficult to hold his gaze.

"I am Alessandro Longo, Count Luigi's chauffeur and bodyguard. I am here to drive you to the Count's moored yacht. Follow me, please," he instructed as he ushered her in a gentlemanly fashion through the hotel's splendid entrance and out into the humid summer evening then into a beautiful burgundy Bentley.

Solo Amore *(Only Love)*. These words were the first thing Belinda recalled about Count Luigi's luxury yacht, even though it comprised six VIP rooms, several private balconies and a fair-sized tennis court which the Count claimed he used whenever he was on board. The burgundy Bentley came to a stop beside the Solo Amore in the marina where Alessandro Longo opened the back door, allowing a bemused Belinda to alight.

He was on deck already walking towards them, his smile beaming and his shimmering pale blue eyes putting the bright lights of the marina to shame. He wore white cotton slacks and an olive-green silk shirt which complimented his deep olive skin. Belinda thought him quite beautiful.

"Belinda!" he called out then, turning to Alessandro, he spoke quietly to him in Italian before his chauffeur nodded in agreement, turned sprightly and walked back to the Bentley.

Returning his full attention back to Belinda, smiling, he said, "Come. mio caro. Come aboard my favourite toy!"

"Some toy!" exclaimed an amused Belinda as Count Luigi helped her onto his luxury yacht and down into the heart of its beautifully decorated living area, where he proudly gave her a detour of the stunning Solo Amore.

She had no idea how wealthy the Count was, although it was a notable fact that gifts were bestowed upon those fortunate enough to be born into Italian nobility. Belinda was somewhat surprised that this was still the custom in Italy today.

"I hope you will allow me to serve you dinner, Belinda," he murmured as he poured Champagne into her tulip glass, tall enough, he remarked, to allow the bubbles and aromas to develop to the full.

"I have given my staff the evening off, mio caro. I am sure you and I can manage without them," he whispered, his eyes gazing at her.

Belinda was piqued with herself for feeling so attracted to him. His every word and flourishing body language mesmerised her. It was like being in the presence of an archangel.

During the delicious four-course meal, heartily eaten and downed with the finest Italian red wines, the two friends chatted endlessly, both becoming a little tipsy and light-headed as the evening wore on. Belinda found herself often bringing the conversation around to Frank in her quest to remind the Count, as the wine flowed freely, that she was, and always would be, in love with the American.

"Let me put it this way, cara mia," said the Count, his voice becoming a little poignant as he savoured the last drop of wine in his glass. "Frank is my greatest friend! My brother! He and I have a special bond and I would give my life for him and like brothers, we share many similarities and opinions."

Belinda was overwhelmed by Count Luigi exposing his true emotions. She adored his vulnerability, his willingness to show her his heart and soul. The wine had slyly taken control of her astuteness as she became less able to think through potential consequences.

"That is so sweet of you, Luigi!" she replied. "I know Frank feels the same about you too," she revealed, cautiously rising from her dining chair.

He moved closer to her, chivalrously steadying her.

She felt a sensitivity to the loneliness deep inside him and her heart began to beat quickly as he murmured quietly, "Frank is a very lucky man to receive your love!"

She smiled feebly at his remark.

"I had a wonderful evening, Luigi, but I must leave now. We are working again tomorrow." She brushed out the creases in her purple dress as she tried desperately to compose herself.

"You want to leave me, cara mia?" he asked, taking her hands in his and bringing them gently to his lips, seductively kissing each of them.

Suddenly, passionate emotions were flooding her senses. Reaching up, she placed her arms around his slim, tanned neck and began to return his sensual kisses.

The haunting words of a well-known Old Tyme Music Hall song resounded unsympathetically in Belinda's head the moment she opened her eyes early the following morning.

"Have some Madeira, m'dear!"
The words seemed to ring in her ear...
Until the next morning she woke up in bed,

With a smile on her lips and an ache in her head,
And a beard in her ear that tickled and said:
"Have some Madeira, m'dear!"

The Alitalia flight back to London proved pleasant enough, seeing Charlie and Elaine sitting together chatting and laughing. Belinda sat some rows behind them, staring at the pages of her open book, her mind too busy to read, continuously replaying the events from the evening before.

This morning, she had awoken with the aroma of the Count's exotic aftershave filling her sense of smell. She could feel his lean body beside her under the ivory silk sheets. He breathed evenly and quietly, laying on his front.

Desperately recollecting her thoughts, Belinda's heart sank as she slowly realised that she had deceived Frank with his greatest friend! His brother!

Devastation and remorsefulness overwhelmed her. Frank would never ever forgive her, she was quite sure about that, unless, of course, he did not find out.

Naked, she slipped quietly out of the large oval-shaped bed and gingerly made her way to the bathroom which proved to be as stunning as the rest of the Solo Amore and, of course, its owner. Taking a quick shower, Belinda quickly replaced her purple dress and searched for her red sandals, finding them abandoned outside the master bedroom door where she had left them in the height of passion. Again, her heart sank.

It was already ten o'clock and she had arranged to meet Elaine and Charlie in the hotel foyer at twelve noon sharp, ready for Giovanni to accompany them all to the Film Festival which was to be their final day.

Checking her red clutch bag for the hotel key card, Belinda was startled when the Count, his voice husky with emotion, asked, "Mia cara, are you leaving me without saying goodbye?"

He had turned in the bed and was watching her closely. She could not read those blue-grey eyes any more now than she could when they had first met.

Suddenly rushing to him, Belinda declared, "No! No! Of course not, Luigi! You know I am due at the Film Festival in a couple of hours. I must go!"

He pulled her to him and held her close.

"Alessandro is already outside ready to drive you to your hotel, mia cara, but first we should talk," he said quietly, stroking her dark auburn hair.

Belinda was distraught. Why had she allowed herself to drink far too much wine, causing her to throw caution to the wind which gave rise to her making love to Frank's closest friend? Count Luigi Boggia was an astute man.

Before Belinda had the chance to beg him not to mention anything to Frank, he had assured her that their secret was safe with him because he did not want to lose the lifelong friendship of the American any more than she did.

"Before you leave me, mia cara," murmured the Count, his mouth close to her ear, "you must know that I am deeply in love with you and have been since first we met."

His words caused Belinda to catch her breath before asking him, "Luigi, you have your choice of beautiful woman, many of nobility. Why then do you choose me?"

"If I could answer your question, mia cara, I would be a very wise man indeed!" came the Count's reply, wrapping the ivory silk sheet around his lower body as he left the bed.

"The affairs of the heart are predestined, Belinda. Determined in advance by divine will or fate," he added solemnly, disappearing into his walk-in dressing room.

Minutes later he reappeared, dressed in a knee-length ice-blue towelling robe. She thought him quite exquisite.

He walked up to her and held her close to his body. She could feel his beating heart beneath his robe as he whispered quietly, "You must leave me now, mia cara, but before you go, please know that I would never willingly hurt Frank. He is my dearest friend and I shall never forgive myself for deceiving him."

Now completely overcome with guilt, a sob escaped Belinda's throat as she wailed, "He will never ever forgive me! I wish I were dead!"

Gently holding her at arm's length, Count Luigi stressed quietly yet purposefully, "Mia cara, Frank must never know what happened between us. What the eyes does not see, the heart does not grieve over! You understand, Belinda?"

"Yes! Yes! Of course I do, Luigi, but I will never forgive myself!" she declared, eyes full of remorse.

"I understand completely, mia cara," he replied. "Yet we must put this behind us and continue living," he advised, walking her up the stairs leading out onto the deck.

"This will be our secret. Just yours and mine," he murmured before assisting her to safely step off of the Solo Amore.

"Always remember, mia cara. Ti amo." *(I love you.)*

It was a breezy morning and the sun shone gloriously over the beautiful Lido di Venezia but Belinda's heart was heavy with contrition. Vaguely, she noticed Alessandro waving to the Count as he alighted from the driver's seat of the Bentley, then smiled and nodded to Belinda as she climbed inside for the short journey back to the Hotel Excelsior.

Chapter 54
Secrets Shared

The sun promised more than it could relinquish as it fought gallantly to burst through the overpowering clouds, as Belinda arrived late at Top Drawer Agency the following Monday morning. She found herself reminiscing more and more about her time spent with Count Luigi, realising he had occupied most of her thoughts since the flight out of Marco Polo Airport the previous day.

Pushing open the heavy oak door, Belinda could feel herself blushing as her mind drifted back to his gentle yet sensual lovemaking.

"Here she is!" called out Camp Freddie excitedly, as little Queenie ran towards Belinda, promptly laying on his back demanding she tickle his tummy.

Whisking the little dog up in her arms, Belinda buried her face affectionately into the poodle's furry body, her mind grateful for a respite from the continuous visions of her sexual rendezvous with the Count.

Promptly popping her head out of her office, Dawn, a wide smile on her pretty face, walked over to Belinda and hugged her.

"Great job done in Venice!" she exclaimed. "Our Italian clients were most impressed with not only Top Drawer Agency, but with the calibre of lookalikes that we appointed them," she added, stepping back and looking fondly at Belinda. "We will have coffee and you can tell Freddie and me all about it!" she urged, taking the younger woman's arm and ushering Belinda into her office.

Disclosing to her intrigued audience that everybody attending the Film Festival was convinced that Charlie Fox was indeed the real American icon, even though he was in the company of La Collins and La Loren lookalikes, Belinda paused and sipped the pleasingly hot coffee.

"A wealthy oil magnate and his wife from Texas would not listen when Charlie tried to explain that he was not Tom Cruise. So, after a while, Charlie went along with it!" declared Belinda, hunching her delicate shoulders and smiling. "Didn't want to disappoint the gentleman, I suppose!" she added quickly in Charlie's defence.

"Fair enough!" agreed Freddie, his deep blue eyes studying her.

"Now! Dear heart! Did you or did you not come across the Count?"

Almost choking on her last drop of coffee, Belinda was taken aback by Freddie's directness.

Giggling, Freddie sprung up from his chair and, slapping her gently on the back making sure she would not choke, glanced knowingly at Dawn who pursed her heavily painted lips and raised her eyes to the ceiling.

Trying desperately to sound unemotional and realistic, a blushing Belinda admitted that Count Luigi had come across the lookalikes at the Film Festival and that he had insisted they all dine with him on their last evening in Venice. Taking a deep breath, she explained how Charlie and Elaine had already decided to have dinner with the rich oil magnate and his wife, so she had no option but to accept the Count's kind invitation on her own.

"After all," she reasoned, "he is Frank's dearest friend and I did not want to appear discourteous."

"And?" asked Freddie.

"And we had a lovely dinner on his luxury yacht!" replied Belinda, knowing exactly what Freddie was driving at.

"And?" questioned Freddie again, his dark blue eyes watching her.

"And? Nothing, Freddie, dear!" replied Belinda assertively, lowering her head as a deep sigh escaped her.

Turning away and completely disregarding her answer, Freddie asked, "Anyone for more coffee?"

Although Belinda had been away for only five days, the two agents spent the following hour catching up on the latest news and gossip concerning the agency. Dawn updated Belinda on the many lookalike and tribute artistes who had been provisionally pencilled in for contracted jobs in the following weeks. A pleased Dawn enlightened Belinda that Lady Denise Ava, their foremost Madonna, had suddenly become flavour of the month again after the agency received half a dozen enquiries for her availability from agents all over Europe. Belinda was pleased for Lady Denise, knowing that she had become increasingly anxious about her lack of job enquiries over the last few months.

"That is the nature of this business! All or nothing at all!" Dawn murmured philosophically before continuing. "The nicest surprise was that out of the blue, one or two of our clients have been enquiring about Anthony Newley tribute artistes!"

"Oh! That is good news," replied Belinda. "It is about time he was properly recognised!"

"Yes, I completely agree," replied Dawn. "Freddie and I have sent out advertisements for tribute artistes and we have already had quite a response," she clarified to her junior partner cheerfully.

Spreading a dozen black and white photographs across her highly polished mahogany desk, Dawn remarked that she had decided to hold an open day to discover whether there were any virtuosos out there because as far as she was concerned, Anthony Newley was one of the greatest talents to have ever come out of the UK.

"This is amazing!" exclaimed an excited Belinda. "Have we received videos?" she enquired, shifting through the photographs, selecting just four from the pile.

"Yes, we have the videos here, but to tell the truth, I have not had time to listen to them as yet," replied a pensive Dawn. "Maybe you could do that, Dame Collins, seeing as you were once married to Mr Newley!" she quipped, opening one of her desk drawers and retrieving the aspirants' recordings.

"Clever!" replied a laughing Belinda, collecting up all the videos and photographs before leaving Dawn's office. "You are a virtuoso in your own right, Mrs Jarvis!"

During a short lunch with Freddie at the local pub, little Queenie sitting contentedly at their feet, Belinda found herself confessing to her dear friend the truth about her evening and night spent with Count Luigi Boggia. Freddie listened silently, his head nodding understandingly every now and then, as she blurted out how terribly guilty she felt about deceiving Frank, and how she loathed herself for having feelings for the Count.

Although she had made a pack with Count Luigi that their clandestine tryst would be 'their secret', the relief Belinda now felt since entrusting Freddie with the truth was immense. Knowing she could trust Freddie with her life, Belinda assured him that in due time, she would take both Dawn and Tanya into her confidence but for the moment, Freddie was to be her only confidant.

Surprisingly, for early September and to the delight of everyone, London was experiencing a mini heatwave. Belinda and Tanya sat at the dining table enjoying a prawn and avocado salad. The two friends chatted and giggled endlessly about Venice and the Film Festival, each savouring their wine before allowing it to slide pleasantly down their throats, Belinda taking care to sound unemotional and practical whenever Tanya mentioned Count Luigi. Certain that Frank would be calling her from New York that evening, Belinda dreaded the prospect of having to lie to him, but lie she must; the secret pact had to be adhered to, for all their sakes.

As Tanya began to clear the dining table, pouring herself another glass of red wine from a fresh bottle, Belinda, suddenly feeling exhausted, walked towards the large winding staircase.

"I will be in my bathroom, Tanya," she called, ascending the stairs slowly. "Desperate for a refreshing soak while I wait for Frank's call," she added, disappearing from view.

"No problem. I will be here!" came Tanya's reply as she busily rinsed the used plates and cutlery before placing them into the dishwasher.

Picking up her glass of wine and carrying it into the beautifully refurbished lounge, she sat on the beige chesterfield sofa and stretched out her legs, allowing her slippers to drop to the parquet floor. She switched on the TV – the news was on. Tanya was becoming restless, even though, since leaving Aarne, she had resumed her career as a Pamela Anderson lookalike with Top Drawer Agency and was doing well, having had three mix and mingle jobs in the last two weeks. The Finnish beauty was happy to be back impersonating the glamorous American actress but somehow, she found she was discontented. Although Tanya adored the highly desirable life bestowed on those fortunate enough to be part of the copycat world, latterly she realised it was no longer completely fulfilling her.

Picking up a magazine from the oval-shaped coffee table and idly flicking through it, Tanya listened carefully, as she thought she heard a knock at the door. Silence.

Suddenly, disturbing the quietness, a male voice called out, "Good evening! Jehovah's Witnesses!"

"Oh no! Not again!" murmured Tanya under her breath.

Irritated with the intrusion, she decided to explain to these 'unique' Christians once and for all that they were wasting their time calling at her friend's house.

Rushing to open the door, Tanya was struck dumb as muscular strength pushed her roughly back inside the house. She had completely forgotten to put on the heavy security chains before opening the door.

Slamming the front door shut behind him, the trespasser, acting quickly, grabbed the petrified Tanya and proceeded to clasp one of his large hands across her mouth, stifling her piercing scream from escaping. Pale blue eyes darted fleetingly around his surroundings, perspiration appearing on his forehead.

His voice was hoarse as he brusquely demanded in Finnish, "Lopeta! Lopeta huutaminen!" *(Stop! Stop screaming!)*

Tanya felt faint; she was sure her legs would have collapsed from under her if Aarne were not holding her up, his rough hand still covering her mouth.

"Why did you leave me? You told me you loved me!" he whined, the grip of his hand loosening somewhat, allowing Tanya to gasp for air.

Seeing her for the first time in weeks, suddenly Aarne's threatening behaviour became one of heartbroken victim as he grabbed his ex-lover and, holding her tightly to himself, sobbed and wailed unabashedly and pitifully.

Falling now to his knees, between sobs the Finn begged his beautiful countrywoman to give him just one more chance to prove he would never try to control her life again. He wept, whimpered and whined, desperately needing her to know that he could not sleep or eat without her. He could not concentrate or function without her. He could not live without her. He would not live without her!

The now highly emotional Tanya reached out and wrapped her shaky arms around the piteous figure at her feet, attempting to quieten him. His shuddering muscular shoulders becoming more subdued. She knew instinctively that she was now in control, although the adrenalin sweeping through her body caused her to tremble and her heart to pound.

She spoke to him as if to a child. She had to make him understand finally that although she loved him very much and was, at times, desolate without him, she could not, would not, be controlled; not by anyone, not by any man, and not by him.

She reminded him gently he had been fully aware when they first met that she was a modern, strong, capable woman and would not live under his increasingly dictatorial and controlling ideology ever again. They talked and talked, they cried and cried; she, the knowledgeable educator; he, the attentive pupil. She, the victor; he, the transformed.

❧

As if on cue, having just walked into her en suite bedroom, Belinda's mobile began playing *New York, New York*, a smile appearing on her mouth as Sinatra's incomparable voice filled the air.

Before he spoke, she sensed it was Frank. He was in good spirits, she thought, and seemed much more relaxed than he had done for some time now. For a while, they expressed their deep love for each other and how miserable each of them were at being apart. Belinda again promised him that soon she would have a precise date of when she could be free to move permanently to New York to be with him. He mentioned that he was being kept busy by the Society, flying here, there and everywhere, but that there were no plans for him to return to London at the present time.

"Looks like you may have to pay the Big Apple another visit real soon," he teased her. "By the way, did you see the Count in the beautiful Venice?" he asked, too casually.

She was conscious of a flutter in her tummy at the mention of his name but she replied shrewdly to the American that she and the other lookalikes did come across the Count at the Film Festival, the day before they were due to fly back to London in fact.

"Luigi sends his fondest love to you, Frank," she heard herself murmur. "He invited all three of us to dinner that evening but we had already accepted an invitation from a rich American oil magnate who actually believed Charlie Fox was the real Tom Cruise!" she heard herself giggle but even to her own ears, it sounded false.

"Is Luigi well?" Frank asked soberly. "I must give him a call," he added before waiting for her reply.

As their call ended, a disquieted Belinda was sure she could hear voices coming from downstairs. Gingerly, she walked out of the bedroom and down the winding staircase, curiosity getting the better of her as her mind wondered who was talking to Tanya. Of course, it could possibly be Jenny from opposite; she was always making herself busy with the neighbours.

She stopped in sudden shock halfway down the stairs as her disbelieving eyes tried unsuccessfully to focus on the scene being play out in front of her.

Reminiscent of two betrothed swans, necks entwined as the female swan soothed her 'forever' mate to peacefulness, she hummed a treasured Finnish lullaby to him, his desperation at losing her now fading as she calmed his trembling. Instantly, Belinda knew that these two swans belonged together and, come what may, she realised they would never be truly apart.

Her eyes widened the following morning when she explained to Dawn about the unimagined reconciliation of Tanya and Aarne. The senior partner was not amused; in fact, she was quite angry about the whole scenario.

"How long do you think it will be before Ms Christianssen is back in the same position as before?" asked a ruffled Dawn, focusing on Belinda.

Sitting at his desk, his eyes darting between the two ladies, Freddie nodded his head, declaring, "I am with Dawn on this one! I am mortified! After all the lies I told Aarne on her behalf!"

"So sorry, Freddie. I have tried to make her see sense, but you know Tanya!" replied Belinda, apologetically.

"And I suppose Aarne has promised her that he will change for the better?" cut in a sarcastic Dawn.

"As a matter of fact, yes, he has," confirmed Belinda glancing at Dawn. "I have told Tanya that as far as I am concerned, if she makes her bed, she must now lie in it!"

"That is all very well, Belinda, darling, but she has not only brought you into this drama but me, Freddie and the agency, for goodness sake!" exclaimed a tetchy Dawn. "By the way, how did he find out where you lived?" she queried as an afterthought.

"He followed me home from Top Drawer one evening!" an embarrassed-looking Belinda quietly admitted.

"OMG! He has been watching too many gangster movies!" squealed a now flustered Dawn, rising to her feet and pacing up and down the office.

Glancing at each other, Freddie and Belinda burst out laughing at Dawn's indignation at the whole sorry saga of Tanya and Aarne's inconceivable reconciliation.

Chapter 55
From a Place of
Malevolence

I n sunny California, Zac Lewis was falling deeper and deeper in love with Kay Carney. The bigger her belly became, the better he liked it.

Feeling fat and unattractive for the first time in her life, poor Kay tried desperately to think positively about the quickly approaching birth. There were many days, when looking at her reflection in a full-length mirror, that Kay would curse her pregnancy for turning her into a fat sow, albeit temporarily.

She was determined that her beautiful voluptuous figure would return once the baby had been born. No matter how many hours in the gym or how many personal trainers it may take, her Marilyn Monroe shape must and would return.

"You have never looked more beautiful," Zac incessantly reassured her, even after she had suffered a bout of the dreaded morning sickness, her usually groomed hair limp and dishevelled.

Annoyingly to her, nothing seemed to faze him; he lived and breathed Kay and their forthcoming baby. From the moment she had enlightened him about her pregnancy and the fact that he was the father, it seemed as if Zac had undergone a complete transformation, his whole world now surrounded by just the three of them.

As for Daniel, both Kay and Zac were somewhat surprised how well he had taken the news of their sexual relationship and how gratifyingly he had bowed out gracefully from his betrothal with the superstar. Daniel assured his ex-lover that he understood completely how his feelings had grown and become sensual for the beautiful Marilyn Monroe lookalike.

"I am almost in love with her myself!" he quipped, wrapping his toned tanned arms around Zac who tried to explain his predicament in faltering tones.

Because of his understanding and congeniality and the fact that he did not want to leave either of them, Zac agreed that Daniel should remain living at his Californian mansion for as long as he wished.

"After all," mused Zac, "my baby will need a doting uncle!" which brought tears to an emotional Daniel's beautiful green eyes.

During these days of exciting anticipation waiting for his baby to arrive, Zac accepted very few invitations for performances that would entail him staying away from Kay overnight. Although he knew she was surrounded by his supreme bodyguards and house staff, Zac hated the thought of being parted from her while she was heavily pregnant and vulnerable. Of course, he knew one day he would go back on the road to tour, but by then the baby would have been born and both Kay and the little one would accompany him.

Now as he replaced the eighteen-carat white gold receiver back on the dagger-shaped telephone in his opulent office, Zac knew undeniably that he would accept this latest invitation. It had been a very long time since he had performed at the world's most famous arena, and he could not find it in his heart to refuse. When later discussing with Kay that he would have to stay overnight in New York, she tried everything in her womanly power to persuade Zac to take her along as she adored New York. However, the music legend stood firm, profusely refusing to hear of her travelling over three thousand miles in her delicate condition.

No matter what she said or how long she cried for, Zac was extremely resolute that she should stay in California where Daniel would keep her company or she could ask one or two of her girlfriends to come and stay.

"My darling, I will only be gone one day and night!" reasoned Zac to a sulky Kay who had thrown herself onto one of the chesterfield sofas. Although she would not even look at him, he continued. "If it had been anywhere else other than Madison Square Gardens, I would have refused, but to perform again in one of the world's most famous arenas, I just couldn't say no. Please try to understand, my darling!" he pleaded.

With the patience of a saint, Zac then spent the following hour cajoling a very peevish Kay. It was only after he promised to bring her a very special surprise back from New York that Kay finally relented, agreeing to his performing in New York, even if it meant he was 'abandoning' her.

Gently pulling the moody Kay close to him, her baby bump pressing miraculously into his stomach, Zac, his voice full of sentiment, proclaimed, "Abandon you, my darling? I would rather die than abandon you and our baby!"

A week later, Zac Lewis arrived at Madison Square Gardens. It had not changed since Zac had last performed there.

The music legend shivered, remembering the icons who had performed at The Garden. Now his own name would be listed again alongside the likes of Frank Sinatra, Elton John, Billy Joel, Eric Clapton, Bruce Springsteen and many others.

His thoughts returned to Kay far away on the West Coast and he hoped Daniel would keep his word and make sure the mother of his forthcoming child wanted for nothing while he was gone. He knew Daniel was extremely fond of Kay and she in turn was looking forward to spending some bonding time with Daniel without the usual distraction of his zany friends, just the two of them.

When Zac telephoned Kay earlier that day, she had just come out of the shower. She sounded relaxed and admitted how much she was looking forward to having a picnic with Daniel in the Hollywood Hills, situated high above the city. She told him she would be preparing the food herself, even though the kitchen staff were happy to help her.

"Be careful in the Hills, my love," advised Zac. "Text me as soon as you are home again, otherwise I shall be anxious all day about you and the baby," he added forlornly.

"Oh, Zac, please!" implored Kay. "I am with Daniel! We are going to enjoy the Californian sun and the amazing picnic I have prepared. We shall talk and talk and talk, and then he will drive us back home and I shall have an early night and dream about you!"

"Well, in that case," replied an amused Zac, "I shall try to relax and have some lunch with the boys before the show."

"You do that!" exclaimed a giggling Kay. "Say hello to everyone for me, will you?"

"Yes, of course, and remember, my angel, I love you!" he said, his voice again full of emotion.

Kay quickly responded. "And I love you too, my darling. Now go knock 'em dead!" and with that, the call was ended.

Daniel's red Porsche Boxster – an engagement present from Zac more than a year before – made its way through one of the most affluent and most scenic areas in Los Angeles – Hollywood Hills. Although Kay had been to the Hills before, she was in agreement with Daniel that because of the breathtaking panoramic views, this is where they would enjoy their day and picnic together.

As they drove through the streets, Daniel taking every twist and turn very carefully, ensuring the safety of the precious cargo he was carrying, Kay laughed out loud at her companion's urban myths and anecdotes. She was mystified by the extravagant mansions and spellbinding views of the city. Homes that seemed to cling vulnerably to the face of the cliffs sent a quiver through her body. How she adored California! It was everything she had ever imagined, and now this breathtakingly beautiful corner of the world was to be her forever home.

"Can you feel the heartbeat of the city?" asked Daniel, glancing fleetingly at her. His large eyes were as green as emeralds.

She turned to him as she fought with the warm wind to keep her sun hat in place. "Why, Daniel Dafoe, heartbeat of the city? What a lovely expression!" she declared.

"Yes! As a matter of fact. I do feel the heartbeat of the city. For me, this certainly is *California Dreamin'!*" she muttered almost to herself.

Bringing the Porsche to a halt some forty metres from the edge of the Hills, Daniel then found a quiet spot for them to enjoy their picnic. From there, they could see the spectacular views which were awe-inspiring and exciting. He carried the picnic hamper from the boot and helped Kay lay out the blankets for them to sit on.

"We should have brought Goldie and Sunny with us. I bet they would have loved it here," remarked Kay, emptying the picnic hamper and arranging the delicious food on the white linen tablecloth she had brought with her.

"No, no! Far too dangerous for dogs, especially Sunny as he is so volatile!" replied Daniel, opening a bottle of lemonade and proceeding to pour it into two plastic mugs, the bright sun highlighting the streaks in his blonde hair.

"If anything bad happened to those dogs of his, Zac would string me up!" he chuckled, his eyes raising to the sky overhead, producing a girlish giggle from Kay. "They are adorable though and I am very fond of them both!" added Daniel, breaking open an oyster then allowing it to slide slowly down his throat.

Under the spirit-lifting Californian sun, they chatted for quite some time, discussing everything and everyone, both revealing to each other little secrets about themselves that they had never divulged before.

To Kay's pleasant surprise, she found she actually felt relaxed with Daniel. There was a time when she felt it difficult to even look him in those accusing eyes of his after Zac had spoken to him about the pregnancy. Of course, she completely understood how shocked and hurt Daniel must have felt when Zac explained to him that he had fallen in love with a woman and was going to be a father and, worse still, that their engagement would now have to end.

Reaching over to where Kay sat across from him, Daniel refilled her now empty mug with lemonade. Smiling her thanks at him, Kay took a pallet of large strawberries from her picnic basket and offered it to Daniel, who, tutting, shook his head.

"Sorry, darling, but I am allergic to the revered strawberry!"

"Really?" queried Kay, her eyes full of amusement. "Good! More for me and the bump then!" she giggled but as soon as the words came out of her smiling mouth, she regretted them.

Instantly, the expression in Daniel's eyes changed, albeit fleetingly, but she had caught sight of the dark clouds passing across them and she felt dismayed.

Luckily, Daniel seemed not to take note of what she had said and continued to explain about how, as a young child, he had found out that he was indeed allergic to strawberries.

After clearing away the picnic hamper and blankets into the Porsche, Kay decided she wanted to take some photographs. Checking her point-and-shoot Sony camera, making sure the settings were correct, Daniel suggested they walk closer to the edge of the Hollywood Hills sign so that Kay could capture the spectacular views that surrounded them.

Life for Luke Cohen had brought not only daily sunshine since relocating from London to Los Angeles a year ago in his search for the American Dream, but also newfound fame. The multi-talented Luke Cohen was by far the greatest Charlie Chaplin lookalike and tribute artiste that ever graced the stage and film studios since the original 'little tramp' captured the eyes and hearts of the whole world many years before.

Luke, in the same way as his hero, could turn his hand to anything concerning show business. Although he was held with the highest esteem in both the UK and Europe, his mind and soul were forever restless, then Hollywood called.

The magic that is Luke Cohen did not waiver when he made his way to his first audition at the famous Universal Studios.

Within one week, he was toddling up and down their Hollywood theme park, meeting and greeting tourists and visitors in his greatest role as Charlie Chaplin's 'little tramp'.

Together with the many Marilyn Monroe lookalikes, Luke was the most photographed icon ever at the Studios. To those who were fortunate enough to see his act, Luke's impersonations would linger in their minds forever. The North London-born Luke Cohen commended and applauded the 'little tramp', knowing in his deepest soul that had he not looked exactly like the South London-born genius that was Sir Charles Chaplin, he would probably still be a tailor's assistant in Saville Row.

Since arriving in LA, Luke had accepted almost everything his agent, Billy Mocca, offered him. After all, although still adored and in demand, the 'little tramp' could not alone bring in enough money for the lifestyle that Luke was now becoming accustomed to. Besides his lookalike stints at Universal Studios as Charlie Chaplin, Luke won many parts in the Los Angeles small theatre scene, enjoying the different characters he portrayed.

Billy Mocca was an astute agent and well-respected in the show business world. When Luke first entered Billy's tiny office in downtown Los Angeles, the agent could instantly see the charisma and appeal of this Englishman with the remarkable face.

"You don't just look like Charlie Chaplin, you *are* Charlie Chaplin!" he exclaimed, eyes gleaming with admiration.

From thereafter, Billy Mocca dedicated much of his time to finding work for Luke, believing that his multi-talented client deserved no less than his own television show.

"One of these days, my boy, I shall land that TV contract for you!" he would perpetually tell Luke at the end of their conversations.

"Well! I won't hold my breath, old chap, but nevertheless, I shall be waiting!" was Luke's tongue-in-cheek reply which never failed to cause Billy Mocca to roar with laughter.

"You Brits kill me!"

Some days before, Kay had telephoned Luke for a chat and to invite him to join her and Daniel on their picnic whilst Zac was in New York. Sadly for Kay, Luke graciously declined the invitation, saying he had masses of lines to learn for an upcoming play.

Before their conversation ended, Kay made him promise that he would visit her and Zac very soon. Kay was extremely fond of Luke.

On the day of the picnic, Luke Cohen rose early and began in earnest to revise the many lines for his forthcoming play at the Fountain Theatre.

After a short while, a restless Luke was suddenly aware that he was feeling quite melancholy as he half-heartedly went over his lines.

An overwhelming desire to see Kay, Zac – someone, anyone, from home, London – engulfed him, prompting him to lay down his script and decide instantaneously to join Kay and Daniel on the picnic. Now that he had made up his mind to go, Luke was excited about surprising Kay who had explained to him exactly where she and Daniel would be picnicking in the Hills, just in case he should decide to join them.

Pointing his silver second-hand Ford Mustang convertible towards the Hollywood Hills, Luke hoped to arrive before Kay and Daniel had finished their picnic. Driving through the streets, Luke, like Kay before him, was amazed by the mansions and panoramic views of the city. He closed his eyes briefly as the hot Californian sun, lingering on his head and shoulders, brought his mind back to the last time he had seen Diane. He missed her today, he missed her yesterday, he would miss her tomorrow and forever, but he had shattered his chance of real happiness when he allowed the beautiful Diane to walk out on their relationship. Luke knew she was right when she accused him of putting his ambitions of stardom before anything or anyone.

Often waking up in a sweat during the lonely nights and calling her name, Luke had decided when Diane had left that he would stay single and hopefully create his future happiness through his show business career. Deep down, he knew nothing could compensate for love and that the greatest gift a man could receive was the love of a good woman. However, he had settled for second best and had thrown himself wholeheartedly into his quest to become one of Hollywood's, and, in turn, the world's, brightest stars.

It was quite deserted when Luke reached the area of the Hills where Kay had told him they would be, close to the 'D' in the famous Hollywood sign. Driving his car off the road and onto a grass verge, he brought his Mustang to a stop and was instantly conscious of the quietness as the wind eerily danced seductively over the Hills.

"It is so quiet, it is deafening!" he muttered to himself as he leapt out of the car, his field binoculars in his hand.

"Now, where are you, Ms Monroe?" he murmured, peering through his binoculars into the distance.

Suddenly, he froze; his head began to pound and he felt as if he were to be sick. Squinting several times and rubbing both eyes, Luke peered again into the binoculars and into the distance. He could just make out Kay, her blonde hair glowing in the sunshine.

He was not sure but it looked as if she and her companion were struggling with each other. He hoped he had made a mistake and that they were, in fact, dancing around and just having fun.

Shaking his head and wiping his eyes again with a white cotton handkerchief, Luke could now make out Daniel's height and physique. What were the two of them doing, he wondered, as a feeling of despondency overwhelmed him. He instinctively knew that something bad was going to happen but he did not know what and he did not know why; he just knew that his instincts were alerting him of something dreadful.

Rushing back to his Mustang, Luke reached inside the back seat and retrieved his famous Charlie Chaplin bowler hat and cane. Only yesterday he had left them in the back of his car after a Universal Studio lookalike job, ready for his next appearance on the Studio's Hollywood theme park. Placing the bowler on his thick black curly hair, Luke Cohen once again became Charlie Chaplin's 'little tramp'.

Luke called the police from his car before venturing out on to the clifftops. Urgently, he ran towards the two figures in the distance, swinging his cane high above his head, hoping he would be seen as he yelled at the top of his lungs "Hello!" but the robust wind did its best to drown out any attempt he made to attract Kay and Daniel.

He was becoming breathless as he now fought his way frantically through the high coarse grass. The nearer he came to the scene being played out ahead of him, the more he was certain this was no dance routine!

Daniel's strong tanned arms were holding Kay captive in his grip as he roughly shuffled her heavily pregnant body towards the Hollywood sign and the edge of the Hills. Poor Kay! Her screams were silenced by the angry wind as she fought against Daniel who suddenly froze as he turned and spotted Luke, now almost upon them. Blinking for a few seconds, Daniel could not apprehend what his eyes were telling him and instantly released his grasp on a distressed and shaken Kay, who quickly moved away from the dangerous edge of the Hills, the Sony camera still hanging around her slim, pale neck. What happened next could only be described as incredible.

The 'little tramp' weaved his way towards a startled Daniel and began using his famous walking cane as a sword, flickering it into the taller man's face menacingly.

Ducking and diving, Luke prodded Daniel's taunt tanned physique, pushing him further and further away from Kay. He continued digging Daniel in the ribs and backside, emulating the 'little tramp', all the while smiling, his bright blue eyes shining with devilment. The iconic bowler hat sat defiantly upon his dark curly hair as he expertly twisted and turned his svelte body. His fists now clenched after throwing his cane to the ground, he began to box a startled Daniel. Luke Cohen sprung forward like lightning.

"Put 'em up, sir!" he demanded, as he quickly glanced around to make sure Kay was safe.

"Are you completely insane?" Daniel yelled at him. "We were dancing, you idiot!"

Fists still raised in anticipation as he bobbed and weaved in the defensive technique of the great boxers, the 'little tramp' yelled back, "That was no rumba, sir! Me thinks you were trying to do the Dance of Death, Mr Dafoe!"

An enraged Daniel became even more irate and began violently pushing the 'little tramp' away but Luke had, once upon a time, studied the gentlemen's sport of boxing and landed a 'real beauty' on his opponent's perfectly shaped nose.

To both Kay and Luke's surprise, the dashing Daniel yelled out in pain, then began to sob as blood started to flow from his wound.

"I'll see you pay for that, you limey bastard!" he screamed in between sobs, as he dabbed at his bruised and possibly broken nose.

"Don't you worry about that, Mr Dafoe," replied Luke. "What I witnessed with my binoculars from some distance away is what you should be worrying about!" and with that, Luke turned and walked towards a weeping Kay, wrapping his arms around her.

"He tried to push me over the edge, Luke!" she stammered, shuddering with fright.

"Yes! I know, sweetheart! I saw everything!" he replied, breathing deeply.

"You saved my life, and the baby's!" she whimpered through her sobs. He could feel her body shivering so squeezed her tightly.

Turning again to affront an enraged Daniel, Luke yelled at him again, "Put 'em up, sir! One on one! Man to man! No elbows! No headbutting!" The 'little tramp' had taken over again, weaving and bobbing around a fuming Daniel.

Between blaspheming and dabbing at his wounded nose, Daniel recovered control of his emotions sufficiently enough to scream the following words, "You are a fucking nut!"

Then astoundingly, on that hot windy Thursday afternoon high in the Hollywood Hills, Daniel made a threatening move towards the Englishman, knocking the 'little tramp' to the hard, coarse ground, prompting a piercing scream to escape from Kay's throat as she stood transfixed in horror at the surreal scene unravelling in front of her.

Suddenly, jumping swiftly atop a startled Luke, Daniel kicked viciously at the 'little tramp', causing not only his bowler hat to topple off his head, but also leading to Luke slipping and rolling dangerously towards the edge of the famous Hollywood sign.

Clutching hopelessly at the rough and prickly grass, desperate for it to stop him rolling any further as it slid from his grasp, pictures of Luke's life flashed fleetingly before him, convincing the 'little tramp' that he was about to meet his God. He became oblivious to Daniel's vicious kicks as each one connected excruciatingly with his bruised body.

Somewhere in the far distance of his mind, he could hear Kay screaming hysterically and then suddenly, before he lost full consciousness, he was sure he heard a gunshot.

There were four of them running speedily towards a seemingly deranged Daniel Dafoe. The classy dark blue uniform that distinguishes the Los Angeles Police Department now giving Kay a feeling of security and comfort as tears flowed down her ashen face. Her eyes, red and sore, transfixed on Luke's lifeless body. Whimpering softly as a female police officer placed comforting arms around her, Kay let out a startled scream as she heard the single shot, gratefully allowing the policewoman to carefully usher her back up the hill towards the waiting police cars.

As the bullet from the police officer's Beretta handgun lodged painfully in his right thigh, Daniel moaned and groaned in agony as he squirmed on the coarse grass, completely forgetting his injured nose. The police officers were unanimous in their decision that Daniel had appeared unhinged as he frantically continued to kick at Luke's unconscious body. He had ignored or failed to hear the shouted command from the Police Captain to kneel and raise his hands above his head.

Within minutes, a large white ambulance arrived and safely carried an unconscious Luke, together with a handcuffed Daniel, to Cedars-Sinai Medical Center. Accompanying the talented paramedics and their patients was one of the police officers, eyes alert and focused completely on the perpetrator.

The following hours seemed to fly by so quickly that it was past seven o'clock by the time a much-calmer Kay arrived at Zac's palatial Californian mansion in a black and white patrol car, escorted by two female police officers. All of Zac's staff and bodyguards had been made aware of what had happened earlier in the Hills and many of them were waiting patiently outside in the cool evening air to welcome their future mistress safely home.

Since hearing about Kay's terrible ordeal, Juan, Zac's valet, had tried several times unsuccessfully to contact Zac in New York. However, the Californian time zone being three hours behind the Big Apple made it impossible to locate the music legend, who would have been on stage performing. Juan assured a weary Kay that he would continue to try and contact Zac until he had reached him.

If Daniel had succeeded in his evil quest to get rid of Kay by throwing her off the edge of the Hollywood Hills, he would have now been sitting on death row. Daniel was to be charged with grievous bodily harm regarding Luke. Had the Englishman not made such a remarkable recovery from his beating, Daniel Dafoe would have been incarcerated on death row for double murder.

With respect to Kay, he was charged with intent to cause injury and possibly death to both her and her unborn baby. The Californian Justice System is a harsh one as it carries the death penalty, and a shocked Daniel knew it would be a very long time before he was able to party all night again with his long string of avant-garde gay lovers.

Desperately, Daniel pleaded with an incensed Zac to remember the good times they had shared, but the music legend quietly assured his ex-fiancé that if he had harmed Kay and his unborn baby in anyway at all, then Zac himself would have shot Daniel straight between his green eyes.

"The trouble with you, Daniel, is deep down you hated the fact that you could not compete with Kay's pregnancy," declared a weary Zac. "You were always so sweet with Kay, deceiving me, her and the whole world with your artifice, so that nobody would ever suspect that you could ever do her any harm."

Before he turned his back on his imprisoned ex-lover and walked smartly out of the Los Angeles State Prison, Zac Lewis silently thanked God that the heroic spirit of Charlie Chaplin's 'little tramp' empowered Luke, enabling the actor to fight for the damsel in distress.

Word of Zac's pregnant girlfriend's ordeal in the Hollywood Hills quickly dominated social media and the front pages of every newspaper around the globe, as well as taking centre stage on the entire television network. Zac's face was suddenly splattered on every magazine cover, and although he was accustomed to living in a goldfish bowl, he refused to talk to the media, no matter how much they offered him, instructing his high-ranking team of lawyers to handle in his stead.

This turned out to be a fraught time not only for Zac and Kay, but also for their whole household as the world's press harassed each and every person on the music legend's payroll.

Although Zac arranged for Kay's mother and sister to fly out to Beverly Hills to stay with them for a while, poor Kay became quite teary and often telephoned her close friend Dawn during this crisis. The concerned agent did her utmost to quell the fears and tensions of her favourite ex-Marilyn Monroe tribute artiste.

"Doting uncle indeed!" snorted Zac some days later, as he read yet another report in the *Los Angeles Times* of Kay and Luke's terrifying ordeal at the hands of Daniel in the Hollywood Hills. "You know they are calling Luke a hero!" he stated, glancing at a pensive Kay as she poured more sparkling water into a tumbler.

"Yes, I know they are, and nobody deserves it more than Luke!" she replied, leaning back and swallowing the soothing water.

"Exactly!" agreed a thoughtful-looking Zac. "If it wasn't for Luke Cohen, you and our baby may have been lost to me forever!" he stressed, his voice catching with emotion.

Rising slowly from her chair, Kay walked towards a now distraught-looking Zac and placed her arms around his strong neck. Her stomach, large with impending childbirth, pressed unashamedly into this amazing man as he brought his head down to her uplifted face and kissed her gently on her red-painted lips.

Releasing Kay and gazing into her eyes, Zac stated as if the idea had just come to mind.

"I want Luke to be our baby's godfather!"

"Oh! That is a wonderful idea, Zac!" squealed Kay, clapping her hands gleefully.

"That is settled then!" he declared jubilantly, before quickly adding as an afterthought, "After all, my love, our baby owes 'the little tramp' his or her life!"

Chapter 56
A Tragic Turn of Events

"Do good, reap good; Do evil, reap evil."
Chinese proverb

Meanwhile, back at Top Drawer Agency, Dawn was seething. Word had got back to her from other lookalikes yet again that Crystal was still being patronising and nasty towards her half-sister, Melita Morgan, whenever the two were contracted to work together.

"After everything Crystal promised me when I reprimanded her about her bad attitude towards Melita, the little minx is apparently still bullying and vindictive!" declared Dawn, rising from her office chair and walking over to the window, her head shaking from side to side with frustration.

"A leopard never changes its spots, sweet pea!" echoed Camp Freddie from his kneeling position, having difficulty clipping little Queenie's red leash onto the dog's diamanté collar before leaving for the evening.

Belinda glanced up from her computer.

"Look, Dawn, I will have a word with her if you like," she offered, a frown settling on her forehead.

"Actually, Belinda, that could prove beneficial," replied a thoughtful Dawn, turning away from the window and the threatening dark clouds. "Do you have a few minutes now to discuss our next move?"

A little more than half an hour later, the agents had decided to give Crystal one final chance to either change her attitude towards Melita and other lookalikes, or have her name permanently removed, not just from the agency's A-team, but from the agency altogether.

"Call her in for a meeting as soon as possible, would you, please, Belinda?" requested a now appeased Dawn, her mind trying to decide how best she should approach the narcissist Crystal.

For Dawn, this was a double-edged sword. Now the foremost Marilyn Monroe lookalike and tribute artiste in the UK and Europe, it was important the agency had Crystal on their books. However, Dawn realised she would have to forfeit the girl if she were to keep Top Drawer Agency running professionally.

Checking several confirmed dates for contracted jobs in respect of Crystal on the present month's calendar, Belinda, glanced up and meeting Dawn's eye, declared, "She is busy again this month, but mostly working alone, apart from a couple with The Rat Pack."

"Excellent!" replied a smug looking Dawn. "Find a date that suits all three of us. I shall give that young lady the length of my tongue once and for all!" she exclaimed.

There are incidences that occur in life that are completely out of our control and which are considered by some to be fate.

Such an incident happened barely two weeks after the conversation between Dawn and Belinda regarding their troublesome Marilyn Monroe.

As Crystal was extremely busy for the following few weeks, the two agents, not wanting to upset the apple cart, had agreed to delay speaking to her until after her imminent jobs had been completed.

Crystal had been chosen and booked by the newly-elected presenter and team of the up-and-coming Reminisce TV channel. She was to perform the iconic song *Diamonds are a Girl's Best Friend* made globally famous by Marilyn Monroe in the 1953 film *Gentlemen Prefer Blondes*. This was to be the last show of the present series and the production company had planned to keep the greatest icon until last.

Hardly glancing at the other photographs and videos forwarded by Top Drawer Agency of other Marilyn lookalikes, the casting team had unanimously chosen Crystal and had no further wish to peruse other contenders.

Being auspicious and at the top of her game, Crystal unwittingly held in the palm of her hands, in a rather distorted and unfair way, the career paths of the less fortunate B-team Marilyn Monroe impersonators. Had Crystal not been available, then one of her 'rivals' would most certainly have performed the iconic song in her stead.

The whole crew – directors, producers, lighting engineers, cameramen and the gofers – were fascinated and mesmerised by the beautiful and talented Crystal, the replica of Marilyn Monroe in the famous pink satin dress. The narcissistic Crystal basked in the admiring looks and whispered compliments not only from men but from the many women on set. Her inflated sense of her own importance and a deep need for excessive attention and admiration had seen her many troubled relationships fizzle out and fade away. Poor Crystal lacked empathy for others and was swiftly becoming somebody to avoid; quite friendless, in fact.

The elation she felt in front of the cameras as she performed *Diamonds* made her dizzy with delight in her power to compel the whole world to fall madly in love with her, just as Marilyn Monroe had done many years before. She giggled girlishly when the director pulled her gently to one side and quietly assured her that, although she had been amazing, the producer had requested the whole scene be staged again because one of the chorus dancers required extra make-up.

Flicking an escaped blonde curl away from her beautiful eyes, Crystal giggled again as she blatantly turned and focused on the unfortunate dancer.

Looking the girl up and down contemptuously, she then turned back to the smiling director and, in a stage whisper, declared, "Oh dear, yes! I see what you mean. A real plain Jane!"

"Exactly!" exclaimed the director very quietly under his breath, not wanting to upset the dancer, who stood a little way behind them with the other chorus girls.

"So, why on earth was she given the job?" asked a frowning Crystal, now becoming irritable. "I want this to be perfect in every way for me!" she hissed through her expensive porcelain teeth.

In the dancer's defence, the director quickly replied, "To be fair, she is probably the finest dancer we have and besides, her hourglass figure is quite eye-catching!"

"Eye-catching? Personally, I think she is overweight!" came Crystal's sarcastic response.

Now patting a tetchy Crystal on the arm, the director assured her that the dancer would look much more attractive after the make-up artists had used their magic on her and with his assurance, the whole *Diamonds* scene was shot again to perfection.

Having overheard much of the hurtful things Crystal had been saying about Penny, their friend and fellow dancer, the other chorus girls exchanged knowing glances.

The directors and producers of Reminisce TV were to hold a barbecue in the grounds of the studio after filming. This was a thank you to all who had been involved with the whole series.

Being escorted by two handsome young men to the barbecue, Crystal, wearing a tight black pencil skirt suit, turned back to look mockingly at the chorus girls, who in turn glared coldly back at her.

Shuddering involuntarily, Crystal glanced at her two young companions and quipped, "I feel as if someone just walked over my grave!"

"Oh, my God!" exclaimed the more handsome young escort. "We are being very morbid, aren't we?" setting all three of them laughing.

The grounds of the studio were decorated with an array of colourful flowers that had everybody catching their breath as their eyes focused on the displays. Their nostrils also filling pleasantly with the many perfumes on offer. Crystal's two escorts vied for her attention, striving for superiority as they both tried to outdo each other, but she had decided to leave their company and mix and mingle with the crowds.

Before strutting away from them and imitating perfectly the icon's voice, she suggested, "Hey, boys, why not escort the chorus girls for a while? God knows they could do with a little flattery!"

And with that, she disappeared into the crowds, her Ted Baker trolley bag pulled close behind her.

When a bored Crystal had exhausted herself working the crowds, receiving many business cards handed to her from interested agents, managers and unsavoury characters, she decided it was time to leave the jollity and revellers who were becoming quite gregarious. She was tired and a sense of melancholy had descended upon her. No matter how hard she tried to brush this feeling aside, she could not dispel it.

Making her apologies for leaving early to the director and producers, the only people that mattered to her, she then walked purposely towards the entrance of the car park where her yellow Volkswagen Golf waited.

Being a Londoner, Crystal enjoyed time spent in the country. She hummed to herself as the words of *Diamonds* ran incessantly through her head. She adored the quiet country lane whose many tall trees made every effort to hide the Reminisce TV studios from the inquisitive eyes of the passing traffic.

Finding the car park was now full, a disgruntled Crystal realised she would have to complete a very tight three-point turn in order to drive straight out of the studio. She made a snap decision to reverse the car out of the large double-gated driveway into the quiet country lane.

Checking her mirror several times and being completely satisfied that the lane was quite empty, Crystal continued to reverse slowly out of the studio's driveway.

As if commanded by the dark angel, no sooner had she completed her delicate manoeuvre, than out of nowhere a large black saloon car came speeding down the leafy lane. As it sped past Crystal's yellow Volkswagen, it clipped her outside back wheel, causing the Golf to spin out of control, halfway across the road before crashing into a lamp post opposite.

Although a very competent driver, the delicate Crystal had lost control of the car completely and had been knocked unconscious when her forehead hit the steering wheel. Like the dark angel himself, the driver of the black saloon car did not stop but continued to drive away at full speed from the near-fatal accident.

Hearing the sickening sound of screeching tyres and the noise of battered metal as the Volkswagen Golf crashed into the lamp post, several people in the car park, together with many of the revellers, came rushing out to see what on earth had happened in this usually quiet little part of the world.

By the time most of the people attending the barbecue had hurried to the scene, somebody had already called for an ambulance which, thankfully, had arrived unusually quickly. The entire Reminisce TV team were shocked and saddened on seeing such a talented and beautiful young woman unconscious and bloodied, lying face down on her steering wheel.

When Crystal was stretchered carefully into the ambulance by the paramedics and driven at high speed to the nearest hospital, the police were dealing with the smashed Volkswagen, questioning any witnesses and moving curious partygoers back to the barbecue.

The group of chorus dancers stood huddled together by the double-gated car park driveway and nodded their heads in unity, when one of them declared knowingly, "Haven't I always told you, ladies? What goes around, comes around!"

That same evening, Crystal's distraught father, William Dunn, a slim man of medium height in his early sixties, sat by her bedside in the Intensive Care Unit of St George's Hospital. The tears were threatening to overflow onto his unconscious daughter's pillow where she lay motionless, her ventilation machine only adding to his distress for his youngest child. He panicked when he first saw her laying on the crisp white sheets, the natural healthy colour drained completely from his beautiful girl.

"Nurse! Nurse!" he called out hysterically. "What has happened to her left eye? Why is it bandaged up?" he stammered, deep down not wanting to hear her answer.

The nurse walked up to the overwrought gentleman and, laying her hand gently on his arm, explained that the eye had been injured in the car crash but that the world-class surgeons would do everything in their power to save it.

"Oh, my God!" was all he could utter, before breaking down in tears.

The young nurse, being full of concern for the gentleman, asked if there was anybody who could support him through this most tragic of times when suddenly, Melita Morgan appeared and walked towards her comatose half-sister's bed.

Abruptly, a surprised William wiped his bloodshot eyes and nodded in greeting to his elder daughter from his first marriage.

With a look of concern shadowing her face, Melita nodded back at him then turning quickly away, she spoke quietly to the nurse, who asked the newcomer if she would like to sit by the patient's bed for a while. Shaking her head in non-acceptance, Melita explained to the young woman that she would visit her sister again, but not while their father was present. The nurse, a little confused, smiled understandingly nevertheless.

It had been difficult for Melita to hold back the tears that rose quickly to her expressive eyes after coming face to face with her father after so many years. He looked older than she remembered; still handsome but somehow more life-weary. His natural blonde hair had thinned somewhat and was beginning to turn silver grey. Shuddering, she recalled, as if it were only yesterday, that cold November evening when, out of the blue, her father had proclaimed to her mother that he was leaving her. There was another woman whom he had been seeing and who now carried his child.

Melita remembered with sadness how her lovely mother Jenny had begged and pleaded with her husband to stay with her and their young daughter, but her pleas had withered in his ears. Brutally, he had screamed at his wife that he did not love her anymore and would be moving out immediately.

Before he walked away from his eldest child to be with his unborn child, Crystal, William Dunn had confessed to his crushed wife that he was truly sorry but could not help himself falling in love with the other woman.

Melita had spent that night, and many other, soothing Jenny's sobs as she wept grief-stricken into her pillow. Melita, the child, lay with her young arms wrapped around her heartbroken mother.

Suddenly, after all those years, coming face to face with her estranged father in the Intensive Care Unit had opened the wound she had long ago buried in her subconscious but which she still carried in respect and support of her darling mother.

Everyone at Top Drawer Agency was in shock when they heard the terribly sad news of Crystal's hit-and-run car accident. Although she was extremely disliked by most of the other artistes, it is never good to hear such tragic news of another person, even if that person was so nasty to the less fortunate than herself. Regrettably, there had been no witnesses to the crash and so the mysterious perpetrator remained at large. The case was placed on the 'Unsolved' pile.

Over the following days, Dawn and Belinda learned that the ill-fated Crystal, the most beautiful Marilyn Monroe lookalike of all time, had not only broken her perfectly shaped nose, punctured one of her lungs and broken her collarbone, but had also lost sight in her left eye. Sadly, although surgeons worked tirelessly into the early hours, due to complications, they had no other option but to remove the severely damaged organ.

"Mirror, Mirror on the Wall,
Who is the Fairest One of All?"

With the pitiful Crystal requiring convalescence for many months to come and still desperately trying to come to terms with the tragedy of losing her coveted beauty, requests for the Marilyn Monroe lookalikes were nevertheless, forthcoming.

By an unfortunate twist of fate, Melita Morgan was fast becoming the new principal lookalike and tribute artiste for the greatest icon of all. At long last, the girl who stood in the shadows, who for the most part was usually second best, had risen like the legendary phoenix from the ashes to become not only one of the finest Marilyn Monroe impersonators, but also the most kindest.

Both Dawn and Belinda were happy for the upturn in Melita's career, although this came at a terribly tragic price.

Chapter 57
Business is Buzzing

Top Drawer Agency was buzzing, and so was Dawn Jarvis. Many of their lookalikes and tribute artistes were contracted out on jobs, not only in the UK, but all over Europe. An enquiry had come in only this morning from a New York client, requesting photographs and videos of Melita for a potential Marilyn Monroe photo shoot in the Big Apple.

It was late September and the south-east, especially London, was enjoying an unusually warm spell of weather, living up to what the Met Office defines as "an Indian summer".

"Another enquiry for Anthony Newley!" remarked Camp Freddie, looking up and focusing on his two agents simultaneously. Little Queenie, sleeping soundly at his master's feet, whined quietly.

"Excellent!" replied a smiling Dawn, stretching to pick up the phone as it suddenly rang out demandingly on her mahogany desk.

"I am so pleased Anthony Newley is making a comeback, even if it is posthumously!" remarked Belinda, smiling at Camp Freddie. "I have always thought him an amazing talent," she added, nodding her head and returning to her computer.

"Yes, indeed he is!" agreed Freddie jumping up from his desk and breaking into an Anthony Newley hit, causing little Queenie to yelp in protest as Freddie pranced around the office.

"Up and down the City Road,
In and out the Eagle,
That's the way the money goes,
Pop goes the weasel.
Pop Pop Pop, Pop goes the weasel!"

With her eye make-up running down her face, Belinda roared with uncontrollable laugher at Camp Freddie's foolish and outrageous behaviour.

Finishing her call, a startled Dawn, eyes widened in disbelief, retorted loudly, "Listen to me, Freddie! You will be up and down the City Road searching for a new job if you are not careful!" which only caused Belinda to laugh even louder.

Marina Greenslade and Louise Rickman, the two principal and rival lookalikes for Queen Elizabeth II, were contracted to work alongside each other for a new documentary that was to be televised some time during October. Dawn was well aware of the problematic history between these two women. Not only did they loath each other, but also loathed working together. She had decided to call the bitter rivals, reminding them that they would have to bury the hatchet and put their differences aside for the duration of the television documentary. Dawn was determined to emphasise that she would have no qualms about passing the job to other Queen Elizabeth II lookalikes waiting in the wings.

Most of the Royal lookalikes were kept busy with a variety of contracted jobs. The Duke and Duchess of

Cambridge were swiftly becoming the most popular royals while the Duke and Duchess of Cornwall were also firm favourites with the clients.

Just as Dawn had predicted some months earlier, the demand for Harry and Meghan, the ex-Duke and Duchess of Sussex, had diminished alarmingly.

Lady Denise Ava, the wonderful Madonna lookalike and tribute artiste, was still proving to be very popular with clients. Often, they would call the agency, complimenting on its professionalism.

Tanya, now back in the arms of Aarne, had recently been busy with an array of enjoyable Pamela Anderson lookalike jobs, and it appeared that all was now tranquil in their relationship. Aarne prepared to accept his lover for who she was, rather than who he wanted her to be.

Huey Lewis, as Sean Connery's 007, and Meyrick Sheen, as the incomparable Jack Nicholson, were becoming extremely popular again with the clients. The charming debonair Huey seemed to be contracted on every prestigious job that came to Top Drawer Agency.

The agency was now fortunate enough to feature four excellent Anthony Newley lookalike/tribute artistes on their books. The most talented was Jimmy Wise, an attractive young singer and impressionist, possessing the debonair good looks of the late, great Anthony Newley. When he sang, you would say it was the superstar himself.

During those bustling and exciting days, Belinda often thought about Count Luigi, of how special he had made her feel during the time they had spent together recently. But her heart belonged to Frank Lanzo; she knew this. He was her true soulmate and, as soon as possible, she would take up his offer for her to move permanently to New York.

Every week, he would telephone her, and each and every conversation was precious to Belinda.

The call came on a dull Thursday morning late in September. Camp Freddie had just opened the agency and was busy removing little Queenie's red lead. It was almost eight o'clock.

Her voice was low as if she were trying not to disturb someone or something, and her accent was strong and foreign.

"Is that Freddie Lawlor?" she asked so quietly that Freddie squinted, pressing his left ear against his mobile in order to hear more clearly.

"Yes, yes. It is Freddie. Who is this, please?" he asked, feeling quite baffled.

"Annalisa, the sister of Claudio," she answered before continuing quickly, "I have an urgent message for you from Claudio. He asks that you come to him as soon as you are able."

Freddie could hear the despair in her voice.

"Oh, my God!" he cried out, fearfully. "I will get a flight to Milan on Sunday!" he assured her.

"That is good. My partner and I will collect you at Malpensa Airport, if that would help?"

His heart was racing but he could hear her sniffing as if she was quietly weeping. Before he could answer, she continued, "Claudio wants you stay in his apartment. He says it is close to the Angels of Mercy Hospice where he now is."

Stuttering with emotion, Freddie thanked Annalisa and agreed to accept Claudio's kind offer. Before they said their goodbyes, they exchanged mobile numbers so that

Freddie could message Annalisa with his flight number and arrival time in Milan.

Throughout the poignant telephone conversation, little Queenie, unusually quiet, curled up in his basket, kept one knowing eye on his beloved master.

We humans can never ever keep the truth from our beloved best friends, for they have insight into our souls.

Although Dawn was due to start a week's holiday with her family the following Monday, she and Belinda agreed that Camp Freddie should fly to Milan on Sunday to say his goodbyes to Claudio. He would be gone a week, which would leave Belinda alone to run the agency in their absence.

"Call Ruby Clement! I am sure she has no lookalike bookings at the moment," suggested Dawn, peering into her gold inlaid compact as she retouched her lipstick.

"Oh! Yes, of course! Ruby!" declared Belinda. "She has always said she would be happy to help us out. I will call her after lunch."

Ruby Clement, the Diana Dors lookalike, readily agreed to help her agents out and work in the agency for the following week. She assured them that she would make arrangements to take holiday leave from her barmaid's job while her very supportive mother would care for her young son. Ruby had had several lookalike jobs since being placed on the agency's books and was quickly becoming the clients' favourite British blonde. Her resemblance to the curvaceous icon was uncanny and the agency felt fortunate to have her on their books.

"That is settled then!" announced Dawn. "The agency is far too busy at the moment for anyone to cope with alone!"

Chapter 58
Arrivederci, Claudio

His dark blue eyes instantly filled with hot tears. Freddie felt as if he would scream out in protest to God for allowing the spectacular Claudio to be so riddled with the dreaded cancer, that the opera singer was now emaciated and appeared skeletal. He felt as if he were watching himself in a bad dream; his own body seemed disorientated as he gingerly moved into the quiet, spotless room where Claudio lay waiting for the inevitable.

Annalisa and her partner, Christina, glanced with tearful eyes at Camp Freddie, then silently left the room. The beautiful Annalisa had nodded encouragingly for him to move closer to her beloved brother's bed.

As he stood peering down at Claudio, the opera singer's eyes flickered then opened slightly. Trying to raise his right hand in greeting, his voice was weak, almost inaudible.

"Freddie, thank you for coming to me," he murmured, trying desperately to keep his eyes open, causing a devastated and emotional Freddie to lose control as he sobbed uncontrollably with sadness for his ex-lover.

Suddenly, the door opened and a stern-looking, rotund nurse appeared. Acknowledging Freddie, she nodded to him without smiling before administering morphine gently to the patient who lay motionless on the crisp, white sheets. Turning, she quietly left the room.

Slowly and with difficulty, Claudio opened his eyes again and whispered to the distraught Englishman, "Freddie, you loved me more than anyone and so I ask you while there is still time, will you forgive me for the way I treated you? I ask you this, dear Freddie, from my heart!"

An overwrought Freddie could only answer with flowing tears which caused his body to shudder as each sob escaped him.

Claudio, with the relief of the magical morphine, was now able to touch Freddie's arm before murmuring, "Freddie, this is my dying wish that you have forgiven me," before his hand dropped again on the bed.

Instantly drying his bloodshot eyes, Freddie took Claudio's hand. Holding it up to his lips, he pressed it against his mouth and whispered, his voice coarse with crying and emotion, "I forgive you, Claudio! You know I would always forgive you! Are you not my love?"

Upon hearing these words, words he had been longing to hear for so long, Claudio smiled up at Freddie and mouthing the words, "Thank you, mio caro," closed his weary eyes, joyful in the knowledge that this, his last appearance, had been a success.

With Freddie standing silently by Claudio's bedside, Annalisa and Christina read prayers and chants from the Roman Catholic Missal. Instead of reproaching God, Freddie silently thanked Him for allowing him to arrive in Italy in time to see and forgive Claudio. Everybody knew that the end was imminent but were still astonished when Claudio passed peacefully on Monday morning, the day after Freddie had arrived in Milan.

"It is as if Claudio was waiting for you, Freddie," remarked Annalisa in a half-whisper after they had kissed the deceased on his forehead before leaving him to the care of the hospice staff.

Wiping a random tear from his bloodshot eyes, Freddie answered, smiling weakly, "I am so happy that I was able to say goodbye, although it breaks my heart to do so."

Squeezing Freddie's arm, Annalisa replied, "He loved you, Freddie. Never ever doubt that. Remember, Claudio was my only sibling and we told each other everything!"

Catching his breath at her touching words, Freddie allowed Annalisa and Christina to slide their arms around him as the three quietly and sadly left Claudio and the Angels of Mercy Hospice.

Although Claudio's funeral was not to take place until the following week, Freddie chose not to attend for fear of breaking down. He was nevertheless pleasantly surprised that Annalisa and Christina had encouraged him to stay for at least a few more days in Claudio's apartment where, they said, he could grieve in peace.

"This is what Claudio would have wanted," said Annalisa quietly to Freddie, as she slipped the key into the lock of her deceased brother's home.

"Is that not so?" she asked, turning to her attractive partner, Christina, who, glancing at Camp Freddie replied, "Most definitely it is!"

After lingering for a few days in his beloved Claudio's apartment, the distinctive pleasant fragrance of his ex-lover filling his senses, Freddie oscillated between grieving for his loss and joyousness when remembering the extraordinary amazing days he and the opera singer had spent together, and of how much in love he had been with Claudio.

Freddie was now ready to return to his life in London. He managed to secure an earlier flight on the Friday, to arrive at Heathrow Airport by nine o'clock.

Driving him to Malpensa Airport and promising to call him when she and Christina were next in London, Annalisa handed him a small, square box as he alighted from her black Fiat.

With curiosity, Freddie began to open it as Annalisa looked on, a smile touching her slim lips.

"What is it?" he asked, peering into the box.

"Look and see!" she smiled, her eyes glistening at him.

Suddenly, Freddie caught his breath as unexpected tears burst from him cascading down his navy leather biker jacket. Slowly, he retrieved the object from the small, square box and held it up to the morning light. In his hand, he held Claudio's gold signet ring, the emerald stone flickering in the brightness of the promise of another lovely day.

"Oh! Annalisa! I can't accept this!" he exclaimed, a look of concern clouding his features.

"Oh! I think you can, Freddie! Claudio has bequeathed this to you."

To his surprise, flight BA1442 was quite full. Possibly tourists visiting London for the weekend, mused Freddie, looking around as he found his allocated seat before pushing his hand luggage into the overhead cabin space.

Unconsciously, his hand went to this throat where he felt Claudio's signet ring hanging with pride from Freddie's gold chain. He noticed there were two empty seats beside him and decided he would have a quick nap later if nobody arrived to claim them.

Settling into the aisle seat and retrieving the in-flight magazine from the rack, Freddie glanced at the many advertisements as he flicked impassively through the pages.

Suddenly, rudely cutting through his private thoughts and causing the other passengers to stare in disbelief, a high-pitched voice was heard, loudly declaring, "No! I am sorry, Flat Balls, but I am sitting by the window!"

Immediately looking up, his heart in his throat, Freddie prayed silently that the two late arrivals, lumbering down the aisle, would not be occupying the empty spaces beside him.

The man in the lead was tall and quite thin, his hair, a peculiar shade of ginger, looked coarse, almost rug-like. He wore a bright red button-through cardigan and he moved swiftly, carrying his hand luggage in front of him. The other man following quickly behind was younger, much shorter and of stocky build. His brown hair was long to the nape of his neck and it was apparent he wore a touch of eye make-up. Could this be Flat Balls, thought Freddie, giggling to himself quietly when suddenly they both stopped beside his aisle, grinning down at him.

"Sorry to be a bother!" said the taller man. "These are our seats, I believe?" He grinned at Camp Freddie, who jumped up immediately, allowing the two of them to file past him.

After several minutes of fussing, fidgeting and complaining about the allotted amount of legroom, they both settled down in their seats before turning to Freddie and introducing themselves as Maurice and Norris.

"Most of our friends call us Flat Balls Maurice and Baldy Norris for reasons we never divulge!" divulged Norris, grinning again at Freddie, before turning his gaze back to the window.

Camp Freddie had to fake a coughing fit, enabling him to hold his white handkerchief over his nose and mouth to restrain his laughter from escaping.

Several times during the flight, Flat Balls would lean casually closer to Freddie, who in turn moved further away in his own seat. He learned that the two men were partners and lived close to Richmond Green where Baldy Norris had been left a two-up two-down cottage by his adoring mother upon her demise.

After a short while, breakfast was served by the attentive flight attendants and suddenly the lethargic passengers found a new lease of life as they waited in anticipation for their first meal of the day.

A few minutes after their laden trays had been handed to them, Baldy Norris needed to use the lavatory. Apologising profusely, he squeezed past Flat Balls Maurice and Freddie to answer nature's call and hurried towards the middle of the plane where toilets were situated.

After a while, Baldy Norris came sauntering back from the loo. Freddie watched him as he made his way quickly to his seat and his waiting breakfast.

Suddenly there was an unexpected violent turbulence, resulting in Baldy Norris tripping over a seated passenger's feet, lurching him forward with such force that he was thrown down the aisle. This was at such speed that his ginger toupee shot off his head and went flying through the air before landing smack bang into a prim and proper elderly lady's toast and marmalade, just as she was about to take a mouthful.

Alarmed, she screamed in shock as her blue-rinsed hair bounced around her head. Jaws dropping in disbelief, the other passengers suddenly burst into hysterical laughter while the flight attendants came running, desperately trying to quieten everybody down.

A furious Baldy Norris reached over to the elderly lady's breakfast tray, and instead of apologising, exclaimed indignantly, "I do believe this belongs to me, Madam!" before grabbing his toupee, then, slapping it back onto his bald head, sauntered back down the aisle to his seat.

Chapter 59
A Close Shave

"Oh, what a tangled web we weave...
when first we practice to deceive!"
Sir Walter Scott

Back at Top Drawer Agency, Belinda sighed with relief that it was Friday. It had been a very busy week with one or other of the lookalikes and tribute artistes popping in to sign contracts or simply for a chat, making sure their agents could see for themselves that they were still looking fabulous. All Belinda wanted now was to go home, enjoy a hot bath and wait for Frank's telephone call.

Glancing up at the ornate wall clock embellished beautifully with Raphael's cherubs, Belinda walked into the kitchenette to refill the kettle for coffee. She realised how much she had missed Camp Freddie and Dawn, but, of course, she was grateful that Ruby had kindly agreed to help her out.

Belinda recalled, how, on Monday morning, the younger woman had arrived bright and early and was already waiting outside the agency door when Belinda approached at eight-thirty to open up.

It appeared that over the week, the two women did not really establish a good rapport between them but they communicated well and were polite to each other. Ruby proved to be a very willing work colleague and seemed to enjoy all of the tasks she was given; happily rushing off to the post office every evening on her way home, arms full of envelopes.

There was something about Ruby that Belinda could not grasp. Often during the week, even when some of the lookalikes were visiting, Belinda had, more than once, caught Ruby watching her before flickering her eyes elsewhere.

After pouring herself a hot black coffee, Belinda checked the time again on the ornate clock. It was almost two o'clock. It crossed her mind that Ruby should have been back from lunch by now.

The lunch breaks. This had been another reason why she found bonding with Ruby rather difficult. Belinda, desiring to have a good relationship with the newcomer, extended the hand of friendship to her early on Monday morning, offering to go to lunch with the Diana Dors lookalike.

To Belinda's discomfort, Ruby declined the agent's offer, explaining that she always preferred to lunch alone if that was okay. Deep down, Belinda felt snubbed especially as she had excellent relations with all other lookalikes and tribute artistes. The subject of lunch breaks was never mentioned again, although Belinda found Ruby much more talkative after she had returned from them than she appeared to be before going.

Finishing her coffee and feeling restless, she wandered aimlessly around the office. Noticing a paperback sitting on Freddie's desk, which Ruby was using in his absence, she nonchalantly walked over and picked the book up, reading the title, *The Law of Attraction*. Being somewhat interested, she began to flick idly through the pages.

There are certain circumstances in life in which one may find oneself in a situation so bizarre that it could cause the heart to stop dead in shock. Such a circumstance almost caused Belinda's heart to cease beating altogether as she stared in disbelief as several photographs, hidden in between the pages of the paperback, fell onto the desk.

Quickly retrieving them for closer inspection, Belinda almost fainted as the handsome face of her deceased husband, Matt Flynn, smiled into the camera, his cornflower blue eyes glinting at the photographer.

Still feeling faint, Belinda slumped into Freddie's chair for fear that she would collapse. Her legs felt weak as if they were refusing to hold her up. Now scrutinising the photographs, she was horrified to see Matt with Ruby, arms wrapped around each other, smiling happily into the camera! Another showed them dancing together, both looking radiant in complementing colours as if they were attending a wedding.

However, the photograph that caused Belinda to shake uncontrollably in bewilderment, inciting a loud moan to escape from her, showed Matt looking joyous as his hand rested in triumph on a pregnant Ruby's stomach.

The voice cut into her incredulity as she jumped out of her confused state. Ruby stood watching, her voluptuous figure filling the doorway. Her tight black pencil skirt appeared to strain at the seams as it attempted to cover her ample shape.

Blinking into the room several times, she flicked her shoulder-length peroxided hair back off her comely face. Swaying noticeably, tottering on her green stilettos, her eyes narrowed as she focused them on her agent. She laughed loudly, the piercing sound causing Belinda to shiver.

"In a way, I am glad you found the photos," shrilled Ruby menacingly. "Now at least the truth is out!"

Trying desperately to pull herself together but losing control, Belinda screamed at the Diana Dors lookalike.

"What were you doing with my husband? When were these photos taken? Who are you?"

Before answering, Ruby tottered up to Belinda, still slumped in Freddie's chair and staring down at her, grinned triumphantly.

"Now wouldn't you like to know, Miss High and Mighty?" she questioned. "Surely, even your pea-brain must have worked it out by now, Mrs Flynn!" she provoked, bringing her face closer to a baffled Belinda.

Her breath smelt strongly of alcohol, confirming she'd had a liquid lunch.

"You have seen the photos! Why do you think Matt is touching my stomach?" she taunted. "Because, Mrs Flynn, he and I were expecting a little bundle of joy, that is why!" she sneered, collecting the photographs together and placing them back in her paperback.

"Matt was going to divorce you so he, I and the baby could be together. Did you know that, Mrs Flynn?" she demanded, her eyes narrowing again.

"I don't believe you!" screeched an astounded Belinda. "You are completely mad! Matt had never spoken to me of divorce!"

"That is because he didn't get a chance, Mrs Flynn, did he?" challenged Ruby threateningly before continuing. "He wanted to leave you but never found the courage. Many times, poor Matt told me he would often stay out late just to get away from you!" she hastened to add, staggering clumsily against Camp Freddie's desk.

Now steadying herself, she continued vehemently, "That is why I blame you for his tragic accident, Mrs Flynn!"

"You are drunk!" remarked a recovering Belinda, getting up from the chair but becoming alarmed when a tottering Ruby roughly pushed her back down again.

Belinda froze on the spot, as she realised suddenly that the Diana Dors lookalike was far taller and stronger than she was.

"Now you listen to me, lady!" ordered Ruby, her voice slurring. "I have a proposition to put to you, Mrs Flynn, and strongly advise you hear what I have to say before opening your mouth!" she added demandingly.

To Belinda's astonishment, the inebriated Ruby ran through a list of demands she wanted from her in exchange for her silence concerning Matt Flynn's love child.

Ruby unsuccessfully tried to explain to a seething Belinda that as Matt's only offspring, her baby Mattie would be entitled to an inheritance from his father who had been very affluent before his demise.

Belinda stared dumbfounded as Ruby reeled off everything she wanted for her son.

Moving suddenly to get up from her chair in protest, Belinda could not believe that again she was roughly pushed back down into the seat by the ominous Ruby.

"You and your son will get nothing! Do you honestly think you were my husband's only bit on the side?" screamed Belinda, her face flushed with anger. "Now get out before I call the police!" she yelled, managing to feign enough courage to retaliate.

Upon hearing those words, an incensed Ruby took a swing at the unsuspecting Belinda who cried out in pain as the younger woman's fist connected unbearably with her right ear, instantly bringing on a splitting earache.

Suddenly leaping over the desk, an enraged and wrathful Ruby grabbed Belinda by the hair and yanked so hard that a handful fluttered to the parquet floor, the auburn strands glistening in the office lights.

Desperately trying to muster up enough strength to defend herself, Belinda's green eyes opened widely in disbelief as Ruby grabbed the large scissors laying on Freddie's desk and immediately attempted to stab at her.

To Belinda, the whole scenario seemed so surreal that fleetingly, her mind would not accept that it was actually happening to her. She was aware of a sharp pain in her left arm as she raised it up to ward off the threatening scissors when suddenly, her attacker was pulled violently off her, landing heavily on the wooden floor, the scissors flying across the room, before crashing against the far wall.

He bent down and punched Ruby in the back as she writhed and squirmed to get her ample body back on her feet. He rabbit-punched her again at the back of the head, precipitating the Diana Dors lookalike to lay back down on the floor, whimpering but complying with his demands.

Although her eyes were closing with fatigue and pain, a barely conscious Belinda mouthed his name as he knelt beside her, holding her hand while he dialled the local police...

Freddie!

"We don't need another hero,
We don't need to know the way home."

Oh! But we do!

When Ruby had been taken by police car to the London Psychiatric Clinic for tests and observation, her mother

Judy Smithers had been notified accordingly. Supported by Freddie, Belinda was taken by ambulance and treated successfully for her injuries at the Royal Free Hospital. It was strongly recommended that she be kept in overnight and possibly the following day too.

Before leaving, Freddie promised Belinda he would call her sisters, Sandra and Christine. He would also take charge of Top Drawer Agency until Dawn's return the following Tuesday.

Freddie was a strong believer in destiny and was convinced he had been chosen by the gods to save his dear friend Belinda. Had he gone straight home as intended from the airport, he was certain Belinda could have been fatally wounded by the deranged Ruby in her irrational state of mind.

On reflection, Freddie recalled how, as he hailed a black taxi, he had checked the time on his Gay Pride wristwatch – a lovely gift from boss-eyed Syd – before instructing the chatty driver to take him straight to Top Drawer Agency in Swiss Cottage, where he knew Belinda would still be working. He felt the need to share with her everything about his farewell visit to his beloved Claudio.

Thanking the taxi driver and allowing him a generous tip, Freddie climbed the high steps up to the agency's heavy oak door. It was locked. Searching in his biker jacket, he retrieved his keys.

Walking along the corridor towards the agency's rooms, he stopped in his tracks upon hearing angry raised voices coming from inside. Gingerly tiptoeing up to the door which Ruby had forcefully slammed shut a short while before, Freddie could distinctly hear shuffling noises and groans coming from the main office.

Silently, he placed his hand on the door handle and pressed down. His heart was pounding.

Instinctively, he knew he had walked in on a very menacing scenario that could have had tragic consequences for Belinda.

Acting swiftly, Camp Freddie rushed across the room to where Ruby's ample rear end was in full view and, grabbing her fiercely, pulled her off Belinda and threw her face down on the shiny parquet floor.

Dawn and Freddie had been notified that Ruby would be kept indefinitely in the Psychiatric Clinic for further investigation. Her mother, Judy, had always supported her daughter and taken care of her young grandson while Ruby was working. Judy had readily agreed to take full charge of little Mattie for as long as her daughter needed her to.

Defying not only the police but her family and friends' wishes to prosecute her attacker, a slowly-recovering Belinda refused to press charges against the mother of Matt Flynn's child.

Struggling with her conscience during the sleepless nights she had endured since Ruby's assault, Belinda wept unashamedly into the darkness as she finally realised how ruthlessly both she and Matt had deceived each other.

Chapter 60
The Law of Karma

It was the middle of a pleasantly mild October when Belinda felt ready to join Dawn and Freddie again at the bustling Top Drawer Agency. During her absence, a mix and mingle job had come in for Dame Joan Collins but due to Belinda being indisposed and her reluctance to undertake any jobs, Dawn offered the clients the well-respected Chloe Radlett in her stead.

"It is for this very reason that I insist that this agency will always have an excellent alternative to the clients' first choice of any lookalike or tribute artiste," remarked a smug-looking Dawn, glancing over her Versace designer glasses at Belinda and Camp Freddie after receiving a complimentary call regarding Chloe's recent appearance as Dame Joan Collins.

"I could not agree more!" replied Belinda, selecting her painkiller tablets from her tan handbag before swallowing one with a glass of cold water.

"Oh, by the way!" declared Dawn, glancing at Belinda. "I had a telephone call earlier this morning from Ada Demir's mother, Afet. Apparently, Ada has made it quite clear that she wishes to stay in Turkey for the time being."

"Really?" queried Belinda surprisingly. "I heard she was about to be married to a very nice Turkish boy before she left the UK."

"I heard that too!" confirmed Freddie, sauntering into the kitchen carrying the used coffee cups on a silver tray. Little Queenie groaned in his doggy basket.

"Well that may be so," replied a pensive Dawn, "but as far as Afet is concerned, the arranged matrimony is now postponed indefinitely!"

"I think Ada must have been very fond of Max Rushton to have reacted in such an extreme manner," said Belinda reflectively, glancing knowingly at Dawn.

"Personally, I think Ada was far more sensitive than we gave her credit for," suggested Dawn, stretching her arms above her head and yawning.

"Far more sensitive!"

Although Mehmet Tekin's life without his lovely Ada Demir by his side was sad and lonely, he had enough strength of character – something instilled in young male Turkish Muslims – to appear to the outside world that he was dealing with this difficult situation in a calm and accepting way. He did not bat an eyelid when his friends and work colleagues enquired how Ada was getting along in Turkey and asked why he had not flown out to visit her as yet.

Of course, Mehmet assured them, he would visit Ada but he was certain she would be returning to London soon. This obviously was not true but Mehmet was in complete denial and refused to accept that Ada no longer loved him or wished to marry him.

He had read her short letter through only once before crushing it fiercely in his thick hand then throwing it into the waste paper basket.

A short while later, he decided to telephone her and beg her to honour their betrothal but there was no answer.

Again and again, a distraught Mehmet dialled Ada's contact number, the continuous ringing sending his inner voices into a frenzy.

Those voices in his tormented head continuously rebuked and berated him for allowing such a callous and unworthy creature to take up residency in his mind and remain there. His concerned mother suggested he should make another appointment with his psychiatrist. However, Mehmet convinced her that only last week he had visited Mr Havers in Wimpole Street and had been prescribed new medication for bipolar disorder, which he promised his mother he was taking regularly.

The truth was, he could not face seeing Mr Havers at the present time, being fully aware that his psychiatrist could read him like an open book.

Mehmet knew only too well that both he and Ada's families, with the exclusion of Afet who was still in Turkey with her daughter, had met recently for more discussions concerning the best way forward now that Mehmet's betrothed had decided, in her disorientation, that she no longer desired a husband. He knew instinctively that the North London Turkish community were discussing his problems over their dining tables each evening, causing deep despair to the very private and solemn Mehmet. He felt humiliation, shame, disgrace and worst of all – dishonour.

The ill-fated Max's closest friend, Josh Roberts, had decided again to call the police department responsible for the investigation into Max's case. He had fresh information regarding the mysterious Tom Pike which he decided Duncan Dempsey, the Investigating Officer, should be informed about.

Josh had spent the past weeks speaking randomly to people in and around the Windsor pub, hoping that someone might remember Mr Pike. At last, he spoke to a couple of burly Londoners standing chatting together at the long mahogany bar who told Josh that they did remember Tom Pike but they had not seen him for many weeks now. Thanking them, he turned on his heel to leave, when one of them suddenly grabbed his arm.

"Hang on there, mate!" he exclaimed "Just remembered. Some weeks back, I heard from drinking pals that Tom had flown back to either Australia or New Zealand. Sorry, mate, can't remember which country they said!"

Adrenalin shot through Josh's veins as he realised this could be the break he had been looking for in order to find the culprit.

Chatting further with the burly pair, Josh learned that the man's drinking pals were not even sure whether Tom Pike was in fact his real name. However, they did remember that Lee MacNamara, the young soldier, could not remember Tom at all, although Tom had told everybody that they had gone to school together. When asked, Tom Pike had apparently divulged that Lee MacNamara now had reduced memory together with other cognitive impairments since being wounded in Afghanistan.

Excitedly, the following day, Josh called the Investigating Officer, eagerly confirming what he had learned regarding the possible whereabouts of Tom Pike, if indeed that was his real name! By the time Duncan Dempsey had finished explaining exactly why Max Rushton's case was now closed and placed in the 'Unsolved' cabinet, a disheartened and dispirited Josh came to realise that the promise he had secretly made to his closest friend would now never be honoured.

Duncan Dempsey gently yet assertively reiterated to a crestfallen Josh that as far as the police overseeing Max's case were concerned, the Prince Harry lookalike had been the tragic victim of a brutal mugging and the man hours spent on this case had now ceased.

Deep into the lonely night, less than a week after Ada had found the courage to telephone Mehmet from Turkey, trying with much difficulty to explain gently to her disconsolate betrothed that she no longer loved nor wanted to marry him, a depressed and sorrowful Mehmet finally gave up hope. He, always full of confidence and self-admiration, lacking in empathy for others, slipped unconsciously into a coma, giving up the fight as he surrendered to the never-ending torment of his inner voices, jeering and hissing as he swallowed the contents of a full bottle of tablets, followed immediately by several glasses of Jack Daniel's.

Lying beside Mehmet Tekin's lifeless body, was a note to his beloved mother.

It isn't that you didn't reach for me, it's just that it was too hard to see your hand in the blackness.

But Mehmet had ignored the Law of Karma.

Karma is a boomerang... What goes around, comes around.

Chapter 61
A Marvellous Party

"We were written in the stars, my love
All that separated us, was time!
The time it took to read the map,
which was placed in our hearts,
to find our way back to one another."
Anon

His strong tanned arms pulled her close to him; though a little rough, she liked it. His shining brown eyes appeared to be mocking her weakness for his touch. His hungry lips urgently finding her waiting mouth as a low moan burst from her. The butterflies in her tummy became as excited as she was as his hot tongue forced its way into her waiting mouth.

Now gently, he ushered her backwards until she was standing against the elaborate super-king-sized bed before masterfully pushing her down onto it.

Swiftly pulling her red lacy panties down and off her legs, he then lay on top of her, his hardened manhood pressing compellingly against her quivering body.

"Frank!" she groaned in her elation, opening wide her creamy legs for him. His manicured fingers found her honey pot and gently caressed it. She trembled as he then began to enter her. Hot tears filled Belinda's closed eyes with delirium after waiting so long to feel him inside her again.

"Mio caro. Amore mio," he uttered emotionally. A groan, escaped from deep within her as his talented tongue found her breasts and protruding nipples, standing up for his attention. Simultaneously he lick-kissed and bit them gently.

Now with all his fervent passion, Frank was thrusting and thrusting until he was full length inside this beautiful woman who savoured and responded to his every move. Their bodies were on fire as Frank brought Belinda to her secret euphoria as his throbbing manhood released forcefully inside her. They lay in each other's arms, their glistening bodies entwined, sexuality appeased briefly until her amazing lover would take her again. Their desire was intense.

"Frank!" she cried into the loneliness and darkness of the night... but there was no one there. She was quite alone!

A sorrowful Belinda pressed her face into the pillow and wept uncontrollably when she realised that her spine-tingling sensual lovemaking with Frank had been a mere dream. She knew without a doubt; her future lay with her lover and it was now time to procrastinate no longer. Before falling asleep, Belinda had finally made up her mind that she was ready to relocate to Frank Lanzo and New York.

Autumn's exuberant cloak of colour was in full bloom, inspiring Belinda's good friends, Bryanne and Simon, to receive guests and throw a party at their charming semi-detached house in West London, for the simple reason they loved to throw parties!

An excited Belinda arrived at the white front door, a bottle of Champagne held tightly in her hand as she pulled the collar of her green tweed jacket up around her neck to ward off the sharp October wind.

Almost immediately, Simon appeared as he answered her knock. His greeting, as always, was uplifting and cheering. Both he and his husband Bryanne possessed such warmth, genuineness and zest for life that all who ever had the good fortune to cross their paths would desire to become lifetime friends of the couple.

Within minutes, Simon was greeting Camp Freddie, boss-eyed Syd, Big Gerty and Fanny, who had travelled together in a black taxi. Little Queenie, his bright diamanté collar catching the lights, peeped out cautiously from beneath Freddie's arm, becoming excited when the dashing Simon made such a fuss of him.

Uptempo music was playing as several guests were dancing and already enjoying the renowned hospitality of this fun-loving couple. A smile danced on Belinda's lips when Freddie walked over to her, his arms opened wide ready to embrace his close friend. Almost instantly, her feelings of melancholy vanished as light-heartedness filled her senses. How she would miss these wonderful friends who, over time, had become as close as family.

Unfortunately, Tanya and Aarne could not attend the party having already accepted a prior invitation, but had promised they would be inviting everybody over to their place very soon.

Eileen, the Music Hall Queen, arrived, this time accompanied by her husband Fred, who appeared to be enjoying himself, although he spent most of the evening sitting eating and drinking as he kept his eyes on his still extremely attractive wife. Belinda liked Fred. She thought him a very down-to-earth kind of person and she enjoyed the little chats they had during the evening as the fun-loving Eileen twirled and whirled with Big Gerty and Fanny, her turquoise blue midi dress complementing her shining eyes.

Several other friends began to make an appearance. Hot Dottie and Chilli Bob strolled into the party, each carrying two bottles of Prosecco, handing them to a bemused Simon who bowed as the newcomers entered. Boss-eyed Syd, a can of larger held in his hand, was busy chatting in a corner with Billy Bunions, an old school friend, while Freddie flamboyantly flitted in and out of the dancing area making sure that little Queenie was settled and did not need to cock his leg.

Sometime during the evening, Jerry Twinkle Toes and Snappy Norm arrived and joined the party that was now in full swing. Eileen, ever the performer, entertained the guests by singing two or three iconic Old Tyme Music Hall numbers, grabbing Belinda's hand to help her out during *Don't Dilly Dally on the Way*.

It was a wonderfully flamboyant noisy party and Bryanne surpassed himself when the delicious and appetizing food he had been preparing for most of the day had almost disappeared before being laid on the table.

"Plenty more where that came from, darlings!" called out Bryanne above the clamour, as he weaved his way vivaciously through the dancing bodies. "Don't be shy, sweethearts! Eat up now!" he quipped sarcastically as some of the guests bombarded the lavish buffet, tutting when he noticed, not for the first time, that Snappy Norm really didn't have any idea how to dress!

"A snappy dresser you ain't, Norm, are you, dear heart?" he remarked in jest to the lanky young man who was busily piling his plate up with delicious fare.

"No, of course I ain't, Bryanne, old mate! Why do you think they call me Snappy Norm?" he answered oblivious to his host's satire before rushing off to join Jerry Twinkle Toes.

For Belinda, the party could not have come at a better time. Earlier in the day, she had spoken to Frank, revealing to him every detail of what she had dreamt and of how desolate and gloomy she had felt when realising that it had been nothing more than a dream.

His unexpected response made her further realise that Frank would not wait much longer and she promised him that, come what may, they would be together forever very soon.

In the early hours of the morning when the indulged guests were relaxing on the large comfortable sofas and armchairs after eating, drinking and dancing the night away, like magic, the effervescent Bryanne appeared in a bright pink tutu, black fishnet stockings and white ballet shoes. He nonchalantly sauntered into the centre of the room carrying a limp fairy wand, the well-worn star looking frazzled. Suddenly, there was an uproar as the guests became excited and started to applaud and whistle, realising that the scintillating Bryanne was about to perform his most famous party piece.

"Nobody loves a fairy when she's forty
Nobody loves a fairy when she's old
She may still have a magic power but that is not enough
They like their bit of magic from a younger bit of stuff
When once your silver star has lost its glitter
And your tinsel looks like rust instead of gold
Fairy days are ending when your wand has started bending
No-one loves a fairy when she's old!"

Chapter 62
A Letter to Astound

November came more as a friend than a foe to a cloudy but dry London. After a warm and pleasant summer, everyone had expected a less appealing autumn.

Belinda had hardly noticed the weather as she spent much of her free time obtaining a US immigrant visa for her relocation to New York in the new year. This proved to be an arduous task and Belinda became enlightened about the United States' stringent immigration policies. Any foreign national wanting to move there must satisfy a number of conditions. Frank, being her sponsor, would need to apply for her to come and live with him. A series of steps should then be followed before Belinda could apply for and receive a green card. She wondered if it was just as exhausting to leave the United States as it was to enter!

Although Belinda understood that at times she would be terribly homesick for her family, friends and London, deep in her heart she realised that her life could never be complete without Frank by her side. It was for this reason and this reason alone why she was now willing to leave everything and everyone behind to be with her soulmate.

Dawn was terribly sad at Belinda's decision but was woman enough to realise and admit that there was no other emotion as precious as love. Although she and Maurice had

had their uncertainties from time to time, life's little ups and downs, they adored each other and were still passionately intertwined.

"Your successor will have to be quite extraordinary to take your place!" declared a remorseful-looking Dawn early one morning, prompting the junior partner to suddenly hug her closely.

"I shall issue only six-monthly contracts to the lucky contender in case you ever decide to leave Mr Lanzo and come back home," added a now appeased Dawn as she grinned playfully at Belinda.

"Leave Mr Lanzo?" repeated Belinda in mock horror. "Are you crazy, Mrs Jarvis?" she quipped, pursing her red-painted lips and tutting in jest.

Laughing, Dawn, always insisting on having the last word, replied, "Well, let us call it my safety net for Top Drawer Agency, sweetheart!"

&

It was Monday 8th November and although the dark mornings held the power to spread depression among its people, London was still enjoying unusually clement weather as Sergie Belladoni turned the key gaining him entry into the Soho betting office. It was early and a feeling of foreboding seemed to settle upon the American as he walked straight into the back office.

Casually, he threw the bunch of keys onto the large round table which was still cluttered with boxes of invoices that he had been checking on Saturday. The shop had been busy then with valued customers, eyes focused on the large television screens as the losers cursed loudly while the lucky ones punched the air in triumph, managers and employees professionally commiserating or congratulating, whichever the case may be.

"Morning, boss. Thought you would like something wet!" came the baritone voice of Stuart North, a burly young man with brown curly hair, as he strolled into the back office handing a bemused Sergie a takeaway cup containing a double espresso.

"You thought correctly, Stu! What a lifesaver you are!" replied the American, accepting the cup and removing the lid, his feeling of foreboding slowly disappearing.

"Good weekend?" he asked Stuart, who nodded and winked at Sergie knowingly.

"I'll take it as a yes, then!" he retorted, swallowing the hot dark liquid.

"Yeah! Had a great weekend, thanks, boss. What about you?"

"You know me, Stu, I love a casino! Missed having Joey's company though. Had to make do with my lady friend!" he quipped.

"Oh! Poor old chap!" came Stuart's quicksilver reply. "My heart bleeds for you, boss!"

By midday, Sergie's feelings of foreboding had returned twofold. Joey had not arrived for work. It was unlike him to be so late, even though he had been to Cornwall for the weekend with his latest lover, a young man.

Several times but without success, Sergie tried calling Joey on his mobile. His anxiety increasing rapidly, the American called his second in command, the manager, Mike Grover, into the back office and asked him confidentially if he had heard from Joey at all. He had not. Mike, tall, attractive and dependable, suggested that it was highly likely that Joey had overslept after driving three hundreds miles to Cornwall and back during the weekend.

Although this did not appease Sergie, he nevertheless nodded his head understandingly.

By three o'clock, a concerned Sergie grabbed his knee-length grey cashmere coat off the peg in the back office, entered the shop floor, slipped behind the large mahogany counter and whispered quietly in Mike Grover's ear. One or two of the workers glanced in their direction, curiosity alert in their eyes. The manager assured his boss that he would take care of everything while the American checked whether Joey was indeed back at his London flat or if he had decided to remain a little longer in picturesque Cornwall.

Count Luigi Boggia was extremely unhappy and sadly disappointed with Belinda. Ever since Frank had telephoned him relaying his wonderful news that he and Belinda were to be married on Valentine's Day in New York, the Count had been like a man suffering bereavement. For him, losing the chance of ever again being with the woman he adored and cherished above all women, was unbearable. He was positive Belinda had deep feelings for him, especially after their seductive night of love spent on his yacht. Their passion and sensual lovemaking was surely affirmation of how much in love they were. He, of privileged birth, accustomed to having or possessing anything or anyone he desired, in a strange way felt betrayed since hearing of Frank's imminent plans to marry the beautiful Belinda.

Count Luigi's natural feelings of self-assurance, arising from his appreciation of his own abilities and qualities, were fading swiftly. His heart was heavy with anguish and dejection when, telephoning Belinda in London, under the guise of congratulating her, he could hear the elation in her voice. He had lost her forever. His beautiful Belinda, whom he had fallen deeply in love with against his own wisdom and good sense.

"Frank tells me you wish to be married in St. Patrick's Cathedral in New York," he heard himself asking her, although his voice sounded strange and far away. She professed that she adored the Fifth Avenue cathedral and being a "good Catholic girl", would love to take her marriage vows there.

It was a brief conversation, full of awkwardness and unease, yet neither mentioned their passionate night of sexual abandonment just months before. This was to be their closely kept secret, their skeleton in the cupboard.

When the black taxi stopped outside Joey's luxury first-floor flat in a bustling Covent Garden, Sergie understood why the young American had chosen to reside in the centre of London's Theatreland. During Sergie's conversation with the knowledgeable taxi driver, he learned that Covent Garden had claimed this title since the time of King Charles II as there are thirteen theatres within walking distance.

Walking quickly up the steps to the dark grey door, Sergie raised the brass knocker and banged it loudly several times. No answer. There were people and tourists everywhere, and street performers and buskers were in full swing. He noticed a bell and pressed his large forefinger against it for several seconds before turning to leave.

Suddenly, the door opened. Alarmingly, his eyes focused on a young, golden-haired man with the most exquisite face. He wore a navy tracksuit on his svelte figure. Yawning, he inquisitively looked up at Sergie who immediately asked for Joey Franzini.

Rubbing his large grey eyes, his voice was effeminate and articulate when he spoke.

"Joey? Joey's gone! Sorry but he left early hours of Saturday morning. Said he would call me, but hasn't done so yet!"

Sergie was seized by panic. He felt confused as he asked the young man, "Where did Joey go? Do you know?"

The grey eyes fixed steadily on the American as the beautiful young man replied, "No idea whatsoever! But he did promise that once he was settled, he would send for me!"

As Sergie's panic increased, he could feel his blood pressure surging dangerously.

"Send for you? Who are you to Joey?" enquired Sergie, conscious of perspiration forming on his brow.

"His lover, of course! I am Ethan, the male model!" he responded, preening a little, grey eyes mocking the American.

"Joey told me he was going to Cornwall for the weekend," stammered Sergie, trying desperately to clarify what Joey was playing at.

"Cornwall? No way! You don't need a passport to go to Cornwall!" replied Ethan blithely before asking, "You are not Sergie, are you?" whilst peering ardently at the American.

"Yes! Yes! I am! Why? Did Joey mention me?" he asked urgently, taking deep breaths to quieten his racing heart.

"Thought so! Joey said you were like a man mountain," remarked Ethan giggling as he reached into his tracksuit pocket, retrieving a white envelope with Sergie's name written in large black letters. "This is for you then!" he declared, handing the document to a perturbed Sergie. "Joey made me promise I would get it to you at the betting shop but now you've saved me the trouble!"

Gingerly accepting the letter, Sergie found himself loath to open and read the contents.

"Thank you, Ethan," he mumbled. "Do me a favour, would you? If Joey gets in contact, call me immediately," he asked, handing the young man his business card.

"No problem! Will do! Now I would very much like to get back to bed!" declared Ethan, yawning again before closing the front door.

Hailing a black taxi, Sergie shoved the envelope into his coat pocket, deciding suddenly to wait until he was back at the betting office before reading it.

Mike Grover waved to him from behind the mahogany counter as Sergie entered the shop. Nodding his head in acknowledgement, the American walked straight into the back office and quickly removed his cashmere coat, throwing it over an armchair once he had retrieved Joey's letter. He noticed his hands were shaking as he ripped open the white envelope and focusing his eyes, he read.

Ciao, Sergie,

My dearest wish is that you will not be too disappointed in me for the life decision I am about to make. I want you to know that you have been my strength and lucidity over the months since James Swift was taken from me and I will always hold you close to my heart.

Although I have covered my true feelings effectively, I find I can no longer be a part of the Society. Of course, being a fully initiated member of the Mafia, a 'made man', a soldato, I am acutely aware of the consequences I could face in my future. This is a chance I am prepared to take.

I ask you for one more favour, paesano. Make sure the Society's hierarchy has sight of this letter in order that nobody is blamed for my disappearance other than myself. Please do not concern yourself with my unpredictable future. Money is of no object. I have opened a single personal offshore account in the Cayman Islands under an assumed name. Only my assumed name is on the credit card. Both Vinny and Lukey were agreeable to this knowing and trusting there would be a three-way split of all skimmed money that was placed in that account. Do not worry! I am 'well heeled', as the Londoners would say.

By the time you read this letter, I will be as far away as I can be, apart from fleeing to the moon!

And so, my dearest Sergie, do this last favour for me. I wish you a long and blessed life and always remember, you are more than a paesano to me. You are one of my chosen fathers, Frank being the other. Tell Frank I love him as a son should love his father and always will.

Joey F.

Curious to know if the boss had found Joey, Mike Grover popped his head around the backroom door. Before uttering one word, he was startled to see Sergie sitting staring into space, dream-like, tears rolling down his pleasant rotund face, a single sheet of paper lying face down on the round table.

Becoming perturbed, Mike walked into the office and closing the door discreetly, dropped his voice to a whisper before asking, "What's up, boss? Did you find Joey?"

Suddenly, snapping out of his trance, Sergie pointed to the letter laying on the table, indicating for Mike to read it. Sergie had always been a good judge of character and his intuition had not let him down when he first interviewed Mike, that he was trustworthy, responsible, respectful and most of all, discreet.

As he finished reading Joey's letter, the manager shook his head in disbelief, assuring Sergie that he had his full cooperation and discretion on the matter. To Sergie, having somebody around whom he could completely trust helped to make him feel less anxious.

When the betting office had closed for the evening, Sergie dialled Frank's number in New York. There was no answer. The Uno Capitano was a busy man and it was sometimes difficult to catch him between his many high-ranking meetings. He knew he could not delay any longer before alerting the Society that Joey had disappeared and so he dialled the Consigliere's number.

It was midday in New York and Ronaldo Trapani's secretary answered the telephone call. Yes, Mr Trapani was available, although just about to leave for a lunch appointment.

Within minutes, the headquarters of the Society were in uproar. Not only did the Consigliere speak at length to Sergie, firing questions at him about Joey Franzini, but Leonardo Agosti, the Underboss, took over the inquisition.

Sometime later, just before the call had ended and Leonardo Agosti was completely satisfied, did he thank Sergie for alerting them so promptly.

"Aldo Lamarina will fly to London immediately!" declared the Underboss to Sergie. "We cannot afford to send Frank Lanzo right now," he added quickly, anticipating and answering the very question on Sergie's lips.

Knowing how upset Frank would be when hearing the news of Joey's letter and recent disappearance, Sergie tried several times to contact his close friend. He was only too aware how extremely busy Frank was at the moment, but decided the Uno Capitano, above everyone, should be informed of Joey's discrepancy. After all, it was Frank who was Joey's mentor and had taught him everything he knew.

Annoyingly, Sergie could not leave a voice message for Frank after he was strongly advised by Leonardo Agosti himself not to discuss this delicate matter with anyone, especially over the telephone.

Chapter 63
Act of Contrition

"The truth I have been seeking
This truth is Death.
Yet, Death is also a seeker
Forever seeking me.
So – we have met at last
And I am prepared.
I am at peace."
Bruce Lee, *The Warrior Within*

Although full of brightness, the November day had become quite cold in New York. Thanksgiving was only two weeks away and Frank was looking forward to spending the holidays with his son, Mikey. The two of them, although very close, had not spent enough time with each other over the last year, not only because of Frank's demanding career with the Society but Mikey was now at university and enjoyed spending free time with his buddies.

Whistling as he made his way up the iconic steps of St. Patrick's Cathedral, its spires like giant angel wings reaching for the sky, a relaxed and contented Frank was finally committing himself to Belinda and she to him.

His appointment was arranged for three o'clock and he noticed how dark the sky had become as he slipped quietly and respectfully through the huge impressive titanic bronze doors, catching his breath in wonder at the glorious decor of this breathtaking house of God. He had worshipped in the Cathedral many times before but its beauty and opulence never ceased to amaze him.

As a Roman Catholic and a New Yorker, Frank was permitted to marry in St. Patrick's Cathedral, at a price. Belinda who, although Roman Catholic, was not a New Yorker, and therefore had to obtain letters from her Parish Priest and the Bishop of her diocese to authorise everything.

Glancing around, he noticed he was alone apart from one or two old ladies kneeling in prayer at the back. He suddenly shivered. It was quite dark, the wall lights dimmed, giving the feeling of trepidation.

Now sitting in the spacious and lavish office, Frank handed all relevant documents to the secretary as he sipped his Earl Grey tea, brought to him by one of the junior priests.

By the time the appointment had come to a satisfactory close, Frank Lanzo had willingly paid ten thousand dollars for the coveted privilege to say "I do" to Belinda in St. Patrick's Cathedral.

Shaking hands warmly with the secretary, Frank noticed, as he walked towards the titanic bronze doors, that the light was on outside one of the confessionals, indicating a priest was available. Suddenly, the overwhelming urge to speak to God and ask forgiveness overwhelmed Frank and he turned back towards the wooden structure with a centre compartment.

Hesitantly, he entered through the penitent's door and knelt on the tiny step below the latticed opening where he would make his confession to the priest who sat in darkness on the other side of the compartment.

"Forgive me Father, for I have sinned," whispered Frank through the dark latticed opening then proceeded to confess his sins to the priest who in turn made the sign of the cross over the Uno Capitano as he recited, "May Almighty God and Merciful Lord grant you indulgence, absolution and remission of your sins. Amen."

As Frank, bowed head and kneeling in pray, received God's blessing, a feeling of tranquillity swept over him. He did not hear the door of his confessional quietly open. The built-in silencer on the gun as it fired one deadly shot into Frank's bowed head did not disturb the young priest who sat eyes closed, as he prayed aloud for the soul of the person in the adjoining compartment.

He slumped forward, face down on the little ledge under the lattice window, his hands clasped together in pray. Frank Lanzo, the supreme Uno Capitano, had paid dearly for his compassion towards Joey Franzini.

They carried him from his kneeling position in the confessional, out of St. Patrick's Cathedral and into the waiting ambulance. It was now dark. As the sirens drew attention to the vehicle, bystanders, onlookers and spectators turned their quizzical eyes towards the ambulance, some secretly praying for the unfortunate person for whom the sirens wailed.

The meeting was arranged urgently for the following day. The Underboss and the rest of the Society's hierarchy had decided that everybody should be informed about the Uno Capitano's demise and why he had to pay with his life.

Although Joey Franzini had confessed that he was the only one to blame for disappearing from London and his position with the Society, it was widely acknowledged, without a shadow of a doubt, that the revered Uno Capitano had alerted Joey after he had been privileged with the name of the third culprit in the Las Vegas skimming racket. To Frank Lanzo, Joey was like a son. He had mentored the young Joey to become the talented and confident 'made man' that he now was.

In the end, Frank could not find it within himself to allow Joey to be silenced by the assassin's bullet, so consequently paid with his own life.

"You will achieve more in this world through acts of mercy than you will through acts of retribution."
Nelson Mandela

Chapter 64
Call of Devastation

The following afternoon at Top Drawer Agency, a high-spirited Belinda hummed as she read through her many emails. One of their reputable Dutch clients was requesting photographs and videos of George Michael, David Bowie, Elton John, Mick Jagger and Liberace for a photo shoot in Amsterdam. She squealed loudly as her eye focused on the name of Liberace.

"Freddie!" she cried out, causing little Queenie to bark. "You, or should I say, Liberace, has an enquiry from the Netherlands!"

Camp Freddie shot out of the little kitchenette, wiping his wet hands on his pink flowered pinafore, yelling, "Where? Where? Let me see!"

Giggling, she showed Freddie the email, who jumped up and down with delight at having had an enquiry.

"I just pray that they will choose Liberace this time!" declared a worried-looking Freddie.

"Oh course they will, silly!" mollified Belinda. "They must be interested in Liberace or he wouldn't be on their list of potentials!" she cajoled.

"Can you call the other lookalikes on the list for their availability, please, Freddie?" she requested as she noticed with satisfaction that President Biden and Boris Johnson were becoming extremely popular these days.

Daydreaming and lost in her thoughts of her beloved Frank and their future life together, Belinda jumped as her mobile began to shrill.

Quickly answering it, she became conscious that a feeling of unease had descended upon her.

She knew his voice instantly. His charming Italian accent.

"Ciao, Belinda, I am in London very briefly. Please permit me to meet you this evening before I fly back to Venice in the early morning. If it is possible, please bring a friend with you."

She thought he sounded extremely emotional as if he was trying desperately to hide something from her.

Before she could answer him, Count Luigi Boggia continued, "I have some devastating news to tell you, mio caro, but I cannot do this on the telephone, as I am sure you will understand."